Apricot Sky

by RUBY FERGUSON

As the train carried her northward through the rugged Scottish hills, Cleo MacAlvey grew more and more apprehensive. Had she recovered from her love for Neil Garvine, the tall lean Scot, Laird and master of Larrich? Had America changed her? Could she resume her old place, or would she, after three years' absence, be left helpless and unwelcome among the scenes of her childhood?

· But when Strogue lay in a white huddle about the harbor far below her, and when the door of Kilchro, ancestral home of the MacAlveys, swung open, Cleo knew she was home.

The world of Kilchro and Larrich was a generous, if not a lavish, world. The green countryside was teeming with game; the sky boasted every color from purple to that strange off-orange which Mrs. Mac-Alvey called apricot; the heaving green sea was studded with a lovely profusion of islands like Skye and Eli-oran, where the

(continued on back flap)

Meanwhile, the children on vacation — Gavin, Gull, Primrose, Archie and Elinore — sailed and swam, took themselves seriously and fought to make the summer last

By Ruby Ferguson

LADY ROSE AND MRS. MEMMARY

THE MOMENT OF TRUTH

OUR DREAMING DONE

WINTER'S GRACE

TURN AGAIN HOME

APRICOT SKY

APRICOT SKY

"Here dies in my bosom
The secret of heather ale."
A PICTISH LEGEND — R.L.S.

Apricot Sky

by
RUBY FERGUSON

Little, Brown and Company · Boston

The characters in this book are entirely imagi-
nary and bear no relation to any living person.

APRICOT SKY

CHAPTER ONE

THE VIEW from the bow window in the MacAlveys' drawing-room at Kilchro House was at all times something to rave about. The house stood on a brae, and you looked over the tops of umbrella pines to a huge expanse of sea, dotted with green islands. Highland skies and seas are noted for their opalescent colours, and this particular sky and sea had every-thing in the way of changing shades of rose, saffron, lavender, and pearl, to say nothing of a blue that would often have chal-lenged the Mediterranean.

The charm of islands whose lilac peaks were smudged on the far horizon, of white-capped waves, of distant steamers chugging on their way to remote ports, of little brown-sailed boats scudding before the breeze, of thousands of sea birds planing and diving, of floods of sunshine scattering millions of diamonds upon the dancing water, all this made up the view which so often came between Mrs. MacAlvey and her knitting, causing dropped stitches and a slight variation from the correct pattern.

I want to think! she would sometimes say, and rush off to the drawingroom to turn her chair towards the view. Not that she day-dreamed; her thinking was always practical and revolved round her family, but the sunny seascape — or the stormy one for that matter — seemed to help.

There one summer's morning she sat, happily chatting to herself, as was her habit. Her round gentian-blue eyes and innocently rosy cheeks were so childlike that to those who saw her for the first time it came as a shock to notice her bird's nest of grey hair — too fine ever to be tidy — and her large, comfortable figure.

She had been up early that morning, for in her mind it was THE DAY, in capital letters. She had been looking forward to it for three years and latterly a tinge of apprehension had crept into her happy anticipation. It was Mrs. Aird who was responsible for that — suggesting that America might have changed Cleo, that she might not really want to come home! As if a mere neighbour could know anything about the family! But still, it was a bit of grit in the shoe.

"Of course," said Mrs. MacAlvey aloud to the empty room, "I haven't really a thing to worry about, now that Raine is engaged and there is so much to look forward to, and it's a lovely morning without so much as a sea mist. And changed or not changed and America or no America, Cleo is coming. We got the telegram from London yesterday afternoon, so nothing can alter that." She hesitated, as a sudden vision of Cleo rushing out of the post office after sending the telegram to catch the first boat back to America leapt colourfully into her mind, but even Mrs. MacAlvey's imagination would not entertain that.

She opened the casement windows wider to let in more sun. A very small spider below the sill looked at her anxiously and waited for its end. She picked it up gently and placed it comfortably on a climbing rose leaf.

4

"I wonder where Alexander has got to?" she said. "And can he be wearing his shoes with the heels worn down? He will do it, and the boys were just the same — " Her eyes wandered to the portraits of the two sons of whom the war had robbed her. Then by a natural transition of thought she was with the three orphaned grandchildren now in her care.

"Did we do right to let Gavin buy his own boat? Fourteen, and mad on sailing. Oh dear!" She looked out to the sea again and was reassured by its summer smoothness. "I often wonder why it is," she went on wistfully, "that I can never settle to anything for long. I must be a bad housekeeper. That reminds me, I wonder if Primose is tidying her room?"

Primrose at that moment was not tidying her room. With her two brothers she was standing on the slipway down at the village harbour gazing with vicarious pride at Gavin's boat, *Minnow,* as she lazily pulled at her painter.

"She was a bargain," said Gavin. "Nearly new and absolutely sound. I've got new rowlocks and a new lug, and we'll go to Kilgarro on Friday. We'll have to assemble some food. There'll be loads of it in the larder with the prodigal aunt coming home."

"You people here again?" said a young man idling on the slip, rubbing the bowl of his pipe on his blue jersey. "How much holiday this time?"

"Eight weeks," said Archie. "And we're sailing to Kilgarro on Friday. Is it going to be fine weather, Hamish?"

"It's set fair for days, and the wind in the south-east. You'll have a fine sail on Friday."

"We shan't, you know," said Primrose bitterly. "I've just remembered, our dreary English cousins are coming to stay. It sinks everything. As if an aunt wasn't enough!"

The horror of it sank into their souls, and they all stood gazing out to sea where a small, bluff-bowed steamer went by with a long tail of smoke behind her. The nearest island, Inchcaul, looked remote and misty, a sign of settled weather. It was just a blue-green blur on the calm sea whose lazy ripples slapped with a gentle sound against the slip. A summer's morning gave one a beautiful feeling, like Christmas carols and dogs' eyes, thought Primrose, scratching her ankle.

They turned reluctantly from contemplating the sea, and stared instead at the village, which consisted mainly of a handful of one-storeyed, whitewashed houses clustered round the harbour. There were also two larger buildings, the kirk, and the Stalkers' Arms, and three shops, all facing the harbour and kept respectively by Tam Mackenzie, Ma Mackenzie, and Rabbie Mackenzie, who were not closely related. It was just that practically everybody in Strogue was called Mackenzie.

"I've got an idea," said Archie. "Grannie hasn't referred to our cousins' arrival for about two days. Couldn't we reasonably be supposed to have forgotten they are coming at all?"

His brother and sister looked at him in admiration.

Raine had slept late. It was one of her failings that she could sleep for ever — when she got the chance. She rang the bell, hoping that something would happen. It did. Mysie appeared with a freshly made cup of tea.

"Good morning, Miss Raine," she cried. "You're the last. Primrose couldn't stop in bed, she was that excited about her auntie coming."

Raine doubted this, but she said, "Good show," in an absent voice. Newly engaged, she was always in a semi-conscious state so far as home affairs were concerned.

Mysie sped across the landing to make Mrs. MacAlvey's

bed. First she removed from the bed-table the neat tray with its fluted pale-blue willow-pattern morning set. The cups were full of cold tea which Mr. and Mrs. MacAlvey had forgotten to drink in their excitement that Cleo was coming home from America after three years absence.

"Och, they're daft," said Mysie, happily shrugging her shoulders and thinking like most maids that her mistress was not quite all there.

Mr. MacAlvey came down the brae to the main coast road, and took a survey of wind direction and weather probabilities, to his satisfaction.

Along the road came the butcher's cart driven by Tam Mackenzie himself. Mr. MacAlvey raised his hand, the cart stopped.

"Good-day, Mr. Mackenzie."

"Good-day, sir. A nice bit of weather if it doesn't go back on us."

"It is, Mr. Mackenzie. About that beef on Saturday —— "

"Ah."

"I doubt if it was beef at all. I wouldn't like to put a name to it."

"Think what it means to a man with professional feelings," said the butcher passionately, "to sell the like of that."

"I can't tell you anything about it then that you don't know already?"

"More's the pity." Tam Mackenzie had a limp and ragged moustache which drooped over his mouth ready to be chewed to shreds in moments of mental stress like the present. "A hundred good beasts going from this district every week, and who gets them?" He waited for an answer and, accepting as such the melancholy squawk of a seagull, continued, "And what do *we* get? Carrion! That's what. Carrion!"

7

"Oh, I wouldn't have gone as far as that," said Mr. Mac-Alvey. "The fact is, my daughter is coming home today from America. We don't want to let her down too heavily."

"I see your point." The butcher pondered. "We can't let the lassie starve. You know where my farm is — at Corri-house? If you were to come up to my backdoor one evening, latish —— "

"That's very kind of you," said Mr. MacAlvey. "Of course I don't like the idea of doing anything illegal —— "

"Who does? But we've got to live. You can't deny that."

"I wasn't going to," said Mr. MacAlvey.

"Look, it might be you'd be after doing a bit of fish-ing?"

"I hope so."

"A nice salmon, say. I could do you, say, a prime lamb for a nice fush, say."

"That's an idea," said Mr. MacAlvey. "I'll see what I can do."

"Well, you know my farm. Any evening. Latish."

Mr. MacAlvey nodded thoughtfully. "I don't know what that other was, Mr. Mackenzie, but it wasn't beef. My grand-son thought it was llama. He said a few words to it in Tibetan and a quiver seemed to go through it."

Tam Mackenzie chewed his moustache, said good-day and whipped up his horse. It was understood in the village that none of the MacAlveys were quite all there, though the old gentleman was a wizard with a rod.

Mr. MacAlvey went on his way towards the twopenny library. About twice a year it had a selection of new books, and this week arrived one of those glad occasions.

At the very moment that he was walking down the hill, his daughter Cleo, who had lost sight of her luggage at King's

8

Cross, discovered that it had caught up with her on the local line at Inverness.

The train was in, it was almost empty. Cleo saw her trunk bestowed in the van, and carrying a suitcase in either hand sought refuge in an empty carriage. She would have it to herself all the way to Inverbyne. She put her suitcases on the rack — they certainly looked very new and very American, for she had not been able to resist abandoning her old ones in favour of their slick smartness — and settled herself in a corner facing the engine.

Though no beauty, she was an attractive-looking girl with a sun-tanned skin, honey-coloured hair, good teeth, and a complexion whose unblemished smoothness had resisted steam heating and an inordinate number of ice-cream sundaes. She wore a bracken-coloured tweed coat and skirt bought yesterday in London, an American-tailored blouse, a felt hat to match the tweed, sheer nylon stockings, and low-heeled Oxfords of a pleasing shade of brown. The general effect was good, and this meant a great deal to Cleo, for she was rather anxious about this reunion with her family after such a long break. They might be critical. They must like her.

It was one of the defects of her character that she was so dependent on the good opinion of others. Cleo MacAlvey could think of no worse desolation than that those she liked should not like her. She was a great deal more diffident than her sister Raine, who barged through life without caring whether people liked her or not, and was about as introverted as a fox-terrier puppy.

One thing was certain, after three years in the United States the family would expect to find in Cleo some degree of sophistication. She hoped they would not be disappointed, but she had simply not been able to achieve it. To all intents

9

and purposes, she was the same girl who went away, and this might be considered a matter for congratulation or just the opposite. It was all very difficult. Cleo let out a sigh. That matter of Neil Garvine, for instance. Neil would have forgotten by this time that she existed — he never had noticed her much. It was disconcerting to realise that after three years amid scenes of splendour and distraction she had not succeeded in getting over Neil.

She looked at her watch, to find that there were still five minutes to go before the train was due to start. At that moment the carriage door was resolutely opened and in came a venerable minister with a small hand-case. He glanced benignly at Cleo, said good-day, sat down opposite her, and began to read the *Hibbert Journal*. Cleo rearranged her feet. She did not actually resent the intrusion, but it did occur to her that there were empty carriages on either side.

The door opened again. This time it was a matriarchal party consisting of grandmother, daughter, and grand-child, much encumbered with paper parcels, string bags, and a covered basket containing a cat. The carriage began to seem rather full. More was to follow. Such is the instinct for gregariousness that a middle-aged couple — the man long-faced, dour, in decent blacks, the woman stout to the point of discomfort, red-faced from the weight of too many clothes on such a warm day — having examined the rest of the train decided that no other compartment than this would suit them, and proceeded to lever themselves in.

Carriages on the local line being small and narrow, there were by now far too many people and parcels in this one for anybody's comfort. Cleo, usually easy-going and tolerant where other people's foibles were concerned, found herself entertaining in her breast the kind of feelings that lead to war between nations. She had chosen an empty compartment because she wanted to be alone. There were empty compartments all along the train. And yet she had to be regarded as a kind of bell-wether because of other people's sheep-like attitude to life.

The thing to do in this last minute before the train left was to take her cases down from the rack — the minister, it was certain, would jump up to help her, the mother and child dislodge some of their parcels — and make her departure to the seclusion that awaited her, probably next door. Raine would have done this without a thought. But Cleo could no more have done it than fly. To make herself thus conspicuous, an object perhaps of conjecture, even of ridicule — though the persons concerned might never cross her path again — was unthinkable. Moreover, she might hurt somebody's feelings. Another defect of Cleo's character was that she was incapable of hurting anybody's feelings for her own advantage, and consequently would never go far in life.

The situation was decided by the appearance of the guard with a green flag. The train was moving.

At least, thought Cleo, I have a window seat, and I can pretend I am alone.

She concentrated on the view, on getting her first glimpse of those familiar landmarks which she had shyly hoped to re-encounter in privacy lest pleasure show too freely in her face and intrigue a fellow traveller.

On her native hills lay the sun-shot mist of summer, the heather was turning purple, the sky was of that brilliant tur-quoise which belongs to northern climes. Everywhere was mountain, forest, and stream, picturesquely disposed. A glimpse of a road with silver birches, a glimpse of a motor-car speeding into the wilds, a glimpse of a waterfall tumbling into a green chasm, and suddenly there was Loch Lawe and the dotted cottages of Lawcardale, and as they slid away came the forested slopes of Bheinn Enneir crowned with rocks, and the Garne river flashing in the sun, and then the train was climbing to a reedy moorland and there was little to see but bronze earth and blue sky.

"A stranger in our midst!"

It took Cleo a long time to realise that she was being addressed. The venerable minister was leaning forward to catch her attention, one hand raised, a warm-hearted smile upon his unworldly face.

"A welcome stranger," he continued, "from our great sister-nation beyond the western sea."

He looked so utterly delighted to have made this discovery that Cleo's heart sank. She could not bear to dash the smile from his lips. It was another defect of her character that she would prefer to blot her own conscience rather than mar the innocent pleasure of others. To be placed in such a situation made her miserable — for she was a girl of natural integrity — but she must go through with it. If he wanted an American girl he must have one.

"My!" she said diffidently. "How did you guess?"

For answer he pointed to the bright stickers of the New York hotel where she had spent the night before embarking.

"And what part of the great United States do you come from, my dear young friend?"

"Noo York," said Cleo firmly, for though she knew he would have been better pleased with New Orleans, Denver, or Salt Lake City, depart any further from the truth she would not.

"Your first visit to Scotland, of course?"

Terrified by the chasm before her feet, Cleo shook her head. She gulped. "I guess — I can't talk. I've gotten a sore throat."

His face lighted up with goodwill as he searched his pockets for a tiny box and offered its contents.

"A pastille? I never am without them. You're going to relatives, perhaps? There's so much in our bonnie country you must see. What a privilege to be your guide!"

Cleo smiled weakly, taking the unwanted pastille and feeling she deserved every moment of its stinging unpleasantness, for it proved to be one of the nastiest of its kind. Her heart thumped as she turned away to stare out of the window, for a horrid possibility had occurred to her. This minister might well be on his way to Strogue to take holiday duties. But to her undeserved relief, as the train slowed down at Grieve he began to gather his belongings together and to replace the *Hibbert Journal* in his little case.

The train stopped. He got up, and with an old-fashioned bow said to Cleo, "If ever I can be of service — a stranger, you know, in a strange land — have no hesitation in calling on me — a friend in need — always to be found at Grieve Manse."

He laid a little card on her knee. Everybody in the compartment was staring at her.

"Thank you," said Cleo, acutely embarrassed.

"Good-day, my friend. And a happy holiday."

"Good-bye," said Cleo.

Contrition overwhelmed her. She had only meant to be kind. And now these others might begin to ask her awkward questions, like, "What do the Americans really think of Britain?"

Fortunately they asked her nothing; in fact, their stares were such as one gives to a peculiar animal in a Zoo, not encouraging.

Now that is all over, thought Cleo thankfully, I wonder who will meet me at Inverbyne?

13

She allowed pleasant conjectures to take possession of her mind as the train ran alongside a wide loch, with tree-fringed islands amid its sparkling waves. Her eyes fell suddenly upon the little card on her knee.

Rev. John Beaton, D.D.,
The Manse,
Grieve

An episode to blot out. Cleo was always being made ashamed by the situations into which her kindly impulses led her. Blushing, she began to tear the little card into small pieces; it was the only decent thing to do.

Too late she realised that several pairs of horrified eyes were upon her. The ungrateful, abandoned hussy!

Oh, thought Cleo, feeling smaller . . . smaller . . . smaller.

On the station at Inverbyne where the single-track line came to an end, Mrs. MacAlvey was engaged in an interesting conversation with two tourists, the station-master, and a calf in a sack, when the train came in.

Immediately she caught sight of her daughter, for Cleo had the carriage door open and was ready to leap on the platform before the train stopped.

They met and kissed with rapture.

"I thought she'd be after falling on her nose," said the station-master with restraint, for he knew this family to be mentally unbalanced.

Cleo's luggage was collected and carried out to the car, which looked extremely odd, with leafy trees sticking out of the roof.

"What on earth?" said Cleo.

"I know. But they've been waiting at the parcel office two

14

days. They're for that bare bit by the dog kennel, from Laura Weir; wasn't it kind of her? Two lilacs, two poplars, and a cupressus."

"But isn't July the wrong time for planting trees?"

"Oh, quite," said Mrs. MacAlvey. "But dear Laura doesn't know anything about gardening and had them out of the ground before anyone could stop her. They'll have to take their chance. The others would all have come to meet you if it hadn't been for the trees. They're longing to see you."

"It's nice to be wanted," said Cleo. "I see we haven't got a new car yet."

"New car! There's no such thing as a new car in this country. Oh darling, you *are* American."

"I'm not," said Cleo, rather more crossly than she intended from recollection of her recent shame, settling herself in the car with the cupressus leaning on the back of her neck and the larger suitcase in her arms, wedged between knee and chin. Swiftly her mood changed to happiness as they climbed the stony road out of Inverbyne and saw the sweeping landscape ahead.

"Oh, what do you think!" cried Mrs. MacAlvey, skilfully avoiding the deep ditch at the side of the road as she drew in to let a rakish sports car pass. "The greatest news! Raine is engaged to Ian Garvine. It only happened a week ago, so I didn't write you. Isn't that nice?"

"Ian? Oh, how splendid. I'm so pleased," cried Cleo.

(Ian. Not Neil. Splendid!)

"Yes, we're all delighted. A neighbour and somebody we've known for years, and such a good match."

"My dear Mummy," said Cleo, "I've been away long enough to know that anybody outside Scotland would think you were cracked. A good match! And what has Ian Garvine got but half

15

a tumbledown house and a few cows? He's a grand boy, but ——"

"He's a Garvine of Larrich!"

"As if that meant anything outside Scotland!"

"Well, the name and the land mean everything *in* Scotland, and that's where they'll live all their lives."

"How long has it been going on? And what brought him to the point?" asked Cleo with avid interest. "I mean, they've known each other for years without anything happening."

"Well, they were hardly more than acquaintances until this spring, and then they went to a cattle show together, away to Strathcard. I think that started it, because from then on they were in each other's pockets, and Ian taught her to throw a fly and you know Raine never cared for fishing. But they fished nearly every evening, and Raine was always at Larrich and talking very knowledgeably about the herd and so on, and then people began to couple their names and I suppose the idea crept up on Ian and he thought it was a good one. It's high time there was a wife at Larrich, not just two men in that great empty place."

"I suppose Raine's very happy?"

"Of course she is. But you know that casual way of hers, as though nothing in this world was worth losing your coolth about."

"Coolth!" said Cleo with a giggle. "Do you think we could stop for a minute and reorganise these trees? One of them is in my ear."

They began to haul the trees about, making things no better than before but a little differently arranged.

Soon they came to the top of a hill and saw the open sea ahead, with Strogue in a white huddle round its little harbour. They were nearly home.

"I'm frightened," said Cleo. "I've been away so long, no one will know me."

"Now, don't be silly," said Mrs. MacAlvey, whose emotions were quite uncomplicated. "You know you've only been away three years, and you haven't altered a bit except that your hair is tidier." She looked at her daughter critically and fondly.

Cleo did not think it worthwhile to try to explain to her mother that there were instances in which life had gone on too fast and, like the tide on the sand, filled up the place where one had been. Nobody talked about their feelings at Kilchro House, it was considered one stage worse than talking about your inside.

"You haven't any visitors staying?" she asked, negatively hopeful.

"Not at the moment," said Mrs. MacAlvey regretfully, for she loved visitors. "But," she added cheerfully, "Cousin Maud's boy and girl are arriving on Friday. All the family say that they are extremely well brought up, and I thought they would be good for our children. And then later the Leighs will be coming from England for a fortnight's holiday. Mrs. Leigh is recuperating after an operation, the poor soul. Such a nice, elegant woman. I shall never forget last time she came, she went all round the house altering everything and making it look so much better. Taste, you know. And all in the nicest possible way, nobody could be offended. Of course, if there's any friend of yours you'd like to invite we must make room."

But Cleo did not answer, for they were home at last, and to her eager eyes the old house looked, as it always had looked and always would, solid and ageless and kind, a little tidier than most Highland houses because the white paint was fresh and there were white-railed balconies at the first-floor windows. The hall door was open, and she only had to go in.

Primrose lay on a sun-warmed rock which burned pleasantly through the brown cotton shorts and faded pink thread jumper which were her sole attire. Beside her the glittering sea spray was flung yards high into the air as each wave of the incoming tide smashed itself against her impregnable rock, and fell in a shower of bright drops upon her limbs, off-setting the burning sensation below her. It felt exquisite. She was superbly happy, not thinking at all, just feeling. She felt very good indeed. It would be wonderful to lie in the sun like this for ever, if the sun would go on shining for ever. But it wouldn't. Primrose thought she would like to organise Nature, and arrange for the sun to shine all day every day and a little rain to fall each night, say between the hours of one and four. Then nobody could complain. It's funny, she thought, you can't stop thinking. Even if you think about nothing, you know that you're thinking about nothing. Gavin thinks that nothing is black, but I think it is goldy-pink like the inside of your eyelids when you shut your eyes. Nothing. If you say a word a lot of times it sounds silly. Primrose Primrose Primrose Primrose Primrose — oh it's idiotic. Miss Soper at school said that one is never happy now, but always going to be happy or having just been happy. Well, she's wrong because I'm happy now. I'm spifflicatingly happy. She said that outward circumstances could never make one happy, because the secret of happiness is within. I must be a mixed-up kind of person, because nothing but outward circumstances makes me happy. I mean this rock and the spray and the sun and not having to listen for the bell for second-school. I wonder what the secret of happiness is? I expect it's a grown-up thing, like wanting to waste time

18

drinking coffee after dinner instead of rushing out to sail in boats. Most grown-up secrets boil down to nothing at all and aren't worth making such a fuss about. Now I'm thinking again and I said I wouldn't! You *can't* stop thinking, unless you're an Indian thingummy-bob in a trance.

Her fingers encountered something hard in the pocket of her shorts, and she drew out a lone Minto, unwrapped it, and sucked it lovingly. Somewhere in the distance she could hear someone calling. It was probably Miss Paige calling for her, to tell her to come to tea or some such unnecessary thing. It was pleasant to lie here and think about pinky-gold nothing and listen to yourself being called for.

To Primrose, Vannah Paige was just somebody who fussed too much about cleanliness and punctuality. To the other MacAlveys she was one of the family, undistinguished in form and feature but immeasurably valuable. She had come to Kilchro long ago, before Cleo was born, when Mr. MacAlvey was in France with the Highland Division in 1917, and somehow they had never wanted her to go away. No one knew how old she was, and nobody cared. Mrs. MacAlvey had been heard to say that Vannah looked exactly the same age now as she did when she arrived on that bygone day, thin, brown, and weather-beaten, with her hair in a tight knot at the back of her head and good-humoured helpfulness written all over her face.

Primrose looked along the length of her arm, and wondered why her fingers were so swiftly obedient to her lightest wish. They curl up nearly before you tell them to, she thought in a puzzled way. It all starts with a message in the brain, but they don't wait for the message to finish. Up they come. Suppose I changed the message in the middle and told them to bend back instead of forwards? That would fool them.

She tried it. The fingers were not fooled. They bent back as far as they could and not forwards at all.

Oh, I can't understand it, thought Primrose, it's another of those grown-up things. Gavin says when you shut your eyes they roll over backwards and you're really looking into the back of your head. Boys have beastly ideas, but I'd rather like to go to a boys' school. There! I'm thinking again. I won't think any more, I'll wallow in the sun.

She stretched her limbs one by one to their fullest extent, the cool outward movement was lovely, and so was the sinking back upon the warm rock. She did it several times more. Then she arched her body up and let it sink, the breath jerking out of her in a noisy gasp. A lock of hair fell across her mouth, and she let it lie, tired of action. A great shower of spray drenched her legs. Must be full tide, she thought. Next time I'll lie on a rock that gets submerged, it'll be a wizard sensation.

One of the great things in life, Miss Platt, her headmistress, said, is disciplined thinking. How weird, thought Primrose, to remember one of Plattie's abysmal little 'talks to the school' while I am wallowing in the sun in the middle of the summer holidays, when at school they just go in at one ear and out at the other. (The only decent thing Plattie ever did was to read *Hassan* aloud to them on Sunday afternoons.) Another thing she did was that one ought to spend a part of every day in formulating one's aspirations. Going up and up like that, thought Primrose, you'd probably burst, or fall flat on your face like a gorged seagull. Why do I *remember* the things she says? There must be something wrong with my subconscious. I mean, you've got to draw the line somewhere, and disciplined thinking . . . !

Suddenly she heard her own name being called much nearer

20

and more loudly. That's the end, she thought. You can't ever be by yourself and do what you want to for as long as you like. Now they'll find me and make me go to tea. I might as well be six. The aunt's come, that's what it is, the aunt's come and we've all got to look civilised.

She dragged herself off her rock, sighed heavily, and, carefully avoiding the calling voice, began to crawl through the whins, up the brae, towards the back of the house.

Cleo sat on the end of the bed in her own room. It looked just the same, and somebody had taken care of her things — her books and the china animals and the cushions she worked in cross-stitch when she was at school and regarded as treasures.

They had had the room repapered for her. It was sweet of them, thought Cleo, though I would have liked a plain ivory wash. She switched on the bedside lamp, and it worked. The Virginia creeper had grown right round her window while she had been away, it looked very pretty hanging down between the chintz curtains. Everything was all right now, tea was over and she had met all the family. She was really at home.

The door opened and Raine came one step into the room. She was slight and vivid, with dark-blue expressive eyes, unmanageable hair, and restless hands and feet.

"I just looked in to make sure you had everything," she said. "Do you like your new wallpaper? I chose it. Vannah suggested a plain ivory wash, but I wouldn't have that. Too much like a cell. I knew you'd hate it." She came into the room and began to look in a very interested way at Cleo's open cases.

"Yes, I have brought you a present," said Cleo. "I've brought something for everybody."

"That's what I was hoping," said Raine with satisfaction.

"You can choose what you want. There are nylons and

silk things and very snappy handbags. And tinned fruit."

"Could we have them spread out?" said Raine avidly.

The choice of presents took a long time. When Raine had decided what she wanted and what would be nice for everybody else, Cleo said, "I'm so glad about you and Ian. I didn't say it adequately downstairs."

"I thought you did," said Raine. "I'm glad you've come home, because we want to be married in six weeks and you can help me with everything."

"Six weeks!"

"Why not? It's taken us about twenty-seven years to get engaged, so why wait longer? We'll be middle-aged."

"To think you'll go and live at Larrich!"

"That could be taken two ways," said Raine. "I don't know whether you're congratulating me or wondering how I'll survive it."

"It's a fine old house. So romantic."

"I suppose historic squalor is romantic. I'm not so sure about draughts and rotting timbers and walls that ooze with damp. But there are to be a great many alterations; in fact, the whole place is to be renovated. For me! I do feel important."

Feeling her throat go dry, and annoyed that it should be so affected by inward feelings that did her no credit, Cleo said in a falsely casual voice, "And how is Neil, after all this time? Do you see much of him?"

"Oh, he's all right," said Raine absently, as though Neil were the last person at Larrich she could be expected to notice instead of the laird himself.

"I went to Dunmaig this morning," she went on, "and in the coffee-place I met James. He sent his love and hopes you'll go over and see them. I expect you'll have to."

"And how is our sister-in-law?"

"If you mean, has Trina mellowed with the passing of the years, the answer is on the contrary. The children would be rather sweet if they weren't so crushed. Mother flung discretion to the winds, and sent Angela a pink crêpe-de-Chine dress at Christmas, and Trina sent it back with a note asking if it could be changed for brown woollen stockings. I said I wondered she hadn't sent Angela herself and asked to have her changed for half a dozen laying hens. James wondered if you had acquired an American accent."

"Oh, have I?"

"Well, Primrose told me that Archie was disappointed you didn't say 'gotten' and 'haff-crazy' and 'hiya, folks.' By the way, Mother sent me up here to ask if you'd go round the garden with her; I quite forgot."

They went down together, and on the stairs met Mr. Mac-Alvey.

"So you're still here," he said. "They must have been wrong."

"I don't think we quite know what you're talking about," said Raine.

As it was clear to Mr. MacAlvey what he was talking about, he thought Raine was merely being awkward and explained patiently, "There were some people here to dinner last night who were surprised that Cleo could think of resisting the glamour of American life and coming back to Scotland. It made your mother and me rather apprehensive."

"Well, that was quite idiotic of you!" cried Cleo, blushing hotly. "I'd have come long ago, but the Professor said he'd never be able to find another secretary, and I felt I was under an obligation and it was all rather horrid. In the end I found a girl myself and trained her. Then I ran for my life before the training wore off. It may have worn off now, for all I

23

know, but I'm on the right side of the Atlantic, so what else matters? And who were those people? They don't sound like great friends of yours."

"They were a Mrs. Aird and her English guest," said Raine. "The Airds are newcomers. They've come to live at Grey Cross and changed the name to Tomnahurish. Isn't that horrible?"

"No, I think it's rather a pleasant name for a house," said Cleo. "It means the hill of the fairies."

"I know that," said Raine. "And anything less like a fairy than Mrs. Aird or Mr. Aird, it would be hard to imagine. You can't insult the fairies. Something will probably happen to the Airds any time now."

As all the MacAlveys firmly believed in fairies — touchy little people, always on the look-out for human slights — both Cleo and her father took Raine's remarks very seriously.

CHAPTER TWO

Mrs. MACALVEY always took her letters into the garden to read them because she believed in killing two birds with one stone. The minute breakfast was over she wanted to get out into the garden and discover how all her plants were feeling after a night's rest, and she also wanted to read her letters in peace without being continually asked who they were from and why most of her friends wrote so illegibly. This arrangement didn't actually work out well, for when she came to answering the letters she could never find them. They had been thrown away with the grass cuttings.

On the morning after Cleo's arrival, Mrs. MacAlvey was wandering happily round her garden in the sunshine, wearing an earth-stained smock and clotted shoes. With the aid of an inexperienced gardener, the willing but unimaginative Calum Mackenzie, she had planted everything herself, lavishing individual care upon each plant, especially the feeble ones, not just bedding them out in dozens and then uprooting the bad doers. There was nothing Mrs. MacAlvey loved better than a sickly plant, and she had been known to go down in the night to one, lest it should be thirsty or not sleeping comfortably.

This morning there was nothing to complain of; in fact, the herbaceous border had never looked better, with its clumps of white phlox, purple monk's-hood, golden-rod, bronze heleniums, and lemon antirrhinums, with an edging of alternate light- and dark-blue lobelia.

"There's such a dearth of blue flowers in late summer," said Mrs. MacAlvey, talking away to herself, "that I had to make out with the monk's-hood. I wish Raine's wedding could have been now. All this will be over by September."

She turned her attention from the flowers to a thick letter, which turned out to be from her brother William's wife, Frances, and wandered along the path reading it.

My dear Jean,

I have so much news to tell you that I hardly know where to begin. First and foremost, dear Robert has passed his first law examination with flying colours and we feel our boy is almost a barrister. For a treat, we took him to hear the Vienna Philharmonic Orchestra at Usher Hall, only my cough was so persistent, it seemed to come on in all the quiet bits. However, who should we meet afterwards but Provost and Mrs. Ritchie and we all went and had supper at The Royal George Hotel. Mrs. Ritchie is better dressed than ever, I feel sure she has come into some money, and her pearls were *real*, she saw me looking at them and told me. I never think you get the value for real pearls, only an expert can tell.

And now what do you think? Marget has left me! She has been forty-two years in the family, twenty-six with me and sixteen with Mother before I was married, and she is fifty-nine. She showed me a letter one day that had come from Canada, and in it was a proposal of marriage from a man called Campbell who used to keep a tobacconist's shop in Iverna Street. He said his wife had died and he wanted to replace her with a worthy woman from the old country, and Marget was the only one he could think of or had the address of, so would she please let him know

26

by return of post. It would be a shilling stamp for air mail, but under the circumstances the expense was justifiable.

Of course I pooh-poohed the whole thing and never gave it another thought until she came in one day and told me her passage was booked and she wanted to give two weeks' notice. All I could say to her was no use, I think the older they are the worse romantic they become, and to cut a long story short she left on Saturday and sails next Tuesday and I hope to heaven she fares better than I fear she will. I think I shall try an Austrian, I believe they are very clean, but Marget was so safe and I never thought she'd do a thing like that!

Who do you think is dead? Mrs. Mark Geikie. So she didn't get much good out of her uncle's fortune. She reinvested the whole lot and never spent a penny of it so far as I know, though she might have done a bit of good to her husband's relations if she wasn't interested in her own. Mr. Geikie being an Elder too, everybody thought she would have spent a bit on the church, and it is usual to give a few little presents when one comes into money, but not Mary Geikie! All she said was, "I'm going to put it all away till I've considered a bit." Well, she's considered for six years now, and she's in the cemetery, and we can't wait to hear the Will. It was a curious end too. She had a fit of hiccoughs, and it went on for eleven days till her breath gave out. If ever I get hiccoughs now I shall be terrified, but Mrs. Maple tells me that if you hold your arms above your head it stops, because it shifts your diaphragm or something. I should have thought the doctors would have known about that, for Mrs. Geikie. But I suppose when your hour comes you go.

At last I have sold the old furniture from the drawing-room. I thought I was going to be with it all my life because I couldn't get William interested enough to part, but one day he sat on a broken spring and it hurt him and he said, "Can't we have some decent furniture in here?" So I kept him to it, and I got £23 for the suite and £1 each for the occasional chairs and £3 for the china cabinet, which was more than they cost 26 years ago; isn't life topsy-turvy? And now it has come to replacing, I am in a maze. I bought several magazines about ideal and beautiful homes,

27

and pored over the pictures without really seeing any light. I mean, nobody could possibly live in those rooms. I must seek more friendly advice.

And now to come to dear Raine. I ——

Stubbing her toe on a loose stone, Mrs. MacAlvey looked up from this absorbing chronicle to find herself face to face with a mass of chickweed which had apparently sprung up in a single night. She gave an exclamation of dismay, and hastily placed her letter in the trug, which all this time she had been carrying on her arm. Then she attacked the weed with a will, pulling up great green lush handfuls and bundling them into the trug. Soon it was full to overflowing, and Mrs. MacAlvey carried it to the rubbish-heap and tipped it out. The buried letter went out with the weed, and would shortly be reduced to ashes when Calum arrived and set light to the rubbish, which he loved to do.

"Now how can that weed have escaped my notice yesterday?" said Mrs. MacAlvey aloud. "I must make a careful search in case there is any more." She had quite forgotten that she had not finished Frances's letter, for though she could do two things at once she could only think of one of them.

She set off towards the rockery, chattering away about what a picture it had been in May with three new saxifrages — all successes — and an amethyst lake of pulsatilla.

"And talking of lakes," she went on, as though conducting a tour, "I wish we could have made the water stay in that one I started by the tennis-court. It was so pretty with the clumps of musk, and I spent hours sinking the water-lilies and making the goldfish feel at home. Of course the gulls got those and the water-lilies didn't take, and whatever I did the whole thing just seeped away. It was only a pond, but I hate that word. My lake! Perhaps I was too ambitious."

28

She had just reached the gate that opened into the lane and, still talking and gesticulating to an invisible companion, found herself face to face with a stout little man in a brown suit, with a shock of wild rust-coloured hair and a round solemn face with a very tiny mouth like a sun-fish. It was Mr. Alistair Trossach, the well-known writer and broadcaster, who lived in what he called a hunting-lodge in the middle of a pine-wood, which was really a tumbledown factor's cottage which the factor had abandoned in favour of a house with a proper roof, indoor sanitation, and wooden floors. Mr. Trossach had recently published his autobiography, *Bird of the Glade*, which had become a best-seller, though none of his neighbours were able to recognise his house or himself from his descriptions, which gave the impression of a lean, handsome figure stalking through baronial halls.

He was more than surprised to see Mrs. MacAlvey address-ing thin air, and after looking round to make quite sure there was no one there, he said, "Good morning, fair Mistress Mac-Alvey. Did my sudden appearance give you a start?"

Mrs. MacAlvey blushed and said, "I was just *singing* to myself. It's such a lovely morning. How are you, Mr. Tros-sach?"

(Moses Jobling! she said to herself. Raine shouldn't put such ideas into her head. It was Raine who had said that nobody on earth could legitimately be called Alistair Trossach and that this was obviously a *nom de plume*. They had all argued hotly for some time about what Mr. Trossach's name could really be. Everyone agreed about Moses, but opinion on the surname was sharply divided between Jobling and Strutt, and to this day some MacAlveys called him Jobling and some called him Strutt.)

"I was in the village early," he said, "to despatch a telegram, for my lodge in the wilderness has no telephone, and I could not resist calling upon you to exchange a few of those congenial nothings that make pleasant converse between neighbours."

Mrs. MacAlvey blinked, for she was still following several phrases behind in this rather tortuous sentence. She gathered that anything she said would be dismissed as a congenial nothing, and was not flattered.

"Would you like to come in and see the garden?" she said.

"Oh, very much. I was just waiting for an invitation. I know a great deal more about flowers than you would think to look at me, Mrs. MacAlvey!"

"I hope you don't know too much or you'll make me nervous. Do come in — oh, the latch goes like this! We've been going to get it mended for years, though I always think that having a few things wrong gives a home individuality."

Mr. Trossach stepped into the garden, and looked round him with a coy smile on his tiny mouth. He pointed his toes when he walked, and had a nervous habit of pulling at his fingers till the joints cracked.

"Ah, very nice," he said. "A nice little garden."

Mrs. MacAlvey blinked again at hearing her carefully cultivated three acres described as a nice little garden, but she said nothing. It was just Mr. Trossach's way, and she was too kind-hearted to look for a sarcastic or patronising intention when one was not there.

"Do tell me," he said, wrenching his middle finger till he must have been in agony, "what did you think of that little radio play of mine on Monday night? I'm sure you must have heard it. I saw Mr. MacAlvey in Dunmaig that very afternoon, and he said you wouldn't fail to listen. I keep a little notebook, and record all opinions of my work, you know, taking a broad cross-section of the public."

"Oh," said Mrs. MacAlvey blankly. It was not so much the doubtful pleasure of hearing herself described as a broad cross-section of the public, as finding herself let in for this particular situation without any quicker-witted member of the family at hand to balance the little more with the little less. She had heard the play. They had all heard it. Quite frankly, they couldn't make head nor tail of it, though Raine said the idea of no character ever finishing a sentence was clever and must mean something.

"Let me see," said Mrs. MacAlvey weakly, "what was it called?"

"*Sostenuto*," said Mr. Trossach. "A musical term meaning sustained. Long-drawn-out."

"Yes it was, rather," agreed Mrs. MacAlvey, and realising that she had not said quite the right thing went on hurriedly — with a recollection of a useful phrase once heard under similar circumstances — "It was very well cast."

Mr. Trossach gave a sound like a faint whinny, and said coldly, "Did you think so? I was very dissatisfied with the Thalia. She played the whole part as an urgent positive while a reluctant negative was the obvious key-note. I'm surprised you didn't get that. It must have given you the strangest conception of the play."

"Probably that was what was wrong," said Mrs. MacAlvey, cheerfully snatching at a straw, and immediately realising that once more she had managed to say the untactful thing. She went on hurriedly, "We all thought it was very clever. My daughter said it was the kind of play that you carry about with you for weeks and then the meaning bursts on you."

"Did it strike her like that?" said Mr. Trossach. "It was meant to have an obvious impact, like a child's drawing. I'm sure the expression was simplicity itself." He sounded both disappointed and annoyed, but fortunately a diversion was caused by two of the dogs, which came bounding across the lawn to inspect the visitor and had to be sternly driven away again. Thankful for the break and determined not to go back to the play, Mrs. MacAlvey said, "Now do come and look at the rose-beds, Mr. Trossach. I wish you could have seen the roses last week — such a blaze of them — but we had to cut them back, and now they look a little denuded. Do you care for gladioli?"

"What are those funny little bright flowers over there?" said Mr. Trossach, pointing.

"You don't mean the zinnias!" said Mrs. MacAlvey in amazement.

"Zinnias? Ha!" Mr. Trossach gave a pitying little laugh. "I always think of zinnias as such large, splendid flowers." He wandered on and, examining the herbaceous border, said casually, "It seems to me as bad to put too much in a border as too little. The fault of the zealous amateur."

Mrs. MacAlvey went bright pink.

"At Turningham," said Mr. Trossach reverently, "our flowers grew to their full stature in a profusion that had to be seen to be believed."

Determined not to give him any satisfaction by asking where and what Turningham was, Mrs. MacAlvey, nevertheless, began to wonder if her visitor's earlier days had been spent in some rich baronial scene. Perhaps they had, and perhaps the recollection of it made anything less seem meagre, but he needn't show it quite so obviously. With all her heart she wished he would go, but when she saw him looking in pained dismay at a daisy root in the lawn and realised she was due to be told about the perfect turf at Turningham, she decided it was her turn to talk.

All she could think of to say was a remark she had been told should never be made to an author, "Have you been writing any books lately?" It seemed to her a right and harmless thing to say, but apparently it drove authors almost to the point of murder. So she said, "Do tell me what you are writing now," and this seemed to be the right thing to say, because Mr. Trossach's face lighted up as though he had been wired for electricity and switched on.

"Would you really like to hear about my new novel?" he asked in a tense, vibrating voice, standing quite still and staring at her in a dazzled way.

"Oh, I would!" said Mrs. MacAlvey fervently, for she had caught sight of Miss Paige at one of the windows and was passionately willing to come to the rescue. Miss Paige was going to look up and notice her! No she wasn't, she was only removing something from the window-pane. Yes she was! No she wasn't! Oh, she had left the window altogether and disappeared from sight!

"I think you will see how delicate the situation is," Mr. Trossach was saying. As he spoke he was moving backwards until he stood, apparently content, with one foot on a pansy root. "I have rewritten the chapter in question three times, at morning, noon, and night, my literary quality varying with the diurnal cycle. So far as I can see, I have left no loophole for Agnes. Not one. She is alone with the hideous complexity of her thoughts, her mind is in turmoil, she comes and goes as in a trance. Once she had Guy to rely on. Now it is too late. Unknown to her, Guy lies unconscious in the Monte Carlo hotel with no one to care whether he lives or dies. At this point, Mrs. MacAlvey, I confess I am up a tree. I can't see a gleam of light to proceed by. Now I wonder — as a woman — how would *you* resolve Agnes's dilemma?"

"Well, if you really want my opinion," said Mrs. MacAlvey, who had heard nothing of the beginning of the story but was rather intrigued by its development, "it is that in novels people always spend too much time chewing and worrying at their minds like a cat at its dinner until it's no wonder they do idiotic things, whereas in real life one just takes the obvious, practical course without making a Chinese puzzle of it. I always think the simple way is the right way, though that probably isn't very literary of me. What I feel is that Agnes ought to stop thinking about herself so much, and find somebody who knows where Guy is, and make a dash to Monte Carlo to see if she can do anything for him. I take it she has plenty of money? The people in your books usually have."

"You seem to forget," said the author coldly, "that Agnes is a nun."

"Oh," said Mrs. MacAlvey taken aback. This evidently belonged to the part of the story she hadn't heard while she was watching Miss Paige at the window and hoping she would come out. But she was not going to be daunted. "She breaks her vows," she added firmly.

It was Mr. Trossach's turn to look taken aback.

"Oh, I say!" he exclaimed. "I don't think I could do that with Agnes. It would be out of keeping with her character. Do you really suggest ——"

"There wouldn't be any novels at all if everybody did everything in keeping with their characters," said his hostess stoutly. "And what's more, people love stories about nuns who break their vows. Look at *The Woman of Babylon*, by Joseph Hocking. It's the best novel I ever read."

Mr. Trossach closed his eyes in pain and made a kind of whiffling sound in his throat.

"Would you mind getting off that pansy?" said Mrs. Mac-Alvey. "It's rather a favourite one of mine. You know," she added triumphantly, "I've always thought I could write a novel myself if only I had time."

Raine was fussing and fuming about the way she always lost the buttons off her cardigans. Cleo, looking out of the window, said, "Who is that peculiar-looking man walking round the garden with Mummy?"

Stung with curiosity, Raine came over and said, "Oh that! That's Moses Jobling, the famous author. He lives in the factor's old hut at Glendussit."

"Ought I to know?" said Cleo. "I've never heard of him."

"Don't be silly," said Raine. "You might as well say you never heard of J. B. Priestley."

"What did you call him? Moses — what?"

"Oh, I see where you've gone astray," said Raine as though it were Cleo's error. "We think Alistair Trossach is a *nom de plume*. It's too utter."

"Alistair Trossach! Is that who it is?" said Cleo, almost reverently, gazing at the great best-selling novelist whose latest book, *Reluctant Zodiac*, she had read on the boat coming over. "Oh, he seems to be leaving. Are you sure he's who you said he was?"

Mrs. MacAlvey came in with a good deal of bustle.

"You left me all alone," she said accusingly, "with that pretentious little man. I said awful things to him. I thought he was going to erupt molten lava. I lost my head completely."

"What did you say, Mummy?" asked Cleo with great interest.

"I shouldn't think of telling you. Oh, there's the telephone —— "

She dashed off to answer it herself, for she adored answering the telephone, always having a lingering hope that it might be incredibly good news, and returned to say, "It was James. He's coming to dinner and staying the night."

"Is he bringing Trina?" demanded both her daughters simultaneously.

"I don't think it's nice to speak of your sister-in-law like that," said Mrs. MacAlvey.

"Like what?" cried Raine in a tone of blazing innocence. "We only said, is he bringing Trina?"

"It was the way you said it. We shall be several extra for dinner. I must see about it."

"When am I going to see your young man?" asked Cleo of her sister.

"He's coming to dinner tonight," said Raine, scrabbling through a box of buttons. "And I expect Neil will tag along too. They've always done everything together, and who am I to come between them? None of these buttons match. I give up!"

At the sudden mention of Neil's name and the thought that he was actually coming to dinner tonight, Cleo's unfortunate heart began to do a syncopated rhythm. She cursed herself, called herself every kind of a fool, and, unable to stay in the house a moment longer, went out for a walk. As Highland walks call for a good deal of stamina (for one is always proceeding along a mountain, up a mountain, or down a mountain), and as it is necessary to remove the shoes and stockings every few minutes to cross a stream and put them on again to clamber through scratchy heather, she was away for several hours and arrived back completely worn out.

36

She took some tea up to her room — she had forgotten about lunch — and lying flat on her back on the bed wondered which dress she should wear for Neil. She finally decided on her new chiffon print, red hibiscus flowers on a white ground, and hoped she was not wasting her time.

She spent a long time over her dressing and thought the result quite creditable.

"Where have you been all day?" asked Raine as they descended the stairs together, and without waiting for an answer went on, "The children won't be at dinner, they are out sailing, so that's a good thing. I remembered to ask for Ian's favourite pudding. It's little things like that that make an impression on a man."

"What is Ian's favourite pudding?" asked Cleo, rather hazily.

"Coco-nut *soufflé*. He likes almond sponge too."

"Does he really?" said Cleo. "Is he fond of food? And will you have to do the cooking at Larrich? I forget what their arrangements are, but I should think rather primitive."

"It is going to be a matter of supreme tact," said Raine. "Their old Morag does it now, and all she seems to be able to accomplish is grouse casserole and one pudding, made of watery custard and stony little raisins. I think it was the food here that first attracted Ian to me, though of course Mrs. Mortimer does it all and won't let any of us so much as boil an egg. I told Ian I wasn't much as a housewife. He has at least been warned, and if nobody objects we shall come here for dinner every Sunday. One good meal a week should keep us from dying of malnutrition, if no more. I say!" — Raine stood back admiringly — "your dress is terrific, I do like it! But actually you needn't have changed just for Ian, he never notices what one wears, unless perhaps it might

37

be a pink satin blouse and tartan trews. I'll try that some time."

"Shall I go and take it off?" asked Cleo with a sinking heart, looking at Raine's washed-out blue cotton and wondering whether she should just have flung on a mackintosh; but her sister said, "No, don't do that, I like to see a nice dress, and it won't matter to Ian either way. I once asked him if he thought I was pretty, and he said he'd never thought about it; so I said. 'Have a good look at me now,' and he said, 'Why? Are you feeling ill or something?'"

They went into the drawing-room with its silvery-pink walls and faded, flower-sown carpet, and Raine said, "I wish they'd come. The worst of farmers is, they attend to every single possible want of every cow and hen before they tear themselves away. I'll put out the sherry."

Cleo walked over to the window and stood looking out at the sea, which tonight looked like wrinkled blue silk embroidered with green and lilac islands. The blue of the sky was changing slowly to a soft bloomy gold. Cleo wished she could be sensible and nonchalant and not such a ninny.

On the stroke of seven-thirty the Garvines arrived. The two brothers were very striking indeed, and looked exactly like Highland gentlemen in books are supposed to look but in real life so rarely do. They were both over six feet tall, lean as hawks, with tanned aquiline faces and deep-set vivid grey eyes. Neil's hair was blue-black and Ian's was bronze. Tonight they wore shabby but clean flannel suits with white shirts and plain ties, but prowling the moors in their kilts and leather-bound coats with bare brown knees above their stockings, they looked like something out of a book by Neil Munro. An artist visiting Strogue had once wanted to paint them life-size into a very dim sort of Celtic picture he was doing, but they had turned down the idea flat. They both had a horror of any kind of self-exhibition.

The brothers were unusual in being among the last survivals of a dying breed — Highland men who still clung to the old way of life, getting such living as they could out of their ancestral land. They had no use for town life. They had never wanted careers or been interested in modern ways of making money, and they accepted a hard life with equanimity. It was part of their pride of race. Larrich House had belonged to the Garvines for over 300 years, part of it had been burnt out by Cumberland's soldiers in 1746 and never rebuilt, and very little had been done in the way of repairs during the past hundred years. There had never been enough money.

Neil and Ian let their fishing and shooting, and were lucky in owning a lodge which was rented at a good price every summer by rich English people. They farmed and kept a large number of sheep and a small but good dairy herd, and they also owned two pedigree bulls, called Larrich Titan and Larrich Torpedo, which brought them in a fair income from stud fees. All this didn't amount to a great deal, but because of their name and the past glories of their estate they were looked up to with great respect by the whole neighbourhood.

As Neil was thirty and Ian twenty-eight, the like-aged MacAlvey girls couldn't remember a time when they didn't know the brothers, and without being close friends they had met frequently at local festivities and gatherings. Cleo at twenty had had the misfortune to fall madly in love with Neil. It was inconvenient to be so obsessed with one young man at a time when she should have been enjoying herself with many, but she kept her secret grimly, aware that she had made no impression whatever on the handsome but rather dour laird of Larrich. Neither of the brothers seemed inclined to marry, though desperately sought after, and by now most of the local girls had given up the unequal struggle and found less spectacular but more accessible swains, so it was all the more gratifying and exciting that Ian should have fallen in love with Raine and become engaged to her.

The brothers advanced into the Kilchro drawing-room with their free stride, and Ian went straight up to Raine and kissed her rather noisily, then fell back with a manly blush.

"Don't mind me," said Cleo. "Hullo, Ian."

"Hullo, Cleo!" he cried heartily. "How nice to see you back again. How long have you been away? Seven or eight years, isn't it? Were you surprised when Raine told you our news?"

"Actually Mummy told me on the way from Inverbyne. I'm terribly pleased, Ian. I think it's marvellous, and I never know what's the right thing to say on these occasions and which one I ought to congratulate. Both of you, I think."

"That's generous of you," said Ian, who seemed very much at his ease and in good form. "People say the funniest things to us, don't they, Raine? 'Dear boy,' 'Poor sweet,' and 'I do think it's plucky of you in these hard times.' Well, I think I'm getting the best of the bargain."

"Don't speak too soon," said Raine. "You don't know yet how awful I am to live with."

"She's honest, willing, industrious, and an early riser," said Cleo, "quiet with children, will eat anything."

"Sunny aspect, one owner, rebored 1948," said Raine with a giggle.

All this time Neil had been standing by a small table looking rather out of things, but now Cleo managed to summon up enough courage to look directly at him, and overcome by the realisation that he looked handsomer, more mature, and more

40

attractive than ever, she said with a calmness that surprised her, "Hullo, Neil. How are you after all these years?"

"All the better for seeing you," he answered gallantly but meaninglessly.

"Stands Larrich where she did?"

"Up to the time we left, half an hour ago. Let me see, where is it you've been? Australia, or somewhere?"

Cleo's heart, which up to now had been in her mouth, suddenly shot down to her shoes at this evidence of his lack of interest in her.

"America," she said casually, and added, "We'd better have some drinks."

Australia! she thought bitterly. Australia! And she spilt some sherry on the polished table, but nobody seemed to notice, and then Mr. and Mrs. MacAlvey came in with Miss Paige and they all stood round and murmured "Slainte!"

"Would you say, Cleo," said Ian, "that America was a better or worse country than England?"

"In what way?"

"Oh, just as a country."

"Well, I like America better for some things and England better for other things."

"That's interesting," said Ian. "What do you like better in America than in England?"

Pinned down, and taking fright at the nightmarish tendency of this conversation, Cleo couldn't think of a single thing she liked better in America than in England.

"I'm the only one of you who has been to England or to America," she had the presence of mind to say, "so it's all rather difficult to explain."

"Let's all have another drink," said Raine, coming to the rescue, but now Neil had to pursue the sticky subject and,

41

looking directly at Cleo, "Is America at all like the films?"

"Oh yes, exactly," cried Cleo, relieved, and dashed on madly, "Everyone in America was very kind to me. Of course, everyone I have met in England has been very kind to me too. I must admit I like some English people very much. I like some American people very much too. They are very kind. So are some English people too of course."

"Quite," said Neil.

Feeling rather sick at hearing herself babbling in this idiotic way and conscious that the family were looking at her oddly, Cleo still could not stop but rushed on in a fever, "The summers are very hot in America. The winters are very cold. Of course, they have air-conditioning in practically all the buildings. In summer, that is, not in winter. I mean, they have it in winter too. But not in the outlying districts." She pulled herself up with a gasp, and Mrs. MacAlvey sprang into the gap thus created and exclaimed, "You two boys must be tired with standing after your hard day. Do sit down, both of you. I always picture you getting up at some unearthly hour in the morning and driving cows about all day."

"We don't work quite as hard as that," said Ian, who had spent most of the afternoon asleep in a boat on the loch, "but of course a farmer's work is never done."

Cleo sank gratefully down on the settee, and as there was no other place available, Neil took a seat beside her and said, "I was surprised to hear you'd come back from America. They seem to have such a grand life there."

"I wanted to come home," muttered Cleo, wishing she could think of an excuse to dash out of the room.

Fortunately for her, at that moment the gong sounded, and Raine got them all on their feet and marshalled them into the dining-room, where she had herself set out the best lace dinner-

42

mats in honour of the visitors, and had lighted four yellow candles standing in old silver candlesticks in the middle of the table, flanking a bowl of yellow roses.

Both the young men's faces brightened at this charming sight with its suggestion of a feast to come, and Raine said, "You sit between them, Cleo, because your frock is so glamorous and completes the scene. Isn't Cleo's dress lovely, Ian?"

"Lovely!" said Ian politely, without looking at Cleo's dress.

Mr. MacAlvey said grace and they all began on the fruit cocktail. In spite of being so disturbed by love, Cleo was hungry. The roast chickens came in, preceded by a rapturous smell mingling the odours of bread sauce, rich gravy, and game chips. Both the Garvines ate enormously and looked very pleased. Everyone disposed of large platefuls, and Mrs. Mac-Alvey said as the plates were changed, "Truth compels me to tell you, Ian, that Raine did not cook this dinner, but she can cook if she tries, and I hope she'll do you credit when she gets to Larrich."

"We're easily pleased about food," said Ian with a reassuring glance at Raine. "I suppose venison stew and porridge is in our blood."

"That's about all you'll get from me," said Raine. "One can make enough of both to last a week and warm it up as required. I'll be a lady of leisure at Larrich."

"Don't you count on that," said Ian. "Any spare time you have can be spent on the farm and save a man's wages."

"I can see," said Raine grimly, "that what I'm going to want is a sense of humour."

"What you're going to want," said Neil, "is muscle and fortitude."

During this exchange of pleasantries Cleo felt rather out of it, but now a diversion was caused by the arrival of James. The

43

eldest of the MacAlvey family, he was unlike his sisters, being slow-witted, patient, and industrious. He had married young, and become very much dominated by his wife Trina, who had taken him in hand and moulded his character on her own lines. Unambitious by nature, he was content to manage the tweed mill at Dunmaig, and was devoted to his two children.

Apologising for being late, he sat down in a vacant place on the other side of Raine, then crying, "I almost forgot!" jumped up to greet Cleo with a brotherly kiss that knocked her sideways.

"Welcome home!" he said kindly. "I was quite surprised to hear you were coming back. Somehow I thought you'd have stayed."

"If anybody else says that to me ——!" said Cleo, ready to howl.

"Trina sent her love," said James, "and hopes you'll come and see us soon."

"Thank you," said Cleo, wretchedly polite. "I'd love to."

"Do go on with the pudding, Mother," said James. "Don't let me hold everything up."

"It's Ian's favourite," said Raine. "Coco-nut soufflé – oh!" she added with a scream of dismay as Mysie brought in an obvious apple charlotte reposing in a silver dish.

"Oh, Mysie, it was supposed to be soufflé," said Mrs. Mac-Alvey.

"Mrs. Mortimer couldn't manage it," said Mysie primly.

Raine looked anguished.

"This is just as good," said Neil generously. "We like anything."

"James dear, do you mind sleeping in the little dressing-room, as it's just for one night?" said Mrs. MacAlvey. "The room you usually have is all ready for Cecil Atkinson, who is coming tomorrow."

"I don't mind," said James. "But who is Cecil Atkinson and why should he have preferential treatment?"

"Oh, my darling James, you must know that!" cried his mother reproachfully. "Cecil is your Cousin Maud's son and your second cousin once removed, or do I mean your first cousin twice removed? Anyway, he's the children's quarter-cousin and a rather mature boy for his age, and I think he'll be good for Gavin."

"Gavin may have ideas about that," said Ian.

James looked at his watch and jumped up.

"It's eight-fifteen. May we have the wireless?" He switched on the set without waiting for discouragement and added, "I never miss it. International Cross-currents, by George Grissel."

"Help!" said Raine.

James gave her a bleak look. "People who are flippant," he said, "and turn a deaf ear to serious matters, are responsible for the state of the world today."

"Yes, dear, I do agree," said Mrs. MacAlvey, "and I think we ought to listen to better stuff than we do, but —— "

"Ssh!" said James.

" — so I must leave Yugolsavia and take a brief glance at Indonesia," said George Grissel.

"What for?" murmured Cleo.

"Ssh! Please!" said James.

George Grissel fell on their ears through a deathly hush that carried them over the rest of the sweet, the cheese, and the dessert.

"Next week," he concluded, "I will make a summary of the desperate problems we have already encountered, and express

45

a few of the forebodings which suggest themselves to my mind. Good night."

"God bless!" said Mr. MacAlvey kindly.

"You do get some funny things on the radio," said Mrs. MacAlvey. "That play of Mr. Trossach's on Monday ——"

"Ah!" said James. "Quite the most significant thing we've heard in years. Trina wrote to congratulate the B.B.C. and asked for a repeat. We talked about it all night."

"Did you, dear?" said Mrs. MacAlvey. "Well, shall we all go into the drawing-room and have some coffee?"

Cleo found herself handing round coffee and wondering how the rest of the evening was going to be spent. Up to now, so far as she was concerned, it hadn't been a success, for all through dinner she hadn't been able to think of a single thing to say to Neil, while he had simply sat by her side eating and hadn't addressed her once. Surely there was some way of making him interested in her? If she could get him by himself she might be able to find out what kind of things he liked to talk about. Perhaps Raine and Ian would wander off by themselves and James would stay and talk to his parents, and in that case Neil might suggest that he and she should walk round the garden. That would be her opportunity. She would try to think of a lot of intelligent things to talk about, say, American politics, because Neil was of a serious turn of mind.

"All finished?" said Raine, clearing the coffee cups. "Then what about a crack at some billiards, Ian — you and Neil and Cleo and me?"

"I'm not so hot at billiards," said Cleo, her dream fading.

"Well, you can be a handicap on Neil, he's too good. Ian and I combine rather well, until I let him down, and then we begin to break the cues over each other's heads, but that doesn't happen until later in the evening."

They went to the billiards-room, uncovered the table, switched on the overhead lights, adjusted the marker, and began chalking their cues. Cleo chalked in silent desperation, hoping the chalk would have magic properties.

Raine opened with a useful and competent break of nineteen.

"Good show," said Ian.

"Fluke," she said modestly. "Your go, Cleo."

Cleo, conscious that Neil's eyes were on her and anxious to look like a promising partner, managed to miss the red completely and sank her own ball in a pocket.

"Hard graft," said Neil absently, his air of slight interest fading as he realised what sort of a partner he had got.

"She's out of practice," said Raine gallantly.

"That's kind but misleading," said Cleo. "I never was in."

Ian added twenty-four to Raine's score, and then Neil took the table and went on scoring for so long that Raine said, "Have a heart. We're all supposed to be in this."

"I've only made fifty-one," said Neil, put off his stroke and missing his cannon. But he continued to play so well that even with Cleo's piffling twos and threes, they won two games running.

"Do you want another?" asked Raine.

"Oh, I don't think so," said Neil.

"Do you, Cleo?"

"No thanks," said Cleo bitterly. "Let's do something I *can* do."

"Couldn't we go down to the shore now?" said Ian in a tone that excluded all but himself and Raine.

"Sounds good to me," said Raine, "but what about these two? Would you and Neil like to go round the garden, Cleo?"

47

"Well, I could bear it if Neil could," said Cleo, her heart jumping.

"Is there anything else you'd like to do?" asked Neil politely.

Cleo could have told him of several things she would have liked to do that would have surprised him, but she said meekly, "We might as well go round the garden."

"It looks cool out there, we might do worse," said Neil.

"I do love the smell of night-scented stocks," said Cleo, her spirits rising as she preceded him to the terrace.

"Have a cigarette," said Neil, offering his case. "It'll clear the midges."

"I don't remember," said Cleo, "what sort of a garden you have at Larrich?"

"I shouldn't try," said Neil gloomily. "We don't rise to much beyond rhododendrons."

"Oh," said Cleo. She couldn't think of another thing to say, and apparently neither could Neil. The silence went on for ages. Cleo felt stifled. She stole a glance at Neil, and saw that his eyes had that cool, dark, withdrawn look which made their owner seem hopelessly remote.

She took a long breath.

"When I was in America," she said, descending the steps by the rockery, "I saw President Truman."

Neil came back to earth with an effort.

"Do you mean you had an audience with him?"

"Well no," said Cleo. "I saw him in a car in the street."

"Oh."

"People in America — young people — were, I thought, quite politically minded."

"Really?"

They walked in grim silence right down the long gravel

48

path that skirted the shrubbery and came out by the tennis-court.

"The court looks in good shape," said Neil with an effort.

"Oh yes!" cried Cleo thankfully. "Do you play? You can come over any time."

"Thanks."

That topic had died. They walked on like two deaf mutes, and stopped where the path ended.

"Mother tried to make a lake here," said Cleo with forced brightness, "but the water wouldn't stay."

"She ought to have got a water engineer."

"I don't suppose she thought of that."

"It wouldn't stay if she didn't get a water engineer to it."

"Oh."

They went on in a silence that to Cleo grew more and more tense. If she could only think of something to say! If she could only . . .

She said, "American newspapers are very large."

"Large?"

"Very large. Pages and pages. It takes all day to read them."

"All day?"

"Well, it could. You have to pick out the serious items."

"The what?"

"The serious items."

"Oh," said Neil.

She thought, It's his turn to say something. Why doesn't he start something? Perhaps he thinks I'm not worth the bother. Her spirits sank miserably.

They walked on for several minutes in an unbroken hush.

"I went for a long walk this afternoon," said Cleo in a sort of tonight-or-never voice. "You should have seen me tottering back! I must be out of practice."

49

"I expect so," said Neil.

"I sat down to rest by a ruined shepherd's hut. I couldn't help wondering — who — who had once lived there."

"Some shepherd, probably."

"I expect so," said Cleo.

They walked right round the tennis-court for the second time and came out by the herbaceous border.

"The ground gets very dry," said Cleo, whose throat was no less parched.

"It wants rain."

"I suppose it does."

"We could do with some rain."

"Is it a long time since it rained?"

"It's been rather dry this week."

"It is usually rather dry in July and August."

"It varies."

"Sometimes it's quite wet."

"Quite," said Neil.

They walked to the bottom of the garden, past the rubbish heap, and stood by the gate opening into the lane.

"I hope Ian won't be long," said Neil, making his first direct contribution. "We've got a cow with rheumatism. Wants looking at tonight."

Cleo's heart felt like a water-logged dinghy.

A blue stream-lined sports car suddenly drew up at the gate, and a sleek, beautiful young woman stepped out of it. She was a golden girl, and wore a skin-fitting suit of maize-coloured linen and exquisite shoes.

"Why, Neil!" she cried. "What are you doing here? I was passing, and thought I must stop for a minute and see the MacAlveys."

"It's Inga," said Neil, coming to life.

"Who?" said Cleo.

"Inga Duthie. Wasn't she here when you went away? I suppose not." And opening the gate for the lovely stranger to walk in, he added, "This is Cleo MacAlvey, Inga."

"How do you do, Miss Duthie," said Cleo, remembering that it was her garden.

"*Mrs.* Duthie." The new-comer flashed a high-voltage smile at Cleo. "We bought Ellen Lodge during the war to be our home after my husband came out of the R.A.F., but alas! he never came back, so I finally came up here alone, and now I never want to leave the place. Everyone here has been so sweet to me." She swivelled the smile around to Neil, who said gallantly, "As if they could help it!" with more enthusiasm than Cleo cared to hear.

"Shall we go up to the house?" said Cleo.

They walked three abreast, which was crowding, and Inga said, "There's something about that car of mine, Neil, which brings out the worst in me. I know she's ten years old and wants reboring, but you might as well put a self-starter on the Rock of Gibraltar for all the notice she takes."

"I'll have a look at her sometime, if you like," said Neil.

"Oh, but how sweet of you! You're so busy, Neil, and yet you always find time for tiresome things like me and my dreary car. I do think it's generous of you. May I bring her over to Larrich or will you come to me? Come and have dinner with me tomorrow!"

"I might," said Neil, as though he wanted to. "I'll ring you."

"And, Neil," went on Inga, "please tell me — if you can put up with me just a little longer because I do so value your opinion — what would you do for blue spots on a dog's tongue?"

"Blue? Definitely blue?" said Neil in an interested voice.

"Well, a sort of slate colour and some of them are actually mauve."

"And are they just spots or ——"

"Well, I'd say more splotches than spots."

"Big splotches or little splotches?"

"Oh, all sizes but mostly big ——"

"Has the dog a temperature?"

"No, but he's right off his food, and ——"

"How old is he?"

"Three. He lolls his tongue out as if ——"

"I say, this is very interesting to me," said Neil. "I'd like to have a look at the dog when I come to do the car. I once had a spaniel ——"

Oh, why didn't I think of spots on dogs' tongues? thought Cleo wretchedly, falling behind the chattering pair.

At last they reached the house and went straight into the drawing-room, where everyone fell on Inga with cries of delight.

"Dear Mrs. MacAlvey," she said, "I've only come for the merest minute. I thought you might be alone."

"Why didn't you let us know?" said Mrs. MacAlvey. "You could have joined us for dinner."

"But not for anything! As if I'd intrude upon you just now, with one daughter newly engaged and another back from foreign parts. It's such a family occasion. But I knew you wouldn't want me to pass your very gate."

"Well, now you are here we'll forgive you. Neil, run down to the shore and call to Ian and Raine. They'll want to see Inga."

Cleo wandered over to the window-seat and, sitting down by Miss Paige, began to admire the gros-point stool-cover she was working.

"I began one once," she said, "but I couldn't cope with all those acres of background."

Neil came back with Ian and Raine, who greeted Inga as though they had been waiting for her all day. Mr. MacAlvey insisted on her having a more comfortable chair and a glass of sherry, while Neil offered her a cigarette, Ian a light, and Raine a selection of cushions.

Everybody was talking at once, even Neil. It was all very animated.

"I shouldn't have stayed so long," said Inga after about half an hour. "It's dark now and my car is so unreliable. Well, it's my own fault. I'll just have to struggle."

"I'll tell you what," said Neil, "I'll drive you home in your car and Ian can follow in ours and pick me up. It's only about two miles out of our way. We're not in a hurry."

Not even for a rheumatic cow! thought Cleo.

"Oh, Neil, I couldn't possibly let you — it's too sweet of you ——"

"I insist. Good night, Mrs. MacAlvey, and thank you for a grand evening. Good night, sir. Good night, everybody."

The good nights became a perfect tangle, and they all went to the door and saw the guests go off into the gathering dusk, Inga's golden hair shining out to the last.

"Isn't she a *lovely* person?" said Raine.

Cleo went to bed. The evening had been a failure. It was mostly her own fault. No good, thought Cleo, wearing red hibiscus flowers if you didn't have what it takes. She shuddered slightly at the intruding Americanism, and stripping off the chiffon frock, let it lie in a neglected tangle on the floor.

53

CHAPTER THREE

We've made it!" said Primrose, standing on the slip at six o'clock on Friday morning and gasping in the chill air.

Gavin, full of pride, had already laid *Minnow* alongside the slip and was lacing the new lugsail to its yard.

"Up she goes!" he said with quiet satisfaction, and began to hoist the foresail.

Primrose flung a bundle at his feet.

"The bathing things. You'd all have forgotten them if it hadn't been for me. I'm sorry to say, I could only flog one towel, so we'll have to share it, and I bags first go while it's dry."

"I've collected some food," said Archie, producing half a veal-and-ham pie in a greasy bag. "What did you flog, Gav?"

"A new loaf, and a pot of raspberry jam that has a beastly tendency to leak on my trousers. And cream crackers galore, and cheese *ad lib. con moto perpetuoso*. And the *pièce de résistance!*" He held up a tin with an engaging picture of tropical fruits in luscious colours. "I hope and pray it's peaches."

"You're nuts," said Primrose. "It'll be carrots. You ought

54

to know by now that you can't go by the picture. That's just put on to mislead you. I've got the remains of the apple charlotte from last night's dinner, and the chicken legs that were left because grown-ups with their revolting false teeth can't eat them. And there's the tin of salmon I bought. What a feast! Lucullian, or whatever they call it."

"What about knocking up Ma Mackenzie," said Gavin, "and getting three bottles of lemonade, large size?"

"I'd do it," said Archie, "only I haven't any money."

"It'll be one-and-six," said Primrose. "That's ninepence each for you and me, Gavin, but worth it."

At last they were ready to start.

"Hi, Donald!" yelled Primrose to a passing boy who had stopped to watch the sailing of the *Minnow*. "Shove her head round for us and give us a push off."

The sail flapped in a playful way and swung over to starboard.

"We're off!" said Gavin in the stern.

Minnow slid along under a light breeze from the south-east. The tide was strong though the sea was only faintly rippled. The buoys were passed, and soon she was well down the channel, where the breeze freshened and tiny wavelets slapped her sides with enchanting thuds.

"It's heaven," said Primrose, scratching her ankle.

It was a perfect day, with that unearthly beauty which comes very early on a summer morning. The sky was as blue as a kingfisher's wing, and the mounting sun made the distance hazy and magical. The sea flashed like a silver shield. The dancing boat was a fairy vessel, carrying the children to the Fortunate Land where everything happens as you want it, and lasts for ever.

"Oh!" said Archie. "I forgot the worms."

"You clot!" said Gavin. "Now we can't fish."

"We can swim and eat."

Soon they were in the quiet water off Inchcaul, and rounding the small island Gavin ran the boat ashore on a sandy beach. They all tumbled out.

"Food at last," said Primrose. "I've never been so famished since that day we went to watch the shooting and forgot the sandwiches. I could eat a whole sheep. Let's start on the meat-pie, and then work up to the apple charlotte and the chicken legs and the crackers and jam. Isn't this utter blissikins?"

She lay flat on her back in the warm sand and bit deep into her slice of meat-pie, but had to sit up before she could swallow it. When they had eaten as much as they could, there was still enough food left for the rest of the day, including the original tin of salmon bought for the occasion. They drowsed for some time on the sand, knowing that this was the realisation of all their dreams during the long, long term at school.

> *"Inchcaul, Inchcaul,*
> *I love you all,*
> *You have such charm,*
> *Your sand is warm,"*

said Primrose, making 'warm' rhyme.

"Come on!" said Gavin. "It's time to get aboard if we want to make Kilgarro."

"We could swim quite as well here," said Primrose lazily.

"But there's a diving-place on Kilgarro. Besides, what's the good of having a boat like *Minnow* if we're only going as far as Inchcaul?"

"All right," said Primrose, "but you might let me take the tiller."

"You can have it," said Gavin, "but for Mike's sake keep her in the channel when we get off Kilgarro. If we ground on that mud we'll be there till bedtime."

With Primrose at the tiller, *Minnow* swept up into the wind, her sails well filled. It was ten o'clock when they reached Kilgarro and the tide was on the ebb.

"I'd better take her in," said Gavin.

"I can do it," said Primrose too confidently. Almost as she spoke she heard an ominous knocking on the keel.

"She's touching!" yelled Archie. "Up centre-board!"

Primrose, fumbling among the tangle of ropes, was not quick enough. *Minnow* gave a sudden list, staggered forward, and with a low crunching sound stood still.

"That's torn it," said Gavin. "She's here till four o'clock, so you might as well get out and wade ashore. Rescue the food, Prim, while I run down the sails."

Primrose, who thought this very restrained and forgiving of Gavin, began to collect the provisions while Archie took off his shoes and hung them round his neck by the laces. Then they all waded to the shore.

"Let's dive now, there are the rocks," said Archie.

"It's low tide, you chump. Let's do the deck-tennis thing first and practise bowling. The tackle is all in the locker. Then we'll have dinner and it'll be right for diving."

The morning went happily by. When they were hungry enough for dinner they discovered that no one had remembered to bring a tin-opener, so Gavin had to dig into the salmon tin with a sharp stone, which was laborious and not very satisfactory. The hole was small, and one had to prise bits of salmon out. But the cheese and biscuits were good, and the lemonade particularly fruity and fizzy.

"I'd like to live here all my life, like the Selkirk chap," said

57

Archie. "You know — 'the beasts that rove over the plain, my form with indifference see'."

"There aren't any beasts on Kilgarro," said Primrose, "and it would be foul in winter. You'd have to live on shellfish."

"I'd arrange for a plane to fly me out magnificent meals."

"Isn't it funny," said Gavin, "to think that at this very moment Grandfather is probably getting out the car to go and meet Cecil and Elinore?"

"It isn't *very* funny," said Primrose. "I feel like those people in *Hassan* having one night of love before they went to their doom."

Archie licked the last of the salmon off his fingers and said, "They can't do much to us, not in front of Cecil and Elinore."

"Oh, come on!" said Gavin. "Let's bathe now."

Primrose seized her costume and began to pull it on under her cotton frock. There was a deep sea pool under the diving rocks. The boys were ready and preparing to leap in. She raced after them, appreciating the cool exciting feel of the sand under her bare feet. A deep, deep breath, and then down, down into the tingling water. Out, out to sea, and the big waves to encounter, and that glorious thrill as the ocean received her and lifted her up. Blowing and spluttering, she turned on her back and flailed her legs, flinging up a tremendous spray, then rolling over again she struck out in a swift crawl. "It's the grandest thing on earth!" she thought, swimming out to sea and feeling the enormous, heaving green ocean all around her. At last she caught up with the boys, and they all rested, treading water and flicking their wet hair out of their eyes.

"Magnoocious!" said Gavin. "It's next best to being a seagull."

"That reminds me," said Primrose. "Gull will be back any day now. In time to go with us to Eil-oran."

"Have you forgotten," said Gavin, "that this is our last day of glorious freedom and childish glee? After this, we shall have Cecil and Elinore hanging round our necks, and they probably can't even swim."

"Elinore can," said Primrose. "She's frightfully good at all sports. That's one of the things I hate about her."

"When we get back to shore," said Gavin, "you can time me along 220 yards. We'll pace it out on the beach. I don't know how it is, I can never win the 220 yards at school."

"There's a girl in my form," said Primrose, "whose brother has an Oxford half-blue for swimming. She isn't a bit sidey about it, either."

"How decent," said Gavin.

Archie dived under, bobbed up again, blew a whale-spout and said, "What rhymes with pudding?"

"Gooding," said Primrose.

"Clot! That isn't a word."

"Well, it ought to be."

They turned and raced to the shore. Gavin won easily.

"There!" he said. "Why the Nebuchadnezzar can't I win the 220?"

"I'll tell you what," said Primrose, "after you've done your measured what's-it, we'd better get back to the boat and wait till the tide floats her. There's about a foot of water round her now."

Half an hour later they waded out to the boat. It was very hot in the full sun, so they curled up and dozed. It was a quarter-past four before *Minnow* heaved out of the mud. Gavin ran up the foresail and lug, headed his boat into the wind, and they slipped smoothly homewards.

59

"It's been a voluptuous day," said Primrose, "whatever comes at the end of it. Our maths. mistress says there's an old Spanish proverb, 'Take what you want, take it and pay for it', which means —— "

"We know what it means," said Gavin. "We're not morons. We'll make harbour about six, unless the wind drops."

The wind did not drop, and at ten-past six Gavin moored his boat at the home slip, and three dirty, happy children, soaked in salt water, sunshine, and fresh air, climbed out, their arms full of tackle and wet bathing costumes.

"I feel like the three B's," said Archie. "Bath, blow-out, and bed."

"We're quite liable," said his sister, "to get the third without the other two. Why does nothing ever last?"

"Chins up, boys," said Gavin.

They slipped in at the back door of Kilchro House, and were lucky enough to avoid Mrs. Mortimer and meet Mysie, herself young and sympathetic.

"Have they come?" whispered Primrose.

"Been here since quarter-past three," said Mysie. "I wouldn't be you."

"Have a heart," said Gavin. "What do they look like?"

"Braw," said Mysie. "A braw wee lady and gentleman."

Gavin gave a groan, which died on his lips as Mrs. Mac-Alvey herself appeared and looked at them in a way which made them feel they were oozing out of their own wet shoes.

"I am ashamed of you," she said. "I will give you the credit of supposing that you forgot your cousins were arriving to-day, because anything else would be contemptible, but that doesn't excuse you. I can't send you to bed without supper on *their* first evening, so you'll get off scot-free, but your grand-

60

father and I feel you have disgraced us. Now go to your rooms and make yourselves look less like ragamuffins. I shall expect you in the drawing-room in fifteen minutes."

Feeling utterly abased the three tore upstairs. Fifteen minutes meant just fifteen minutes when Granny said it.

And now for the worst! thought Primrose, performing a whirlwind toilet and flashing downstairs again, a dead heat with the boys, scarlet-faced but immaculate in their school suits.

The drawing-room looked very large and serene, and the scent from the bowls of roses on the low tables was quite stuffy after the scent of open sea with which the children's lungs were filled. After a summer's day out with the wind and the ocean, houses seemed cagey and unbearable.

On the window-seat two people were sitting gazing at the view. They were, of course, Cecil and Elinore.

Cecil was a tall, pale boy of sixteen, with glasses. He wore very light flannels and a tailored striped shirt and school tie, and a very good-looking Shetland tweed sports coat. Elinore, who was fourteen, had one of those long bobs of shiny hair that looks all in one piece, and she wore a pink linen dress that looked as though it had just come out of an expensive shop, and silk stockings and brown-and-white court shoes.

"Children," said Mrs. MacAlvey, "come and meet your cousins. Elinore and Cecil, this is Primrose who's fifteen, and Gavin who's fourteen, and Archie who's only ten."

"Only!" muttered Archie, glaring at his grandmother's back.

"How d'y'do," said Elinore and Cecil, politely and simultaneously.

"How do you do," said Primrose and Gavin.

"I'm all right," said Archie. "I'm always all right."

"I'm going to leave you to get to know each other," said

61

Mrs. MacAlvey. "Dinner is in half an hour. Come straight in when you hear the gong."

She walked out of the drawing-room and closed the door behind her. Everybody who was left stood about awkwardly.

"What time did you get here?" said Primrose.

"Our train reached Inverbyne at two-forty," said Cecil, "and your grandfather met us with the car. We arrived here at about three-fifteen."

"You were lucky," said Archie. "The car usually breaks down and gets here at about eight-fifteen."

"How queer," said Elinore, looking at Archie as though she felt it beneath her to talk to people who were only ten.

"This is quite a nice place," she went on. "It's nicer than I thought it would be."

"The view is supposed to be rather good," said Gavin.

"Is it?" said Elinore. "Of course, when one has been to Norway ── "

"I'm sure it's a remarkably fine view," said Cecil.

"Have you been to Norway?" said Archie to Elinore.

"Oh yes. And to the South of France and Switzerland and the Channel Islands. I think travelling broadens you. I'm always so sorry for people who haven't."

"What do you do here all the time?" asked Cecil.

"Sail, mostly," said Gavin. "I've just got a boat of my own. *Minnow.* I bought her with my own money."

"What displacement?" asked Cecil.

"We don't know," said Archie, "but you can get four in with a squash."

"Oh, I thought you meant a yacht," said Cecil, straightening his tie. Gavin went scarlet.

"What about a mooch round the garden before dinner," said Primrose. "I hate being indoors, anyway."

The others consented, so they walked primly round the garden and looked at the herbaceous border, which wasn't a success, as Cecil knew the Latin names of all the plants while the MacAlvey children didn't even know the English ones.

It was a relief when the dinner gong sounded. The children made their way to the bottom of the table, where they usually sat in unobtrusive silence, avoiding any awkward questions from their elders, but this did not suit Cecil and Elinore, who waited to be given places by Mrs. MacAlvey. Very soon Cecil was intelligently discussing the shooting prospects with Mr. MacAlvey, while Elinore chatted in a sophisticated way with Cleo and Raine and was obviously making a great hit.

After dinner — and coffee, which Primrose hated but Elinore said she loved and always took in the drawing-room at home — they all went out into the garden again, and since the paths were not wide enough for five to walk abreast, Primrose found herself on ahead with Elinore while the boys walked a long way behind.

"Tell me about your school," said Elinore fervently.

Primrose, whose one idea in the holidays was to forget that such a place as school existed, looked taken aback.

"What sort of a report did you get?" asked Elinore.

"Oh, I expect it was pretty rugged," said Primrose. "I carefully avoided actually seeing it. There's one thing I will say for Granny, she doesn't hold inquests on our reports with all the gory details. She just says, 'Your report has come, Primrose. I hope you'll try to do better next term'. There's a girl in my form called Diana White, and her father actually has the whole family in and reads Diana's report aloud to them, uttering low moans of pain as he does so. Murder, I call it."

"I have kept all my reports, ever since I was eight," said Elinore. "I have them in a box. They are so interesting. What is your favourite subject at school?"

"Oh, I don't know," said Primrose. "Some are drearier than others, I suppose."

"English is mine," said Elinore. "I got ninety-one per cent. in the English exam. last term. My great friend Pearl Panton got ninety-three. She's doing School Certificate. Her father's a baronet."

"Nice work," said Primrose absently.

"She got a prize too, for a French essay."

"I say!" said Primrose politely. "She must be pretty hot."

"Shall we go back to the drawing-room now?" said Elinore. "I promised to show Miss Paige my embroidery, and I should like to do some more of it before bedtime."

Having deposited Elinore in the drawing-room, Primrose felt justified in making her own disappearance. She found Gavin and Archie kicking their heels into the earth at the bottom of the rockery.

"Where's Cecil?" she said.

"He's gone up to his room to write a letter to his mother to say he's arrived safely. Where's Elinore?"

"In the drawing-room doing some disgusting sewing."

Next morning when she awoke, before she even opened her eyes, Primrose had that grim feeling one gets when something unpleasant is going to happen and one is not sufficiently awake to remember what.

Then she remembered and gave a groan that shook the bed. Opening one eye to see whether the tea had come, she saw it standing coldly on the bedside table. The hour was late. Primrose leapt out of bed and went first to the windows, as weather-wise people do. It was a brilliant morning. You could

64

see for miles out to sea, where a steamer like an ant was puffing on the skyline. Nearer, the island of Inchcaul looked so close that you could have tossed a pebble on to it. The white cottages were very distinct.

"Humph!" said Primrose. "There's a change coming, it's freshening already."

At breakfast Mrs. MacAlvey said, "Cecil wants to see the loch, so your grandfather will bring the car round at ten o'clock and take you five children. You can drive right round the loch and be back for luncheon."

Primrose, Gavin, and Archie were never very taken with the idea of riding in the car at the best of times; it seemed to them an occupation for the elderly and those who had lost the use of their legs, but they patiently submitted to the arrangement. The car came round, and Cecil got in front with Mr. Mac-Alvey while the other four crushed in behind.

Cecil and Elinore were impressed with the Highland scenery. They kept comparing it with the scenery in Norway and Switzerland, which Primrose thought too phoney for words. Places were places in their own right and not meant to be measured up against other places.

The turquoise blue of the loch was slightly ruffled by the wind, and its many tiny islets, some dense with hazels, some bearing a solitary pine, were like blobs of emerald in the limpid water. More colour swept the mountain-sides, with the burning pink of opening heather. On either side of the loch the mountains ran so far into the distance that you could only dream the end of them — if there ever was an end — where somewhere their misty amethyst met the misty blue of the sky.

Cecil said, might he have the car stopped, and he got out and picked something from the roadside. Elinore said it would

65

be a rare fern for his collection. This happened several times and Cecil seemed very happy.

They arrived home for luncheon feeling ready for violent exercise after all that sitting down, so they were quite pleased when their grandmother suggested tennis.

"Don't bother about me," said Archie. "I'm going to catch a dragonfly."

Gavin ran to fetch his own and Primrose's racket and shoes; Cecil and Elinore disappeared up the stairs and fifteen minutes later came down clad from neck to toe in immaculate white, each carrying not one but three rackets.

"Excuse me, but are you looking for Wimbledon?" said Gavin.

"Not at all," said Elinore coolly. "We have a rule at school, and so has Cecil, that you are never allowed to play tennis unless you are absolutely correctly dressed in all white. You more or less get used to it, quite automatically, you know."

Primrose flushed scarlet, looking down at the crumpled cotton dress she had worn all yesterday and today, and the far from white shoes which hung from her racket. She might have said that they had the same rule at her own school — which was true — but with laundry being so difficult and the staff so busy, her granny didn't think it was necessary for them to wear tennis whites for their ordinary holiday games. It was ostentatious to do so, and only made a lot of work for other people. But she nobly refrained from saying anything about this, though she felt furious when she saw Cecil's glance travel from his own snowy trousers to Gavin's grey shorts, hitched up with an old striped tie.

"Come on, if you're ready," she said gruffly and led the way to the court.

"How shall we play?" said Gavin.

66

"I think Cecil and I had better play you two," said Elinore with a look of the caste versus the outcaste. "Shall we toss for side?"

"Heads," called Cecil.

"Heads it is," said Gavin.

"Is there anything in the side?" asked Cecil.

"Well, the end with the delphiniums is the worst," said Primrose, "because the balls keep going in among them and you have to do a lot of crawling about."

"How funny having flowers at the end of a tennis court," said Elinore. "Our court at home has a run-back of eighteen feet at each end. You'd better take the delphiniums, as you're used to them."

She and Cecil proved to be a formidable pair. Cecil had the advantage of height and long arms. He was very accurate and had a sizzling service. If he missed his first service, the second was just as hard. Elinore was a showy player and pirouetted about the court like a ballet dancer, striking spectacular attitudes. When she hit the ball it was usually very hard indeed, and when she missed it she bobbed down, turned round and shouted, 'Out!'

Gavin was the kind of temperamental player who had days on which he couldn't do anything wrong and days on which he couldn't do anything right. This was one of the latter. He struck a bad line of double faults, and all his smashes went about three inches out of court.

Primrose played a good, steady game, keeping a good length and returning a deadly backhand, her best stroke. She was in her school first Six.

The game went wholly in favour of Cecil and Elinore. They won the first set at six-one, and though Gavin and Primrose after a hard-fought second set managed to win it at nine-seven, the other two ran ahead again in the third set and were soon five-two.

It was Cecil's service. His first serve was an ace, which Primrose never touched, for it zipped along the ground without rising.

"Fifteen-love," said Elinore who always called out the score.

Cecil served to Gavin who returned the ball hard and true, but with his usual bad luck it caught the top of the net and fell back into his own court.

"Thirty-love!" sang Elinore.

Cecil served to Primrose, who this time had the satisfaction of pasting the ball back right at Elinore's feet.

"Thirty-fifteen," said Elinore, not so loudly.

Cecil served again to Gavin, and again poor Gavin's strong return let him down and went out of court.

"Forty-fifteen!" chanted Elinore. "Set point!"

Cecil served to Primrose and a grand rally developed. The ball crossed the net again and again. Elinore got enormously excited, dancing on her toes and brandishing her racket like a battle-axe. Cecil drove hard at Gavin who lobbed the ball up. Rushing to the net and leaning well over, her arm and racket outstretched as far as she could, Elinore smashed with all her might. The ball nicked Primrose's racket and sped into the delphiniums.

"Game *and!*" shouted Elinore.

"My sacred turtle!" said Primrose. "You had your racket about a mile over the net. Hadn't she, Gavin?"

"I'll say she had," said Gavin.

"Indeed, I had not!" said Elinore angrily. "I always take the greatest care to stand well on my own side of the net. Actually I was standing a good two yards inside my own court when I smashed the ball, wasn't I, Cecil?"

68

"I didn't see," said Cecil, funking the issue.

"Well, I was," said Elinore. "But of course there's no referee, and if you two are going to stick to your story, it's no good my telling the truth. You can call it forty-thirty. It'll be all the same in the end, anyway. Go on, Cecil, finish them off."

Cecil twisted his body into a corkscrew and unleashed one of his rocket services at Gavin's backhand. Gavin, a little dazed by Elinore's unsportsmanlike behaviour, didn't even see it until a slight swish and a shower of delphiniums told him what had happened to it.

"Game and set," said Cecil and Elinore simultaneously, and Cecil added politely, "Thank you very much."

"I think we'll go and change for tea now," said Elinore, donning a spotless white blazer.

Gavin and Primrose let down the net.

"I say!" said Gavin in a dismayed voice. "Do we have to change for tea? Do we have to *have* tea? I thought we'd have gone to the village and got some pop."

"We could wash," said Primrose scornfully. "I could even put on my Liberty voile." She suddenly gave a yell of fury and sat down flat on the grass. "It's ruined!" she cried. "Our blissibus holiday. All ruined. Oh, Gav, we might as well be dead!"

CHAPTER FOUR

Cleo and Miss Paige were on the bus which ran along the coast road as far as Blain, took a tentative dive into the mountains, thought better of it, and turned back towards the sea.

At that turning-point Cleo and Miss Paige descended and began their walk. A sunny glen, heather lined, lay before them with steep hills on either side, and as the glen ran westwards it was likely at last to reach the coast. The road, which like most Highland roads began with some sort of a surface but quickly lost it, grew narrower until it became a mere track among the whins and heather, pierced here and there by stony streams. A high wind romped over miles and miles of open country. Miss Paige, who had entrusted her locks to a hair-net, soon found it was missing and cried, "That's the worst of long hair in a bun. If it does get loose you look like a weeping willow."

Cleo wore a peasant handkerchief tied under her chin.

Soon the track ended at a cluster of black houses roughly thatched with blocks of turf. Peat-smoke rose in plumes from the primitive roofs. A black cow with a plaintive expression was tethered to one door.

Three bare-footed children with handsome deep-eyed faces and rough black hair stood and stared at the newcomers with the curiosity of mountain sheep. Each wore a single, sack-like, sexless garment.

"What is this place?" asked Miss Paige.

They shook their wild heads with concerted action.

"Oh come! Surely one of you can speak English?"

The two smaller children pointed to the elder girl, who said, "I can speak English."

"What do you call this place?" asked Cleo.

"Inverbedale."

"If we keep on, can we get round by the seashore and back to Strogue?"

"No. There is not a road, only over the rocks, and she would be high tide now."

"Do you go to school?" asked Miss Paige.

"Sometimes."

"Where do you go to school?"

"Over there," said the girl with a wave of the arm that embraced about ten miles of mountain and loch.

Cleo found some pennies in her pocket, and offered them to the children, whose eyes became enormous.

"Don't you know what they are?" she asked.

"Yes."

"Haven't you ever had any pennies before?"

"No."

"Let's go on, Vannah," said Cleo. "I must know what happens when this glen comes to the sea."

She turned as they walked away to wave back to the children, who were staring after them as though they were spirits. There was something unforgettable about these children, who were clean, dignified, and intelligent-looking, like the wild deer of the mountains or the young eagles of the inaccessible heights.

At last Cleo and her companion reached the coast, and stood high aloft on a turf-clad hill whose long slopes ran down to the hard fawn-coloured sands, where the green rollers creamed and broke in a thunder of spray. On the rocks below hundreds of gulls were perched, and farther out the gleaming grey birds bobbed on the swell and dived with a flash of wings. When they rose into the air their cries were flung high by the wind and became part of the sea symphony. Clouds of huge size rolled in the blue sky, taking their shapes from the islands beneath. The air was rich with scents of sea and turf and heather. Cleo lay flat on her back and shut her eyes so that all her senses absorbed scent and sound, and from where she lay a disturbed plover sprang up into the air and added his lament to the elemental music.

"We shall have to go back the way we came," said Miss Paige, "so we might as well have a long rest." She divided a bar of chocolate, one half of which she placed on Cleo's reclining chest, and added, "Whenever I see a black house, I rather wish I lived in one. There's something so appealing about primitive life. I should like to sleep in a wall bed and learn to use the handloom."

"You'd be kippered by the peat smoke before you learned to use anything," said Cleo lazily.

"I do believe," said Miss Paige, "that I once came here with my father when I was a child. Our home was at Rosemarkie, and he was a great sportsman and never happy except when he was out of doors. I was devoted to him and would always follow him when he would let me. My father was a fine-looking man, with a large, broad head and a pointed beard. Of course it was the fashion for men of his generation to look like

72

King Edward. I remember how fond he was of wearing that dun-coloured homespun that the crofters make and which always smells of the peat. Does this bore you, Cleo?"

"Oh no. Do go on. I've never heard you talk about your father, Vannah."

"I remember once being out with him and a ghillie. It was an autumn afternoon and mists were wreathing above the loch. My father didn't want me to go any farther, so he wrapped me in his plaid and made me sit down on a flat rock, and he gave me a small copy of Burns's poems that he always carried, and told me to memorise one of them and on no account to move until he came back for me. Then he and the ghillie went on, and I obediently began to learn the poem, with my fingers pushed into my ears and saying it line by line as a child does; but soon black clouds came racing across the sky and a terrible storm broke. The rain literally washed me off my rock, and I crouched by the side of it, holding on to the plaid which the wind tried to tear from my cold, wet fingers. At last a crofter came by and offered to rescue me, but I repulsed him and refused to leave, saying, 'My father told me to wait here for him and not to move. I won't go away.' He probably thought I was demented! It was two hours later before my father came back to me. I was frozen with cold, half-drowned and weeping, and all I could say through my chattering teeth was, 'Oh, saw ye bonny Lesley, As she ga'ed o'er the Border? She's gane like Alexander, To spread her conquests farther.' I had learned my poem! My father said I had taken his instructions too literally, which in later life was a good excuse for me when I wanted to interpret his wishes to suit myself."

"Go on," said Cleo. "Another story."

"Well — " Miss Paige looked pleased. "There was the time

73

when I lamented because our name was not on one of the clanstones at Culloden. We were spending the day in Inverness, and I begged my father to take me to see the battlefield. At first he wouldn't, thinking it a morbid fancy for a child of eight, but I begged until I got my way. It was a wild spring day, with a bleak wind blowing across that desolate heath. On the farther side of the water were the wild mountains; here were just the lonely graves of the poor Highlanders who never reached their homes again. After the battle, as you know, the country people buried them hastily where they lay, sorting them according to their tartans, and they carved the names of the clans on rough blocks of stone and set them up above the shallow graves. I ran from one to another, searching — not for the name of Paige which is not a clan name, but for Mackay, my mother's name to which I felt I had some right. There was Macdonald, MacGillivray, Fraser, Cameron — but no Mackay. I sat down by the roadside and cried like a waterspout. A lady came up to me and said, 'Why are you crying, little girl?' I said, 'Where were the Mackays? Tell me that!' My father came and led me away. I wept all the way home, and he was disgusted and said he would never take me anywhere again."

"But he did?"

"Yes, many a time." Miss Paige smiled. "My dear father was so indulgent. And I was the queerest child! I remember once he promised to buy me a silver plaid brooch when I had earned it by casting a line, playing and landing six trout. It was a promise lightly made and probably as soon forgotten, but I took it in deadly earnest. How I struggled and worked to win that brooch! Meanwhile my father had to go to Edinburgh on business, and took my mother and my elder sister Alice with him. For some reason I was left at home, I can't

74

remember it now. When they returned they brought me a large box of sweets and a Cairngorm pendant. My sister said, 'Look what Papa bought me in Edinburgh!' It was a silver plaid brooch. I was sick with pain and dismay. To think that Alice had got that for doing nothing, while to me it had been like the Victoria Cross! I went out and threw my pendant and the sweets into the loch. And from that day I never fished again, or wanted to. Nobody could understand it, my father least of all."

"I understand," said Cleo. "I know just how you felt."

She got up reluctantly and said, "It's four o'clock. We shall have to turn back if we want to catch the five o'clock bus. Why is it such an anti-climax to go back from anywhere the same way one came?"

When they got back to Kilchro, Raine was waiting, and cried, "I'm so glad you've come. Ian rang up to ask if we would go to Larrich and decide what is to be done to the house before it is fit for me to live in."

"Oh, but you don't want me," said Cleo, alarmed.

"Of course I do. I haven't any ideas at all, and you always have such a grasp of the situation. I don't quite know what that means, but Father always says it of you. 'Cleo has such a grasp of the situation.' There's a lot at Larrich that wants grasping before I go to live there. You'd better do something about your face before we start."

"Why? Is it scarlet?"

"It looks horrible." (Cleo wilted.) "Stick some of my calamine on, it's on the top shelf of my little book-case in a bottle marked brilliantine, and meanwhile I'll get the car out. I expect you're wanting tea, but there'll be some at Larrich."

Cleo was not sure whether she was dying to go to Larrich or would do better to stay at home, but as she splashed Raine's calamine on her flaming cheeks she decided that at least she would not make the mistake of looking forward to the visit. There was no surer way of blighting anything than by looking forward to it, whereas occasions that one regarded without enthusiasm often turned out to be highly rewarding. So she fanned her face with *Adam Bede* to dry it, and sprang into a clean linen frock, while Raine tooted impatiently below.

They arrived at Larrich a little after six. The house was a cube, square and grey, rather ugly with its flat rows of sash-windows, but owing its redeeming touch of romance to its massive stones, iron-studded door, and four pepper-pot turrets. Behind it was a belt of pines. The surrounding land was mountainous and wild, the farming of it neither easy nor profitable. Every foot of good soil was utilised, and the best of it lay along the southern shore of a small loch a quarter of a mile from the house, which had formerly provided the water-supply. In the loch was an island, the family burial-ground of the Garvines.

The hall door stood open and Raine marched in, followed by her sister, into a hall which was spacious and high, paved with stone flags across which lay a shabby runner of carpet. On the walls hung various horns and antlers, grey with dust. The furniture consisted of a fine old black oak table and massive matching chairs, hand carved, which had stood there since the house was built, and beyond these had been fitted to the wall a line of strictly utilitarian hooks on which hung an array of old coats and mackintoshes, gum-boots standing beneath. Several doors led off from the hall.

Old Morag appeared from the back regions.

"Good-day, Morag," said Raine. "Where is Mr. Garvine?"

"He's away out," said Morag, "and so is Larrich himself. You'd best begin your tea."

76

"Something has gone wrong," said Raine. "That's farming! I'm sure they wouldn't want us to wait."

She led the way through a curtained archway into the dining-room where tea was laid on a round table, on a frayed cloth of finest damask; a dish of freshly made baps, a slab of butter, a grocer's jar of whinberry jam, and a lopsided fruit cake.

"I'll be bringing the tea and the eggs," said Morag.

"Odd cups," said Raine, pouring milk into the thick utility crockery. "What do you think, there is a complete set of Rockingham for twenty-four persons, and a dozen of red and gold Wedgwood, and a dozen of Royal Worcester like museum pieces. Morag has them all locked up for special occasions."

"What does she call a special occasion?"

"Oh, nothing less than a royal visit."

"What a prospect for you!"

"No; she has promised to hand over the keys to Ian's blushing bride."

Morag appeared with a huge, ornate silver tea-pot, inadequately cleaned, and a basin containing six boiled eggs.

"I'll be bringing more eggs if there's no enough," she said.

"I have often wondered," said Cleo, "what it feels like to eat three eggs." She gave a slight gulp, and added, "What will — Neil do when you and Ian get married?"

"Oh, just the same as now," said Raine. "Of course it is really his house, but even if Neil were ever to get married — and I don't think he will because he never takes any notice of girls except perhaps Inga Duthie, and she has so much money that his pride would never allow him to propose to her — he would never hear of Ian leaving. The house is so large it would easily divide into two, but, oh dear, now you have set me off worrying about what sort of a sister-in-law I may get."

"I shouldn't worry," said Cleo, attacking her second egg with undiminished appetite. "I'm sure Neil will never marry, and you will make this place so comfortable for him that he won't want to bring another woman in. He will become one of those selfless bachelor uncles with his brother's little ones prattling round his knee."

"Neil never sits down long enough for anything to prattle round his knee," said Raine, buttering baps; "he is a most restless person, and when he is talking to you his mind always seems to be miles away. I never know with people like that whether they are actually so lofty-minded that they can't condescend to ordinary chatter or whether it is just that they are slow in the uptake. Of course Neil is a dear and very idealistic, he would have made a wonderful Jacobite, but Ian is nearer to the earth and more comfortable company, if you know what I mean."

Stung by the slanderous suggestion that Neil could be slow in the uptake, Cleo was just about to make some heated reply when Ian burst into the room full of apologies, embraced Raine, and shouted to Morag to bring fresh tea and more eggs.

The rest of the meal was a merry one, and when it was over Ian said, "We'd better go round the rooms and see what wants doing."

First they went to the drawing-room, which was a long, beautifully proportioned room with a Regency striped wallpaper in pink and grey, a floor which had once been used for dancing but whose parquet had not seen polish for years, some stiff, faded Chippendale and Sheraton furniture which suggested eighteenth-century conversation pieces, low white bookcases filled with old-fashioned books, many fragile-looking little tables bearing what used to be called bric-à-brac, stiff pink curtains split along the folds, and an all-pervading musty smell.

They stood in silence not knowing what to say, as only the phrase 'How pretty but what a pity' seemed to meet the case, and then Ian said rather awkwardly, "I suppose what you'll want here, Raine, is a less cluttered-up look and some deep chairs and settees. I hardly ever remember this room being used."

"I remember it," said Cleo, "at your mother's silver-wedding party. It looked beautiful then and not a bit neglected — I mean —— "

"You needn't be afraid to say it looks neglected," said Ian with dignity, "because we know it does, and I think we ought to alter it completely before Raine has to sit in it."

"What a pity," said Cleo, "that there aren't any family portraits. Ancestors in dark tartans with frames of soft old gilt wound give this room a kind of substance."

"The Garvine ancestors don't seem to have cared about the fashion for having their portraits painted," said Raine. "I thought it was the custom in the eighteenth century for poor but honest painters to travel about Scotland, calling at the houses and painting the entire family in oils in return for a fortnight's free venison and a sniff of the whisky. Why, oh why, should such a one have missed out Larrich?"

"But he didn't entirely," said Ian. "There were a few portraits, I believe, but a sorry tale hangs thereby. My grandfather was a bit of an eccentric, to put it mildly, and had a passion for clearing out everything he wasn't actually using, so he made a great bonfire and burned the old portraits and a lot of other family things that might have been valuable today. In any case, valuable or not, we'd have liked them."

"What a vandal!" said Raine. "Now you mention it, I've

79

heard that story before, but in a livelier version. I was told he set up his ancestors in the back-yard and took pot shots at them until there wasn't a shred of canvas left on their frames."

"We haven't a back-yard," said Ian with dignity.

"Now, don't take it that way, I think your grandfather was magnificent," said Raine, "even though he has robbed us of our heirlooms. We must manufacture some more for our descendants, *noblesse oblige*. If any hungry painters come to the door, tell Morag to call you immediately, and don't let him paint you with the cows! By the way, will Neil approve of anything we do here?"

"Neil says everything is to be as you want it."

"Then let's leave this room for the time being, and go and look at the sitting-room."

The sitting-room was a real man's den, gloomy and dingy with its red-flock walls and smoke-stained ceiling, but cheerful and warm in the spread of its log-filled hearth, its shabby leather armchairs full of crumpled cushions, and its assembling close at hand of everything that a man's leisure could possibly demand, from piles of books and magazines on the floor to fishing tackle and parts of guns and dog baskets and tins of tobacco and pipe-racks and seed catalogues and bags of cowcake samples, all over the place. Three dogs disentangled themselves from the pleasing chaos and came leaping round Ian.

"This," he said with simple understatement, "will want clearing up."

"Sweet mercy!" said Raine.

"Paint? Wallpaper? More chairs?" said Ian.

"I'd hate to disturb anything you liked so much as it is," said Raine. "There are two other possible sitting-rooms, aren't there? Couldn't we have a go at those?"

"One of them has damp streaming down the walls," said Ian, "and the other one smells."

"What does it smell of?"

"I don't know. Nobody has bothered about that smell for at least a hundred years, so there's no one living who remembers how it started. It just smells." Ian pushed down the dogs, passed round cigarettes, and cried, "Oh, here's Neil!" And Neil himself came striding in, wearing a kilt and short-sleeved shirt, with his hair wet with the sweat of toil and his arms grimed to the elbows.

"Hullo, Raine! Hullo, Cleo," he said. "I was just going to wash. I thought you'd be away upstairs."

"They can go upstairs by themselves now," Ian said, "while I talk to you about that new Milk Board regulation. Go along, girls, and see the worst."

Cleo, who was furious with herself because her knees had gone weak the minute Neil came in so unexpectedly, followed her sister up the shallow staircase, avoiding the holes in the carpet.

At the half-landing they both stopped a minute and began to giggle at the sight of a stripped pine branch in a glass case, supporting a conglomeration of stuffed birds which Nature in her maddest mood would not have thought of bringing together — a grouse, a horned owl, a pair of magpies, a bevy of surprised-looking divers and guillemots, a number of tiny songsters, and a forlorn and crazy-looking bird which Raine with an effort identified as a capercailzie.

"Where do you think that outfit would look nice?" she asked grimly.

The bedrooms all turned out to be much alike, fine lofty rooms of rectangular shape, with shabby carpets, ponderous

81

Victorian furniture, and truly magnificent fourposter beds supporting heavy canopies and dusty drapings.

"Can you see me reclining gracefully in one of those?" said Raine. "I should lie awake all night waiting for the top to fall in."

"I like this one!" cried Cleo, opening the next door and revealing a bed that was gay in green, scarlet, and black with window curtains to match. "A tartan room! Oh, I love this! Don't change it, Raine."

"But it's just as decayed as all the others," Raine complained, "and if you touch those hangings they'll probably crumble into dust and smother you. I don't know where to *begin*. I don't know what to *do* about the bedrooms. Of course the walls shriek for paint or wallpaper, and we must have new carpets, but we can't introduce new furniture along with the ancient. How I envy brides who start their married lives with some nice empty rooms!"

"You don't really," said Cleo. "You're mad with pride in Larrich."

"In a way, yes. But have I got to go back two hundred years and live in that age in that way, or live in the present day as myself? I didn't think it was going to be as bad as this, and so much of it! Now tell me, do we send the antiques to the salerooms and buy new, or is that Philistinian of me? Or do I mean vandalistic? Ian isn't rich, and we might not get much for the old family things, and the modern furniture we could afford to buy might not look right in the old house, and it would all end in a frantic muddle."

Raine gave a desperate sigh, and Cleo said, "Hasn't Ian any suggestions to make?"

"Oh no, he has the most touching faith in me, which makes things harder. Over there is his room" — she led the way across the corridor — "and this one next to it is Neil's. You see! A small iron bed in the middle of about an acre of bare boards, and the bed covered with a plaid in the traditional manner."

The master of the house and his brother certainly slept austerely.

"Here's the last room on this floor," said Cleo. "That makes seven."

"Eight," said Raine. "Eight! Don't try to spare me."

"Oh, this one has the prettiest view," said Cleo, "and it has an alcove, such an agreeable shape after all those hollow cubes. This would make a lovely sewing-room for you, Raine."

"Sewing-room? What do I want with a sewing-room?" cried Raine. "I shall have all my time taken up with chasing hundred-year-old smells and extricating myself from the bed curtains. Cleo, would you *mind* not testing the strength of those worm-eaten floor-boards or you'll find yourself in the cellar, upside-down in the balancer meal."

"Oh, Raine, they're not worm-eaten, that's one of the good things about them. I was just making sure of it."

"You ought to be doing this instead of me," said Raine dourly. (And Cleo thought, Oh, if I were!) "You'd have the place full of dainty sewing-rooms and bowers of beauty in about two weeks. You'd have the Annie Laurie Room and the Pickwick Room and —— "

"Oh, don't talk like an idiot!" cried Cleo, sharply exasperated. "Where do we go from here?"

"The top floor, I suppose."

On the top floor of Larrich House were cupboard-like servants' rooms, relics of an eighteenth-century *ménage* and empty of any furniture.

"Morag sleeps in the kitchen for warmth," said Raine, "and a girl comes in from the village daily to help her. These" —

she flung open a door, revealing a suite of bare apartments with barred windows — "are the nurseries. Anything less than ten or twelve little toddlers would be lost here."

"Would there be a bathroom down below?" asked Cleo. "I quite forgot to notice."

"There would. Just the one, and practically inaccessible. I mean, it is tucked away at the end of a little passage all by itself, and you go up a step to go in and then fall head-first down another step as you enter the door. The arrangements must be seen to be believed, and there is a cistern in the corner which makes gulping noises all the time like somebody being strangled. Surely you remember it, Cleo, when you were here in the old days?"

"Yes, I remember now. It was dark and I opened the door and fell flat on my face, and while I lay there waiting for the end I heard the cistern gurgling in the darkness and thought it actually was somebody being murdered. You'll have to do something about the bathroom."

"Let me write that down," said Raine, bringing out a black notebook and a stub of pencil and finding a blank page. "Thank goodness, I've got something to write down at last. 'Completely reorganise bathroom. Steps. Lighting. Gurgling cistern.' We seem to be making headway at last. 'Induce Morag to sleep in proper bedroom on (a) hygienic, or, if that fails, (b) Biblical grounds.'"

"Biblical!"

"She'd do anything the minor prophets did. I shall tell her they always went upstairs to bed."

"Where have you two got to?" came Ian's voice from below, echoing through the hollow passages.

"We're coming down in dark despair," shouted Raine, and they descended to where Ian and Neil were waiting.

84

"Well, have you got it all planned?" said Ian cheerfully.

Raine gave him a heart-rending look, and said, "I've decided it's hopeless. We'll leave the house as it is and go and live with the cows."

"What's in that notebook?"

Raine showed him what she had written and he grinned.

Cleo wandered back to the room with the tartan hangings and stood at the window looking out at the magnificent view of loch and pinewood. She fingered the old curtains thoughtfully, while the others watched her in a bewildered way.

"This room was my great-grandfather's," said Neil. "He was a grand old type. I can picture him sitting by that hearth with a blazing fire of pine logs shining on the steel fire-irons and yelling for a couple of clansmen to come and pull off his boots, then rolling into his tartan bed to dream of the chase."

"Oh, but that's wonderful, and Larrich is all wonderful!" cried Cleo, for the moment forgetting her diffidence. "It has dignity, and that is the most important thing a house can have, because you can't buy it and you can't destroy it either."

She saw Neil looking at her in a stunned sort of way, and was so overcome that she could have gone through the floor.

"The oracle is about to give tongue," said Raine. "Go on, Cleo."

"Oh, I can't. It isn't my business."

"You've got ideas," said Ian, "and apparently nobody else has."

"Well, I've no right to shove in," said Cleo, wondering what on earth she was expected to say, "but if you insist — oh, this sounds cheek ——"

"Say it!" said Raine. "We're all ears."

"All right. If it were my affair I shouldn't try to alter anything, I'd just restore it. I'd have one big bedroom furnished in

85

modern style — for you, Raine — and as for the others, they should be cleaned and restored to what they were in their days of glory. If the carpets and hangings will bear cleaning, have them cleaned and leave them shabby, it's part of their charm. If they won't clean, then buy some old but serviceable things that the rooms will feel at home with. I would aim at a gentle, faded, past-splendour look in these rooms. Does that sound possible, or —— "

"It is possible!" cried Ian. "And it's good."

"I like it," said Raine generously. "What else, Cleo? Don't stop now."

"You'll have to have some servants, Raine, and they'll be Highland girls, and if you get the right ones they'll love to live in and care for a fine old place like this. And think! Wouldn't your own friends who come to stay with you enjoy sleeping in a room like this one, if the bed were made up with fine linen and the mahogany was gleaming and the old faded tartan gave the final touch of romance? I simply love this tartan room. And the tartan is good, it won't fall to pieces when it's cleaned. I gave it a hard tug. Oh, Raine, you are lucky to have it!"

"Don't go so fast," said Raine, scribbling in her notebook.

"You're never taking it down!" cried Cleo, horror-stricken.

"Of course I am. Ian and I will go into the practical side of it later. Let's go downstairs now because we still haven't done anything about the sitting-room."

"The damp one?" said Ian. "That'll make you think, Cleo."

They all went down to look at the damp sitting-room. The window framed a magnificent view, but the walls had broken out with a horrible grey fungus. Raine covered her eyes and shuddered.

"A builder or plumber could put this right," said Cleo en-

86

thusiastically. "Don't look so Lady Macbeth-ish, Raine. Have it made into a yellow sitting-room with yellow linen covers, it would be lovely, and —— " She stopped dead.

Raine uncovered her eyes and said, "Now what's the matter?"

"Please don't let me talk any more. Anybody would think my needle had stuck."

"Why are you people with brains so modest?" said Ian. "I'm all for Cleo's ideas, and we'll get this room cleaned up if it takes the Lord Provost of Glasgow to do it. I like yellow, it's my favourite colour. Like buttercups."

"Not buttercups!" interrupted Raine. "Spare me buttercups. I'd want that heavenly boiled gold colour you see in the sky when the sun has just gone down. What would you call it?"

"Apricot?" suggested Cleo.

"That's it. *Tinned* apricot. We'll have a tinned apricot sitting-room looking out at a heavenly apricot sky. And now we've done all we're going to do today, and I feel exhausted with so much hard work. Neil, you are an angel to stand there looking dumb and acquiescent while we mess your house about. I'm not forgetting it *is* your house."

Neil smiled and said nothing, and Ian, laughing, took one girl on each arm and cried, "Let's have some more to eat, and play Canasta!"

So they spent a merry evening in the den, in a cheerful atmosphere thick with tobacco smoke, and eleven o'clock came in no time.

CHAPTER FIVE

I KNEW something like this would happen!" cried Mrs. Mac-Alvey. "It's a wet day and the Leighs are arriving!"

She found she was addressing an unresponsive audience, for in spite of the fact that Mysie had entered the room, drawn back the curtains with a particularly grating rattle of rings, and placed a tray of tea on the table between the two beds, Mr. MacAlvey was still fast asleep.

"Wake up, Alexander!" said Mrs. MacAlvey firmly, leaning across until she could prod his shoulder. "It's Tuesday and it's raining, and you have to go to Inverbyne to meet the Leighs."

"Oh heavens, so I have!" roared Mr. MacAlvey as he shot up in bed, the last sentence having penetrated his sleep-sodden brain, and adding crossly as his eye took in the familiar bedroom surroundings, "Why, it isn't time yet. It's only time to get up, I want my tea."

He splashed in milk to his taste, spooned up sugar rather untidily, and lovingly poured his cup full to the brim.

"Oh, Alexander," said his wife, as she had said most mornings for forty years, "you always get it all over the tray-cloth."

She got up at once and went, not hopefully, to the window

to confirm the worst. The whole outside world was one vast billow of dripping mist. There was no sea, no mountains, no garden — just the wet Highland mist.

"The Leighs haven't been to stay here since before the war," she said, "and they didn't have particularly good weather last time —— "

"Now how on earth can you remember a thing like that?" asked her husband, slapping down his empty cup and relaxing on his pillow.

"Well, I do remember it, and I did so want them to arrive on a glorious day like we've been having. One always wants one's place to look its best when guests come, and it so seldom does. The roses were perfect and now they'll all be washed out and soggy-looking, and I'd planned to have tea in the garden, they'll feel so stuffed up after the night journey from London and then coming on from Inverness. I hope it isn't going to be wet *and* hot with the indoor walls streaming, or Mrs. Leigh will think she's taking a cold, after her operation and everything."

"Perhaps it will clear by afternoon. That hot, bright weather isn't so good for the fish, anyway, and Dr. Leigh will be all agog after the trout, if I know him."

"Oh, Alexander, don't settle down again, do get up, it's nearly eight and there's such a lot to see to."

After breakfast Mrs. MacAlvey's first care was to see that her guests' room was ready. She had put them in the green bedroom over the dining-room, which had a little balcony on which Mrs. Leigh could sit if she did not feel up to joining the party downstairs, and even her eagle eye could not detect any flaw in the room. It was as fresh as could be, with its pale-green walls and plain moss-green carpet, its twin green bed-covers and eiderdowns, its parchment reading-lamp and cream

89

cushions in the comfortable chintz chairs, its shining walnut furniture and cream-tiled open fireplace with a fire laid ready to light on Mrs. Leigh's arrival.

Everything that the most exacting guest could need or desire was there, a little trough of carefully chosen books on the tall-boy — Mrs. MacAlvey remembered that the doctor liked Somerset Maugham and had provided his newest novel, specially sent in a parcel from Inverness along with some Florence Barclay reprints for Mrs. Leigh, who adored this romantic but slightly old-fashioned novelist — writing-paper, a tin of biscuits, extra blankets in the bottom drawer, coat-hangers in the wardrobe, magazines on the small table by the balcony door. Everything, except one thing. Mrs. MacAlvey had intended to place a bowl of perfect yellow rosebuds upon the dressing-table this morning, and now she could not do so because of the rain. Perhaps Primrose might be persuaded to go out in a mackintosh and cut the buds, but she would be sure to cut all the wrong ones — no one but Mrs. MacAlvey could choose exactly the right roses — and they would be sodden with rain and drip all over the place. If only she had cut them last night!

She went downstairs and confirmed that Mrs. Mortimer had not forgotten any of her orders about lunch, peeped into the drawing-room to see that the fire had been lighted, thus dispelling a little of the gloom projected from the streaming windows, looked into the morning-room where Archie was lying flat on his face on the floor reading yesterday's paper and the others were sitting hopelessly about doing nothing at all, looked into the pantry where Cleo and Raine were putting out the silver for Mysie, and said, "Well, I think everything's ready."

The next excitement was finding it was twelve o'clock and Mr. MacAlvey had not even got out the car, so he had to be rounded up and hurried off to the station, and then there was nothing more to be done but to wait for the guests to arrive.

Mrs. MacAlvey changed into her grey crêpe, happy as a sandboy. She loved days on which visitors were arriving, and aware that the rest of the family were less enthusiastic, she sang 'Bonnie Mary of Argyll' gaily as she dressed, to cheer them up.

"Listen to Mother!" said Cleo, downstairs.

"Yes, 'Bonnie Mary,'" said Raine. "She always sings that when the family atmosphere is a trifle tense. It means, I'm happy, why aren't we all?"

"Isn't life odd?" said Cleo. "If they hadn't spent two nights at that hotel in Pitlochry years ago, they'd never have met the Leighs and they wouldn't have been coming to stay."

"It would have been somebody else," said Raine philosophically.

"What are we putting on?" said Cleo.

"Need we go into that? I'm perfectly all right as I am."

"Not with dog marks on your skirt," said Cleo. "Mrs. Leigh likes to see the daughters of the house looking fresh and dainty. I've never forgotten her saying that. It was the time we stayed at Aboyne before the war. I was nearly sick."

"I can see you are in no mood, dear sister, to welcome our charming guests. Compose yourself! Think beautiful thoughts!"

"Girls, are you ready?" cried Mrs. MacAlvey, appearing at the top of the stairs. "Oh, you haven't changed! Quickly, quickly. Your nicest frocks, of course."

Triumphantly she drove them before her. It was Her Day, she was at the very top of her form in spite of the weather.

She bustled into the morning-room, made a clucking noise at the sight of Primrose's hair, an approving one as her eyes fell on Elinore, immaculate in blue, and hauled Archie to his feet, straightening his tie.

"Laddie, you go and stand in the porch and give me warning when they're coming," she said. "You'll do that for Granny, won't you?"

"If it wasn't wet, we'd have been out by now," said Archie, "but we're in, so I will."

Stationing Archie where she wanted him, Mrs. MacAlvey surveyed the hall with her head on one side. Perfect! She had spent an hour yesterday — and what a good thing she had not left it till today! — in arranging that great white bowl of garden flowers.

"Oh," she said doubtfully, as Miss Paige appeared, smiling, in a purple jumper-suit to which she was attached and which everybody else hated.

"They're here!" yelled Archie, much earlier than anyone had expected, and before Mrs. MacAlvey had taken her hand off her heart and prepared the words of greeting for her guests, the Leighs were coming in at the door.

"This is wonderful, I'm so delighted to see you!" she cried, kissing her friend. "And Dr. Leigh! How well you look!"

"Doctor is always in the rudest health," said Mrs. Leigh, "and I am wonderfully well considering all things. Of course since my operation I've been up one day and down the next, I can't expect much for a couple of years, people don't understand who haven't been through it, but I'm sure a holiday here at dear Kilchro is going to make me a different woman. And how are you?"

"Oh, we're splendid," cried Mrs. MacAlvey, "and we're all going to take the greatest care of you. You don't think you've taken any harm from your long journey?"

"Oh, I don't think so," said Mrs. Leigh. "Perhaps I might

stay in bed tomorrow just in case, I don't want to be a nuisance and it's purely nerves. I mean, the nervous shock goes on much longer than anybody would suppose, and I was three hours under the operation — but I won't talk about it, I've made up my mind I won't, it can't be of the slightest interest to anybody. How charming the house looks, and neither you nor Mr. MacAlvey look a day older in spite of the war and all you've gone through. It's this heavenly soft Highland air, it keeps you young."

"Would you like to go straight up to your room?" said Mrs. MacAlvey. "Or will you come in the drawing-room first and have something to sustain you until lunch time, in about twenty minutes? Coffee or Ovaltine or sherry?"

"I'd love to go into the drawing-room," said Mrs. Leigh, "and I'd adore a cup of coffee, if it isn't too much trouble. Doctor can be helping to take up the luggage. Oh, if that isn't Miss Paige! Dear Miss Paige, I couldn't picture Kilchro without you, and you've put on weight too, haven't you?"

"Everybody seems to have disappeared," said Mrs. Mac-Alvey looking wildly round, "but come and sit by the fire and loosen your coat. I'm so disappointed in the weather, it has been wonderful up to now but these rain mists come on suddenly and sometimes they go as suddenly and sometimes they stay for days. But the house isn't in the least damp, you needn't have any fear. I always think when one is under par one is susceptible to colds."

"That's so true," said Mrs. Leigh, sitting down beside the fire and holding out her hands to it with a little shiver. "I never used to feel cold before, but since my operation I seem to have lost all my resistance. What a lovely room this is! I used to sit for hours by that window just gazing at the view. I'm looking forward to doing so again. Ever since I knew I was

93

coming I've been thinking, if I could only sit by the big window at Kilchro and gaze at that wonderful view I should feel strength coming back to me, I know I should. You must think me awfully tiresome talking like this when I used to be so full of vitality."

"Oh, my dear, no," cried Mrs. MacAlvey, her voice warm with sympathy. "You have come here to get well, haven't you? That's all that matters. We are so healthy, we must try not to appear too bursting with high spirits, and so tire you."

"Oh, but I am perfectly well too," said Mrs. Leigh. "You must not regard me as an invalid. The great thing after an operation is to forget it, any doctor will tell you that. Lead a normal life, they will tell you, and just forget yourself. I mean, recovery is three parts psychological, isn't it?"

At that moment Raine and Cleo came in, Raine carrying a tray with a silver jug of coffee and some cups and saucers and a bowl of brown sugar.

"Your lovely daughters!" said Mrs. Leigh. "I'm sure I don't know which is the prettier, Cleo or Raine. Oh, but Raine, your tremendously happy news! We were all delighted to hear of your engagement. Did I meet the young man when I was here before? He lives in the neighbourhood, doesn't he?"

"I don't know if you met him," said Raine. "It's Ian Garvine, and you wouldn't remember anything because it only boiled up this year."

"Well, you ought to be ashamed of yourself for getting engaged before your elder sister. That sort of thing wasn't allowed in my day, when mothers had some control over their daughters. What are you going to do about it, Cleo?"

"I can't think," said Cleo with the smile of a sweet little tiger.

94

"Well, don't throw yourself away just to get even with Raine, because I'm sure Mother doesn't want to lose you," said Mrs. Leigh, patting Mrs. MacAlvey's hand.

"And now tell me about all the rest of the family," she went on. "Such masses of them. I wonder how you keep count!"

"I don't try," said Mrs. MacAlvey, admiring her visitor's shoes and wondering how she would look in size threes made entirely of little red straps.

"My mother," said Cleo, still smarting, "holds the record for having mislaid more grandchildren without noticing it than any other woman in Scotland."

"How peculiar!" said Mrs. Leigh.

"Now, really, you mustn't take any notice of the girl's nonsense," said Mrs. MacAlvey. "We have Malcolm's children living here; you'll see them at lunch. Primrose is pretty, and Gavin is clever, and Archie is such a pet."

"She's off again!" said Raine. "These grandmothers. She never raved about her own children like that, did she, Cleo? We were crushed down and held under. That's why we've nothing to say for ourselves today."

Mrs. Leigh gave a thin smile, and putting down her cup said, "That was highly delicious. Now I think I will go up to my room if I might have someone's arm, just for the stairs. So tiresome of me."

Mrs. MacAlvey took the visitor up, and her expressions of pleasure at the arrangements of the green room floated downstairs.

At lunch Mr. MacAlvey and Dr. Leigh chatted happily about flies and the state of the local waters, and the young people behaved so well that they never opened their mouths, thus producing a paralysing effect upon their elders. When lunch was over, Mrs. Leigh said she would go to her room and

95

rest after the effects of the night journey and such an exciting morning.

Mrs. MacAlvey too felt some reaction after so prolonged an expenditure of energy, and was soon drowsing over the drawing-room fire. Her mind, relaxed, sped back to the days of her own well-regulated youth in Edinburgh. She had been a serious girl with aspirations to become a nurse and live a selfless life running a leper colony. Before she met Alexander she had once nearly married an Englishman, a social worker, who was looking for a Scottish girl with ideals to match his own.

How different my life would have been! thought Mrs. MacAlvey, overawed.

She found herself unable to picture it, for she had never been to England, and always thought of it as being full of successful people living in Georgian houses.

Gently she drifted away into delicious sleep. When she opened her eyes it was four o'clock and Miss Paige was saying, "What a surprise for you! The mist has all gone, it stopped raining soon after lunch and the sun came through at three. Now everything is dried up and it feels very warm, so what about tea outside after all?"

"Oh, good!" said Mrs. MacAlvey. "Tell Mysie and the girls, and could you listen at Mrs. Leigh's door to see if she is moving, and if not, cough or something."

"I could start the Hoover."

"Well, that's a bit drastic. It always sounds to me like the war starting again. She should be awake by now."

There proved to be no need to cough or to start the Hoover, for Mrs. Leigh could be distinctly heard opening drawers, and presently she came down in a printed dress of navy-blue and white with a coat to match and said, "I've had a wonderful rest

96

and I dreamed the sun was shining and when I woke it was. Oh, tea on the terrace! It makes one feel *en fête*. I wonder if one of the girls would go up and find my little fur wrap for my shoulders?"

"I'll go," said Miss Paige, and Mrs. Leigh cried, "Oh, but it is too bad to give you such trouble. I can't get used to giving trouble, I used to rush up and downstairs like a two-year-old, but since my operation the spring just isn't there. Thank you very, very much indeed, dear Miss Paige."

At last they were all seated round or near the tea-table, with a splendid tea laid out, three kinds of scones and tea bread and two kinds of jam, strawberry which had been made in June from the Kilchro strawberries and peach which Miss Paige had made from some dried peaches that Cleo had sent in a parcel from America, and a home-made Swiss-roll and fruit cake, and iced buns and coco-nut macaroons.

"The men have already set off away up the Lisswater," said Mrs. MacAlvey. "They had ham and eggs, so we shan't see them till dark or later. And I don't know where the children have gone. I never ask. Children of their age have secret lives of their own, and if there's one thing they resent it is interference."

"I think you're wonderful, Mrs. MacAlvey," said Mrs. Leigh. "When I saw that enormous crowd at luncheon and realised that we should be sitting down twelve to every meal, I was overcome with amazement that you should cheerfully cope with so many and allow yourself to be overrun with people like us. How do you do it?"

There really was no answer to this, and Cleo said, "Try some of the other jam, Mrs. Leigh, if you've finished that."

"Oh, I couldn't. I'm not acclimatised yet to these gorgeous

97

country spreads, not after the birdlike meals we have in London. You haven't told me yet when Raine's wedding is to be."

"It's on September the eleventh," said Raine, "so that Primrose can be a bridesmaid before she goes back to school."

"And what are you going to wear?"

"Oh, I don't know yet," said Raine. "I suppose Cleo and I will have to go to Edinburgh and do a couple of days bumbling round."

"It all sounds so nice and casual," said Mrs. Leigh. "I shall be gone long before then, unfortunately, but I brought your wedding present with me, so you might as well have it now. It isn't new, but it's far better than anything you could get nowadays and it's perfect and not even a crack. It's all nicely packed in a box and it should be somewhere on the floor in my bedroom, a wooden box with straw sticking out of the edges."

"Oh, could I — " began Raine, all excitement, and Cleo said, "I've finished my tea. Can I go too?"

"Oh do," said Mrs. Leigh. "I hope you'll like it."

"Will you believe me," said Raine as she shut the glass door which let them into the house, "when I tell you that I never even thought of wedding presents? That shows how unmercenary I am. Is everybody I know going to send me a wedding present quite unprovoked?"

"I expect so," said Cleo, "and you know such a lot of people."

"It's incredible. I'll die with excitement. I always loved presents, but the most I ever got all at once was the Christmas I had measles and people were sorry for me. I got eighteen. I shall always remember it. I shall probably get more than eighteen wedding presents. I wonder what people will send me, and if I dare give them a little guidance. Is it usual?"

"Not unless they ask you specifically," said Cleo, "and they don't, because they generally have some object put away that

98

they're waiting for a bride to unload it on. Like Mrs. Leigh."

"Oh, Cleo," cried Raine, "what do you suppose it is?"

"You'll know in a minute."

"Yes, but much the most thrilling part of a present is wondering what it is. Turning it over and feeling it. I wish Ian were here to share it. I don't think I've ever done Mrs. Leigh justice. Think of her during the long, long weeks that she lay on a bed of pain, brooding and planning what she'd give me for a present, and saying, 'Doctor! Doctor! The only thing that really matters is to give Raine MacAlvey the most unique, stupendous wedding present.'"

"Such as —— ?"

"Cleo, what do you think it can be?"

"Now how on earth should I know?"

"Cleo!" Raine yelled. "She said it hadn't a crack in it!"

"If it hasn't a crack in it, it must be pottery of some kind," gasped Cleo as they ran upstairs side by side.

"My very first wedding present!" said Raine. "Let's have three guesses each before we open it. You go first."

"Well, it might be what they call a *jardinière* to hold a potted palm."

"Or a huge cut-glass fruit-dish like the one that Isa Abernethy had, and you can't put anything in it but peaches and hot-house grapes because home-grown apples look so sordid."

"Or it might be a little china ash-tray with A Present from Hampstead on it."

"Or a marble bust of Queen Victoria."

"Or a soap-stone model of the Taj Mahal. I saw one once, and the people it belonged to thought a lot of it."

"Or, coming down to earth, it could be five different sizes of pudding basins. I believe a lot of people give kitchen-ware nowadays."

"Well, that's three guesses each," said Cleo, "and there's no prize for the nearest. Here's the thing itself. How do we get the lid off?"

"I'll get some scissors or something and prise it off," said Raine, and when she had done so she made the first dive into the straw and fished up a pink china cup.

"Well, that's it," she said. "A pink tea-service. I think it's very pretty."

"You'll be able to have about five dozen people to tea at Larrich now," said Cleo. "I mean, what with the Rockingham and the Wedgwood and the Royal Worcester and this."

"I must go back and thank her," said Raine, and she ran downstairs again and out to the terrace, and said, "Thank you very much indeed, Mrs. Leigh. I think it's a most frightfully pretty tea-service, and it's my first present and I'll write you a proper letter later on."

"I had hoped," said Mrs. Leigh, "that one day my own daughter Norrie would have had it, but she isn't interested in marriage, I'm afraid." She sighed deeply, and while Cleo and Raine were carrying in the tea-things she said to Mrs. Mac-Alvey, "Don't let Cleo get like that, just drifting on and on into being an old maid. She seems quite happy and gay about her younger sister getting married before her, but I always think it's such a fatal attitude. Norrie used to be like that, and now she's gone all remote and matter-of-fact and never tells me anything. Perhaps when Raine is married she will make an effort and find a young man for her sister. Hasn't her fiancé got a brother or anything?"

"Oh yes, Ian has a brother. That is Larrich himself, but we look on him as a confirmed bachelor. He's thirty and very handsome, but wrapped up in bulls, and we've always thought him rather lofty-minded and idealistic, not an earthy, every-day type at all. Not that Ian is earthy, but he is more ordinary than Neil, and I always think ordinary men make the best husbands."

"Your daughters are so charming to you, I envy you," said Mrs. Leigh. "Before my operation I used to get on better with Norrie, but since then I haven't had the strength to adapt myself to her moods. She's rather an unsympathetic girl, though I wouldn't say it to anyone but you."

"Oh, I don't know," said Mrs. MacAlvey modestly. "My girls make fun of everything, especially Raine, and I've told them till I'm tired they'll never get young men that way be-cause men are frightened of witty girls and always thinking they'll be the next victim, but in spite of it all Raine has got one and a very nice one, so I'm going to stop giving advice. Nothing that was true when I was a girl is true any more."

Mrs. Leigh sighed and said, "Being in the Red Cross during the war didn't do Norrie any good, she got so independent, and now she won't give it up and calls herself a Commandant, whatever that may mean. I'm still hoping and praying that she'll settle down and marry some nice man in our own set, because I do think, and so does Doctor, that the right class is the best basis for a successful marriage, especially in these aw-ful socialistic days when you're supposed to rub shoulders with anybody and like it. Well now, I think I shall have to go and rest until dinner. My strength leaves me suddenly, in a flash." She demonstrated a flash with uplifted fingers. "I know I'm a trial to everybody, and only those who have been through it can understand. After all, it's only ten weeks ago."

Mrs. MacAlvey assisted her guest to her room, and then with a happy expression on her face she sought the cloakroom for her gardening shoes and an old mack and got down to clearing up the viola bed.

Within five minutes of arriving at the water Dr. Leigh landed a fine trout. A lunatic with a rod, he did everything wrong, talked incessantly at the top of his voice, thrashed the stream with his saturated fly, and behaved more as if he were doing the family wash than a delicate angling operation.

"A bonny fish," admitted Mr. MacAlvey who, doing everything right, had caught nothing.

"There was an amusing incident on the train coming up," shouted Dr. Leigh, choosing a fly at random and tying it on with a series of ungainly knots. "We were in a first class corridor carriage at King's Cross and opposite us was sitting a very well-dressed man of about sixty, looked like a barrister. Just at the last minute in rushed a big black dog, recognised this man who was obviously his master, and jumped all over him. By some means he'd followed him from home. There wasn't time for him to get out and take him home, as at that minute the train drew out, and there he was, saddled with him to take to wherever he was going. He'd have a lot of trouble with him, he was leaping about the carriage with excitement and he looked very embarrassed. By the time he got him under control we were well on the way, and then who should come in but the ticket inspector and he went for him and nearly knocked him flat."

"Very amusing," said Mr. MacAlvey, who thought there was something to be said for the ancient Romans being fussy about personal pronouns.

"I've got another bite," said Dr. Leigh, drawing a second leaping silver fish to the bank. "Talking of dogs reminds me of a patient of mine, very well connected, wealthy family, fine house, magnificently appointed, he went in for pictures, you know, didn't mind what he paid for a picture if it took his fancy, had a gallery built on to house them, employed a first-class architect to design it, special lighting, all the rest of it, very bad case of angina but wouldn't take care of himself, used to smoke eight Corona-Coronas every day of his life — by the way, what was I going to tell you?"

"Something about dogs," said Mr. MacAlvey crossly, for he had seen the big fish he was after come within reach of his fly and then flash away at the impact of the doctor's voice.

"Oh yes, dogs. His wife had a Pekinese that used to get under the cushions, and one day my patient sat on it. He didn't realise, of course, and they missed the dog. His wife was in a fine state, rang up Scotland Yard. The body made itself obvious a week later. I think I've got something here! Ha!"

"You're doing very well," said Mr. MacAlvey, looking at his guest's third fish.

"Must be lucky," said Dr. Leigh. "Think I'll try a worm now and drag it along the bottom."

Mr. MacAlvey shuddered as he made his own skilful cast.

"It just isn't your day," yelled the doctor at the top of his voice, and began to sing, *Maire, My Girl.*

"Shall we move up-stream?" suggested Mr. MacAlvey, reeling in his unsuccessful line.

"Yes, let's. It's all the same to me and you may have better luck. Talking of patients, did I ever tell you — by Jove! I think I've got another! No, false alarm." Dr. Leigh laughed heartily. "I call this great! Lovely country, nice bit of sunshine after rain, what more can you want? I've made up my mind to get a twenty-pound salmon this holiday."

"I wouldn't be surprised at anything," said Mr. MacAlvey.

CHAPTER SIX

Next morning when they had finished breakfast and were sitting in a row on the balustrade of the terrace Gavin said, "What are we going to do today?"

"What is there to do?" said Elinore.

"When we haven't planned anything definite and the weather isn't right for sailing, we usually go down to the village and just snowk about," said Archie.

"I say, do you think there's any chance of a round of golf?" asked Cecil.

"Shouldn't think so," said Gavin. "And the men wouldn't want you, anyway."

Cecil, who played to a handicap of four but creditably refrained from mentioning this, was silent.

"The village looks so dirty," said Elinore.

"Oh, it is," said Gavin. "Pounds of oil and tar and decaying fish all over the place."

"I think I shall stay here in the garden and read."

"Good show," said Primrose. "That's one of you settled. What are you going to do, Cecil?"

"I think I'll read too," said Cecil obligingly.

"I should sit in the summer-house if I were you," said Gavin kindly. "It's in the nicest part of the garden and has a marvellous view."

"And," he pointed out to his brother and sister as they cantered down the hill, "the summer-house can't be seen from the house windows, so Granny won't spot them and think we've neglected them. Strategic, see!"

They reached the quay and looked out to sea.

"Squally," said Gavin. "It's freshening from the sou'west. Shall we risk a soak?"

"I'll tell you what," said Primrose. "Let's go to Kininver and see if Gull's back. If she is she's sure to be down there catching crayfish. The tide's out, we can walk along the beach."

Kininver, which lay about two miles south of Strogue, consisted of a cluster of houses and a small handloom factory. It also had a broad rock-strewn beach which at low tide yielded a harvest of stranded sea-creatures.

When they were still half a mile away, Primrose caught sight of a small figure poised on the rocks and gave a shriek.

"There's Gull!"

They all began to run, yelling, "Gull! Gull! Hoi, Gull!"

Gull heard them and straightened up. Her whoop came to them on the breeze, which by now was very fresh indeed. She was thin, brown, and twelve years old, and dressed in shabby shorts and a darned blue sweater. She had bright, sapphire-blue eyes, a thick plait of hair, a big mouth, and freckles.

"Got anything?" said Archie as they came up.

"Six. Savage brutes too. There's one under this rock where I'm standing, but I can't reach him. Take the stick, Gavin, you've got longer arms than me. Go on, shove harder than that."

Gavin drove the stick as hard and far as he could under the

shelving rock, stirring the sea-pool vigorously and scooping as he drove.

Out rushed the angry crayfish and Gull, pouncing, soaking herself to the shoulder, grabbed him by the back of his shell and held him up.

"Biggest I've ever seen," said Archie.

"That's seven," said Gull. "I don't need any more. Let's go and squat over there and eat my chocolate. Albert, the boy at the lodge, gave me his coupons this month. He's bilious."

"I hope he'll stay bilious," said Archie.

They threw themselves on their backs on the hard white pebbles above the tide-line.

"Where have you been all this time?" asked Gull.

"I like that!" said Primrose. "All what time? When did you get back?"

"Yesterday, but it seems ages ago. Staying with my relations makes Time behave in a peculiar way, they're so civilised. I wore stockings all the time." And Gull stuck out a long bare leg which ended in a holey gym shoe.

"I've got a boat, I bought her myself," said Gavin. "*Minnow.*"

"We went to Kilgarro in her," said Archie. "It was pretty good. You'll like her, Gull."

"We'll all like her," said Primrose, "provided that Cecil and Elinore can be persuaded to read in the summer-house every day for the next four weeks."

"Who on earth are Cecil and Elinore?" asked Gull.

"Our cousins. From England. They're clots."

"What sort of clots?"

"Well, they say, Is it dirty? And if it is, they won't go or won't do it."

"Elinore is the worst," said Gavin. "Cecil would often be

quite human if it wasn't for Elinore. She really is the most binding clot."

"Well, what have you done with them today? Lost them?"

"We left them in the summer-house, reading, but we'll never be able to pull that one again. We shall have to take them everywhere with us, and *Minnow* won't hold us all, so how can we go sailing?"

"Last night after dinner," said Primrose, "we went in the drawing-room and had coffee. In the drawing-room, I tell you, on a summer's evening in the hols. And Cecil offered to recite. He recited practically a whole act of *Romeo and Juliet*. And everybody sat round in a sort of drunken stupor."

"As a matter of fact," said Archie, "it was *Hamlet*."

"Oh well," said Primrose. "It's all the same. The only thing that's worth reading in English literature is *Hassan*."

"Well, let's not think about your cousins," said Gull. "Let's play the Cloud Game. And you can go first, Archie, because you're the youngest and jolly impatient."

They sprawled on the stones, blinking up at the sky. It wasn't cold, but there was no blue up there today, only a great many different shades of grey as the cloud-wrack lightened and darkened and was blown about by the wind.

"I am on a cloud," said Archie, "and I am sailing above the ocean. Below me a school of whales is playing. There are big whales, middle-sized whales, and microscopically small whales. They are spouting away like mad. I can count two hundred different whale-spouts, some a mile high. One of the whales is as big as the *Queen Elizabeth*."

"That's impossible," said Gavin. "And they couldn't be microscopically small either."

"They're my whales," said Archie, "and I should know. Your go, Gull."

"I am on a cloud," said Gull, "and I'm following a train. The train is whizzing along, it's one of the newest streamlined trains doing about ninety-five miles an hour. I don't have to make any effort to keep up with the train, I'm above it all the time. It goes faster and faster —— "

"It couldn't go much faster than ninety-five," said Primrose.

"Shut up and don't spoil it. I can see the fireman lean out of the cab. Then the whistle shrieks and the train dashes into a tunnel. When it comes out the other side I shall still be hovering over it on my cloud."

"It'll never come out, not at a hundred miles an hour. It'll blow its valves," said Archie. "Go on, Gavin, you next."

"I am on a cloud," said Gavin. "I am sailing above the city of Baghdad. I can see right down into the city. The streets are full of gold and jewels and pomegranates and Persian carpets and Persian kittens. A hundred sheikhs on splendid stallions are dashing through the colonnades yelling 'Allah — Allah — Allah.' "

"Haven't you got yourself into the Sahara?" asked Primrose scornfully.

"Well, isn't Baghdad in the Sahara?"

"Oh, is it?" said Primrose. "I wasn't sure. Well, it's my turn now. I am on a cloud and floating over Kilchro House. In the garden Elinore is sitting in a deck-chair dressed in absolutely correct tennis white. But she isn't playing tennis, she is doing some embroidery to show Granny. So I unbutton the cloud I'm on and let about fifty thousand gallons of rainwater down, and Elinore is now swimming round and round like Alice in the Pool of Tears. She does look silly."

"I say! You've got Elinore on the brain," said Gull. "You're obsessionated with her."

108

"Yes, I have sort of got her in my hair," said Primrose.

"She has a friend called Pearl Panton," said Gavin, "whose father is a baronet, no less, d'y'see?"

"Oh, did she tell you that too?" said Primrose.

"And Pearl Panton says that one ought always to aim at absolutely correct behaviour, if only to set an example to one's inferiors."

"What are inferiors?" asked Gull interestedly.

"Dunno," said Gavin. "P'raps it's something we haven't got."

"Well, I vote we put Pearl Panton and Elinore out of bounds," said Gull, "and the next person who mentions them will be held under water by all the rest. Let's go along the rocks now and look for *something*, we can't sit here for ever."

"What do you know about that!" cried Archie, holding up an empty sack. "The crayfish have all got away."

"That fixes us," said Gull. "We've got to catch seven more crayfish. Come on!"

While they scoured the pools, soaked to the skin, Primrose said, "I'll tell you one thing we want to do these hols., Gull, and that's to go and explore Eil-oran. You know — that island out beyond Inchbar."

"Sounds all right," said Gull, "but it's supposed to be haunted, isn't it? Nobody ever goes there. And it's a dickens of a long way."

"We thought we'd make a day of it when the wind's right. Of course there are about a million snags, including you know who, that I hadn't to mention."

"I always think it's a pity," said Gull, "that the world is full of People — like us, and Un-people — like your cousins."

"Um," said Primrose. "And isn't the world just an Abominable Tomb when there isn't any sun."

Archie, lying flat on his stomach, was trying to coax an invisible crayfish out of its lair. Gavin suddenly tired of the game and, throwing himself down on the rocks, thoughtfully dabbled his hands in a clear pool to the consternation of a family of sea anemones.

He thought of boats and of ships. He had a collection of hundreds of pictures of ships cut out of papers and magazines, which his grandmother had allowed him to paste on the plain white walls of his bedroom. His room was a magnificent sight with all those ships — yachts and schooners, frigates and destroyers, brigantines and galleons, Cunard liners and Chinese dhows, red-sailed fishing boats, and even coal-barges. And of course *Cutty Sark* from several different angles. No picture of a ship was ever refused. He had several school friends looking them out for him. In the dentist's waiting-room at Inverness he never dared to open the *Illustrated London News,* because there was always a picture in it that he wanted badly and it was agony to have to drag his eyes from it. Having no conscience at all and finding himself alone in the waiting-room, Archie had once torn out such a picture and later presented it to his brother. Gavin took it as though it were red-hot and for days suffered torments. Impossible to send it back to the outraged dentist. It lay on his hands like a *corpus delicti.* Finally he forgot his scruples and pasted it to the wall. It was a picture he wanted very much, but even to this day he felt a criminal's pang every time he looked at it.

He looked down at the pool wherein he dabbled, and thought of it as a tiny sea, himself a giant. If he had paper and matches he would make a fleet of small boats, fairy-size boats, and guide them over that limpid water, fouling their keels perhaps in the drift of feathery weed that sprayed from the rock — just for fun. He would stir the pool, make waves with his fingers, and round and round the fairy fleet would go, gallantly breasting the storm he had created. He loved miniature things, perhaps because there was dawning in him a love of power. And yet there was no desire to wreck or destroy; he was too gentle by nature, too easily captured by beauty. The anemones, for instance, were beautiful in a queer sort of way. With a finger-tip he stroked their soft pink mouths and felt the sucking motion of their lips with strange pleasure.

He had forgotten the others till Gull came up to him and said, "What are you doing?"

"I like this place," said Gavin.

"It's not bad. Nearest to the sea for me. But it only seems to attract coal-boats. Remind me, I've got a picture for you at home. I cut it out of a magazine while I was staying at my aunt's."

"Oh, did she mind?"

"I didn't ask her." (Gavin winced.) "She has a very grand sort of smoke-room with piles of English papers, and I just hooked out what I wanted. Yours is a big one — full page. It's an oil-tanker berthed in the London Docks. Have you got an oil-tanker?"

"I don't think so," said Gavin. "Thank you very much, Gull."

"Sea anemones," said Gull. "Aren't they pretty? When you take them out of the water they aren't any colour at all."

"I'm soaking wet," said Primrose, coming up. "But you can't get cold from sea-water; I read it in a book. I have enjoyed this morning. I've just had an idea. Hamish might lend us his boat, the big one."

"That old tub?" said Gavin. "It might do."

"I wish the sun hadn't gone away," said Archie, trying to shake water out of his dripping jersey.

"It'll come back," said Gavin. "And we're going sailing! Stick to that, *mes enfants*. We're going sailing!"

They got all the crayfish they wanted, and then discovered that it was ten minutes to one and they had two miles to walk home. They said a hasty good-bye to Gull and promised to see her soon, but run as hard as they could they were still twenty minutes late for luncheon. For this they got into a really serious row. Gavin sulked all the afternoon, and not unjustifiably, for he was fourteen and felt it *infra dig.* to be scolded like a child before Cecil, who was treated like a man and a guest.

"But, after all, he's never late and never in a mess," said Primrose moodily, "and we always are."

"I won't be happy," said Gavin, "until I've made him hours late *and* smothered in oil."

All the afternoon it grew darker and stormier, and by tea-time the sea was blotted out by rain. All night and all the next day it rained. Cecil didn't mind, as he was busy pressing his ferns and learning some speeches out of *Coriolanus;* for he was secretly very proud of his elocution and thought he might go on the stage and become a second Laurence Olivier. Elinore finished two corners of her embroidery and began a third. Gavin and Archie put on their macks and snowked about the village with their wet hair plastered to their heads. Primrose, who had been refused permission to go with them, sat on her bed all day reading *For Whom the Bell Tolls,* which Raine had got out of the threepence a week library at Dunmaig. She decided that it wasn't much fun reading when you hadn't anything to eat at the same time, and the sweet ration was finished days ago.

By night she was glad to see the shapes of the islands beginning to loom out of the mist. The sea was a heaving, tossing waste.

"We'll soon be sailing now," said Gavin next morning at breakfast.

"You children are not to go out in the boat until I say so," said Mr. MacAlvey.

"It wouldn't be safe, would it?" said Elinore, and everybody else except her brother glared at her.

"But, Grandfather, there's not much wind really," said Archie, "and it'll probably drop altogether with the ebb."

"And work round to the west with the flood," said Mr. MacAlvey. "No sailing till I say so, do you hear? I'm well aware that no element on this earth could drown you children after the times you've been capsized under a boat, but I won't have you drowning Cecil and Elinore."

"We never thought of that," said Gavin simply.

It was three days before the weather was right for sailing again.

CHAPTER SEVEN

Raine said that unless they went to see James's wife soon, Trina would consider herself slighted and the family repercussions would not bear thinking of; so on the first fine morning she and Cleo found themselves on the Dunmaig bus climbing the long hill out of Strogue, with the sea sparkling on their left and on their right the peaks that guarded the blue flash of Loch Maig.

"When I was in America," said Cleo, "I used to think of this. I thought of it practically the whole time."

"What — the Dunmaig bus?"

"You know what I mean."

"Is there anything in this exile business?" asked Raine.

"Oh, there is. It's like being hungry and *not* knowing that you're going home for tea. Sometimes I used to dream that I was climbing over the rocks, over the black slippery bobbles of seaweed, and smelling it and hearing the water gurgling in the caves and the gulls wailing. I nearly used to believe it was true, and then I'd slowly open my eyes and it wasn't."

"Oh, poor Cleo, how awful. I never thought of you feeling like that."

"Then you ought to have done!" said Cleo indignantly. "You can't have had much imagination. The only thing that kept me alive was thinking that you were thinking of me. And you say you weren't!"

"But we were," said Raine. "We thought of you every day or nearly every day. But we always thought of you eating fried chicken and not having to keep your hands off the butter ration."

"It's a good thing I came back," said Cleo.

Soon they reached the little town of Dunmaig, clustered round its harbour.

"Shall we go and see Trina straightaway," said Raine, "or shall we have some strengthening food first?"

"Don't you think we'd better go and get it over, and then we can enjoy ourselves?"

They made their way to James's house. It was a small square stone house in a road of similar houses, with five very clean windows and a front door with a sunblind arrangement above it. Cleo and Raine were impressed with the sunblind, for they had never had anything like it at Kilchro.

"Come on, do," said Cleo as Raine dallied, trying to find out how the sunblind worked up and down.

"Trina always makes me feel like a small, dull child of six who has come to school without a pocket handkerchief," said Raine, tapping the well-polished door-knocker. Trina herself opened the door with such rapidity that she must have been watching them from one of the windows while they fiddled with the sunblind.

"Do come in," she said. "So this is Cleo!"

"Now, don't pretend you don't know me, Trina," said Cleo. "I've only been away three years, I can't have changed as much as that."

"I remember you as looking much younger," said Trina, leading the way down the narrow hall which had a little pathway of white drugget to save the carpet. Practically everything in Trina's house was covered up with something to save something that was underneath.

They went into the sitting-room, where the venetian blinds were dropped to keep out the sun, and the result was a greenish twilight that smelt of geraniums and furniture polish.

"You've just come at the right time," said Trina. "I'm going to enrol you in my League of Watchers. It'll be five shillings each. You're not very good material, but if I get ten new members before the end of the month, I shall hold the record for our area."

"What on earth is the League of Watchers?"

"Need I go into that?" said Trina. "Think! All we need to do is to Watch. It's a Biblical injunction, isn't it? In these days we interpret it as being alert about the trend of world events. If there had been enough people on the Watch, say in Wallace's day, the whole course of history might have been altered. It mustn't happen again."

"But there had to be *some* history," said Cleo, "so why should one lot be better than another? I mean, what have we lost?"

"I'm not going to argue about it," said Trina, going an unbecoming red, for she had no sense of humour and merely lost her temper if provoked. "When we have a lecture in Dunmaig, and I'm trying to organise one, I'll let you know and you can come and hear all about it, though I think it will be above your heads. Only you might give me the ten shillings and help me to get my ——"

"All right," said Raine, holding out a ten-shilling note. "I'll try anything once, even altering the course of history."

116

"I'll go and find my receipt book," said Trina in a very dignified voice.

"We could have got four peach sundaes for that," said Cleo.

"We shouldn't have got out of here alive," said Raine. "It saves time to give in at once when it's Trina. Here she comes."

"And how are all at Kilchro?" asked Trina, handing them their receipts.

"In rude health," said Raine. "And such a lot of them too! We have four visitors besides the family."

"Your mother," said Trina, "will be collapsing one of these days."

"We hope not," said Cleo, and added, "Mother is not the collapsing sort, none of us are. We may explode, but we don't collapse."

"It sounds like one of those plastic beakers," said Raine, "that fold up on you at picnics."

"It's easy to make a mock," said Trina, "but there's many a true word — I need not go on. I suppose you've come to Dunmaig to enjoy yourselves? It must be lovely to have so much free time."

"We've really come to do some shopping," said Raine, and added, too late for politeness, "and to see you, of course."

"Your mother told me she did all her shopping in Strogue. She said she felt it was only right to support the village shops."

"Well, we do get the essentials in Strogue," explained Raine, "though even after ten years of rationing Ma Mackenzie still hasn't got the hang of it, and you have to be strong-minded and argue it out. But we come to Dunmaig for the extras, such as sliced tongue and those nice little three-cornered cheeses, and biscuits. Ma Mackenzie only stocks thin arrowroot and cream-crackers."

"I see," said Trina, with a look that said more plainly than words what she thought of people who came from afar to strip Dunmaig residents of the small luxuries that were theirs by right.

"Besides," said Cleo, trying to make their visit look less like a descent of locusts, "Raine wants to go to the hairdresser's."

Trina gave an indulgent laugh. "It seems so funny to me," she said, tittering. "I've never had anything done to my hair in my life."

(Why is it, thought Raine, that people who boast about never doing anything to their hair or faces are always such a poor advertisement for the fact?)

"Aren't we going to see the children?" said Cleo, changing the subject to something apparently innocuous.

"Oh certainly," said Trina. "They're in the kitchen. I'll call them. No one can ever say I thrust my children forward until they're asked for. I've been to houses where you fall over a horde of children the minute you enter the drawing-room. Armitage! Come, dear, and bring Angela! They are doing their homework," she explained.

"Do they do home-work in the holidays?" asked Cleo.

"Each day," said Trina, "we do just one hour's study. It keeps our little brains in fine fettle."

Raine made a slightly strangled sound and put her hand-kerchief to her face.

"Trina, do you think we could have the blinds raised just a little? It — it seems to strain my eyes."

"You probably need glasses," said Trina, going over to pull up the blind about a foot, adding, "I dare say a minute or two of sun won't do the carpet much harm."

Armitage and Angela appeared in the doorway. They were sallow-faced children, with very long, thin white legs which somehow had resisted all efforts of the summer sun to tan them.

Armitage wore glasses and had a high wrinkled brow; Angela had prominent teeth which prevented her from quite closing her mouth and made her look like a young, hungry rabbit. Though they were ten and twelve years old, they both wore holland overalls belted at the waist, to cover up whatever they were wearing underneath.

"Say good morning nicely to your aunties," said Trina. "And shake hands."

"How do you do, Auntie; good morning, Auntie," said Armitage, extending his hand to each politely. Angela followed suit, but made no remark beyond a gulp.

"Hullo, Angela," said Cleo. "Goodness, you've got tall!"

Angela gulped.

"I don't believe you remember me," said Cleo, trying hard. "I must take you for a walk some day."

Angela gulped.

"So you've been doing your home-work!" said Raine to Armitage, gallantly holding up her end of the conversation.

"You should just see his arithmetic book," cried Trina proudly. "Ten out of ten all the time. Quite perfect. You'd hardly believe it unless you saw it. Fetch your arithmetic book, Armitage, and let your aunties see."

"Oh, please don't trouble," cried Raine. "We do believe it, honestly. I'm sure Armitage gets ten out of ten every time."

She had had it in mind to invite the children to come over and spend a day with their cousins Primrose, Gavin, and Archie, but she was beginning to have her doubts about the wisdom of such a course.

"Yes, I always get ten out of ten for my arithmetic," said Armitage earnestly. "I find it very easy. I'm sitting for a scholarship in December, to go to Lyons College at Inverness, and I think I have it in the bag. I don't think there's a doubt of my getting it, is there, Mother? My weak spot is Latin prose. I think the summer holidays are too long, I get out of touch."

"I say, Angela, do you like ice-cream?" said Raine.

Angela looked blank, nodded her head and then shook it.

"You should come over to Strogue, Armitage, and have a day out with Gavin," said Cleo. "Wouldn't you like that?"

"Yes, I would," said Armitage.

"But we don't like playing with wild rough boys," said Trina with an arch little smile, "and we're the weeniest bit afraid that Cousin Gavin is a wild rough boy."

Armitage scratched his leg and said, "May we go back now, Mother?" Some complicated telepathic communication seemed to be taking place between the children, and he added, "Angela would like to listen to the wireless. May we turn it on?"

"Angela must learn to ask for herself," said Trina firmly. "Do you want to hear the wireless, Angela?"

"Yes," murmured Angela in an agonised whisper.

"Well, first of all Mother must know what's on the programme."

"It's Botany for Juniors," said Armitage.

"You're sure it's for juniors?" said Trina anxiously.

"Yes, Mother. Oh, please, Mother."

Trina shook her head.

"Don't bother now, Armitage. Mother will come and find you a nice programme when the aunties have gone."

With that the two seemed contented, and obediently and silently melted from the room.

"You have to be so careful what a child hears," said Trina. "Or what an adult hears, for that matter. One pernicious little seed is sown and ——" She pulled a long face and shook her head gravely. "Actually," she went on, "the only programme worth hearing is International Cross-currents."

"Does Armitage listen to International Cross-currents?" asked Cleo.

"Indeed he does. My children are both well-informed," said Trina proudly. "I consider that people who are flippant and turn a deaf ear to serious matters are responsible for the state of the world today."

"I seem to have heard something like that before," said Raine.

"I suppose it's true," said Cleo gloomily, and thought, Now I've done it! as she saw Trina turn to her with boiling eyes.

"Do tell me!" cried Trina. "What do the Americans really think about Britain?"

"You'll think me feeble," said Cleo, "but I never heard any of them say."

"What a pity. You must have moved in shallow circles. I was listening to a remarkable play the other night — *Sostenuto*, by Alistair Trossach —— "

"We heard it," said Raine. "We thought it was absolute nuts. Nobody ever finished a sentence."

"Oh, but surely you understand what that meant!" Trina was a tall woman, but broadly cylindrical in shape and the same width all the way down; so now in her tight red dress with her face turning a keyed-up scarlet, she looked like an aggravated pillar-box. "It was illustrating how modern political life is just a series of loose ends."

"I don't believe it," said Raine. "Alistair Trossach — I mean, Moses Jobling, or do I? — has no brains, only a superficial cleverness, and he tries to see how much the credulity of the public will stand."

"I don't agree, I don't agree!" shouted Trina.

"I'm not asking you to," said Raine, "It's just my own silly, worthless opinion."

Thinking it was time she interposed to save bloodshed, Cleo said, "I wonder what the children are doing? They're very quiet, Trina. Angela doesn't look very strong. Does your doctor see her?"

She could not have made a more unfortunate remark. Wheeling round from Raine and more scarlet in the face than ever, Trina exclaimed, "Doctor? I tell you, I've never had a doctor in my house and never shall. They know nothing. Nincompoops, that's all doctors are. If I had time I could tell you what my poor neighbour suffered. And as if any doctor could tell a mother anything about her own child's inside! Angela is highly strung, she gets it from my family. She's a very intelligent child."

"I'm sure she is," said Cleo. "And so pretty."

Soothed, Trina calmed down and took a seat.

"To change the subject," she said, "I haven't congratulated you on your engagement, Raine."

"Thank you very much," said Raine.

"Oh, I haven't congratulated you *yet*. I'll want to know a great deal more about the young man first. James says he is very nice, so I hope it isn't all on the surface. You'd better be sure that you're doing the right thing before you go any further."

"I haven't a doubt," said Raine with great self-restraint.

"Ian is an absolute dear!" said Cleo warmly.

"Ah," said Trina, as though her gloomiest doubts were realised.

"I really think we shall have to go," said Raine, trying not to sound so happy about it. She and Cleo rose thankfully.

Trina too jumped up with alacrity, and as they made their way to the front door said, "I suppose you'll be getting lunch in town. I'd have asked you to come back and share ours, but I don't think you'd be satisfied with our simple food."

"Oh, but we're not fussy —— " began Cleo, and Trina interrupted, "When I said Simple Food, I was speaking advisedly. I don't suppose you've read Adelaide Amble MacPherson's book, but we all have the greatest faith in it. She says that to obtain the maximum of nourishment, food ought to be simplified to the nth degree; that is to say, colourless, formless and practically tasteless. We've been practising this for three weeks, and we're all wonderfully better for it. It seems to have made our lives quite different."

"I'm sure it has," said Cleo.

And Trina said, "I'll lend you the book some time. It's been so nice to see you, do come again, won't you?"

"Thank you very much," said Cleo, and Raine added, "Tell James we called and were sorry we couldn't wait to see him. I suppose he'll be home soon?"

"Well, they're rather busy at the mill," explained Trina, "and it means he has had to get his lunch at the hotel this last fortnight."

"It's not the same as coming home, is it?" murmured Raine, and they made their good-byes and set off thankfully down the street.

"The only thing I can think of that's colourless, formless and practically tasteless is ground rice," said Cleo.

Once in the town they soon did the necessary shopping and then wandered along to the small stone pier and sat on a bench to rest, for it was a humid day and their feet ached. The sea looked dark and oily, and the fish-peat-tweed smell which characterised the town was much in evidence. Close by them a cloud of sea-birds shrieked and fought over a pile of refuse.

123

"I never felt frightened about getting married until now," said Raine. "I say, Cleo."

"Yes?"

"Will you promise me something?"

"What is it?" said Cleo apprehensively.

"Will you promise to shoot me if I ever turn into a frightful person?"

"But you couldn't!"

"You don't know that. I think it creeps upon you. I mean, if you are a frightful person you don't think of yourself as a frightful person, you think you are fine and everybody else is frightful."

Cleo thought for a moment, and said, "You know, James is very proud of Trina."

"Oh!" said Raine, horrified. "Promise on your honour you'll shoot me before Ian gets proud of me!"

"All right. I promise."

"I've often wondered," said Raine, "how parents can love unattractive children. I suppose when Ian and I are parents, I'll understand."

"You and Ian couldn't have unattractive children."

"That's just wishful thinking."

"Look," said Cleo, "let's go and have some ice-cream meringues. We need uplift."

Coming out of the café, feeling stronger, they blinked for a moment in the sunlight.

"Oh, look!" cried Raine. "There's Neil — over there, going into the saddler's."

Cleo's knees went weak. It was like swallowing ice-cream too quickly.

"Let's go over and surprise him," said Raine, and so it happened that when Neil came out of the shop he found the two girls in their blue and yellow summer dresses pretending to examine a string of brushes hanging outside the door.

"Hullo!" he cried. "What are you two doing in Dunmaig?"

"Shopping," said Raine. "How weird to meet you like this."

"Yes, isn't it odd?" said Cleo.

"I've been here all morning," said Neil. "I've been to the post office and the library and the corn chandler's and the vet's."

"What about taking us to lunch?" said Raine.

"Can't do it. I've got to get back, but there's a yacht anchored in the harbour that I'd like to look at. Will you come along?"

"Tell you what," said Raine, "you and Cleo go, and I'll slip into Jeanie's and see if·they can give me a shampoo and set."

They say that life never gives one a second chance, thought Cleo, hardly able to believe that she was walking down Nevison Street alone with Neil — but this is mine. And she tried desperately to think of something casual yet interesting to say. Of course what she really wanted to know was whether he had gone to dinner at Inga's and whether he had repaired her car and looked at her dog's tongue, but those were questions that could never be asked nor would she ever know the answers.

Paralysed with love and the bad luck that seemed to dog her footsteps, all she could think of to say was, "Doesn't Dunmaig smell?"

When she had said it she wished she had died first, but Neil replied without surprise, "Yes it does, but I rather like it. I mean, there's nothing wrong with fish and peat-smoke and tweed separately, so why should we mind them when they're mingled? The smell is Dunmaig, and Dunmaig is where one belongs. When I was at Alamein I'd have swopped every smell there was for the smell of Dunmaig."

As that seemed to be the end of that, Cleo thought hard for several minutes and then said, "Are all the animals flourishing?" And was pleased when he replied enthusiastically that they were, and added, "We've got three new calves, I don't mean new-born, they're about six months old and we've had them sent from Aberdeen to rear for the herd. I wondered if you and Raine would care to name two of them? They'll have to have Larrich names."

"I'd like to very much," said Cleo, bursting with happiness that he should have chosen her for this honour. "Do you think we could call mine Harebell? I've always wanted to call a calf Harebell."

"Harebell? I think that's rather good. Raine can choose something beginning with H too — as a matter of fact, it works in very well because Inga Duthie has already named hers Heather."

"Oh," said Cleo, her joy running out fast like the last pint of water down the bath-pipe.

They walked on in dull silence until they came to the slip. It was a dirty slip, with rusty iron rings lurking among the uneven blocks of stone ready to trip you up, and the water that slapped on the slimy foundation below was purple with grease and phosphorescence.

A little way out there rode at anchor a white yacht which clearly did not belong to the locality.

"That," said Neil, "is what I call a bonny boat."

"Would you like one like that?"

"Wouldn't I!"

"If ever I come into a fortune," said Cleo, "I'll buy you one."

"You're not likely to," said Neil.

Cleo went dumb. They stood for several seconds more staring at the white yacht, and suddenly Neil said, "Well, that's that. I'll have to be off now."

They walked back without saying a word to where his car was parked on a spot enclosed with a white line.

"It's been nice to see you," said Cleo.

"Yes, hasn't it?" said Neil, and bade her good-bye.

It gave Cleo some satisfaction as she walked away to reflect that his last remark was just as silly and ambiguous as anything she could have said herself, and it only proved that other people said things they didn't mean and probably went hot over afterwards. Though it wasn't to be expected that Neil would care a row of pins whether anything he said to Cleo MacAlvey was well or ill expressed, he would be too delighted about Inga Duthie choosing the name of Heather for his new calf, and just by luck Cleo had chosen a name beginning with H too — if she hadn't he would have requested her to — and now it didn't matter in the least what Raine called hers, she could call it Hosepipe or Horrible for all anyone cared. The only thing that matter to Neil was the H, because Inga had chosen it, and he would treasure the calf Heather and probably sell the other two at the first opportunity.

Cleo wandered up and down Nevison Street waiting for Raine to come out of the hairdresser's, and bought some knitting-wool and hair-grips and a magazine, none of which she really wanted, to pass the time.

At last Raine came out with little soft curls all over her head and said, "Have I been ages? This is a new style for me, and I think it's rather a mistake. I thought perhaps Neil might have taken you to lunch, after all."

"He had to go back," said Cleo with a touch of irascibility in her voice. "And I don't seem to want any lunch, it must be the meringues."

She dropped several parcels as she spoke and the knitting-wool fell out of its flimsy wrapping.

"Whatever possessed you to buy that colour?" said Raine.

"I thought I'd knit some of those little coats for the dogs for the winter," Cleo said, bitterly improvising.

"Well, even dogs have feelings, and that green! Did Neil have anything to say?"

"Not much."

"He's just a wee thocht dour," said Raine. "He doesn't get on with people easily, so don't think it's your fault, you're only one of dozens. Look, it's ten to two, and I for one am going to get something to eat."

CHAPTER EIGHT

"While the nice weather lasts we really ought to give a garden-party for the Leighs," said Mrs. MacAlvey.

Realising that as usual she had spoken her thoughts aloud, she looked guiltily round to see if anyone had heard her. Some-one had. Georgina the purple cat, who was lying on what was left of the *Erica carnea* on the rockery, washing her kitten, was looking at Mrs. MacAlvey in a very surprised sort of way.

Mrs. MacAlvey felt embarrassed, for Georgina was no ordinary cat. She was unusual in every way, and Mrs. Mortimer the cook said she understood everything that was said to her just like a human being. If this was so, Georgina had a right to feel surprised when Mrs. MacAlvey, alone in the garden, suddenly began to talk to thin air about garden-parties for the Leighs.

"Nice Georgina!" said Mrs. MacAlvey ingratiatingly, with a slight cough.

Georgina's colour was one of the most curious things about her. The offspring of an unauthorised union between a Kilchro tortoiseshell and the blue Persian belonging to the Strogue minister's wife, she was neither blue nor tortoiseshell but a rich dark purple, with a copper sheen when the sun shone on her. Visitors to Kilchro would blink their eyes and say, "Is there something unusual about that cat, or am I——?" Georgina knew perfectly well that she was different from the common herd, and it made her supercilious and patronising. She noticed things. She noticed now that Mrs. MacAlvey — after talking out loud to nobody at all with acres of empty garden around her — dropped her gardening gloves and hoe, scraped the earth off her shoes on a bit of rock, and made for the house, muttering to herself, "I'll have to do something about it. At once!"

As soon as she got into the hall she began to call, "Girls! Vannah! Where are you? I've been thinking, we ought to arrange a little garden-party for the Leighs while the weather ——"

Raine came bursting out of the dining-room.

"Oh, Mother, the invitation cards have come! They look marvellous. Honestly, I never really felt as if I was getting married until now, but when you see your name down in silver print it gives you the most incredible feeling, as though you were sitting on the throne of Scotland eating a strawberry ice with fireworks going off all round you. It's wonderful! It says, 'Mr. and Mrs. Alexander MacAlvey request the pleasure of the company of' and then there's a blank, and then it says, 'at the marriage of their younger daughter Raine,' etcetera, etcetera, etcetera, and then a blurb about Ian. And it's all in silver with silver edges. And Cleo and I are going to address the envelopes this afternoon, and I must ring Ian up at once and get his list. Fortunately most of our friends overlap, but he's got some relations in Aberdeen who have to be asked, and two old aunts at

Banff who never go anywhere, but they're sure to come, he says —— "

Raine gasped for breath and began to fan herself with somebody's hat which she had just picked up off the floor.

Cleo came leaping down the stairs.

"Oh, Cleo," said Mrs. MacAlvey, "I've been thinking, we simply must arrange a little garden-party for the Leighs while the wea —— "

"Oh, Mummy," Cleo cried, "we're going to do Raine's invitations, did she tell you? And she says that Ian has two old aunts at Banff who never go anywhere, but they're coming, and they wear high net collars and collar supports up to their ears and Alexandra fringes, and they never talk about anything except the day they went to the garden-party at Balmoral in 1904. And —— "

"Garden-party!" said Mrs. MacAlvey firmly. "That's what I want to talk about. The Leighs — I mean, we —— "

"Losh, Mummy, they're not going to Balmoral, are they? Daddy and Dr. Leigh have gone fishing. They won't be back for hours, so we won't bother much with lunch, and Raine and I can get on with addressing the invitations. There's Raine on the 'phone now."

Raine was pouring out the story of the invitations to Ian with many embellishments. Nobody else could make their voice heard until she finished, and then she clamped down the receiver with a triumphant ping, and cried, "Ian wants me to go round at once because the decorator is coming, and he's sent a lot of chintz patterns in advance for us to choose from, and he's got some Regency wallpapers — oh, and stair carpet; we'll have to do the invitations when I come back. I'll go and put a clean frock on, thank goodness Daddy didn't take the car to the loch."

She sped upstairs like a tornado, and Mrs. MacAlvey said, "Well, she's gone! Where's Mrs. Leigh, Cleo?"

"She forgot her operation for once and walked down to the village, Mummy, to get some stamps, but she'll remember it again when she comes back up the hill."

"Oh, Cleo dear, I don't think you ought to talk like that. I mean, you'll be saying it when she's here. And I was down the garden when I suddenly thought that we ought to get up a little garden-party for her and Dr. Leigh so that they can meet some of the neighbours, and I said so out loud and Georgina heard me and looked so surprised."

"Well, Mummy, I suggest that you and Georgina and Mrs. Mortimer all get together and decide who you'll ask and what they shall eat, and we'll fall in with whatever you arrange."

"There's Vannah at last, thank goodness," said Mrs. MacAlvey, as Miss Paige appeared at the top of the stairs, staggering under the week's laundry. "Is anybody in this house serious-minded? Vannah, come down quickly, I want you to help me to get up a little garden-party very quickly, for the Leighs. Put those sheets and things down, this is much more important."

So Mrs. MacAlvey got her way, and the invitations went out by telephone, and the garden-party took place three days later in brilliant weather.

All the previous day, the children had behaved with a strained perfection that was almost painful to see, hoping that by so doing they would earn the right to be 'let off' the garden-party. They got their wish. It was to be a grown-ups' garden-party (Best news since Hitler conked out! said Gavin), and after they had helped in the morning by setting up little tables on the lawn and carrying out chairs, Primrose gave the word to escape, and like wisps of smoke in the air, one minute they were there and the next they were gone. Even Cecil and Elinore.

"You do think it's going to keep fine, don't you, Vannah?" said Mrs. MacAlvey, peering from the morning-room window at the speckless sky. "Do you remember that time when it started to rain just as we got the tables laid outside and we rushed everything into the drawing-room, and then the sun shone and we put everything out again, and almost at once it began to rain and we had to bring it in, and —— "

"Spare us, Mother dear," said Raine. "It's like 'another little mouse brought another grain of corn' that used to irritate me so when I was small."

"I've got over the stage of having nervous prostration over garden-parties," said Miss Paige. "Everything has happened to me that can happen."

"Not it," said Raine. "You've not had my wedding yet. You won't know what anti-climax is until you've had my wedding."

"You haven't a thing to worry about," said Cleo. "The food looks wonderful and there's plenty of everything —— "

"Oh, don't say that, darling!" cried Mrs. MacAlvey. "It's so unlucky."

Mrs. Leigh was the first to come downstairs, dressed for the party. She had excelled herself, as a compliment to her hostess. She wore a white silk dress lightly dotted with red, a large drooping black hat with a bunch of silken poppies, and long black suède gloves, which seemed to lift the whole affair from a country garden-party into a Highland Social Event, or so thought Mrs. MacAlvey as she glanced out of her bedroom window while trying to do up the buttons of her new brown two-piece which fastened awkwardly at the back.

"Mrs. Leigh is down already and looking like *Vogue*," she said to her husband, adding as she turned, "Oh, Alexander!

133

You're not going down in that old tweed suit? Impossible!"

"What's the matter with it?"

"Well, you *fish* in it. Anybody can smell that."

"What am I to put on, then?"

"Your nice grey or —— "

"I thought this was a homely affair, just a few neighbours."

"Yes, I know dear, but it's for the Leighs, and I think we should try to look a little festive. Mrs. Leigh has taken such trouble with her appearance, and I'm sure the doctor will wear his best. Oh, and she's talking to somebody who must have arrived early —— "

"I'll only feel uncomfortable the whole afternoon," grumbled Mr. MacAlvey, hunting in the wardrobe for his grey.

"Alexander, please, please don't be obstructive. I have so much to do and — here's your grey. And you can't possibly wear those shoes!"

From below Mrs. Leigh's voice drifted up and in at the open window, "The hydrangeas are so gorgeous they make you blink, don't they? And the palms! People in London don't realise how warm it is in the north of Scotland. They have the impression it's exactly the same as the Arctic Circle. But you know, the sea is positively steaming. It's the Gulf Stream or something, I believe. No, no, I don't bathe. I did long ago, but I had a very severe operation —— "

"Who on earth can she be talking to?" said Mrs. MacAlvey, trying with shaking fingers to clasp her pearl necklace while peering round the window curtain. "Oh, it's Mrs. Abernethy. She's introduced herself. I simply must go down before anyone else comes."

Raine was dressing with her door open so she could call across to Cleo.

"Isn't it a pity," she said, "that Ian and Neil can't both be

134

away from the farm together? So Ian will come until tea-time, and then he'll go back and Neil will come for tennis."

They were both ready at the same moment, and bounded out of their rooms overtaking their father on the stairs.

"Do you feel gay?" said Cleo. "We do."

"Well, I don't. I don't feel like a garden-party at all. I feel like lying in a boat on the loch listening to a ghillie crooning to the fish."

"Poor, poor Father!" said Raine. "Oh, look at all the people!"

Already people were gathering on the lawn in chattering groups, for everybody knew everybody else, and already some of the keen gardeners were poking about in the borders and reading the rose labels, and telling each other how much bigger their own phloxes were.

"Oh, Dr. Leigh," cried Mrs. MacAlvey, leading up a stout little man with a bristling red beard, "this is Dr. MacArthur. Now you two can get together and talk about the B.M.A. I'm sure you've got lots in common."

She was as happy as a sandboy. She had got her garden-party, it was actually in full swing, nobody was standing about looking lost or neglected, and the sun was shining. What was more, the long-awaited big dahlias were out and Mrs. Kennedy, queen of the local gardeners, was standing looking at them, unable to hide her envy.

She darted off happily to talk about Latin names and seeds and cuttings and compost heaps, and — in a spasm of hostess-like responsibility — to greet a few more people.

"Now don't trouble about me," said Mrs. Leigh. "I shan't wait to be introduced. I shall simply talk to everybody who looks interesting."

She was having a wonderful time, and was gratified by the way these West Highland people seemed to hang on her

135

words. She thought them charming and such good listeners.

Over there beside the hollyhocks an elderly man was standing alone, gazing into the far distance. He was tall and white-haired and very quiet-looking. Mrs. Leigh thought she would have a little chat with him, so she made her way over and said brightly, "Isn't it a delicious view? They say you can see Skye when it is clear, but I suppose it is never quite clear enough. Or is it? And tell me, is that pinkish smudge an island or just a cloud?"

He did not reply but remained quite motionless, staring out to sea. It was like trying to make conversation with the statue of William Wallace.

"I wonder if I am near-sighted?" said Mrs. Leigh. "The other day I said to Mrs. MacAlvey, 'Oh, look at that patch of sunlight on the hillside,' and it wasn't a patch of sunlight at all, it was a white cow."

This time he turned his massive head slightly in her direction and looked at her, or rather through her, for his eyes had a weird, unearthly expression which made Mrs. Leigh's blood run cold and reminded her of banshees. Or was that Ireland?

"Of course to a Londoner like me," she said, "Scotland is quite, quite enchanting."

This strange old man was getting on her nerves. There was an air of ancient grandeur about him, as though he were hundreds of years old or had fought and died in some long-forgotten battle and come back as a ghost. Mrs. Leigh's knees began to shake, and she wondered if she was as strong as she thought she was.

"Oh dear!" Mrs. MacAlvey was saying, a little distance away. "Mrs. Leigh has got hold of Ardmunch and she won't be able to make sense of him. I must go over and save her."

And she went over and said, "Good afternoon, Ardmunch, I'm fine and glad to see you here. This is my friend Mrs. Leigh from London."

With the look of a caged eagle the old man made a stately bow and returned to his occupation of staring out to sea. Just then his wife came up, a short, sonsy woman with a merry red face who cried, "Och, Mrs. MacAlvey, you must just introduce me to your London friend. I've often thought myself I'd like fine to go to London, but I've never been able for bringing my mind round to it."

"This is Mrs. Mauchlin of Ardmunch, Mrs. Leigh."

"I've just been talking to Mr. Mauch — to your hus — to Ardmunch," said Mrs. Leigh, quite exhausted by the effort of getting it right at last, "and asking him if he can see Skye from here."

"I shouldn't be surprised," said Mrs. Mauchlin. "I'd like fine for you to come and see me and tell me all about London, but you can only get to our house by boat and some people don't take kindly to it. Our friends girn at us, but I've always lived on an island since I was married forty-two years ago, and I couldn't sleep without the sea round me."

"How romantic it sounds!" said Mrs. Leigh. "I shall always be sorry that I wasn't able to visit the islands, but the sea does dreadful things to me. I can't tell you what this visit has done for Doctor and me. We're so enthusiastic about Scotland and are going to adopt it as our second home. I'm really very well up in Scottish history and all those foolish controversies with the English about this and that, and I've come to the conclusion that in many cases the Scots were right."

"There now!" said Mrs. Mauchlin, looking nervously at her husband.

"I'll tell you a secret," said Mrs. Leigh. "Doctor and I have

137

been collecting material for a book about our holiday. We thought it would be such fun to write it together in the long winter evenings, and we thought of calling it 'Our Life in the Highlands.' "

"It's been done before," said Raine, who had arrived to rescue her mother, "by Queen Victoria."

Mrs. Leigh looked after Raine's retreating figure a little coldly. She had doubted for some time whether she really cared for Mrs. MacAlvey's second daughter. She didn't for a moment believe that anyone had previously used the title 'Our Life in the Highlands,' which had taken her hours to think out for herself. Raine was merely trying to be difficult. And as for suggesting that Queen Victoria had written a book! If she had, Mrs. Leigh would have heard of it. There was no worthwhile book of which she had not heard.

She felt quite put out and her enjoyment of the day was temporarily clouded, but presently she noticed two ladies casting glances of admiration at her dress, and she went over to them and introduced herself and found them very much to her liking, so all was well once more.

Meanwhile Cleo was walking round the garden with Raine and Ian, whom everybody was bombarding with questions about their approaching wedding, for the invitations had been duly sent out and had been received that very morning.

Cleo felt gay and contented, looking round at the bright summer colours, the emerald grass and the pigeon-grey stones of the house, the charming hues of light dresses, the white flutter of tablecloths and the cool gleam of cups and saucers. Almost like a painted background was the slope of blue-green hillside to the sea where the silver-blue waves tumbled lightly, laying creamy bands of foam on the fawn-coloured sand, and farther away the islands lay like shadows on the ocean's

138

face and there was not a cloud to mar the azure of the sky.

Here in the garden were flowers like butterflies and butter-flies like flowers, all happy in the sun, and there were even tiny flies enjoying life as they crawled up the stalks of the roses and tumbled into the large pink hearts.

Cleo was happy, but at the same time she could not help wishing that she did not have to make a three with Ian and Raine — kind as they were and glad to walk with her — and she wondered whether all her life she would find herself making up a three with some lucky pair.

Presently she saw Miss Paige on the terrace trying to catch her eye, and it was time to shepherd all the guests to tea.

"Oh, Mother," cried Raine, rushing up, "do you realise that all this time you've left poor Dr. Leigh with Dr. MacArthur who can't talk about anything but statistics, and already he'll have gone through all the cases of notifiable diseases in every town in Scotland for the last ten years. You must find Dr. Leigh somebody amusing to have tea with."

"How awful," said Mrs. MacAlvey, knitting her fingers. "What about the Erskines? I see there is room for another at their table."

"That'll do," said Raine. "But if you value your social sense, keep Mrs. Leigh out of their way. If she starts telling the Erskines that she's very well up in Scottish history and she thinks that in many cases the Scots were right, you'll have to call the police to stop a war."

"What a responsibility an affair like this is!" said Mrs. Mac-Alvey.

The tables were each laid for four persons, and the family divided themselves up among their guests. Mrs. MacAlvey self-sacrificingly placed herself with the two Miss Tods, who were known to be difficult, and their cousin Miss Drummond, who was stone deaf. Mr. MacAlvey thoughtfully went and sat with Ardmunch and Mrs. Mauchlin and their daughter Fiona, who was, to put it kindly, a little absent-minded.

Raine and Ian were with their great friends, Bobbie and Margaret Ferguson; while Cleo, looking round for congenial company, found herself seized and pressed firmly into a chair by kind, fat Mrs. Dalgleish and her two enormous daughters, who talked about nothing but dieting all through the meal, which they devoured with great zest.

Mrs. Leigh was safely disposed of at a table with Mr. and Mrs. Beattie, who had both recently undergone operations far less severe than her own, and with Mrs. Aird, who adored all things English.

Tea was just over when a car drew up and out stepped Inga Duthie, in white sharkskin and looking dazzling, accompanied by three young men in tennis flannels with Air Force tunics slung over their shoulders. They were officers from the R.A.F. station at Dunfaul.

Welcomed, they said they didn't want any tea but had come on purpose for the tennis, and at once they took possession of the court and began to play a spectacular game, while the garden-party took on an air of Wimbledon and everybody drifted over to watch.

"Inga always brings her own partners," said Miss Paige to Cleo. "It's awfully good play, isn't it?"

"It doesn't seem to occur to them that anybody else might want the court," said Cleo, so crossly that Miss Paige was surprised.

"Oh, I don't know," she said. "Most people enjoy watching."

"Vannah," said Cleo, "if you could have just one gift, what would you choose?"

140

"Just one?" Miss Paige thought for a moment and said, "I've always thought I'd like a fitted dressing-case if money was no object. I know it's silly and they weigh about half a ton and you can't get a porter, but —— "

"I didn't mean that sort of gift. I meant, like the fairies give you at your christening, Beauty and Virtue and so on."

"Oh, I see. Well, one sole gift sounds rather meagre, though it might do if it was the right one. I should say health is as good as anything."

"That's dull," said Cleo. "I'd like to be magnetic."

"But you are. All you MacAlveys are magnetic. It just describes you."

"That's not what I meant," said Cleo, walking away. She didn't feel happy any more about the garden-party, and at the same time she was furious at having to admit to herself that the mere arrival of Inga could put her at a disadvantage on her own ground.

She stood digging her toe into the soft earth of a flower-bed when all of a sudden she saw Neil arriving, in white flannels with a shabby tweed coat over them. Her heart gave its usual blow against her ribs, for he seemed to be walking straight towards her, but the next minute she saw that the tennis had stopped and that Inga was running across the court, waving to Neil, who looked pleased.

"At last, Neil!" cried Inga. "You've just come at the right moment, because Bingo has to go and you can take his place. Or perhaps you'd better play with me against Rusty and Mac."

"I'm not very good," said Neil, looking bashful and taking off his coat, but Inga only flapped her eyelashes and cried, "Now, darling, don't be modest."

They began a new game, and Cleo could not tear herself away from the hateful scene, though it did her good to see that

141

Neil was playing badly and hitting everything out of court or else poaching Inga's balls and putting them into the net. When the game was over and Neil and Inga had been well beaten, she strolled across to where the men were falling over one another to help Inga on with her cardigan, and Neil noticed her at last and said, "Hullo Cleo. Where have you been all this time?"

"None of you have had any tea," she said, trying to sound cool and hostess-like. "Won't you at least come and have a drink? I'm sure you'd like something, Mrs. Duthie."

"Oh no, thank you," said Inga with a brilliant smile. "It's too sweet of you, Cleo — I may call you Cleo, mayn't I? And please don't call me Mrs. Duthie, because simply nobody does — but I'm going back with the boys to a party at the Station. By the way, Neil, why don't you come along? It's going to be quite an affair, in honour of the new C.O."

This is the end, thought Cleo in despair, but to her surprise Neil declined and Inga said, "Well, I suppose I'll see you soon, Neil, and thank you over and over again, Cleo, for such a maddeningly lovely party, and do thank your Mother for me, won't you, because I don't want to drag her away from her guests. Neil, what on earth are you going to do with yourself if you don't come with us?"

She slipped her arm affectionately through Cleo's and said, "Do say you'll come and have tea with me one day at my funny little house! Could you come next Saturday? Splendid! And we won't have any men there at all. They're so obtuse, they can't even see when a poor woman is longing for a cigarette."

At this there was a kind of battle-charge on the part of the three men, all holding out their cases to Inga and striking lighters which promptly went out. Inga thoroughly enjoyed the situation, and finally accepted Neil's cigarette and somebody else's light. Cleo, standing a little outside the gay scene, found herself in the end with no cigarette and nobody bothering, and didn't know whether to laugh or scream.

However, a few minutes later Inga and her party drifted away, and to her amazement Cleo found herself alone with Neil. She was so cross that she didn't even try to charm him.

"If you're quite sure it isn't too much trouble," she said, "I should like a cigarette."

He looked dismayed. "Oh, didn't you get one? Here you are."

Three puffs took her bad temper away and she said, "Won't you come up to the house, Neil, and have a drink?"

"I have to go straight back now," he said. "The bull has strained a tendon." And he looked so handsome and noble as he said it that Cleo had to shut her eyes, and found herself saying in a shaky voice, "These midges!"

Neil said sympathetically, "They always begin to bite at this time. They say it was the midges that got Prince Charlie down, not Culloden."

"Oh, Neil, must you go so soon?" cried Cleo from the depths of her heart, so that he looked startled and said, "I don't want to go, but the bull —— "

Damn the bulls! thought Cleo, who hardly ever used strong language, not even in her thoughts.

"It's been a lovely afternoon," he said simply, fastening his racket into its press. "I did enjoy the tennis. Inga's a fine player."

"Terrific," said Cleo, her spirits sinking lower and lower. "Would you — would you care to come and play tennis with me — with us one of these nights?"

"I might," said Neil, indifferently.

"Oh, there you are!" cried Raine, coming upon them sud-

143

denly. "Have you all been playing tennis? Listen, Ian has had a bright idea, and I've left him lying in a darkened room to get over the shock to his brain."

"Hasn't he gone home already?" gasped Neil. "The bull —— "

"It's better," said Raine, who didn't know what he was talking about. "The idea is that we should go to Skye, the four of us, on the steamer on Friday. Now, don't say you can't leave the farm, Neil, because Ian says it can easily be arranged for once."

"I wasn't," said Neil. "It would be a fine idea."

Cleo was so pleased that she couldn't say a word except, "We'll have to get up at three in the morning because the steamer leaves at four because of the tide or the fish or something."

"Well, that's settled," said Raine. "Cleo, I think Mother wants you to go and talk to Mrs. Abernethy. You know how she adores talking about Balmoral and what the Queen wore at Crathie Church last Sunday, and none of us can stand it any longer."

"I'll go," said Cleo, realising that it was time she did a little social duty. "Good-bye, Neil," she added, wishing that she could sound a bit more nonchalant, and finished with great daring, "If there's a sea mist or anything on Friday, I think I'll die."

"Why? Are you so keen on Skye?" said Neil, but Cleo fled without answering, and Raine said, "She hasn't been to Skye since she was about twelve, and neither have I. I expect that's why she's so keen."

Mrs. MacAlvey greeted her daughter with joy, for though some people were leaving, others of a clinging type lingered on and had to be entertained; but at last all the good-byes and thank-yous were said and everybody was gone, and in the early evening hush where the shadows of the firs crept long across the lawn the garden lay quiet and weary-looking, and a kind of sighing shiver went over the grass and the heavy roses drooped.

"Hasn't it gone quiet?" said Miss Paige.

"Yes, and hasn't it been a wonderful party?" cried Mrs. Leigh. "I have enjoyed it, and I think it was so very kind of you all to do it for me. I quite forgot that I have to be careful, which just shows that it's all psychological, isn't it?"

"Was the tea all right?" asked Mrs. MacAlvey anxiously. "I mean, the cakes just tasted like dust and ashes to me, but it's always like that, when it's your own party."

"Everything was beautiful," said Raine, "and Ian ate an enormous tea, and you should have seen some of the old people enjoying the lobster patties. There'll be some queer dreams on feverish pillows tonight!"

"Oh, I hope not," said Mrs. MacAlvey. "I wouldn't like — there's Alexander! Alexander, was it all right? And you can go and take your grey suit off now."

"Thank you, I'm quite comfortable. How many more times have I to change my clothes?" he said perversely.

"And here comes Dr. Leigh," went on Mrs. MacAlvey, a little anxious. "I do hope poor Dr. MacArthur didn't bore you, Doctor? He means well, but he will talk about —— "

"I thought he was tremendously interesting," said Dr. Leigh. "Most knowledgeable. He gave me some astounding figures, quite astounding."

Mrs. MacAlvey drooped into a chair.

"I can't remember when I last sat down! My feet! Oh, Raine, go and find me some slippers. Great big ones, your father's will do."

"Yes, Mother," said Raine. "And what do you think? Everybody was asking Ian and me what we'd like for wedding presents. Fancy having people actually asking to give you presents! We couldn't think of a single thing."

"Well, it was very stupid of you, when you need clocks and sets of pans, and you can never have too many sheets, and even cushions and table-lamps and fish-eaters."

"Oh!" said Raine. "I never thought of things like that."

Cleo came up the garden alone, bemused, smiling to herself in a fatuous dream that was made up of Skye and sunsets and Neil and the feeling you get on a still summer evening when the scent of cooling earth comes to you, and the tobacco plants open their crumpled rose-and-white petals and give out a deep fragrance, and one sleepy thrush is singing his late silver song.

"Ah, here's Cleo," said Mrs. MacAlvey. "Now we're all here, and a cold supper is in the dining-room and we needn't talk. Do you think it went off all right, Cleo?"

But Cleo didn't hear the question. She walked straight into the house, determined not to look forward to Friday.

"Considering how unpretentious the MacAlveys are," said Mrs. Leigh to her husband as they changed in the privacy of their room, "and I do think one can be too unworldly, they know some very nice people. Very nice. I spoke to at least three people who were connected with the Scottish nobility. But it is such a pity about the Scots, they eat too heartily and dress so badly."

146

CHAPTER NINE

Gavin had gone down to the quay to rig the sails on *Heather Bell*, Hamish's big boat, kindly lent for the occasion. He had hoisted the lug and foresail before the others arrived, and when he saw them he slipped the mooring rope and ran the boat alongside the slip, showing off how well he could handle her.

"We're here!" shouted Primrose, tottering up with her arms full. "Archie and I have got the food and the bathing things, and Granny made us bring waterproofs too, in case."

"What's the food like?" Gavin asked.

"Oh, a bit sordid," said Primrose. "Mrs. Mortimer wasn't feeling inspired, so I'm afraid it's mostly fish-paste sandwiches and some of those biscuits that went too soft for the dining-room, and the cake that Mrs. Leigh told Mysie was too sad for her. I never knew that cakes had feelings. Stick all this junk in the locker, Gav, and then you'd better get Cecil and Elinore aboard. Shove them on the port side, because you'll be carrying your boom to starboard. Hasn't Gull turned up yet?"

"She's doing about thirty knots along the beach now," said Archie.

"Old Mother Mac has got some South African plums in the window," said Primrose yearningly, "and some boxes of those very soft fat dates. I wish we had some. Have you got any money, Gav?"

"I've only got one-and-four."

"I've only got eightpence." Primrose displayed the coppers and said, "No can do. The dates are three shillings a box and the plums are four shillings a pound."

"Oh, let's have them by all means," said Cecil patronisingly. "Get whatever you want." And he produced a ten-shilling note from his trousers pocket and held it out.

"Thanks most awfully," said Primrose. "Do you mean I can spend all this on food?"

"Certainly," said Cecil. "Get some chocolate too, if you like. Here are my coupons."

Gavin scowled heavily at Cecil's lordly, take-the-children-out-for-the-day manner, but Primrose, who never looked a gift-horse in the mouth, was already on her way to the shop.

When she got back Gull had joined the party. She had brought her contribution in a jam-jar.

"It's a whole wine jelly," she said, "and I've got stacks of dull sandwiches in my rucksack too. Oh I say! Are we going in *Heather Bell*?"

"This is our great friend, Gull Tordoch," said Primrose, "and these are our cousins Cecil and Elinore Atkinson."

"Cheerio," said Gull with a wide grin.

"How d'y'do," said Cecil in a bored drawl.

Elinore took one look at Gull's shabby kilt and washed-out jersey and looked away again, ignoring her.

"Come on," said Primrose, boiling with rage, "get aboard. Hey you, Angus what's-your-name, shove her bow round for us, will you?"

148

Gavin took the tiller, paid out the main sheet, and let the boom swing forward. *Heather Bell* slid away from the quay, passed buoy after buoy, and soon was bobbing gaily as the little waves of the open sea met her bow. The wind behind her, she danced over the water, headed straight for the channel. It was impossible not to be brimming over with happiness when the sky was so blue and the sea so enchanting, when the white sails curved above you and the fresh salt wind blew cool through your hair. Far ahead the islands seemed to sparkle in the sunlight, and crying gulls followed the boat, gracefully wheeling.

"Where are we making for, Gavin?" shouted Primrose against the breeze.

"I thought Kaista. There's a farm where we can get milk, and a good bathing beach. And it isn't too far in case anyone who isn't used to it feels sick."

"If you mean me," said Cecil with a condescending smile, "I have done some real yachting in the Solent."

"Never heard of it," said Gavin.

"It would be fun," said Gull, "to work out a plan to visit all the islands."

"You couldn't do it in a summer holiday," said Primrose, "even if you did one a day. Anyhow, when are we going to Eil-oran?"

"Let's go now," said Archie.

"*Heather Bell's* slow. We'd have to start a lot earlier to go to Eil-oran."

"It's an awful pity we can't go in *Minnow*," said Archie, "but four's the absolute maximum she'll take."

"Shut up, Archie," said Primrose, thinking his remark would sound rude to Elinore and Cecil, but they didn't seem to have heard. They never did take any notice of what Archie said, considering him too much of a kid.

149

"I wish," said Elinore in an affected voice, "that I could remember a poem about the sea."

"I can remember about a million poems about the sea," said Primrose.

"This one is rather special. Pearl Panton recited it at our Speech Day. It was awfully impressive and she recites marvellously. By the way, her father's a baronet."

"You've told us already," said Gavin. "Let the poor bloke rest."

"Really," said Elinore, "you know nothing. Imagine going to a Scotch school! Nobody has ever heard of any Scotch schools."

"Give me strength!" yelled Gavin. "What about Fettes?"

"What about it?" said Elinore. "I never heard of it."

"Then you're an ignorant little English —— "

"Oh, be quiet, everybody!" shouted Primrose, thinking that Elinore was really the limit but one had to have the sense not to start a war with six people in a boat at sea. However, she could not keep her mind in a state of exasperation for long when the day was so glorious and she was at her favourite sport of bounding over the main, so she began to divide up the chocolate and generously offered the first piece to Elinore.

Twenty minutes later Gavin cried, "There's Kaista!" — pointing ahead to a bright green island with a sharply shelving shore. It was only about half-tide, and the island seemed to be surrounded by ugly looking rocks pushing up their brown seaweed-coated backs from the sea. But Gavin knew his way in, and putting down the tiller he hauled on his sheet and, running neatly through a narrow channel, he laid *Heather Bell* ashore on a sandy beach.

"All out!" he cried.

"I say, you did that quite well," said Cecil, impressed by Gavin's handling of the boat.

"I've been doing it since I was about two," said Gavin modestly, and Primrose added, "Our father was a sailor."

They both thought suddenly and sharply of lovely summer holidays spent in boats with their sailor father before the war came and took him away from them, never to return, for he went down with the *Jervis Bay*.

"Shove her well out, Gav," Primrose said as she and Gull began to unship the provisions. "It's no fun being caught on the ebb with that old tub high and dry and having to lug her down the beach."

Gavin lowered the sails and dropped anchor. *Heather Bell* rode smoothly at the end of her anchor rope.

Cecil and Elinore stood looking about them with interest. It was the first time they had been on an island; except for the Isle of Wight, which was so different and hardly an island at all. Primrose, Gull, and Archie carried all the food up the beach and dumped it on the sand; then they went back and fetched the bathing things.

Gavin waded ashore.

"The tide's not bad for bathing," he said. "What about a bathe now, and then eat?"

Cecil and Elinore were very fussy about finding suitable changing places among the rocks, and complained a lot about sharp stones, seaweed, and oil, but at last everybody was ready and rushing into the sparkling sea. The sun shot through to the depths and made bright patterns on the sand.

"All in a ring!" yelled Gavin. "Join hands, feet to the middle, make a wheel."

They turned on their backs, feet to the middle, hands joined, kicking up mountains of spray.

"Now heads to the middle, feet out, splash!"

A great wheel of splashing flashed towards the sun.

Then Cecil obligingly did his trick, which was to stand on his hands on the bottom with only his feet showing above the water, and everybody else tried to do it but was less successful than Cecil. Afterwards they swam out a long way, and turned on their backs to rest, with the broad ocean all around them, emerald green and heaving, and the tremendous sky above.

"I call this the ultimate blissikins," said Primrose, treading water. "I don't know about you people, but I'm boiling hot. I could stay in for hours."

"I'm starving," said Archie. "Let's go out and eat, and then come in again."

The mention of food appealed to them all, so they swam lazily to shore. Primrose and Gull began to spread out the food on a large sheet of brown paper which they had discovered in the locker of the boat.

"It looked a lot when we started," said Primrose, "but it doesn't look much now. I could eat it all myself."

"So could I," said Gavin, Archie, and Gull simultaneously.

"This sandwich tastes slightly — just slightly but unmistakably — of paraffin," said Gavin.

"Oh, that's only the last lot of marge," said Primrose. "Mrs. Mortimer explained to me that Ma Mackenzie told her it had come in at the same time as the paraffin and she hoped we weren't fussy. I'm not fussy, but I do think she oughtn't to keep them on the same shelf in the shop. You know — they grew in beauty side by side."

"What about the farm up there?" asked Cecil. "Couldn't they produce some food?"

"Only porridge," said Gull, "and it's the most awful lumpy

152

muck. It's what they live on. But they might have some milk. Go on, Archie, and see if they have."

"Give me tuppence," said Archie to his sister, and added, "Don't you eat everything while I'm away."

"I say, I like these sandwiches," said Gull. "You don't notice the paraffin if you eat them with the plums. Look, Elinore" — she went on generously — "you can have the sandwiches I brought. They don't taste of anything. Would anybody like a go at the wine jelly? There aren't any spoons, but if I tip it out on the paper you can lap it up."

Elinore and Cecil declined to lap, but the others all got some wine jelly and left a portion for Archie, who was by now to be seen coming down the field with a brown pitcher carefully held in both hands.

"Glory, he's got it!" said Primrose.

"Here's the milk," said Archie, arriving. "She milked the cow for me. It's all warm and frothy."

"Oh! Ugh! It hasn't been strained!" cried Elinore.

"Strained?" said Archie. "How do you mean, strained?"

"You can have first drink, as you're the guest, Elinore," said Primrose. "Sorry we haven't any cups."

"I don't want any," said Elinore, pale with disgust.

"All the more for us," said Primrose. "What about you, Cecil?"

Cecil condescended to take a drink, for he was very thirsty, and then the others quickly emptied the jug.

"Swill it out in the sea and then take it back, kid," said Gavin.

"Not me," said Archie. "Let somebody else mug."

Gull offered to go. Afterwards they bathed again until they were too tired to swim another stroke. They came out and lay in a drowsy row on the hot sand.

"I'm hungry again," said Primrose an hour later. "We ought to have saved something for tea."

"Last summer holiday," said Elinore, "I stayed with Pearl Panton, and we used to take a picnic basket with us in the car. It had green cups and saucers and plates, and flasks for tea, and silver forks and spoons, and glass dishes for fruit and cream."

Primrose opened her mouth to make what she thought a brilliant retort, but with singular restraint shut it again. It just wasn't worth wasting one's strength on a pachyderm like Elinore.

"I say," said Cecil, "do you think I could explore a bit? This looks the kind of place where I might find some specimens for my collection."

"Explore all you want," said Gavin, "but the only specimens I know of on Kaista are children and goats. They both look alike, only the goats have little horns — up here."

So Cecil went bounding off across the rocks in his nicely tailored grey flannels and striped blazer.

"If we were on Eil-oran," said Archie, "he might find a specimen of a monster for his collection."

"What is this Eil-oran?" asked Elinore.

"It's an island. Nobody ever goes there. There's supposed to be a monster on it."

"It belongs to the *Sithe*," said Gull.

"The what?"

"The Little People. What you call fairies."

"Is that actually true?" asked Elinore, obviously very impressed.

"No, it's a lot of rot," said Primrose. "But we're going to have a look at Eil-oran as soon as we've got time and the wind's right."

"It will be something to tell Pearl Panton," said Elinore. "She has been to Corsica."

"Never heard of it," said Primrose cheerfully.

Elinore gave her a cautious glance to see if she was being mocked, but Primrose looked as innocent as a baby seagull, and Elinore said, "I think Eil-oran is a pretty name. I'm rather keen on names, actually. I think Elinore is a beautiful name, and I have another. Felicity. Elinore Felicity. Don't you think that's musical? Have you got another name, Primrose?"

"As a matter of fact, I have," said Primrose, dragging one leg out of the sand to scratch the ankle. "But I don't like it much. It's Hephzibah. Primrose Hephzibah."

Archie gave a snort of joy. "I've got another name too," he volunteered. "It's Brontosaurus."

"I think Neurasthenia is an awfully musical name for a girl," said Gavin. "Don't you, Prim?"

"Oh yes, and so's Lethargy."

"They only call me Gull for short," said Gull. "My real name is Seagull Nightingale Cuckoo Stork Tordoch."

"I thought there was a Vulture in it somewhere," said Gavin.

"Of course, I forgot. Seagull Nightingale Cuckoo Stork *Vulture* Tordoch. My old Nanny called me Vulture because she's awfully keen on names, *actually*."

"I don't think you're a bit funy," said Elinore, going red. "I think you're just a pack of silly kids. I'm going to find Cecil. We both think you're all awfully childish." And she got up with dignity and walked away.

"We oughtn't," said Primrose. "She's our guest."

"Rot," said Gavin. "She asks for it."

"Yes, but it isn't gallant Highland courtesy towards the English."

155

Archie and Gull were rolling over and over, shrieking with laughter.

"Vulture!" yelled Archie.

"Brontosaurus!" screamed Gull.

At last Cecil and Elinore were seen returning together. Elinore still looked to be on her dignity, but Cecil was quite excited and cried, "What do you think, I actually found a specimen of *Fonta rarifloris* in the bed of a stream up there in the field. At least, I'm almost sure that's what it is. I can't wait to get home and compare it with the illustration in my book. I could have stayed searching for hours, but a very dirty kid stood staring at me all the time. I told him to go, but he took absolutely no notice. It was very putting-off."

"That would be Hector Mackenzie," said Primrose.

"You don't mean to say you know him?"

"Not him in particular, but they're all called Hector Mackenzie. If you throw things at them, they'll go."

"Have I time to go back?" said Cecil. "There are one or two most interesting ponds."

"All the time in the world," said Primrose encouragingly. "We never bother about time."

"I'd like to come with you," said Gavin for no reason at all, and Elinore said she would go too, so when they had disappeared Primrose, Gull, and Archie spent an interesting hour clambering over the rocks and looking for caves which were not there.

When they were tired of this they went back to the beach, and were just deciding that they were hungry again when they saw the others coming towards them down the field. Gavin and Elinore looked merely dirty, but Cecil was hardly recognisable, for he was plastered almost from head to foot with wet,

156

dripping mud. It was greenish too, and had bits of weed stuck in it. His beautiful trousers were quite ruined.

"Cecil has been in the bog," announced Gavin unnecessarily.

"Right in the bog!" wailed Elinore. "Oh, what shall we do? Oh, look at his clothes! Oh, Cecil, are you wet? You know you always get a cold when you get wet, and Mummy said you weren't to."

"Oh, shut up!" said Cecil in justifiable fury.

"In any case, we're going home now," said Primrose. "It's nothing, Cecil. We've all been worse than that millions of times, and we're still alive."

"None of us will be alive long," said Gavin grimly. "I've just noticed, it's half-past five and it'll take us all of two hours to get to Strogue. And dinner's supposed to be at seven."

Rather chilled by this revelation, they embarked as quickly as they could. Gavin pushed off, leapt into the stern, and set course for home. The wind was light and the speed not so good as it might have been.

"But whatever our retribution," said Primrose, "it has been a frabjous day." And she sighed noisily from pure pleasure.

They cast anchor in Strogue at seven-forty, and the luckless Cecil was not yet finished with trouble, for the slip was greasy and in trying to spring lightly out of the boat — like Gavin — he fell on his knees and rose with a jagged gash in one trouser leg, while a lot of blood began to mingle colourfully with the green mud.

"Well, I got my wish," said Gavin to Primrose later that night. "I brought Cecil back plastered with dirt, but somehow I wasn't so thrilled as I thought I would be. After all, I never heard anything so decent as the way he told Granny it

157

was all his fault for walking into a bog and making us late. And then asking her not to stop us sailing, like she threatened to do. You've got to hand it to Cecil, whether you want to or not. I always said he wasn't bad — if you could prise him away from Elinore."

CHAPTER TEN

IF THERE IS one thing more likely than another to damp one's enthusiasm for a day's outing, it is to begin it in the cold dusk before dawn, standing on a slipper quay, listening to the melancholy slap of an oily sea against the stones, and trying to keep one's teeth from chattering.

"And this is called pleasure!" said Raine, hugging her tweed coat round her. "The worst of starting off at this time for a whole day is that you never know what to put on, and whatever you put on is sure to be wrong by the middle of the morning."

"One of us ought to have come in thickest tweeds and ghillie shoes and the other in a cotton frock and sandals, and then one of us would have been right," said Cleo, whose fingers were numb.

"Not necessarily. It could be pouring on Skye, and then we'd want oilskins and rubber boots. And I do think it is most ungallant of the men to let us arrive here first."

"That's probably because we're ten minutes early owing to all the clocks and watches at home being different," began Cleo, and added, "Here they come now."

The Larrich car rattled up, and Neil parked it, and both the Garvines jumped gaily out, wearing kilts and open-necked shirts and tweed coats with leather patches on the elbows.

"We're cold," said Raine accusingly.

"Why didn't you go on board?" said Ian. "The steamer's waiting."

"There'll be lots of room," said Raine. "Sane people don't start off for a day's enjoyment in the middle of the night. Only lunatics like us."

"But you wanted to come," said Ian.

"You mean, you wanted to come, but you didn't tell us how dreary it would be. My teeth are rattling like very skilfully played castanets."

"Is that a sea mist coming up?" said Cleo, pointing.

"No, it is not, that's a mist for heat," said Ian, exasperated. "Now don't you start being a little ray of sunshine!"

"What about getting on board?" said Neil.

"He's determined to go," said Raine. "How I wish I were back in bed!"

"I couldn't have believed it would be as dark as this at four o'clock in the morning," said Cleo. "Perhaps there's an eclipse or something?"

"It's always like this just before an earthquake," said Neil. "Now, if you can't think of anything worse to say we'll go on board."

There is something magical in the moment of a ship's sailing, whether it be the *Queen Mary* in all her magnificence, or an oily tramp leaving London River for the mysterious East, or a little steamer chugging out at dawn into the cold, fresh, western sea.

That moment came with a thrill to the four adventurers as they leaned on the rail and watched the pier recede and the

160

strip of black water grow wider between them and the shore, and Strogue itself suddenly become a blur beneath the dark hills of the mainland as they looked back at it from the sea. Ahead lay grey mist, and the nearer islands were hidden. They had the feeling of explorers setting out into the unknown, lured on by the tang of the salt spray and the desire for new worlds. It was that hushed hour just before the sunrise, and the sea was still asleep, silvery dark with phosphorescent gleams. There was no sound but the determined throbbing of the steamer's engines and a faint swish as the bow parted the sluggish water.

"If you really want more sleep," said Ian to Raine, "we'll sit down on that seat over there, and you can put your lovely head on my shoulder and hog it to your heart's content."

They arranged themselves accordingly, but Neil strode away to the bows and stood gazing out to sea.

Cleo thought there could be no sight more noble than that of a kilted Highland man standing squarely in the bows of a ship, as Neil was now. Of course she was dotingly prejudiced, but he certainly looked rather splendid with his dark head and eagle profile.

She went up to him and said, "Do you think we shall see the sunrise, Neil? I've always wanted to. Once I got up early on purpose and pushed out a little way in a boat, but it was a grey morning like this and absolutely nothing happened except that the grey went lighter and lighter and then stopped. I've never been so disappointed."

"There'll be a sunrise this morning," said Neil kindly. "The mist is nearly gone already, and if you turn round now and look at the land you'll see that the hills have bright edges."

"How clever of you to know that through the back of your

head!" cried Cleo, turning round and discovering that he was right.

Already the summer dawn was broadening across the pearl-grey sky, and eastwards behind the land there was a red flush which paled to lilac, changing to rose and then to azure. The sun suddenly sprang aloft with one joyful leap, and all the sea-birds of the coast seemed to be wheeling and screaming, filling the air with wings.

"How good of Nature to do it on purpose for us," said Cleo.

"It's there most mornings," said Neil, "only people don't realise what a good show it is. Here comes the wind, and look! the waves are rising and nearly jade-green in colour. The last time I stood on a ship and watched Scotland fade from sight was on a transport going to North Africa."

"I suppose you thought you might never see it again," said Cleo, her heart missing several beats.

"No, I didn't think that. Soldiers are optimistic blokes. I only wondered how Ian would cope with the farm alone."

Before Cleo could grow any sadder, contemplating those bygone days, Ian and Raine came staggering up — for the steamer was pitching merrily by now — and Raine said, "Let's have a soak of the sun in our old bones. I can't count a joint in my body that isn't smitten with rheumatism, and Ian has shooting pains, and we're hungry and we want to see Skye."

"Well, there she is!" said Neil, and the others were silent, awed by that first sight of the fairy isle as she lay like a cloud with her mauve peaks on the far horizon.

"Och, the lure of it!" said Ian in a mocking tone. "You only have to say, there's Skye, and everybody in the ship drops whatever they're doing and stares like a cow."

"I don't stare like a cow," said Cleo. "Neither does Neil. You're just utterly unromantic, Ian."

"The sight of the cuillin always makes me feel drunk with enchantment," said Raine. "It's terribly dramatic, Ian. Skye is the only island with a sense of drama in the western sea, so don't you dare to say it is only another island or the fairies will have their revenge on you, and next time you come to earth they'll send you to live on the Bass Rock with a lot of gulls and guillemots and no atmosphere at all."

"There won't be much atmosphere on Skye now that they have the buses there," said Cleo.

"But there aren't many buses," said Neil, "and none at all at Loch Coruisk. I should like to walk up Glen Sligachan to Loch Coruisk again when the streams are running wildly and you can't hear yourself speak for the wind and the water-falls."

By now the strong wind was whipping their hair madly across their faces and they had to shout to make themselves heard, so they stopped talking and watched the coast of Skye draw nearer, until at last they could discern the outlines of the mountains and the deep indentations of the sea-lochs, and soon the island was bright with colour and turned from a painted backcloth into a real place and they were steaming into Portree harbour.

The little white town was hardly awake at half-past seven, but they found an hotel open and had breakfast with ham and eggs and toast and coffee, and then they lit cigarettes and sat on a bench in the sun, utterly contented.

"When you go out with some people," said Raine, "you enjoy it so much you want it to last for ever, and with others you wish it was over."

"I know," said Cleo. "People that say, I wonder if I turned

163

the gas off, and wouldn't poor Aunt Susan have liked this, and I haven't eaten so much since Hogmanay, 1896."

Ian said, had they come so far just to sit on a bench in Portree? Raine said she could think of many things worse, and this led to an argument which was finally clinched by Cleo saying, "Let's stay till the shops open. It's nearly nine now, and we ought to take something home for Mother to show we've been."

The men good-naturedly agreed to wait, so as soon as the shops opened Cleo and Raine went window-gazing and finally Cleo bought a spoon with a coat of arms of Portree on the handle, and Raine a paper-knife made of horn with *Eilean à cheo* burnt on it in antique lettering.

"Anybody would think you were English tourists!" said Ian in deep disgust, examining the trophies, while Neil kindly said, "If there's anything you girls would like, I'll buy it for you as a souvenir."

Cleo had a hankering after a little framed picture of rocks and waves, and she thought if Neil would buy her that she would be able to keep it for ever, but Raine dashed her hopes to the ground by exclaiming, "No, thanks, Neil, we'll save you from your own rash generosity. My tastes are devastatingly expensive and so are hand-knitted Shetland twin sets."

"I wasn't meaning anything like a hand-knitted twin set," said Neil bluntly, and Ian called impatiently that a bus left along the coast in five minutes' time, so they went and took their seats in it and half an hour later were at Sligachan, leaning on the parapet of the bridge and staring up at the fantastic shape of Glamaig, that mighty cone which springs from sea-level to an incredible height, and at Sgurr nan Gillean, where snow lay even yet in the deep corries of the north face.

"Let's get sandwiches from the hotel and spend the rest of the day climbing," suggested Neil.

"Oh no, I want to go to Dunvegan and see the fairy flag," cried Raine. "You do too, don't you, Cleo — and Ian?"

"Yes, I think Dunvegan is good romantic value," Ian said, and Cleo, shading her eyes to gaze along Loch Sligachan, said, "I came here when I was about twelve, and we bought a guide-book which said that the hill-slopes abounded in herons, so we climbed about for hours looking for them but we didn't find any. It shook my faith in all writers of guide-books, and I've doubted them ever since."

Neil agreed and added, "I shall come here by myself some day and climb Sgurr nan Gillean by the old track where the marauding Macdonalds came down to harry the Macleods."

"And take a Thermos flask to put snow in," said Raine, "or nobody will ever believe you've done it."

Neil looked at her coldly, and after they had rambled around for a while they had lunch at the hotel and took the bus to Dunvegan, only to find they had been unlucky enough to come on a day when the castle was not open to the public.

Bitterly disappointed, they wandered back to the road.

"When they opened the door and told us we couldn't go in," said Cleo, "I think I caught a glimpse of the fairy flag; anyway, it was something fluttering and yellow."

"But the fairy flag is green," said Ian.

"Oh no, Ian, it's yellow."

"I tell you, it's green. Of course it's green."

"No, Ian, yellow. The Macleod colour is always yellow."

"But everyone on earth knows that the fairy flag of Dunvegan is green. It's practically the first thing you learn at your Nanny's knee after ABC."

"Raine knows it's yellow," said Cleo.

"I don't," said Raine. "It could be shocking pink for all I care, and I'll never feel the same towards the Macleods again for bringing us all this way for nothing."

"Cleo's right," said Neil suddenly. "It is yellow, Ian."

"Well I'm —— " began Ian, and slowly shut his mouth, and in that instant Cleo realised that she had been thinking of the Macleod tartan and that of course the flag was green, and the scarlet rushed to her face because of Neil's chivalry. Or perhaps, knowing her to be in the wrong, he had merely intervened to stop such a silly argument. In any case, he must think me an idiot, thought Cleo, the brightness of the day quite eclipsed. But she soon cheered up again as they walked along the coast road towards the rolling hills and saw the great breakers crashing in upon that wild shore.

"I feel as though I ought to break into poetry," said Raine, "or else into some runic chant. Nature speaking to me from the deep, and so on."

"It does speak to you," said Neil. "We don't listen enough."

"All it says to me," said Ian, "is that these hills and that sea will last for ever and in a few years I shall be gone and forgotten."

"But not quite lost," said Cleo, "because no sound is ever lost, and this conversation of ours will go echoing on until it finds a remote little corrie in the heart of the hills, and there it will rest for ever and the fairies will play it over to themselves on Sunday afternoons on their little gramophones."

"And on that spot," said Neil, "no heather will ever grow, and even the hardy mountain ram will avoid it because it belongs to the Little People. There's a fantasy for you!"

"More like a Celtic lament," said Raine. "We shall come here again some day, shan't we, Ian?"

"Of course we shall. And bring all the children."

"Ha!" said Raine. "You'll be standing on a rock raving about the view, and I shall be in the background administering slaps all round."

"No child of mine," said Ian with sudden vehemence, "will ever be slapped."

"Nonsense," said Raine. "Of course they'll be slapped if they need it. I don't intend to have undisciplined children."

"And is that your idea of discipline?" said Ian hotly. "Striking a helpless child is not only cruel but the act of a lazy, incompetent parent. My children will be disciplined by reason."

"You can't reason with a child under seven," said Raine. "If it's naughty, the only thing it understands is a smacking."

"Woman, you appal me!" said Ian. "The child, inexperienced in the ways of life, makes a mistake, and promptly the adult, to whom it looks up with trust, clouts it over the head and maybe marks its little soul for life."

"What utter rubbish!" said Raine. "You were smacked, I was smacked, Neil was smacked, Cleo was smacked. There's something satisfying to a child in being smacked. Defend me from these nicely balanced psychological punishments. They only muddle up a child's mind. The only things that left marks on my soul were the dreary little lectures I got when I was too old to be thrashed. My children may have a soft father but they'll have a granite-hearted mother."

"Now we'll stop this!" intervened Neil. "Take no notice of him, Raine. Wait till Ian finds his son and heir leaving the field gate open, and he'll forget his theories and hand him a dunt."

"Thank you, Neil," said Raine. "Where were we when all this started?"

"I don't know," said Neil, "but I know where Cleo is, half-way up the brae to photograph that neat little but-and-ben with the old couple sitting at the door."

"I've got a lovely snap," cried Cleo, coming back. "I only wish it was in colour, the white cottage and the yellow thatch and the bright blue sea beyond the bright green field. The old woman had a pink apron and the old man a scarlet handkerchief round his neck, and they both had shocks of pure white hair. They only speak the Gaelic, but they smiled and looked so sweet, and I peeped inside the but-and-ben and it looks so bare and poor. I suppose they live on their own potatoes and keep a few hens and haven't a penny in the world."

"And I wouldn't put it past them," said Neil, "to have brought up three children, and one of them is now an advocate in Edinburgh and one an ear specialist in Glasgow and one the managing director of a motor works. The great men of Scotland come from homes like that."

"But you must make it four children or else wash out the motor works, Neil," cried Cleo, "because one of them would certainly be an eminent divine."

"Of course. How did I come to forget the divine?"

"But I call it abominable," declared Raine. "What use are all these eminent people that they've pauperised themselves to educate when the old father and mother haven't got a single comforting child to lean on now they're old?"

"Wh-what use?" stuttered Ian, hardly able to believe his ears. "A famous advocate — and a divine — and you say what use?"

"Yes, what use! They'd be better employed looking after Pink Apron and Red Scarf."

"But you can't mean that, Raine. To have given four eminent sons to Scotland is the finest thing that old pair could do, and they don't consider they've made a sacrifice."

"Well, that's the conventional view," said Raine coolly, "and it may be found in all earnest Scots novels, but I don't believe in it."

"*You* don't believe in it! *You* don't believe in what every eminent Scots writer and thinker —— "

"Oh, stop using that word 'eminent,' Ian. Such a silly word. I think that family life is much more important than fame. Those sons should have been made into nice crofters or shepherds or fishermen. Then the family would have been together now, with the daughters-in-law knitting and spieling and turning the bannocks — or whatever it is they do — and the weans prattling round the door, instead of just two lonely, pathetic —— "

"There's an ignorant, worm's-eye view if ever there was one!" broke out Ian rousingly. "Where would Scotland be if its great men hadn't left island homes like that one? And where would Scotland be if parents didn't make sacrifices to educate their clever children? One's children are not one's own."

"My children will be my own all right!" said Raine vehemently. "They'll be born West Highland, and they'll stay in the West Highlands, where they began. And if they have brains, well, Larrich needs their brains more than Edinburgh does, and I'll not end up a lonely old woman with a noble expression and a feeling of having been done in the eye."

"That," said Ian, "is the most narrow-minded bit of blind selfishness and bigotry I ever heard."

"And now we're back at Raine's children again," interrupted Cleo, rolling up her eyes while Neil yelped with laughter. "Do stop it, Raine, I'm exhausted with all this arguing."

"You're exhausted!" shrieked Raine, turning a fiery glance

on her sister. "What about me with the prospect of all this incompatibility?"

"And what about tea?" said Cleo. "Let's wander back to Dunvegan and find some. Nobody can argue over that."

"Don't worry over Ian's argumentativeness," said Neil to Cleo as they found themselves walking behind the other two. "It's just a hobby with him and doesn't mean a thing. He brings out a new set of theories to suit the occasion, and has forgotten them by next day."

"Oh, I'm not worried," said Cleo. "Raine is never happy unless she is being stimulated, and the more nonsense she talks the less she means it. Do you think we could stop and just get a few of those harebells? They look like an amethyst lake."

"They don't last very long," Neil pointed out as they climbed the grassy bank to where the harebells were growing.

"I only want a few. They'll remind me of what fun we had today."

Neil picked half a dozen harebells and added them to Cleo's small bunch, whereupon without his seeing it she separated the ones he had given her and put them safely in her pocket, so sentimental and besotted was she.

They walked on towards the village, some fifty yards behind the other two. Raine turned and cried, "Don't linger behind, you two. Come and save me, Ian and I are at it again. It all began with tea, and now we're shouting each other down about whether China is an aspiring nation or a world menace, and if we had broadswords one of us would be dead."

In the village they found a café and ordered tea, and while it was being prepared they wandered out on the turfy slope that led down to the sea and found it gay with sea-pinks.

170

"Here's a flat piece like a stage," said Raine. "Let's dance a foursome reel!"

This spontaneous suggestion seemed to be part of the sunshine and the wine-like air and the exciting feel of the turf beneath their feet, and the next minute they were all gaily at it, springing about with flashing feet on their improvised dance-floor, making exaggerated gestures and clan cries.

"Encore! Encore!" cried a hearty nasal voice as they finished, and shocked at having been observed they looked round and saw two people sitting on an outcrop of rock, a man in bright tweeds and a woman in a white suit and toeless sandals with a tartan snood on her hair.

"Say, that's the purtiest thing I ever saw," said the woman. "Tell me, was it spontaneous or were you performing some ceremonial?"

"It was just a dance," said Cleo, gasping for breath. "We didn't know anybody was watching or we wouldn't —— "

"But I wouldn't have missed it for worlds," said the woman. "Would you, Elmer? We just love anything primitive. You couldn't be professional dancers, by any chance? We'd be happy to engage you to give a show at our hotel, wouldn't we, Elmer? It would be something noo."

"Oh no, no, thank you!" said Cleo, backing away and nearly falling over Raine. "We're not — we didn't — we only —— "

She recovered herself and grabbing Raine by the arm made a rapid escape towards the village, but Neil and Ian stood as if petrified, drawn to their full height, the picture of outraged Highland dignity, their eyes flashing and their fingers twitching, those clansmen's fingers which in an earlier age would have snatched the dirk to avenge the insult.

171

"Oh, come on, you two!" cried Raine, turning back and waiting for the brothers to join her.

By the time they reached the café they had all cooled down and were ready to laugh off the episode, but the next minute the American couple also entered the café — which was not surprising considering it was the only one in the village — and beamed upon the four young Scots as though greeting old friends.

"Would this place have any ice watter?" asked the woman.

"I guess nat," said Elmer. "I guess this isn't the Savoy."

They sat down at the adjoining table. The woman produced a coloured book of tartans, flipped over the pages, and with complete unself-consciousness began to match it up against Ian's kilt.

Raine and Cleo collapsed on the table, weak with laughing, and Elmer looked at them with interest and said, "I heard the Scotch never laffed."

"Somebody told them a joke two weeks ago," said Neil grimly.

"We'll miss our bus," gasped Raine, stifling herself with a handkerchief. They all swallowed their tea hastily and fled.

"I saw Elmer casting an envious eye on your kilt, Ian," said Cleo as they took their seats. "I think he was about to make you an offer for it."

"They don't know how lucky they are to be alive," said Ian.

"I liked their car," said Neil. "It looked so rich and strange standing there in Dunvegan."

"I thought they were sweet," said Raine.

The bus slid away from the tiny village on the wild shore, and soon they were in the wilderness of mountain and valley that lies between Dunvegan and Portree, with the great glassy breakers of the open sea on their left hand and on their right the brown moors and the olive-green hills under the turquoise sky. On the wind came the tang of peat, for there were great stacks of it by the roadside, and men, women, and children were working to bring in their harvest of warmth before the winter. Herds of Highland cattle with their shaggy umber coats, fierce horns and timid faces stood knee deep in the emerald bog. The sun poured down in full brilliance and laid a burning bar across Cleo's bare arm, already reddened and sore, but the foolish girl would not show her pain lest Ian should offer to change places with her and take her from Neil's side.

For twenty-two miles the road climbed and fell. It was hot in the bus.

"That last signpost said four miles to Portree," said Ian. "Who's for getting out and walking the last bit?"

"All of us," said Raine, jumping up. The bus stopped and they descended. The wind was boisterous and smelt of the sea and heather. They turned towards the downward slope of the road.

"This is grand," said Cleo, striding joyfully. "Who's for going back and dancing the Gay Gordons for Elmer?"

A car came up behind them and the driver stopped and offered them a lift.

"No, thanks," said Neil. "We're walking for pleasure."

By the time they reached Portree and the steamer, they were too tired to do anything but limp on board. A day begun at three in the morning seemed like a week. At last the steamer sailed, and once again the four of them were leaning over the rail, this time to watch Skye slipping away into its magic mists until the houses and the harbour and the jagged tops of the mountains were all one, a memory beyond the steamer's white wake.

A path of gold seemed to run clear to the horizon, where the sunset was flushing the clouds with crimson and the whole western sky was aflame.

Cleo felt melancholy and romantic as she gazed at the setting sun and thought the others might be similarly affected, but quite unmoved by the beauty of sea and sky Raine and Ian were now arguing away about the renovations at Larrich, and Neil was listening to them intently, and they might just as well have been standing in an attic surrounded by pots of paint.

"There seem to be so many men working at so much an hour," said Raine. "I never thought I should live to count the minutes clicking away like half-crowns down a helter-skelter. I do hope you're not going to be ruined, Ian."

"I think it might be a good idea," Ian said, "to ask for the bills up-to-date. Then we can see how much more we can stand."

Raine gave a noisy sigh and said, "That would be one sure way of nipping all our enthusiasm in the bud. I think one big square bill at the end would be better than dozens of sickening little ones."

"How can you stand there looking at the most gorgeous sunset and chunnering about bills?" cried Cleo, exasperated.

"That's what the prospect of marriage does to you," said Ian. "Destroys your finer susceptibilities. Keep out of it, Cleo."

"I shall!" said Cleo, grimly reckless and turning her back on Neil, who was struggling to get his pipe alight in the breeze.

Raine went on, "Of course we shall economise like mad after we are married and live in frugal squalor, and get the reputation of being misers until we have made up for our extravagance. And I'm sure the new dairy herd will turn out very

174

profitable with all the work that you two men will put in."

"There's no money in milk nowadays," said Neil, gloomy at the failure of his pipe.

"You'll have to get the cows to try something else," said Cleo tartly, disappointed at the turn the conversation was taking.

By now Ian and Raine were arguing about their wedding, for Ian wanted it to take place in the hall at Larrich — as traditional Garvine weddings did — and Raine said, "Aren't you thinking of Young Lochinvar? And what's the matter with Kilchro, it's a good home and my own? In any case, you know my mother would have a fit at anything but a kirk wedding."

Soon they became conscious that the evening was turning chilly and that they were too tired to talk any more. They all crushed on to a narrow seat, huddled together for warmth, Neil on the outside because it was the draughtiest, then Ian and Raine, with Cleo at the sheltered end.

The rest of the journey seemed long. Cleo found herself going over the day in a rather profitless way, thinking of all the things she might have said and the things she wished she had not said. Her feet were cold and she was hungry, sensing the same depressing sensations in the others.

At last the harbour lights of Strogue appeared through the silver-grey dusk.

"It's been a lovely day," said Raine dreamily. "Quite the second loveliest day of my life."

"What would crown it," said Ian, "would be roast potatoes."

"I'm glad we came, aren't you, Neil?" said Raine.

"Yes, of course," said Neil.

"Aren't you, Cleo?" said Raine.

"Yes, of course," said Cleo.

175

CHAPTER ELEVEN

"OH, IT IS SATURDAY and I must go and have tea with that frightful woman at Ellen Lodge," said Cleo unthinkingly at breakfast.

A startled hush filled the room and pieces of toast on the way to mouths were poised in mid-air. All eyes were turned on Cleo, who realised that she had caused a sensation.

"What frightful woman?" asked Primrose eagerly.

"Cleo! Really, dear!" said Mrs. MacAlvey.

"You *can't* mean Inga Duthie ——" began Miss Paige.

"Doesn't that charming Mrs. Duthie live at Ellen Lodge?" said Mrs. Leigh. "I'm sure somebody told me she did. Or am I wrong? I'm sure you all told me she was a wonderful person. Or am I thinking of somebody else?"

"This is very interesting," said Raine, planting her elbows on the table and gazing at her sister. "Do you really think she's frightful, Cleo? And why? Actually I've never been able to make my mind up about Inga, and now you go and react like this. Why frightful?"

"Listen," said Cleo. "This isn't the Spanish Inquisition, or is it? I don't know why I said it. It slipped out. Do I have to account for every single adjective I use when I'm not thinking?"

"Keep your hair on," said Raine, slitting open an envelope from the pile on her plate and creating a diversion with a joyful yell of, "Oh, it's a wedding present. A cheque from Uncle William."

"How much for?" asked Primrose artlessly.

"How rude!" said Elinore, and Mrs. MacAlvey put in a hasty, "Get on with your breakfast, children."

"But the only point of a cheque," said Archie, "is how much it's for."

"If you give her a chance," said Gavin, "she may tell us how much it's for."

"That will do, Gavin," said his grandfather.

"Actually it's for fifty pounds," said Raine, "and I don't mind who knows. I feel weak with excitement. Now I shall be able to get twenty-five yards of that brocade curtain material at two pounds a yard. I must go and ring Ian at once."

"What a waste!" said Primrose. "Fancy spending fifty galumptuous pounds on curtain material when you could use old sheets or anything and buy a ciné-camera."

"You'll think like Raine when it's your turn to be married," said Miss Paige.

"I doubt that," said Primrose. "I shall put on the bottom of the invitations, please send money if you're going to send anything. It's the only way I'll ever get a ciné-camera."

"Is anybody using the car this afternoon?" said Cleo desperately.

"What for?" asked her father.

"Alexander, you heard Cleo say she wanted to go to tea at Ellen Lodge," said Mrs. MacAlvey.

" 'Wanted' is good," said Raine.

177

"Please can I have the car, Daddy?" asked Cleo.

"I can't say if I'll be needing it or not. Doctor and I talked of running over to Drimmont this afternoon. We could drop you at Ellen Lodge and pick you up on the way back."

"Oh, no! You'll be hours later than you say. It's so dreary waiting to be picked up on people's way back when it's a sticky visit and you have to hang on, trying to think of things to say."

"There you go again!" said Raine. "Why have you taken such a dislike to Inga?"

"I haven't taken a dis —— "

"She's the most harmless person. A bit showy and full of herself, but I think she's genuine at the bottom. Of course I've never come up against her, but why should I? Or why should you? It doesn't make sense."

"Will you please, please, please shut up!" said Cleo. "I'm walking to Ellen Lodge. It's only four miles. It won't kill me."

"You could have the bike," said Gavin helpfully. "The one in the garage that's called Primrose's, but anybody rides it."

"Strange as it may seem," said Cleo, "I can't ride a bike."

"Can't ride a bike!" yelled the chorus.

"If everybody has finished," said Mrs. MacAlvey, "will they please leave the table? Cleo dear, I'm sure there's no reason why you should go to tea with Inga if you don't want to. I can't understand what all the fuss is about."

"If I may make a suggestion," said Doctor Leigh, "why shouldn't we go to Drimmont tomorrow? Then Cleo could have the car."

"All right," said Mr. MacAlvey. "You can have the car, Cleo."

No less irritated by the time she went up to dress, Cleo could not imagine why she didn't ring up Mrs. Duthie and

178

make an excuse not to go, and yet the visit to her rival —
for so she had come to regard the attractive young widow —
held a fascination for her. She wanted to see Inga's house and
Inga herself at close quarters, as Neil probably saw them, with
the same instinct that drives the tongue to press on the aching
tooth.

"Of course I am a fool," thought Cleo, joylessly applying
lipstick, "and I have a diseased mind. No wonder nobody likes
me."

In this low-spirited mood she found herself putting on a
green linen coat and skirt which did not suit her and an or-
gandie blouse which was wilted from having been worn before.

"As if I cared," she told her unpromising reflection in the
mirror. "I'm not competing."

A slight altercation with the self-starter of the car did not
improve her mood, and by the time she reached Ellen Lodge
she was quite ready for the wave of depression which sweeps
over any woman at the sight of another's perfect house and
garden. Other people's paint is always such a good colour, their
windows are so bright and their curtains so well hung, their
drive so weedless and their flower-beds so controlled and gay,
their bell-push so highly polished, their lawns so newly mown,
their general arrangements contrived in so superior a way to
one's own. And of course Mrs. Duthie was said to have a
great deal of money. She had certainly made a dream house of
Ellen Lodge, which had formerly been an untidy shooting-box
inhabited by a happy-go-lucky family whose ponies roamed
into the dining-room and ate the food off the table.

Mrs. Duthie had had the long, low house painted cream,
and it gleamed like a pearl against the dark-green pinewood on
its north side. Before it the brilliance of rose-beds caught the
eye, and the scent of them made waiting at the nail-studded

179

oak door a pleasure. The elderly parlourmaid in traditional black-and-white uniform, which Cleo thought no one could be induced to wear nowadays, showed her into a white hall carpeted thickly in beige, with one superb oak chest under a Venetian mirror, two Jacobean chairs with gros-point seats, and a tall urn of white pottery filled with magnificent flame-coloured gladioli.

There was a welcoming cry from above, and Inga came dashing down the stairs, with her hair in a silken sweep on her shoulders and wearing an expensive white silk shirt over pale-blue slacks.

"I'm so glad you could come," she cried. "Wouldn't you like to see the garden? People always ask to see the garden first in this part of the world. You see, I'm getting into West Highland ways. Anybody would think I was planning to stay here all my life."

She laughed musically and asked Cleo if she wanted to take anything off. Feeling hopelessly overdressed, Cleo declined and followed her hostess through the glass doors at the back of the hall, remarking, "These are new."

"The doors? Oh yes, practically everything is new. Did you know the place before? I put it in the hands of a really good London man, and he literally pulled it to pieces. It's liveable now. I mean, there's a lot I could do, but I have simple tastes and don't bother."

The old wilderness of a garden which Cleo remembered had been completely cleared to make space for three terraced gardens, which descended a slope and ended in a natural glen where silver birches fringed a stream whose splashing sounded like cool music. The house, the garden, and the glen were such a blend of artistry and natural beauty that Cleo was dazed with admiration at what money and the really good London man had achieved. The first terrace was a formal garden, paved and ornamented with a low maze of box; the second a lawn with borders blazing with all the appropriate flowers; the third was taken up by a lily-pond and a white summer-house with a small pillared portico in the classic style.

Did Neil sit there sometimes of an evening with his lovely hostess, and gaze at the pink and white lilies and think of shabby Larrich and the power of wealth? It was comforting to think that whatever else he was, Neil was the least materialistic person who ever lived. But he probably sat in the summer-house, all the same.

Cleo began to feel depressed. She had known this would happen from the very moment that perfect house burst upon her view, and when she felt depressed she was always at her worst. She should never have come.

"Like it?" said Inga in careless pride.

"I can't think of anything flattering to say that all your guests haven't said already."

"How do you know what my guests say?"

"I'm assuming they say the only possible things. Perfect. Exquisite. Breath-taking. I could add lots more."

Inga beamed, and said, "Don't you know that Highland guests never say anything but humph?"

It was a slight relief to Cleo to know that Neil had probably said humph.

"They say the house was built by a Miss Macdonald of the same family as Flora," said Cleo. "It is a beautiful shape. She is supposed to have seen it in a dream, and got up in the middle of the night and drawn the design without rubbing out a single line."

Inga contorted her lovely features.

"I haven't heard that one, but it's a pity there wasn't an

india-rubber handy. I had to spend a fortune in getting the kitchens moved over to the other side of the house. They were the only rooms that got any sun."

Cleo tried to think of something to say. Continued praise was cloying, but there didn't seem to be anything else.

"Your roses," she said, "must be the best in the district."

"Oh no, never!" said Inga with maddening modesty. "An Edinburgh firm did the garden, and I think they were rose-mad. Actually I never have them in the house, as I hate the smell. Too much like the Petit Trianon."

I shall have to go on like this for hours! thought Cleo, taking a long breath and exclaiming, "How lovely the glen is! Is it part of the garden? I don't remember it before."

"Ah, that's special," said Inga, waving a casual hand towards the silver birches and the shaded stream. "It was a wilderness when I came. It was separated from the garden by an ugly fence over which I used to lean, frantic with frustration. But now the fence has gone and the whole place is trimmed up, and I wander down there in the evenings and feel it is really mine. You see, the owner has given it to me and named it after me. It is Glen Inga. I'm terribly proud of it."

A dreadful thought dawned on the unfortunate Cleo.

"But that is Larrich land!" she cried.

"How clever of you. Yes, Neil Garvine is my landlord, and it was he who gave me the glen and named it after me. I'm glad you think it pretty."

Pretty! thought Cleo. This is the very end! In her confusion she snatched at the lavender hedge and pressed a handful to her nose.

"Darling, don't do that," said Inga sweetly, "or you'll smell all eighteen-eighty. Come and see the dogs."

Unhappily, Cleo followed her hostess to some modern kennel-runs, where several large dogs were springing about uttering hysterical howls at the sight of their mistress.

"Aren't they fiends?" said Inga proudly.

"Yes," said Cleo.

Inga looked at her sharply, and added, "Don't you like Alsatians? Down, Boompsie!"

"I don't know a thing about them."

"Really? I am surprised. Then it's no use showing you their finer points. The bitch has won seventeen firsts, though I don't suppose that means a thing to you."

"I think they're marvellous," said Cleo.

"Oh no, no. Not really."

"Yes, absolutely wonderful dogs."

Inga smiled angelically, shook back her hair, and said, "You know, you look awfully sweet in that little green thing."

"Thanks," said Cleo, feeling like an ingenuous sixteen-year-old in a little frock run up by Mummy on the sewing-machine.

"Shall we go back to the house?"

They went back and into the drawing-room, a finely proportioned room which ran the whole width of the house. Cleo didn't like the drawing-room. She felt that the really good London man had rather missed the bus here. The walls were painted silver and were starkly bare, while the ceiling was bright blue. The floor was covered with jade-green carpet of such deep pile that one instinctively lifted the feet while crossing it to avoid entangling the ankles. The original wide fireplace had been taken away and in its place was a silver electric fire flush with the wall, and above it a shelf of frosted glass bearing seventeen jade Buddhas in diminishing sizes.

For the rest, the room contained two blue settees of extremely modern design, an odd chair or two, and a striking cocktail cabinet made of looking-glass and bearing a large framed photograph of an R.A.F. officer, who was presumably the late Mr. Duthie.

"Just hurl yourself down," said Inga, and Cleo meekly chose one of the smaller chairs. Her little suit would have looked quite ghastly on a blue settee.

"Cigarette?" said Inga, picking up the largest Buddha. She did something to the back of his neck and his stomach opened, revealing a row of Player's. Rather as an anti-climax, she then produced an ordinary box of matches and struck one on her heel.

"Now I wonder what we'd better have?" she said, as though destiny hung on it. "What would you like?"

"I don't mind," said Cleo. "What do you usually have?"

She was wondering whether Neil ever sat on this horrid little chair or if he preferred a settee. There was something revoltingly intimate about a settee.

"Tea? Or is that too obvious? I don't usually bother with anything when I'm alone."

"Neither do I," said Cleo, trying hard to hold her end up. "Don't order anything specially for me."

It was hard even to picture Neil in this exotic room, but he undoubtedly came. He came to look at Inga's car and to offer her first choice in naming his calves, and to give her glens and call them after her.

"As a matter of fact, I'm quite thirsty," said Inga. "Let's have some tea." She stretched her arm to press a concealed bell, and with a continuation of the same gesture to pick up another Buddha, flick his stomach open, and say, "Put your ash in that. Your sister," she went on, "is the sweetest thing."

Cleo was so surprised at hearing Raine described as sweet

184

that her eyebrows shot up and she missed the Buddha by inches. A curl of ash lay on the carpet.

"I adore all your family," said Inga.

"Oh," said Cleo, thinking that Inga's conversation was the sort you couldn't possibly reply to. She began to wonder if the best defence wasn't to let herself go and chatter madly, but somehow she couldn't do it. The atmosphere paralysed her. Inga was horribly in control of the situation, sitting like a bird of paradise in the midst of her rich surroundings.

The door opened and the parlourmaid, looking too perfect to be real, pushed in a chromium trolley bearing an imposing silver tea service, some blue glass cups and saucers, and enough food for about eight people.

Inga perched herself on the arm of a settee and poured a cup of tea for her guest and one for herself. The blue glass cups, though in themselves attractive, gave the tea an unfortunate appearance as of liquid mud.

"This must seem tame to you after New York," said Inga.

"I didn't much care for New York," said Cleo.

"How odd. I thought everybody adored New York."

"Perhaps it depends on what one is doing in New York."

"Oh, that's frightfully subtle!"

"Is it?" said Cleo.

"Do you think it extraordinary of me," asked Inga, "to bury myself in a place like this?"

"I never think anybody is extraordinary doing anything."

"Oh!" said Inga, and added, "I think you're rather deep."

"Shall I pass you the scones?" said Cleo, who wanted one herself and found she was near the trolley which Inga had pushed disdainfully away.

"Heavens, no!" said Inga. "I never eat a thing. Do help yourself."

185

"Thank you," said Cleo, and proceeded to make a very good tea.

"By the way," said Inga, "what would your sister like for a wedding present?"

"Oh, just some little thing. She wouldn't want you to bother."

"What has she already?"

"Well — a tea-set and some aluminium pans and a rather nice thing for putting fruit in. And of course, cheques."

"I was thinking something old and rather beautiful. For Larrich. Like an eighteenth-century door-knocker."

"They've got an eighteenth-century door-knocker at Larrich already," said Cleo. "It's been on the door for about two hundred years."

"But how silly of me! I really have hardly ever been to Larrich. Of course, when there's a hostess there it will be different, and I expect one will be running in and out all the time. We are sure to see some social life there."

"Oh surely!" murmured Cleo, vividly aware that she herself would witness little of all these intriguing ins-and-outs with their inevitable conclusion.

"But what shall I get for Raine and Ian? I mean, they are both rather fastidious people, and one just can't give them anything."

"Why not ask Raine herself?" said Cleo, making up her mind that nothing on earth would force her into continuing this talk about Larrich and the Garvines. "In these days it is so much better to know what people really want."

"But doesn't that under-value the element of surprise?" Inga jumped up, swung back her golden hair, and said, "Have you finished tea or would you like some more?" — at the same time casting a disdainful glance over the piles of provender left on

186

the trolley, which convinced Cleo that had her hostess been alone she would have polished off the lot.

"Thank you, it was a lovely tea," said Cleo enthusiastically. "I always eat an enormous tea. Everybody in Scotland does."

"That's what makes you all so sonsy," said Inga, looking at Cleo as though she weighed twelve stone. "And now you must tell me, what are your plans?"

"My plans for what?" said Cleo suspiciously.

"Well, I suppose you'll be going off to take some awe-inspiring post or other. Everybody in the neighbourhood has told me how efficient you are."

What a revolting word 'efficient' is! thought Cleo, and aloud she said, "Oh, I'm not so efficient as all that. I shan't do anything until after Raine's wedding, and then I suppose I'll look out for a new job."

"I should," said Inga with a frank smile. "I think the very worst thing is to waste one's talents, and I can see that you have talent for all kinds of clever things, like typewriters and being a great man's right hand."

"What about your own talents?" said Cleo daringly. "I should have said you were wasted here. I picture you in the midst of a glittering throng."

"Ah, but I've had all that," said Inga, trying to look nostalgic. "And now I'm starting a new life, and it suits me. One changes — one's aspirations, one's values. I'm in love with West Highland life, and I don't know how I could ever have borne a crowd. And talking of crowds, how wonderful your mother is! To see her sitting there serenly at Kilchro surrounded by *generations* of family! It must be killing. And to that she adds guests. Guests!"

"But Mother loves having people to stay."

"Now don't tell me that. Nobody loves having people to

stay. To a certain extent it satisfies one's conceit to show them how superior your domestic arrangements are to their own, but that doesn't make up for the nuisance of having to organise their time at the sacrifice of your own leisure. Oh, I know it all! You have only to take a place in the country as I did here to get hopeful little letters from all your friends and relations who have a fortnight's holiday due in September and don't know quite what to do about it. I decided that the only course for me was wholesale alienation, so I left the letters unanswered."

"With a lovely place like this," said Cleo, "that was downright selfish of you. Besides, supposing you want to go and stay with any of those people?"

Inga gave a little scream.

"For sheer human misery can there be anything to compare with staying in other people's houses? What I've been through! One's bedroom is always searchingly cold and the bed placed in the draughtiest position, with no bed-light and blankets like sheets of lead. You daren't go down in the night to look for a heartening drink, or the whole family come down in their dressing-gowns and ask you if you are ill, and you know that for years after they will talk of you as 'that eccentric woman who prowled about the house in the dark.' They give you the wrong things for breakfast, and afterwards thrust you out for a bracing walk when all you want is to crawl back to bed with the newspapers until lunch. And the rest of the time is taken up with ghastly little parties where you are expected to get excited about meeting their dreary friends."

Cleo could not help laughing. Inga certainly could be very amusing, and there was fascination in her drawling voice and the way she couldn't quite manage her r's, to say nothing of her undoubted beauty and her gestures and her clothes. And

188

if she liked anyone and wanted to please, she must be quite irresistible.

"Don't let's sit here any longer," said Inga. "I wonder if you would mind coming out on the court and throwing up a few balls for me? I want to practise my backhand volley. It really would be self-sacrificing of you."

"Not at all," said Cleo. "But I'm not dressed for tennis and I haven't any shoes."

"Oh, just take your coat off. I won't make you run about, I shall do all that. You won't actually be playing, I only want you to smash balls at me, the more erratic the better. What size shoes do you take?"

"Fives."

"Oh dear! Mine are only threes. But I can probably find an old pair in the boot cupboard. I think the Grant girl left a pair behind and she had enormous feet too."

The Grant girl's shoes when produced were about size seven, but Cleo accepted them without a murmur and knotted the laces round her ankles.

They went down to the court, which lay at the side of the house and was in perfect condition.

"Now," said Inga after an orgy of net measuring, "you stand over there and keep pelting them at me on my backhand, that's your right, my left. Don't be afraid of hitting them."

Cleo obligingly sent over balls, some of which Inga drove into the net and others which she smashed all over the place with more style than accuracy. These Cleo had to collect. She became very hot, and tiring of her role of stooge began to return the balls with a force and precision which made Inga in her turn have to do all the running about.

"I didn't know you played," said Inga, trying hard not to pant. "Shall we have a game?"

189

"I'd love to," said Cleo, blessing those hours of practice she had put in at the Long Island Club with a first-rate coach.

She then had the time of her life while proceeding to beat Inga in two straight sets with the loss of only four games.

"Thank you so much," said Inga without enthusiasm. "You really would make a player. You've caught me on one of my off-days too."

"Fluke," said Cleo modestly, conscious that her blouse and skirt had parted company and her size seven shoes were full of shale.

Inga came round the net after letting it down.

"You do get hot, don't you?" she said, looking at Cleo as though she were a blowsy middle-aged aunt. "There's one thing I'm thankful for, I always keep cool. It's probably due to my Norwegian blood."

"Oh, have you a dash of Norwegian too?" said Cleo with pardonable felinity.

They walked back to the house, and Inga said, "I simply must change at once. I don't know about you."

"Oh, don't bother about me," said Cleo. "I'm going home now."

"It's been marvellous to have you. Do come again. You might not think it, but I'm a very selective person. A one-person person, if you know what I mean. I never, never could bear a crowd, only one person at a time. But that person must be the right person, and it's all so difficult. Ah well! You should take up tennis, you'd be quite good at it."

"I might," said Cleo.

"And do give my love to Raine, and tell her I'd welcome any idea about the present. I'm sure she won't mind being asked, but it must be something for Larrich."

"I'll tell her," said Cleo.

She changed back into her own shoes, put on her coat, and thought that if the car wouldn't start it would be the last straw, because Inga would say 'You should learn to drive a car, you'd be quite good at it', and would send for the gardener to give her a shove. To be shoved off Inga's premises by Inga's gardener would be the utter depths.

But the car started at the first attempt, which it rarely did and must have been helped by Providence, and with a final well-timed wave Cleo set off at such a pace that she missed the gate-post of Ellen Lodge by only a couple of inches.

She reached home and parked the car on the shady side of the drive.

"You're back early," said Raine, lounging in a deck-chair. "Tell me all about it. What did you do?"

"Played tennis."

"Not in those clothes?"

"In these clothes. My blouse was out at the back and my placket was round at the front and I wore size seven shoes that belonged to the Grant girl, and I beat her in two straight sets and only lost four games. Six-three, six-one."

"What Grant girl?"

"No Grant girl. I beat Mrs. Duthie."

"But you couldn't! She's the best player for miles round."

"That's what she thinks."

Raine said, "I can't think what you've been up to at Ellen Lodge, but I hope you behaved better than it sounds. What did you have for tea?"

"Oh, lots and lots of things. I ate and ate."

"Disgusting. By the way, Noreen Leigh is coming."

"Noreen? Coming here?"

"She rang up from London to say she had to accompany a

patient in the Red Cross ambulance to Inverness, and she would come over and spend a night and go back with Doctor and Mrs. Leigh on Friday."

"Good. I haven't seen Noreen since before the war. I liked her."

"We all did. Do you remember when we took that house at Aboyne? 1938, wasn't it? Noreen was such good company and thought of things to do when it poured with rain, and so far as I remember it poured with rain solidly for a month."

"I'm glad she's coming. I wish she was staying longer than one night."

"So do I. I cannot think of a worse fate than to be Mrs. Leigh's only child. I'm sorry for Noreen. I think her whole life has been one long nag about not being different from what she is. She's courageous and independent and adventurous, and Mrs. Leigh can't see any good in that because what she wanted was a jelly-fish daughter to walk two paces behind her with a cushion and say 'Yes, Mamma.' I'd like to have half an hour alone with Mrs. Leigh telling her how to appreciate Noreen."

"Be careful," said Cleo. "She's probably resting in her room and hearing every word you say."

"It can't do her anything but good," said Raine, trying to fold her deck-chair, trapping her fingers and dropping the whole thing on the ground.

"By the way," said Cleo, "darling Inga wants to know what you want for a wedding present. It has to be something you can hang up in the hall at Larrich. She suggested a door-knocker."

"But there is a door-knocker. It's on the door."

"So I told her."

"And I don't want anything to hang in the hall. You should

192

see the moth-eaten stags' heads they're taking down! I don't believe you, Cleo."

"All right. Go and ask her yourself."

"But what a curious idea!"

"Ah, here's Cleo back again!" cried Mrs. MacAlvey, bursting out of the house followed by Mrs. Leigh in a shady hat. "Had a lovely tea-party?"

"Terrific, Mummy."

"And isn't Ellen Lodge a picture? What taste Inga has! But she must be lonely there by herself, so young and pretty. It doesn't seem right. All her money won't buy her happiness."

"No, Mummy."

"She seems to cling to this district where people have been kind to her, poor girl."

"Yes, Mummy."

"Cleo is being difficult today," said Raine.

"And have you heard my news?" said Mrs. Leigh. "My little girl is coming to travel back with us. What a long time since you saw Norrie! But it means my lovely holiday is over, and it's much too long a journey to come back for your wedding, Raine, though there's nothing I'd like better. Still, I never thought it possible that I should feel so well. In two short weeks I've completely forgotten my dreadful ordeal. I just never think about it. And I took so much persuading to come, because I didn't think I should be equal to it; yet here I am, a new woman. I'm afraid that when I came I was a great trial to you all with my fads and fancies."

"Not at all!" cried Mrs. MacAlvey. "Think how happy it makes us that we've been able to build you up."

"I shall never forget how sweet you've been," said Mrs. Leigh, "and neither will Doctor. He feels a different man, and now he'll be able to face a hard winter in London, with all its fogs and influenzas."

Mrs. MacAlvey was gazing at her daughter in surprise.

"Did you go to Ellen Lodge in those clothes, dear? I don't call that a becoming outfit, do you, Raine?"

"It's what they call Crazy Tennis Wear," said Cleo. "The very newest thing."

"I never know when you're talking sense," said Mrs. Mac-Alvey. "Now, dear Mrs. Leigh, I'm going to settle you in a deck-chair where you can watch me, and I'm going to dig all those daisies out of the bottom end of the lawn. Here's my little spud, and I'll have a clear hour before supper if nobody interrupts me. Just relax and have a wee doze if you can."

CHAPTER TWELVE

Mysie with the early tea tapped on Raine's door and sidled into the room.

"Morning, Mysie," said Raine, sitting up in bed in her washed-out pyjamas. "I've had the weirdest dream. I dreamt the house was burnt down, only nobody seemed to care, and I was eating ice-cream on the lawn in a pink chiffon kimono, but what worried me most was that I was wearing Wellington boots. Mrs. Leigh came up to me and said, 'Now we're actually in the East Indies,' and Doctor Leigh was driving a butcher's cart full of haunches of meat."

"The fire means your own wedding, of course," said Mysie eagerly, for she was an expert on dreams. "And anything about the East or about meat is gey lucky, so you'll get a fine day. I don't know about the chiffon, that's an English kind of thing, and I'm vexed at having to tell you that pink is not a good colour, not according to Mrs. Mortimer's dream-book. It means trouble with an elderly relative, but then you're always having trouble with your mother about what you wear, so I don't doubt she'll take exception to your wedding dress. As for the Wellington boots, I canna bring myself to mind anything about them. Wellington boots? U'mm."

"I'm sure they mean something good," said Raine. "Perhaps I'm coming into a thundering great fortune."

"Whatever Wellington boots mean," said Mysie, "it isn't money. If it had been silver slippers, now!"

"Can you see me in silver slippers?" said Raine.

"I've got a premonition," said Mysie, "that any kind of boots means a tiff with your lover."

"Oh, that's nothing," said Raine disappointedly. "We have that every day."

"Oh, I know what I was to ask you," said Mysie. "Miss Cleo wants to borrow some of your old clothes. She's going fishing with her father while the doctor writes his letters."

Arrayed in old slacks and waders, Cleo was tying flies. "There!" she said. "You've got a Magnet and a Red Hackle and a MacAlvey's Special. Three-course menu for some old trout."

"Ha!" said her father, fluffing up the speck of brown feather he called his Special. "If we don't catch anything here, we'll move over to the loch and take the boat."

"Remember, I've got to go back and meet Noreen Leigh's train."

"Och, you've hours yet."

"I only wanted to remind you. You'd be here all day!"

The river was flecked with sun and shadow, and under the bank and the dipping hazels lay dark amber pools where the fish loved to bask. Cleo watched while her father made delicate casts. Something silver broke the surface and danced at the end of the line. It was a half-pound trout, and Mr. Mac-Alvey cried, "The Special! I told you it was good!"

The Special took two more trout and then there was a long lull.

"Let's move up-stream."

"All right, if you think the fish here are tired of us."

Cleo obediently moved along the bank while her father made tentative casts across the deep green stream. There were other occupations which appealed to her far more than fishing, and yet there was something peaceful and carefree in strolling like this along the river-side in alternate sun and shade, listening to the soft slap of the water against the stones and hearing its deep gurgle among the roots of the alders, the thin flute-like song of the running line, and the rustle of drowned grasses trailing in the stream.

"You're day-dreaming!" said Mr. MacAlvey accusingly. "No good angler day-dreams. Pull yourself together and come out here and have a cast."

"I'm no good. I'll only tangle the line."

"Don't make silly excuses. I'm ashamed of a daughter of mine who can't fish. Here, take it!"

Cleo waded thigh deep and with the green river flowing all around her made a stiff and cautious cast. The float hit the water with a plop like a falling pebble and the flies sank.

"Tch!" said Mr. MacAlvey.

"Well, I warned you!"

"Be more careful. Try again."

"By now I'll have scared off every fish within miles," said Cleo, reeling in, thankful to see her line was not fouled. She cast again, and cried, "I've got one!"

It was a seven-inch baby salmon, pure silver. Cleo carefully disentangled the hook from the tiny aristocratically curling lip and flipped it back into the water.

197

"There are some big fish in this river," said her father.

"Then you'd better get them before I do any real damage."

The fishing went on quietly for a few minutes.

"Cleo, what are your plans for the future?" asked her father.

She was completely taken by surprise and said, "I shall have to do something about a job quite soon."

"Your mother's going to be very lonely after Raine is married and the children off back to school and the winter coming on. If you go too, we'll be quite alone for the first time. We were hoping you wouldn't be in a hurry to take another job."

"You mean, stay at home? Me? Oh, I couldn't. I always intended to take a job when the holidays were over. I'd hate not to be working."

Her father began a sigh which turned to a kind of snort.

"I suppose all that American hustle has got into your blood. Your mother and I were rather counting on your staying at home awhile. You see, we've always had Raine about, and ——"

"But Raine won't be far away, and if I know her, she'll always be running over."

"I dare say she will. Would it be too much to *ask* you to stay? You'd find plenty to do and it would make us happy."

"It's too much to ask anybody, Daddy. Honestly it is."

"I don't mean permanently. Say, just for the winter."

Cleo, standing thigh deep in the water, stared along the river into its blur of green. If the fish had climbed the banks and hooted she would not have noticed them. This was awful, the worst yet. To stay at home — without Raine; to be the old-maid sister cheering the declining days of the old folks and doing the shopping and entertaining the neighbours to tea and dinner — was that to be her Fate? Because there wasn't really any 'just for the winter' about that kind of life. It got its hooks into

198

you and you sank down and drowned in it. After 'just for the winter' came 'just for the summer,' and years slipped by. Parents got really old, helpless, then there was no question of escape. You became a fixture, part of the landscape. Miss Mac-Alvey, and then 'that nice Miss MacAlvey,' and then 'old Miss MacAlvey.' You had only to look at Miss Murdie or Miss Reay — who had probably forty years ago consented to stay at home for the winter because the other sister was getting married and Mother would miss her so.

For the first time Cleo's affection for Raine was shot through with envy. Mrs. Leigh's stupid little digs about letting your younger sister beat you to the altar hadn't even registered before. Now she knew just what they meant. She wished madly that she had married that nice Mr. Pulham they had seen so much of when they were in Washington in '47. She had been crazy not to marry Mr. Pulham. She could have come over on the *Queen Elizabeth* as Mrs. Pulham and paid her folks a lovely long visit, and nobody would have suggested that she didn't go back to America and Mr. Pulham. (Why did she keep saying Mr. Pulham in this fatuous way?) She couldn't even remember his Christian name, she hadn't known him long before he proposed to her. And the gist of what she had said to Mr. Pulham was that she couldn't contemplate settling in America, that all she wanted was to get back to her Scottish home and take a job in Scotland, and it was very decent of him to understand. Because Mr. Pulham had been really understanding, and the sort of person one could have married on a sensible friendly basis.

And now this! Of course Raine would be kind and would tell her to run over to Larrich just as often as she wanted, but everybody knew that young marrieds wanted to be with young marrieds, and it was likely that Inga would become Raine's best friend. And the next garment that Cleo bought after her bridesmaid's dress would be a nice printed silk to wear at Neil's wedding.

In a way it was her own fault that she was the last of the MacAlveys. It sounded like a coronach played on the pipes — Lament for the Last of the MacAlveys. To think that in 1939 there were five of them, and now there would be only James at Dunmaig absorbed in his own affairs, and Raine at Larrich wrapped up in her new home and husband with the pardonable selfishness of brides, and Cleo who had no ties and a doubtful right to any life of her own, left at Kilchro. The Last of the MacAlveys.

"All right," she said aloud. "I'll stay."

"That's a good girl."

He gave another snort, eloquent of his relief, and casting freely and violently landed a magnificent trout.

"That was the Red Hackle," he said.

"Nice work," said Cleo. "On the understanding that it's only for this winter, of course."

"Of course."

Nothing like maintaining a pleasant fiction. This is being noble, thought Cleo, and I don't feel a bit uplifted like the saints and martyrs of old. I feel awful. I feel like a landed trout. I'll never go fishing again. Never!

All she wanted now was to get home.

Soon, by dint of making a nuisance of herself by constant reference to her watch, she persuaded her father to pack up the expedition, and they returned home, one joyful, one deep in thought.

Raine was running round the house with her hands full of tissue-paper. Every post now brought presents.

"An electric clock," she said. "And an electric toaster. And from Ian's aunts at Braemar a magic machine, also electric, that wakes you up at seven o'clock, lights the lamp, twitches off your night-cap, sponges your face with ice-cold water, and thrusts a cup of tea under your nose. And electricity was one of the things that Ian and I had decided to be economical about! By the way, am I coming with you to meet Noreen?"

"That's entirely up to you," said Cleo.

"What's the matter with you? Has something put you out? Not Mrs. Duthie again!"

"I'm not in the least put out," said Cleo. "Don't be silly. By the way, I'm not taking another post. I'm stopping at home for the winter to be company for Mother."

"Good!" said Raine casually. "That's frightfully sensible of you."

"So you won't have to feel that you're plucking the last fledgling from the rifled nest, so to speak."

"I say, are you all right?" said Raine. "And do you think we ought to invite Mrs. Leigh to go with us to meet her erring daughter?"

"Heaven forbid," said Cleo. "Get in the car quickly, and don't let's give her the chance."

Noreen's train was twenty minutes late at Inverbyne, but that was nothing unusual. The MacAlvey girls chatted to the stationmaster, who was a great gossip and wanted to know all about the wedding and what was being done at Larrich.

"The decorators are in now," Raine told him, "and I actually saw a plumber lying on his back doing something to a pipe."

"Did you now? And a muckle of money it'll be costing, I haven't a doubt. It's the laird you ought to have been marrying on, no his younger brother."

"Who wants the laird?" said Raine. "The bulk of the work

will have to be done after I get there, but when I'm once on the spot I'll push those chiels around."

"They'll need some pushing," said the station-master. "Yon train's here."

Noreen leapt out of the train in her Red Cross uniform, looking just that little bit different after twelve years, but still noticeable for her hyacinth-blue eyes and beaming smile.

"How decent of you both to come and meet me!" she cried. "I feel awful in these clothes."

"Did you really come all the way to Inverness in an ambulance?" said Cleo. "Did the patient survive?"

"Only just," said Noreen with a grin. "And how is the fluttering little bride?"

"That's enough of that!" said Raine. "We're awfully glad you've come, Noreen. Why can't you stay longer?"

"I've only come to take the parents home. How lovely the air smells here! Pines, I think."

"Probably railway sleepers," said Cleo. "Wait till you get to Kilchro."

"On the train I was thinking about that holiday we had at Aboyne before the war ——"

"We were talking about it too, last night ——"

"Wasn't it fun ——"

"The best ever ——"

"And it rained all the time," said Noreen. "How's Mother?"

"Flourishing."

"Has she stopped talking about her operation yet?"

"Since the question comes from you, and to be devastatingly frank, the answer is No."

Noreen laughed and said, "I've brought you a wedding present, Raine. Fish servers."

"Jolly appropriate," Raine cried. "One of the economical

202

things Ian and I are going to do is live on fish out of our own loch."

"Do I remember your young man? Did I ever meet him?"

"Probably. But I wasn't interested myself at that time, so you'd hardly notice. He's tall, lithe, and handsome. Highland laddie type."

"Sounds good."

"Rather!" said Raine. "I always said I'd marry a professional man, didn't I, Cleo? — and live outside Edinburgh in a big white villa, and yet here I am stuck for life to a poor Highlander, and a farmer too."

There was enough conscious pride in Raine's voice to make Cleo uncomfortable. Pardonable egoism, perhaps, in one who was already singled out by the importance of her coming brideship, but a little jarring to the nerves of two old spinsters like Cleo and Noreen. Why Noreen was not married at thirty-four was one of life's mysteries, since everybody seemed to fall for her at sight. There had been an affair long ago and some suggestion that Mrs. Leigh had interfered, but nobody knew the truth of that story.

They drove off from the station, talking about everything that had happened since last they met.

Back at Kilchro House, Cleo took Noreen upstairs.

"Have you given up your room for me?" said Noreen. "How you must have cursed me for coming. The one person I can never forgive is the guest for whom I have to give up my room."

"The house is full," said Cleo, "and I didn't mind a bit. Raine and I are sharing for tonight. We've decided to read all night if we can't sleep."

"Let me get into a dress," said Noreen, tearing off her blue tunic and struggling to release the links in her white shirt-

203

cuffs, "then I'll feel like something human. By the way, I couldn't bring a lavish gift of E.P.N.S. for Raine and nothing for you, so I got you a book token. Here —— "

She ransacked all her pockets, and finally found the book token, which she handed to Cleo.

"A guinea! It's too much. You shouldn't, Noreen."

"Hope it isn't a white elephant. Can you buy books here in Strogue?"

"No, but there's a bookshop in Dunmaig. I shall have fun choosing."

"Curse!" said Noreen. "I've dropped my front stud."

"It's under the bed," said Cleo, diving and picking it up.

Noreen, in an orange-coloured cotton negligée, was changing her shoes and stockings.

"Oh, do you wear mules!" cried Cleo, lifting a pair from the bed. "I never could. They make me feel like a horse with loose shoes."

"You get used to them," said Noreen, taking a lime-green and pink printed dress out of her case.

"How frightfully Rue de la Paix," said Cleo.

"It's a bit of ancient glamour. Prewar, I assure you."

As she zipped up the dress, Mrs. Leigh rushed in crying, "Oh, there you are, Norrie darling. I'm sorry I wasn't here to greet you, but I've been down to the village."

She kissed Noreen, who said, "Well, Mother, I'm glad to hear you're quite well again after your holiday."

"I walked up that hill out of Strogue without even thinking of it," said Mrs. Leigh. "I hope I'm not going to suffer for it later."

"Well, don't think of it now," said Noreen bracingly, and Mrs. Leigh turned to Cleo with a forced smile and said, "Did you ever hear anything so unsympathetic?" She looked back at her daughter and said, "What's all this about an ambulance? Whoever would think of sending you to accompany a patient? I hope she wasn't very ill."

"She was before I'd done with her," said Noreen, patiently ironical. "Really, Mother, I am normally intelligent and responsible."

"Your father was quite concerned," said Mrs. Leigh, putting into her husband's mouth — as she often did — sentiments she thought he ought to express. (Friends of the Leighs who knew just how prosaic the Doctor was were surprised at the flowery speeches Mrs. Leigh credited him with having made to her in private. . . . 'The Doctor said to me only this morning —,' or 'The Doctor made the quaintest remark to me the other day —' heralding flights of verbal felicity far beyond the scope of anything the Doctor had ever been heard to achieve in public.) "Your father said, 'I hope Norrie isn't imagining she's a trained nurse or she may find herself in serious difficulties, and that wouldn't be fair to the patient.' He said —"

"Come down when you're ready," said Cleo, making her escape.

On the stairs she met Raine charging up.

"Who" said Raine dramatically, "do you think has come?"

"Lord Louis Mountbatten."

"Idiot. It's James — with Trina and the children. Trina hasn't deigned to visit us for two years, and now she has to turn up on the very night that Noreen is here. But I suppose she couldn't resist watching me open the parcel."

"What parcel?"

"They've come to bring my wedding present. Do come down, Cleo, before Trina goes all over Mother like a steamroller."

In the drawing-room a small group was gathered, consisting

of Mrs. MacAlvey, James, Trina, and the two children, standing in awkward attitudes round a square cardboard box.

"Is that really for me?" said Raine, darting in. "Can I open it now, Trina?"

"You'd better," said Trina. "If you don't like it I'm afraid you'll have to lump it, as it can't be changed."

Everybody held their breath while Raine tore off the string, and from a heap of shavings lifted an ornate silver cake-stand supported by two gorged-looking cherubs.

"Oh, but it's magnificent!" she said. "Utterly regal!"

"It cost the earth," said Trina, "but I expect all the presents will be on show at the wedding, and I wasn't having it said, Is that little thing all Raine MacAlvey's brother can afford?"

"Here's the card to go on it," said James. "It says, 'From James and Trina, Armitage, and Angela, to Raine with every wish of love and happiness,' and I wrote seven before I was satisfied."

"Oh, thank you over and over again!" cried Raine, nearly capsizing the cake-dish in her anxiety to look sufficiently pleased, and kissing James heartily and not kissing Trina, which didn't detract from the tension of the moment. "It's the most spectacular present I've got so far."

"I don't know why we're all standing," said Mrs. MacAlvey, on whom her daughter-in-law always had the effect of a crocodile on a weak swimmer. "Won't s-s-some of you sit down?"

"Grandmother," said Armitage, "please could Angela and I go and find Gavin?"

"But he's not in, dear. They're all away out somewhere in Gavin's boat."

"Oh, I did want to see them," said Armitage, anxiously wrinkling up his forehead. "Well, could we go down to the beach? Mother, please let us. We won't go near the sea, and we won't run about and get hot."

Poor little wretches, thought Cleo. What's the point in being twelve years old with a beach handy if you can't go near the sea or run about and get hot?

"Pull your socks up and push your hair out of your eyes," said Trina fussily, "and keep together and don't go near any rocks. I know a little boy who fell off some rocks, and —— "

Angela gave a loud gulp, and Armitage said, "We won't go near anything we shouldn't, Mother. Thank you, Mother, for saying we can go."

"We shall be having a cup of tea in a minute," said Mrs. MacAlvey, "and then supper later. You'll all stay, won't you, Trina? You see, we've got Noreén Leigh here, she's just arrived from Inverness."

"Shall I come to the beach with you two?" cried James jumping up, and both children gave squeaks of delight, while Trina said, "If you make them over-excited, James, I'll never bring them here again."

The departure of James and his children seemed to thin down the crowd in the drawing-room, and presently Mrs. Leigh and Noreen came in and were drawn into a long argument about just when it was they had met Trina before.

"Come and sit by the window, Noreen," said Cleo, "and you can gaze at our famous view while you drink your tea."

"I should think it is rather depressing to look at the sea all the time," said Trina. "It always makes me think of the poor sailors."

"I remember when we met you last!" cried Mrs. Leigh. "Your little boy was still a baby in a shawl, and he had inflamed eyes and Doctor gave you something to use on them."

"I remember that," said Trina, and added ambiguously, "It's a wonder he ever got his sight back."

Tea was rather confusedly served and drunk, and Mrs. MacAlvey said, "Come and see the garden, Trina. There'll be some fruit and vegetables for you to take back."

She seemed to have struck the right note, for after a tense moment in which one could almost feel Trina struggling not to say that of all foods, fruit and vegetables were the most likely to upset the children, she allowed herself to be led off.

Meanwhile Miss Paige was holding her thumbs and willing Primrose and Co. not to come home for supper. But something went wrong with her absent treatment, for not only did the three of them arrive starving at six o'clock, but Cecil who had stayed in with a cold decided that he was well enough to appear at table, along with Elinore who had stuck by his side all day, so there had to be a frantic last-minute rearrangement of the dining-room, and finally seventeen sat down to the meal.

"Oh dear, we're all sitting in families!" thought Mrs. MacAlvey as her eyes swept the large circle, but she had not the strength to demand a general post. Perhaps it was a good thing that Trina should have her children on either side of her — for they had returned from the beach without a hair out of place — and there was Noreen sitting between her parents and apparently with very little to say.

Trina put on her glasses and looked round fussily to see what Mysie was bringing in.

"Would it be too much trouble," she asked her mother-in-law, "if we could have a little bread-and-butter and some sliced apple?"

"Mother," said Armitage with a sensational outburst of independent thought, "as we are here, might we not have what the others are having?"

"That's a good idea," said James. "We don't want to put Grandmother to any trouble." And he seized the plate of veal-and-ham pie which was offered him.

The meal could not be called a success, for it was eaten in a kind of paralysed silence for which no individual person could be held responsible. When it was over they all went into the drawing-room for coffee.

"This ought to cure people who think they like large families," Raine whispered to Cleo.

"We don't want any coffee, Granny," Primrose was explaining. "We're going up to Darluin to see a pony that's for sale, not to buy it of course, but for something to do. It's actually an auction and ——"

"You are not going to any auction sale," said Mrs. Mac-Alvey. "You are going to take Angela and Armitage for a nice walk."

"Oh help!" said Primrose. "Need we?"

The seven youngest members of the party, ordered to get together over their coffee, sat in an uncomfortable circle and in total silence. Only James's pair, desperately anxious to please, wriggled like pleading puppies until Angela's cup fell with a crash on the floor, and coffee poured over Primrose's none-too-clean ankles.

"Oh! Oh! Oh! I am sorry!" cried Angela, vocal for the first time in history and bursting into frightened tears.

"What are you scunnering about?" asked Primrose, to whom the dropping of cups was a normal occurrence.

Trina jumped up, fussing and fuming. The carpet was ruined, Angela was not fit to bring out in company, it was all James's fault for persuading them to come.

"Oh no, no!" cried poor Mrs. MacAlvey, to whom the shattering of her party meant more than the dropping of a cup.

"It's nothing, Trina. It happens every day with children."

"Not with my children," said Trina. "They are not allowed to behave like hooligans."

All the adults present felt acutely embarrassed and slightly sick at the sight of poor Angela trying to thrust back her hysterical sobs by pressing both bony tear-wet fists to her mouth, but it was Primrose who saved the situation. Some spark of pity or understanding must have penetrated the tough exterior of her school-girl soul, for she jumped up and said, "We'll all go down to the beach. Come on, Angela, you stick to me and forget the beastly coffee." And she extended a queenly hand which Angela grabbed, relief and adoration struggling in her puffy little face.

"I wish they could spend more time with their cousins," said Mrs. MacAlvey, snatching at any spar. "It would be good for them all. If we had more room we'd invite them to stay." And you could see her mentally sorting bedrooms.

"That's quite unnecessary," said Trina, "thank you all the same. Any change in their routine would be absolutely disastrous and upset them for weeks. You don't know what it's like to have highly strung children."

Mrs. MacAlvey, who hardly knew what it was like *not* to have highly strung children — and grandchildren — opened her mouth feebly, and shut it again. To start an argument with Trina — especially in mixed company — was like challenging Juggernaut.

"Come on, Armitage," said Gavin, grabbing Archie's arm as he spoke and hustling towards the door after Primrose and Angela before anything else could happen.

"If you don't mind, Auntie," said Elinore, "Cecil and I would like to go upstairs and read."

"By all means," said poor Mrs. MacAlvey, thankful to see the roomful thinning out.

Those left behind grouped themselves about the drawing-room and somebody had the bright idea of turning on the radio. Cleo and Raine, who had looked forward to a merry evening with Noreen, sat in silence, listening to Victor Silvester's ballroom orchestra and wishing that Trina would feel the urge to go. But Trina, strangely enough, was by now enjoying herself. She was having one of the best evenings of her life for, thrown into proximity with Mrs. Leigh, she was deep in an absorbing conversation about nervous diseases, their causes, symptoms, and effects. Mrs. Leigh as a doctor's wife considered there was nothing about such matters she did not know, while Trina as a sworn enemy of the entire medical profession contested every point hotly, and the conversation soon took an acrimonious turn, to the delight of the contestants — for they were well matched and could have done battle for hours — and the complete demoralisation of everybody else in the room.

"And to prove my point, let me tell you about one of Doctor's cases!" cried Mrs. Leigh, regardless of her husband's furious glances. And soon the words "At the time of my operation" rang out clearly, drowning the radio alike with poor Mrs. Mac-Alvey's final attempts to divert the conversation.

There was no hope now of saving what was left of the evening, and relief came at ten o'clock when the children returned and James, who hadn't opened his mouth since supper, said they must be off if they wanted to catch the last bus back to Dunmaig.

Armitage and Angela looked happy and had a touch of bright colour in their sallow faces.

"Father," cried Armitage, "Gavin says I could play rugger. He says I would make a good runner."

"You'll do your running by running off to bed," said Trina with dampening effect. "You're flushed already, and if that doesn't mean one of your headaches coming on, I'm very much mistaken."

But she achieved quite a pleasant smile when saying good-bye all round, and said, "I must say I've enjoyed myself. I think it does me good to get out, only James is such a stay-at-home, aren't you, James?"

James, who was laden down with carrier-bags of vegetables from the garden, gave an acquiescent smile.

At last they were gone, but it was too late to pick up the shreds of the evening and make them into something.

"Do you mind if I go to bed?" said Noreen. "I didn't sleep much last night."

"It's been a beastly evening for you," said Raine, "but we couldn't help it."

"I do think we have got some rummy relations," said Archie, appearing in the doorway and talking through a mouthful of plum. "There's Armitage and Angela, and Cecil and Elinore, and ——"

"You needn't go into details," said Cleo.

"I wasn't going to say you," said Archie, surprised.

"I'll go up with you, Noreen," said Raine, "to see you've got all you want. Archie, go to bed at once. And wash! I never saw anything so disgustingly dirty. You're soaked in plum juice."

They all drifted away, and Cleo took a book from the shelf and held it in front of her, unseeing.

Presently Mrs. MacAlvey came in and began plumping up cushions.

"A minute's peace never did anybody any harm," she said.

The cushions arranged to her liking, she loosened her shoes and kicked them off thankfully, sitting idly for a moment on the window-seat.

"I expect," she said, "you're glad of a nice quiet read after all that crowd. I'd better slip away and not disturb you."

"I'm not reading, Mummy. I just picked the book up."

Mrs. MacAlvey let out a large sigh, which seemed to sum up the day and close its agenda.

"Father has told me you're going to stop with us after Raine goes. I'm so happy, I can't tell you!"

"That's all right, Mummy. You'll miss Raine, but it won't be so bad if I'm here to see you through the winter."

"Perhaps it isn't right to let you sacrifice yourself for us, Cleo."

"Sacrifice? What rot. No such thing."

"I've always firmly believed," said Mrs. MacAlvey, "that duty unselfishly done will bring its reward. I suppose you'll laugh at that and call it old-fashioned."

"Not a bit," said Cleo. "It's just one of those charming Victorian fantasies, like eating flies makes cats thin, and he for God only, she for God in him."

"I don't know," said Mrs. MacAlvey, "why I should have better children than I deserve."

"You'll find the answer to that one in any nice Victorian novel," said Cleo, smiling. "I can see Daddy and the Leighs on the lawn in the gloaming. Could they, by any chance, be waiting for you?"

"Mercy! I said I'd go for a stroll with them. Where are my shoes?"

Left alone, Cleo found nothing to do. The house was quiet. She didn't really want to read. She went upstairs, for there

213

seemed nothing left but bed, and Raine came out of Noreen's room and said, "Is that you, Cleo? Come in and talk. It's the last chance we'll have with Noreen."

"I thought she wanted to go to bed?"

"Not really. She only wanted to get away from downstairs."

Noreen was standing by the open window, gazing out at the rising moon and stroking the petals of the yellow climbing roses that reached to the sill.

"I should like to live here," she said. "I envy you all."

(Live here? thought Cleo. What as? Maiden aunt?)

"I'm surprised to hear you say that," said Raine, "after the shattering evening we've just endured. I sometimes think family life is over-rated."

"You'll soon be escaping from it," said Noreen, turning from the window with a sigh, to sit down with one leg beneath her on the bed.

"Oh, but I'm not looking on marriage as an escape," said Raine. "I suppose some girls do marry to escape from home, but it's rather a sordid reason."

"You're one of the lucky ones," said Noreen. "You can afford to call other people's reasons sordid. It's a bit obtuse and patronising of you."

"She didn't mean it like that," said Cleo. "Of the three of us, Raine *is* the lucky one. Not that I want to escape from home; there's nothing for me to escape from so far as I'm concerned, and I've just committed myself to becoming my aged parents' prop and stay, and we won't talk about that. But what about you, Noreen? Do you still find it awful at home?"

Noreen made a pattern on the bedcover with her finger.

"I suppose it's my own fault," she said, "for being what I am. I'm a double disappointment to Mother, and that's very hard luck on her. Double, because first I'm not the kind of daughter

214

she wanted, and second I am the kind of daughter she didn't want."

"But you've got to be You. Everybody has got to be an individual."

"That's another way of saying that everybody has a right to live their own life."

"But haven't they?"

"That comes well from you, Cleo!"

"I suppose it does. It's all very involved. I do hate to see anybody's life wasted."

"What do you mean by wasted?"

"Well — not as free and full and exciting as it might have been."

Noreen shrugged her shoulders and said, "So far as I am concerned, I must be the reincarnation of Wordsworth's dreary Lucy. 'A maid whom there were none to praise and very few to love.'"

"The poem ends," said Raine. " 'But she is in her grave, and oh! the difference to me.'"

"It's nice to think that somebody missed her," said Cleo thoughtfully, "but not much help to Lucy."

"What are you going to do all winter, Noreen?" asked Raine.

"I don't know. It depends."

"You've got something on your mind, haven't you?" said Cleo. "I could sense it all evening."

Noreen looked up quickly, then looked down again and said, "I don't know that I have."

"It doesn't matter if you don't want to tell us," said Raine. "We're such old friends, it would be all right and wouldn't go any further. But I expect there are some things you can't put into words. I mostly tell people if I've got anything on my

215

mind, but it takes different people differently. I mean, Cleo and I are awfully anxious to help, but it doesn't matter if —— "

"Thanks very much," said Noreen awkwardly, but she did not offer to continue the conversation.

There suddenly seemed to be nothing to talk about, after all, and Cleo said, "Well, I suppose we ought to go to bed. If you're hungry in the night, Noreen, the stillroom is at the back of the hall and through the little door. There's lots of food there. I always think it is mean of people not to tell their guests where the food is kept. I'm always awfully hungry in the night in other people's houses."

"*Dormez bien*," said Raine, uncoiling herself from the floor.

"Wait," said Noreen. "I'd better tell you what's been worrying me. At least, not exactly worrying — because it hasn't anything to do with me, you understand. It's about a great friend of mine."

"I had a friend like that when I was at school," said Raine helpfully, since Noreen didn't seem quite able to go on. "She was always wanting to do weird things, and giving other people the responsibility of deciding whether she should or not. Is your friend like that?"

"Oh, yes," said Noreen thankfully. "That's just it. I'd better tell you about her. She's an only child and her parents are a bit — well, difficult. They have awfully high standards, social and otherwise, that she has never been able to attain to. She is, in fact, the wrong sort of daughter."

"Like you —— " began Raine, and Cleo said, "Why be so unselfish and self-deprecating? I dare say the girl is awfully nice and the parents are wrong."

"Well, she has a frightful time at home," said Noreen. "They've been trying for years to marry her off to the right man — I mean, right socially, and now she's — well, she's in love and she wants to get married, and the man is wonderful and her parents would die of shock."

"Why?"

"I'd better go back a bit. She met this man during the war. He was a Flight-Lieutenant in the R.A.F. After the war they went on being friendly, and writing. They've been in love for the last three years, but the girl wanted to be sure. I think three years is a good test, don't you? She's absolutely sure."

"Well, what's the matter?" said Raine. "Why doesn't she clinch it?"

"One met a lot of people in uniform during the war," said Noreen. "One didn't ask what they were in private life — hardly thought of it. My friend never thought of it. She didn't care. She isn't conventional in her ideas and not in the least snobbish. Her parents —— "

"Are conventional and snobbish," finished Cleo for her. "Oh, Noreen, what on earth did he turn out to be?"

"A ringmaster," said Noreen simply. "In a circus."

"A ring —— " began Cleo, slightly stunned, and Raine cried, "Do you mean the handsome man in the red dress-coat with a riding whip who —— "

"Yes," said Noreen.

"But how wonderful! I never think of circus people as being real, but of course they must be, and in spite of being so fantastic they are probably quite as — quite as —— " Her voice faded away as she caught Noreen's eye and saw Noreen's cheeks growing pinker and pinker.

"If you mean steady and reliable," said Noreen, "my friend has met many of her fiancé's colleagues in the circus, and she says they are just like our own kind of people, but usually nicer."

217

"I'm sure they are," said Raine. "But the ringmaster, is he handsome?"

"Very — or so my friend says. Not that that matters."

"And they are really in love," said Cleo, "and it has already lasted for several years. Then why don't they get married? What are they waiting for?"

"Her people," said Noreen, "would never speak to her again."

"No, I quite see that. At first of course. But don't you think they'd get used to the idea?"

"Never! Not my friend's people. They're rather like Daddy and Mother, ultra-conventional, London-suburban, ambitious socially. I mean — a daughter in a circus!"

"But has the girl decided?" said Cleo. "What is she going to do?"

"What do you think she should do?"

"I'd marry him," said Raine. "If it was Ian and he was a clown in a circus, let alone a dignified part like a ringmaster, I'd marry him. It's the most romantic situation I ever heard of."

Noreen got up off the bed and shook out her skirt.

"Yes," she said slowly. "I think she will marry him — in fact, I'm sure she will. She knows this is the real thing, and she won't let it go."

"Oh good!" said Cleo. "By the way, where will they live?"

"Oh, he has a caravan. It's a travelling circus — and ——"

"A caravan! A real ——"

"The very newest kind of motor caravan, with calor gas and a real bathroom, carpets, curtains, a radio-gramophone, a Cairn terrier called Patch ——"

"If he likes Cairns," said Raine, "he must be all right. I

218

think your friend is lucky, and it's going to be the most exciting marriage that will put mine quite in the shade."

"Her people —— " began Noreen.

"Time," said Cleo, "is a great healer."

"Time," said Raine, "will prove to them that she did the right thing."

There was a moment's silence.

"We really must go to bed," said Raine. "Come on, Cleo. Good night, Noreen, and do come and stay with me at Larrich, won't you?"

"I'd love to," said Noreen. "Good night, Raine. Good night, Cleo. It's been marvellous to see you. I'm glad I told you about my friend."

"So are we," said Raine. "Wish her luck from us, and if she's ever up this way, we'd love to know her and her husband, wouldn't we, Cleo?"

They went across to Raine's room.

"Which side of the bed do you want?" asked Raine.

"I don't mind," said Cleo.

"Well, you can have the side by the wall, and then if anybody falls out it'll be me. I always like to do the generous thing."

They undressed thoughtfully and, pulling back the curtains, opened the window wide to the summer night, so soft and scented.

"Cleo," said Raine, "you understood that there wasn't any friend, didn't you?"

"Oh, right from the start, I knew it was Noreen herself. I'm awfully glad, aren't you?"

"We advised her. It's partly on our heads. I never was so glad about anything since Ian and I got engaged."

Cleo sat down on the bed and laughed helplessly.

219

"Oh, Raine! Think of Mrs. Leigh with a son-in-law in a circus!"

Breakfast next morning was a hurried affair with the restless quality of a last meal for departing guests. The Leighs looked too heavily dressed in their travelling suits, and Noreen wore her uniform.

The usual things were said, too frequently.

"Now do eat a good breakfast, goodness knows when you'll get anything else."

"They'll be able to get something in Inverness if the local train gets in on time."

"It never does."

"Don't forget what I told you, there's always an empty first-class carriage at the very back of the London train."

"I really don't think I dare travel at the back of the train," said Mrs. Leigh plaintively. "I mean, in a wreck — telescoping. Thank you for suggesting it, all the same."

"Oh, I hope you won't find the journey too tiring and undo all the good your holiday has done you."

"I dare say I shall need a few days in bed when I get home," said Mrs. Leigh, "but what can I expect? How I detest being an invalid! Norrie, do you have to travel dressed like that, dear? I can't tell you how I dislike it."

"I happen to be on a job," said Noreen.

"Perfectly ridiculous!"

Just as they were ready to start, Raine cried out suddenly, "Why shouldn't we go with them, Cleo? We have to go to Edinburgh some time about the dresses and things. I can be ready in five minutes, can you?"

"Of course," said Cleo. "I'll dash and pack."

"But you can't rush off like that!" shrieked Mrs. MacAlvey. "The money! The patterns! The sizes!"

"You get those ready while we're packing," shouted Raine, already upstairs. "I must ring Ian."

"Listen to her!" said Mrs. MacAlvey helplessly. "I shall die!"

Raine and Cleo, like a whirlwind, were upstairs, downstairs, in and out the rooms, telephoning, calling, shouting, contradicting.

So in the end the Leighs — through no fault of their own — left in a turmoil, luggage all over the place, dogs under everybody's feet, people downstairs calling up and people upstairs shouting down, Mr. MacAlvey ringing the hotel to borrow the roomy old Daimler to take all the people and all the luggage to Inverbyne, Mrs. MacAlvey crying at least six times, "Girls, if you can't get in at a nice quiet hotel in Edinburgh be sure to go to Auntie Kat's," and the children standing round and making audible comments about the Leighs' lovely pigskin cases and Raine's fibre one with one corner bashed in.

At last they were off, everybody waving, calling, blowing kisses, Mrs. MacAlvey in tears as she always was at any departure.

"What a magnificent send-off!" said Doctor Leigh. "Ah, the warm Highland hearts!"

"Dear Kilchro!" murmured Mrs. Leigh fondly, putting her head out of the car window for a last look at that hospitable house.

CHAPTER THIRTEEN

THE NEXT DAY seemed so quiet that after lunch Mrs. Mac-Alvey said "I think I'll take the opportunity to go over and see Lady Keith. I've been going all the summer, and she does appreciate a visit now that she can't get out, with her rheumatism, poor soul."

"You go, my dear," said Mr. MacAlvey brightly, "it'll do you good. I'll run you to Drumpegge and come back for you, pick you up at the gates."

"Oh, but you're coming too."

Mr. MacAlvey groaned.

"Of course you're coming, Alexander. Drumpegge likes a crack as well as she does, and what would he think if he saw you slinking away from the gates?"

"While you're gone," said Miss Paige, "I'll get all the covers off the drawing-room cushions and wash them. It's such a chance."

"You'll do nothing of the kind, Vannah," said Mrs. Mac-Alvey. "You're coming with us. Both Drumpegge and Lady Keith are very fond of you, and they'll only keep asking me why you haven't come."

"But he always says to me, aren't you married yet?" said Vannah reluctantly.

"Well, you must just say no you're not. So that's settled. We'll all get ready and start at three."

Drumpegge House was a perfect example of Victorian Gothic, a square fortress-like block with a pointed turret at each corner and a stone porch like a frowning eyebrow. Its setting was not good, for it stood in the middle of some flattish fields, and its unattractive background was a disused quarry and a belt of half-dead stone-pines, but tourists would gaze at its exterior and say, "That's just my idea of a romantic old Highland home."

Inside, the romantic and the Gothic ended abruptly, and all was prettily Edwardian, in a manner rarely preserved at the present day. The Keiths had money — unusual in Highland families — for the present laird's father had married an Australian heiress who, after spending ten years in raising a family of six children, had let herself go on the house with flowery carpets, polished mahogany, wallpapers festooned with sweet peas, wistaria and trellised roses, fretwork brackets and Sheraton whatnots, water-colour paintings of Highland cattle with their feet in a blue loch and masses of purple heather behind them, mirrors painted with bulrushes, water-lilies, and storks, dainty breakable little chairs and occasional tables, silver photograph frames, silk cushions, china cabinets full of egg-shell porcelain, plaster figures of pretty children, puppies and angels, candlesticks with dangling lustres, rosewood pianos with pleated silk fronts and gilt candleholders, lace curtains tied up with bobbly cords, Chinese draught screens, velvet *portières*, bead hassocks, and silver-plated fire-irons. When the present Drumpegge inherited all this, his wife was so delighted with it that she vowed to dedicate her life to preserving its delicate charm, and this she had faithfully done with the help of a crowd of hard-working young housemaids from the village. Everything at Drumpegge always looked as though it had been laundered or polished five minutes before you arrived. Some people found this depressing, among them Mrs. MacAlvey.

Sir Haris himself saw them coming across the strath, and rushed to meet them, his beard flying in the breeze and his loud check tweed trousers flapping madly round his legs.

"This is a treat!" he cried. "Come in with you, come in. The old girl will be excited. And you've brought Miss Paige! Not married yet, Miss Paige? It beats me. I could find you a' husband tomorrow, if you'd let me."

"I don't believe in forcing the hand of Providence," said Miss Paige.

"Ha! ha! You know how to take a joke. I've always said, MacAlvey, that the greatest thing in life is to be able to take a joke."

"Surely not the greatest," said Mr. MacAlvey, who was inclined to be literal.

"But why not? You believe that the greatest thing in life is to be able to take a joke, don't you, Miss Paige?"

"I am reminded," said Miss Paige, "of a nurse we used to have when I was a child, and how she often used to say that the greatest thing in life is to learn to fa' soft. She came from the Borders."

The laird roared with delight and slapped his thigh with a sound like slapping cast-iron.

"To learn to fa' soft! My, my, that's a grand bit of philosophy. I must remember that. Best thing I've heard in years."

Miss Paige thought he looked exactly like one of his own Highland cattle. She had often trembled at the sight of him barging about his delicate satiny drawing-room, looking in fact like a bison in a bun-shop, but somehow he always contrived to avoid any sort of collision, for like many enormous, clumsy men he was light on his feet and had that sixth sense of cats and bats, which always look as though they are going to hit something but never do. This was all right for Drumpegge himself, but didn't help the nerves of onlookers.

"And how are all the good neighbours at Strogue?" he cried, changing the subject. "Not that I care, but a Keith always says the polite thing, ha! ha!"

While he was talking, he was shoving them before him into the house, and presently they found themselves in the sitting-room where Lady Keith was sitting with a plaid rug over her knees, doing a bridge problem out of *The Scotsman*.

"Look who's here, Jean," cried Drumpegge. "Why isn't there any whisky in this room? If I've told those girls once there's to be whisky in this room, I've told them fifty times."

"Not for me," said Mr. MacAlvey hastily. "I never drink whisky in the afternoon, and the ladies don't take it at all."

"Well I do," said Drumpegge, "and I want some now." He rang the bell and gave his order, then turned to his guests and said, "What made you come? Nothing better to do?"

"Really, Haris!" said Lady Keith. "It would serve you right if they went away again."

"MacAlvey won't go until he's told me about the big fish he didn't catch," said Drumpegge, flinging himself into a deep chair with a guffaw and pushing a footstool towards Mrs. Mac-Alvey with the toe of his shoe.

"We really came to ask how Lady Keith is," said Mrs. Mac-Alvey. "How is the rheumatism, Lady Keith? What a trial it must be!"

"She's shamming as usual," said the victim's husband.

"Of course I am, everybody knows that. But a lot of nice people come to see me and I like it, so I shall go on shamming. I've heard about one of your girls getting married soon. Tell me when it's to be."

"In three weeks' time ——" began Mrs. MacAlvey, when her host interrupted, "So she's marrying Ian Garvine of Larrich. That's the sort of match I approve of. One of the things that's the matter with the Highlands at the present day is that so few of the young men marry local girls. They go on their holidays to England and marry Torquay typists with English voices like road-drills, and tartans they're not entitled to wear, bought at Woolworth's."

"I don't think you can buy tartans at Woolworth's," said Miss Paige.

"That's beside the point," said Drumpegge. "What I mean is, the MacAlveys have got their daughter off to the right man, and I'd like to know how they did it. We've got four still on the shelf and likely to stay there."

"On the shelf indeed!" said Lady Keith. "Flora is only twenty-one and Roberta is fifteen. The twins come in between, eighteen last March."

"Well, not one of them has had a bite yet, and I say if a girl hasn't had a bite at twenty-one she hasn't much hope. And talking of bites, how about this angling competition they're running at the Lockit Arms next week, MacAlvey? I'll enter if you will, though Heaven knows I'm the worst fisherman north of the Clyde."

The men began to talk argumentatively about fishing, while the women got together on the pleasant subject of Raine's wedding.

"Raine and Cleo are in Edinburgh now," said Mrs. Mac-Alvey. "They've gone to buy the dresses and a few odds and

226

ends that Raine needs. She never was a great one for clothes, and I never could get her to wear pretty nightdresses, she preferred the boys' pyjamas. She's capable of going on her honeymoon in striped winceyette."

"Where are they going for the honeymoon?"

"Oh, they won't decide till the last minute, but it'll be either North Berwick or Carnoustie. They're not for going too far from home. Raine had some idea of being married in a coat and skirt, but I told her I'd have no wedding from Kilchro without a white bride."

"I should think not," said Lady Keith. "Oh, how I envy you! I wish I was planning a wedding for Flora. It must be such fun."

"That's it!" shouted Drumpegge, who seemed to have the gift of carrying on a conversation of his own and listening to everyone else's. "You get some advice from Mrs. MacAlvey on how to get your girls off. You've certainly missed the bus up to now."

"I take no notice of him," said Lady Keith. "He doesn't mean a word of it. Marie brought a nice young man home that she met at a party, and Haris was so rude to him that he never came again, and I don't blame him."

"He was a Glasgow man," said the laird. "No Keith ever married a Glasgow man, or ever shall if I can help it. Let's have some tea in — filthy drink, but I suppose you'll be disappointed if we don't offer you some."

"Civic pride," said Mr. MacAlvey, "compels me to tell you that my father was a Glasgow man and I was born in Glasgow myself."

"Well, I didn't say there was anything wrong with you. I dare say in ten years' time we'll be glad for the girls to marry anything, even Campbells."

The tea came in, brought by a young maid in an Edwardian starched apron and goffered cap with long lawn strings, a uniform which must have been carefully preserved for about forty years, or copied. The cups were finest Wedgwood, the tea service highly ornate silver, and the hot scones and honey kept everybody — even Drumpegge — speechless for ten minutes.

When the maid returned to remove the tea, three wild-looking dogs burst into the room at the same time, and looked as though they were about to attack Miss Paige, who was still struggling with a piece of very gluey fruit cake she had rashly taken. Then they seemed to change their minds and sat up on their haunches, begging.

"Oh, may I give them something," said Miss Paige, "or will it spoil their dinner?"

"Spoil nothing," said Drumpegge. "They don't get any dinner. They're not lapdogs. When they're hungry they can go and dig out a fox, can't they?"

"Don't be silly, Haris," said his wife, "you know not one of them could kill a mouse, they're far too soft and over-fed. That brown-and-white mongrel belongs to Elspeth and she gives him chocolates, I've seen her."

"Then cake can't hurt him," said Miss Paige, thankfully dividing her soggy incubus into three parts and seeing them wolfed down in about a twentieth of a second.

"Our dogs are spoilt too," said Mrs. MacAlvey. "Archie bursts into indignant sobs if we offer to whip the wretches."

"It's a pity we couldn't have wished little Patience off on to Archie," said Drumpegge. "Isn't it, Jean?"

"Patience is a Corgi," explained Lady Keith, "and belongs to a cousin of mine who has recently been staying with us."

"That dog had a devil," said Drumpegge. "And so had its

228

mistress. She'd never been in the Highlands before, and said she wouldn't be getting her money's worth unless we had a piper to screech round the table and drown the noise of the girls drinking their soup. Well, I haven't had a piper here since old Jock died of D.T.s in 1934 or thereabouts, and I had to go out and borrow one off Duncan of Bonnymile, and he was about ninety and I had to get him as tight as a lord before he'd consent to play. A bottle of whisky a day that woman cost me, just for a piper. But we had her leg pulled beautifully. She said the dream of her life was to see a Highland toast drunk, and was it true that every time we did it we broke the priceless crystal goblets in the fireplace? We said, oh yes, it was, and the girls went and dug out a lot of prewar Woolworth glasses — the table looked a treat — and then we all got ourselves up and asked a few people in for the spirit of the thing — seven different tartans, I tell you, and Lord knows how much tattered lace — and we did the whole thing with our feet on the table and crashed all the glass into the fireplace, every bit of thirty bob's worth. Hilda was impressed, said it was the most thrilling moment of her life, and she'd tell all her friends about it for years to come. Heaven help you, Jean woman, you've got some funny relations."

"No funnier than yours," said Lady Keith. "What about your English cousin's daughter Maud who came to spend a week with us at Fort William? I took her round the West Highland museum and showed her all the Jacobite relics and the secret portrait and the tartans and everything, and she looked perfectly blank until we were coming out and then she beamed and said to the Curator, 'I get it now, this Charlie would be the one that grew up to be the Merry Monarch.' I could have gone through the ground."

She still looked a bit overcome at the memory, and Miss

Paige said, "You don't have to apologise for relations. I mean, everybody has got ones who — I mean —— "

"Who'd be better dead," said Drumpegge, combing his beard with his fingers. "Why make any bones about it?"

The three dogs, who had been sniffing about the room, now came and draped themselves round the laird's feet and went to sleep.

"They're simply not allowed in here," said Lady Keith, ringing the bell for the maid, who made some ineffectual dabs at the dogs while everybody else got up and shoo-ed. After a final mad scamper round the room, they were ejected.

"I was reading in a magazine," said Mr. MacAlvey, "about a poor Scots lad who went to America and made a fortune of millions. When he died he left a clause in his will which said that his greatest treasure would be found in a small steel box in the safe. His family were expecting something sensational in the way of an enormous diamond, but what the box contained was a mere handful of dusty earth and a note which read, 'This is Scottish soil brought by me from Scotland sixty-two years ago and every grain is dearer than gold.'"

"How interesting!" said Lady Keith. "Is that fact or fiction?"

"It was said to be true."

"Well, I think he was screwy," said Drumpegge. "If he'd cared that much about Scottish soil, why didn't he come over with his millions and do a bit for the Highlands? Meaningless sentimentality. Blah!"

"I thought it was a lovely story," said Miss Paige. "We're all so afraid of being called sentimental in these days that we never show any feeling at all."

"Well, I'm sure you do, Vannah dear," said Mrs. MacAlvey, "with all those photographs of your old home on your mantel-piece, and the hoof of your pony done up like an ink-stand and

230

everything, and that locket you wear but won't tell anybody who's inside. I think it's sweet, and I'm sentimental too and don't care who knows it."

"I only made a secret of the locket to tease the children. As a matter of fact, there are two film-stars in it. I'll show you when we get home."

"I always wanted to wear a locket with miniatures of the girls in," said Lady Keith, "but Haris said I hadn't the right kind of neck."

"Neither had you," said her husband. "A locket on you looked like a prize-card on a show heifer. You're too sonsy."

The maid suddenly entered and said, "There's the Reverend Waddy in the drawing-room and he's after asking for madam."

"Who the hell is he?" growled the laird. "And why does he ask for you and not for me?"

"Hush, Haris! I think he must be the new young minister from Glensnood. Possibly he's come to ask me to preside at their sale of work at Glensnood."

"Well, say you can't and give him two pounds. It comes cheaper in the long-run."

"Two guineas would sound better."

"Two pounds, I said! Do you think I'm made of money?"

"All right, Haris, you needn't bellow," said Lady Keith, getting up with the aid of her sticks and walking slowly out of the room.

"That woman has to argue every blessed little thing I say," grumbled Drumpegge, with a fond and anxious glance after his wife. "Well, MacAlvey," he went on, "have you heard of anybody getting a bit of shooting?"

"Can't say I have. The only people who get any shooting round here nowadays are the rich English who've bought up the moors."

"You've said it. My word, how things change. When I think of the old days — Stewart with his 20,000 acres and Macdonald with his 15,000, and the others, and now it's all pared away — well, I swear there'll never be a square foot of Drumpegge land sold while there's breath in my body."

"You happen to be one of the very few lairds who can afford to say that."

"There's something in that," said Drumpegge, turning over the remark as though he were tasting it.

"There's everything in it."

"And look at this," went on the laird, snatching up the *Glasgow Herald* and waving it about. "Four pages about this infernal Government's doings and not a word about what's going to happen to Inverness-shire. And a photo of Gromyko! What am I supposed to do with a photo of Gromyko? Wear it on my chest? Some sense if they'd put in a photo of a Galloway bull or a thirty-pound fish."

He gave a hearty slap at a wandering wasp, squashed it flat, and said, "That's all newspapers are good for."

"It was better in the old days," said Mr. MacAlvey. "I can remember when there were hardly any trains out this way, no motor-cars, none of these smelly buses and only a smattering of tourists."

"Tourists!" cried Drumpegge. "My old father hated them. I mind when he was ninety, half paralysed and well past going out after the stags, he could still sit at his bedroom window with a shotgun and pick off a brace of tourists as they went along the strath. They never knew what hit them."

"That's a lie, Haris," said Lady Keith, coming in at the open door. "Yes, it was about the sale of work," she went on, settling herself in her chair, "and I said I couldn't come, and gave him the two guineas."

232

"Why, you double-crossing female!" roared Drumpegge, whipping out an enormous cigar like a torpedo from his coat pocket and thrusting it upon Mr. MacAlvey.

"Your old father was always the worst shot in Ross, Inverness, and Argyll," said Lady Keith calmly. "If he ever did shoot any stags, which I doubt, they were led up to him blindfold."

"I think we really must go," said Mrs. MacAlvey, rising. "We have enjoyed our visit, haven't we, Vannah?"

"We've enjoyed it too," said Lady Keith, "and I do hope you'll come again and tell us all about the wedding when it's over. To think that if you hadn't come I shouldn't have known when it was to be."

"Oh, but you've had your invitation? You must have. They were sent out ages ago."

"We haven't had any invitation," said Lady Keith. "Have we, Haris?"

"Now, how should I know?"

"But one was certainly sent to you," said Miss Paige. "I know, because I wrote the envelope myself and I asked Mrs. MacAlvey whether Drumpegge had an 'e' at the end."

"Well, we never got it," said Lady Keith, "and I can guess what happened. Haris goes down the drive to meet the postman and stuffs the letters in his pocket. Then he goes out on the moor to read them and throws them all away. I've told him about it dozens of times. It's too bad."

"I probably thought it was an advertisement," said Drumpegge.

"Then we'll send you another as soon as we get home," said Mrs. MacAlvey, "and we shall expect you all on September the eleventh, the girls too."

"All of them?" cried Drumpegge, rubbing his hands with

delight. "Good! Good! They say one wedding always leads to several, so if we can't get at least one of the girls off at Raine's affair, there must be something wrong with them."

"Roberta will have gone back to Roedean," said Lady Keith, "and a good thing too. Talking of marrying a child off at fifteen!"

"I never said a word about Roberta, did I, Miss Paige?"

"Roedean?" echoed Miss Paige mockingly. "Oh, Drumpegge, you don't mean to say you have your daughter educated in England!"

"Oh, they choose their own schools nowadays," he said, "and why shouldn't we take the best from England? They've milked us often enough." He glanced at Mrs. MacAlvey, and then looking down affectionately at his coat with its leather patches and check trousers, now covered with dogs' hairs, added, "I suppose it isn't one of these dressy affairs? I can come as I am?"

"You'll wear your good kilt and doublet," said Lady Keith firmly, "or you'll not go at all."

"Well, just a drop before you leave," cried the laird, seizing a full bottle of *Highland Laddie*.

"Oh no, thank you, really," said Mr. MacAlvey.

"Come on, man, you can't refuse a *deoch an doruis!*"

"Well, a very small one."

"And small ones for the ladies too," said Drumpegge, splashing hearty drams into the glasses.

On the way home Miss Paige said, "Well, there's one thing about going to Drumpegge. You don't come away with a sore throat from having to talk too much."

234

CHAPTER FOURTEEN

How KIND of Ian to ask us over to see how nice he is making the place for Raine!" said Mrs. MacAlvey the following evening as she and her husband descended from their car on the paved way before the door of Larrich House. "And so convenient to be able to come when Raine is away, because I know how she would rush us round, and never give us time to see anything properly before we found ourselves outside and going back."

The door was opened by old Morag, with her spectacles on the end of her nose and a piece of long grey knitting in her hands.

"The laird's no in," she said when she saw the visitors, "but Mr. Ian's aboot somewhere."

"Hullo!" cried Ian, bounding out of the back regions. "Can you get into the place? Mind those planks, Mrs. MacAlvey. The workmen seem to use the hall as a dumping ground, seeing they're not supposed to be doing any work on it."

"Good evening, Ian," cried the guests simultaneously, and Mrs. MacAlvey added, "The house looked fine from the road as we came along with the sun just lighting on the old grey walls. It put into my mind some lines of Robert Louis:

> *A pickle plats and paths and posies,*
> *A ring o' wa's the hale encloses*
> *Frae sheep or men,*
> *And there the auld hoose beeks and dozes*
> *A' by her lane."*

"She's an Edinburgh woman," said Mr. MacAlvey gloomily, "and she was brought up on Robert Louis."

"It sounds very nice and appropriate," said Ian, "though I haven't the least idea what pickle plats are. They sound rather tasty. And as for the posies, you'll have to teach Raine to be a gardener, Mrs. MacAlvey, or else come yourself and make us a flower garden."

"I might even do that, and I'm so glad you can't do anything to the outside of the house. I love its old grey, grim, four-square look."

There was certainly a great deal of upset inside Larrich House. The doors of dining-room and drawing-room stood open, and inside were to be seen stripped rooms with erections of planks, billowing sheets splashed with whitewash, and many overflowing pots and tins of paint. Ian led the way to the back, saying, "Come and look at our new sitting-room. There! They've stopped the damp and replastered the walls and are putting in a modern grate made of little tiles. Isn't it a fine view of the loch? Raine wants a window-seat here, and the whole room is going to be done in a soft shade of mellow yellow."

"Did you say melon?"

"No, I said mellow. Melon isn't the colour at all, it's more of a tinned apricot. Raine says it gets the evening sun. You know, it took a woman to teach us that rooms 'got' such things as evening sun. We always took it for granted that if you wanted the sun you went out and found it. Now let's go and take a look at the dining-room."

"You're not having anything modern done to this fine old panelling!" said Mr. MacAlvey in horror.

"No, no. It's only being cleaned and restored, and the ceiling is to be whitened. Then we can see the plaster garlands and the foxes' masks that disappeared into black smoke sixty or seventy years ago. And let me tell you that we have always used our dining-room table decently covered with a red frieze cloth and a white damask one on top of that, and now Raine says we are to eat off the bare board. I call it going back two hundred years. She'll be wanting rushes on the floor next and a half a pine-tree burning across the fire-dogs."

"Quite right," said Mrs. MacAlvey. "You've hurt the feelings of that grand old table long enough with your damask cloths. I don't know what your great-grandfather would have said. And another thing, Ian Garvine, your father had a piper until not long before the war —— "

"Oh, don't remind Raine of that! Well, now you've seen the room where you'll attend our first dinner-party, shall we go upstairs? Mind the planks."

The bedrooms were all very much in the workmen's hands.

"The carpets and hangings and the valances of the four-posters have all gone away to be tenderly cleaned," explained Ian. "And if any of them give way under the strain — and I'm afraid a large proportion of them will — they are to be replaced by others as near like them as possible. The credit for the idea must go to Cleo, she thought of it."

"Good for Cleo," said her father.

"Yes, it was much the brightest idea that emerged from our original chaos. As you see, they've got the floor-boards up in this one and are replastering most of the walls. Larrich must be wondering what has happened to it. There hasn't been such an upheaval here since the place was built, and when it is finished it will all be ship-shape and trig for the next two hundred years."

"And by then," said Mrs. MacAlvey with satisfaction, "Raine and you will be ancestors."

Ian laughed at the idea of himself as an ancestor, and Mr. MacAlvey said, "You're spending a great deal of money."

"We won't go into that. It doesn't bear thinking of! But Raine and I are prepared to spend the rest of our lives re-trenching, hoping that posterity will bless us. We're going to write a full account of what we've done and how much we've spent and of our lives of penury, so that there won't be the slightest doubt in our descendants' minds of what they have to bless us for. We haven't any intention of being noble and anonymous. Neil has helped us no end, which is fine of him considering that he only benefits indirectly."

"Supposing he takes it into his head to get married?" said Mr. MacAlvey. "Have you thought of that?"

"The house is so vast that it would easily divide into two," said Ian, "and we would be content with the lesser part be-cause, after all, Neil is Larrich, and in a way I have stolen a march on him and am almost behaving as though the place were mine. But he'll never marry, and he'll share all the extra comforts that having Raine about the place will bring. This" — continued Ian, opening a door — "is a corner room with two windows that get the sun all day, and Raine says it is to be the nursery. Do you think we should have bars put to the windows at once, or does that look a little ostentatious? There's a suite of nurseries on the floor above, but Raine says it reminds her of an orphanage. I suppose it is a bit over-facing to start one's married life with accommodation for ten children and two nurses. That's probably what made my parents falter and produce only two of us."

"Raine said she wasn't very taken with the bathroom," said Mrs. MacAlvey.

"Oh, but that's all being altered now, and is being made much less like a dog kennel with a bottomless well in it. And I have a surprise for Raine. I'm having the small room next to her bedroom made into a luxurious bathroom with blue-and-white fittings, and she isn't to know a thing about it until it's finished. We keep it locked, and she thinks the workmen use it as a store."

"How proud and happy you are both going to be!" said Mrs. MacAlvey with a sigh of deep satisfaction. "I can hear it ringing in your voice, Ian."

"I wish I could show you the tartan room," said Ian. "It took Cleo's fancy. We sent the old tartan away to be cleaned, curtains, bed valances, everything, and it has already come back, rather shredded, but tartan is something that can be replaced. It will look truly eighteenth century, that room, and there is a wide hearth that would roast if not an ox a goat, and a genuine broad-sword to stir the fire with. Whoever sleeps in there will be fighting 'bluidy battles' in their dreams all night and yelling old clan cries."

"Mercy! You're not going to put Raine to sleep in there?"

"Not on your life. It's enough to turn her into a Lady Macbeth. Raine is having a modern bedroom in twentieth-century walnut and the latest thing in curtains. Cleo says the tartan is to be our guest-room, but we shall have to choose rather unsusceptible guests."

"Or else very romantic ones," said Mr. MacAlvey. "Are we to climb any higher?"

239

"I shouldn't," said Ian frankly. "It's a bit of a howling wilderness up above. It's finally going to be licked into shape and made into pleasant staff bedrooms, and Raine had the idea of a couple of small flats for the factor and another estate man, if we ever get back to having another estate man. You see, she's already developing the clan state of mind, everybody under one roof."

"And, mercy! what is she going to do for maids in this great place?"

"I'm thankful to say that that isn't going to be such a problem. The renovation of Larrich has caused such interest in the district that we are being bombarded by young women who want to come and work here. We thought of promoting Morag to the position of housekeeper without portfolio, and getting her three or four good girls with the right feudal ideas."

"Feudal?"

"Yes. Proud to work in the laird's house for their keep and the honour of it. We can pay them something of a wage, you understand, but no fantastic modern notions. Gaelic-speaking girls with bare feet and blue eyes and plaidies on their shoulders, that's what we want at Larrich."

"And I hope you get them!" said Mr. MacAlvey, laughing heartily.

"Well, let's go down and see what we can find in the way of supper. I'll have to ask you to eat in the den and put up with all the clutter."

The den was more cluttered than ever, seeing that it was now the only habitable room in the house, and three wolfish-looking dogs rose up and fawned on the visitors.

"Nice doggies!" said Mrs. MacAlvey nervously. "They'll be nice company for Raine's Pet, won't they? Pet has fretted like anything while Raine has been away. I keep telling her that she'll be coming to live at Larrich and have lovely doggies to play with."

"H'm," said Ian doubtfully, bundling the shaggy hounds out of the room.

"Oh, and a pussy! Up on the mantelshelf. Pet loves pussies."

"That one might as well go out too," said Ian, seizing the animal and pushing it through the open window, whence it soon sprang back again and took the most comfortable chair.

There was an abundance of good food on the table, rather chancily laid out — a whole roast ham, a cold chicken, salad, buttered rolls, a dish of plums, a glass jug containing about a pint of cream, biscuits, butter, and home-made cream cheese.

While they were eating, Neil came in and greeted them.

"How are you, Larrich?" cried Mr. MacAlvey. "It's a shame to inflict ourselves on you when you're so throng already."

"Very glad to see you," said Neil. "What do you think of the house?"

"Well, it's what I'd call an ordered chaos, and it's going to be remarkable when it's finished."

"It wanted doing," said Neil.

After supper Ian·said, "What about a game of bridge?"

"I have to go out," said Neil, "but why don't you get Duncan? I know he plays."

"Duncan is the clerk of works, who's boarding with us," Ian explained. "He lives in one of the top rooms, and makes his own porridges because he says nobody else on earth can get them to his satisfaction."

"I'll go and fetch him down," said Neil. "He comes from Lanark and he's a character."

Duncan had a long stony face, a cold blue eye, and the look of a U.F. elder, but admitted to a passion for bridge.

Oh, I do hope I get to play with Alexander! thought Mrs.

MacAlvey, who had little faith in her game except with a tender partner.

Ian spread the cards and they drew for partners. Mrs. Mac-Alvey drew a three and looked eagerly to see what followed. Mr. MacAlvey drew a ten, Mr. Duncan a five, and Ian a King.

"That's Mrs. MacAlvey and Mr. Duncan against you and me," said Ian. "My cards."

Mrs. MacAlvey prayed silently and opened her cards. It was just the kind of hand she dreaded, four spades to the Jack, three small hearts, three small clubs, and three negligible diamonds.

"No bid," said Ian.

"No bid," said Mrs. MacAlvey.

"No bid," said Mr. MacAlvey.

"One nae trump," said Mr. Duncan.

"No bid," said Ian.

"Oh dear," said Mrs. MacAlvey. "I suppose I've got to give you my longest suit. . . . Two spades."

"No bid," said Mr. MacAlvey.

"Five spades," said Mr. Duncan.

Mrs. MacAlvey gave a stifled cry. "Oh but — " If there was one thing she hated more than another it was a partner who left you in what you had never intended to be a call.

Mr. MacAlvey led the five of clubs and Mr. Duncan put his hand down. It was a very good hand, its strong point being four aces, two of them singletons. There were five spades to the ace.

Mrs. MacAlvey put on the singleton ace of clubs, Ian put on the two and she added the three from her own hand and picked up the trick.

"Oh dear!" she said, looking at her remaining two clubs and her partner's trumps. "I'll never get into my own hand."

She made six tricks from her partner's hand and went down five.

"Two-fifty to us," said Ian.

"Wull I be tellin' ye hoo ye should ha' played yon hond?" said Mr. Duncan.

"Oh, please don't!" said poor Mrs. MacAlvey.

She dealt the cards and looked at her own hand. It added up to fourteen points, so she ventured, "One heart."

"One spade," said Mr. MacAlvey.

"Three hairts," said Mr. Duncan.

"No bid," said Ian.

Knowing that she had been given a double raise, Mrs. MacAlvey looked unhappily at her hand and dared not.

"Pass," she said miserably, and looking up caught the full glare of her partner's baleful eye.

He put down his cards. It was a good hand, and Mrs. MacAlvey, playing with intense concentration, was able to make her contract. She had never been so relieved about anything in her life.

"Gin ye'd led yer Queen o' clubs and finessed yer Jack o' diamonds we'd ha' made twa mair tricks," said Mr. Duncan in the voice of a hanging judge.

Mr. MacAlvey dealt the cards, and called "One heart."

"Twa diamonds," said Mr. Duncan.

"Two hearts," said Ian.

"Five diamonds," said Mrs. MacAlvey, gritting her teeth and grasping a very ordinary hand. It was some satisfaction to give Mr. Duncan as good as he gave.

Mr. Duncan played the hand without turning a hair and made his five diamonds.

"Losh! Ye're an awfu' rash bidder," he said reprovingly. "Ye fair mak' me scunner."

He dealt the cards, picked up his hand, and declared, "Three nae trumps."

"No bid," said Ian.

"No bid," said Mrs. MacAlvey, hardly glancing at her hand.

"No bid," said Mr. MacAlvey.

Mr. Duncan scooped in the tricks very quickly and said, "Game and rubber."

"Thank you very much," said Mrs. MacAlvey, feeling as though she had been playing with a boa constrictor. "Now we really must go."

"Oh, but we've hardly begun," said Ian. "You must play another rubber."

Apart from a game taken by Ian in hearts, the next rubber was played practically single-handed by Mr. Duncan.

"I never held such cards in my life," said Mr. MacAlvey.

"I'll be awa' back to ma room," said Mr. Duncan with a fierce roll of his eye. "Guid-nicht to ye all."

"Oh, but we owe you some money," said Mr. MacAlvey. "Let me see, eleven from fifteen ——"

"Gin I ever lower maself to play for money," said Mr. Duncan, "I'll let ye and the deil knaw."

"He's a great old boy," said Ian when the clerk of works was gone and they had finished laughing. "Now you know why all our eighteenth-century renovations are being carried out in the strictest Presbyterian manner. What shall we do now? Would you like to come out and see the calves?"

"Oh no, we must go," said Mrs. MacAlvey, but her husband was anxious to see the farm, so they went out.

Everything was admirably kept, and the calves were as pretty as a picture.

"This is Heather and that's Harebell," said Ian. "And this one Raine has named Holly."

"I can see Raine spending a lot of time out here on the farm," said Mr. MacAlvey. "It'll all be new to her, and she never could resist anything to do with animals."

"And won't it be fun for little Pet!" said Mrs. MacAlvey. "She'll learn to be a farm dog and drive the cows, but I'm afraid she's rather naughty with hens."

"Oh she is, is she?" said Ian grimly.

"Yes, but rather sweet the way she sidles up to them so innocently and then gives a sudden grab at their tail feathers. She'll make you laugh, Ian."

"Oh she will, will she?"

"Dear little Pet, I must tell her about the farm, she'll love it. And Raine will be home tomorrow. We've had a lovely evening, Ian, and it was kind of you to ask us here and show us everything. We're longing now to see it finished, but mercy! it'll never be done in time for you getting back from your honeymoon."

"We shall be lucky if it's finished by Christmas," said Ian; "but we don't care. We think it will be fun to live in the midst of the muddle and gradually watch it clear itself. And when Raine's on the spot she'll be able to watch the men mixing the paint, and not let them make the yellow too yellow and the blue too blue."

"She'll be a genius if she has any influence over them at all," said Raine's father. "My experience of painters is that they'll have their own way about colours, however much you argue."

"Well, before you go you must come in and have a *deoch an doruis*," said Ian.

"Oh no, thank you!" said Mr. MacAlvey. "We had one

yesterday at Drumpegge and it will last us for quite a while."

Ian walked with them to the car and stood waving as they drove away, and Mrs. MacAlvey waved to him until Larrich was out of sight.

" 'And there the auld hoose beeks and dozes,' " she quoted dreamily for the second time that evening.

"Beeks?" said Mr. MacAlvey. "What's that, anyway? Beeks!"

"I don't know either," said Mrs. MacAlvey. "But it's an awfu' nice word."

CHAPTER FIFTEEN

"As MILTON or somebody said, 'Even the weariest river winds somewhere safe to sea,' " said Primrose contentedly.

She was eating an apple and trailing her hand in the water, as Hamish McInnes's boat with Hamish at the tiller rushed on its way to Eil-oran at last.

In the boat, as well as Hamish and Primrose, were Gavin, Gull, Archie, and Elinore. Cecil had caught another cold and had had to be left behind in bed. It seemed rather mean, perhaps, to leave him all alone, but for one thing the wind was just right for Eil-oran and for another Hamish had a day off and had offered to take them, and he certainly knew how to handle *Heather Bell* to the best advantage. It was quite a squash with six in *Heather Bell*, no other boat could have taken them, and Gavin and Primrose were secretly very glad that Cecil hadn't been able to come.

"I don't think it was Milton who said that," said Elinore. "Pearl Panton says you should always verify your quotations."

"I shouldn't think it would matter when anyone has been dead as long as Milton," said Gull.

"I wasn't talking to you," said Elinore, who still continued to be slighting towards Gull, whom she considered beneath her notice.

"I can't see the point of Primrose's quotation," said Hamish, giving a snort of laughter as Primrose absentmindedly dipped the apple in the sea instead of her hand.

"It doesn't have to have a point," said Primrose. "I just felt like saying it. That's what poetry is for. 'Emotion recollected in boats.' That's Wordsworth."

"My favourite line in poetry," said Elinore, "is, 'Hearts at peace under an English heaven.' What is your favourite line, Primrose?"

"Oh, I couldn't really say, not straight off like that," said Primrose, her mind darting wildly from 'Lars Porsena of Clusium' to 'Oft had I heard of Lucy Gray.'

"My favourite line," said Archie, "is, 'And their carcasses are whirling in the Garry's deepest pool.' "

"Shut up," said Gavin. "Don't you realise we're on the sea at last and actually going to Eil-oran?"

They had already left the nearer islands behind them, and were running before a strong wind through deep green seas. The sense of adventure and freedom were exhilarating as the bubbling water tore past the gunwale and the white sails gleamed above. There is no motion in the world as thrilling as that of a heeling boat making impulsive rushes through a sun-lit ocean. They had been on their way for three hours. Nobody wanted to chatter.

For those who are interested, Eil-oran is the outermost of the group of islands that extends to the west of Strogue. It is about a mile long, never more than half a mile wide and in some places only about two hundred yards. By some freak of Nature, or owing to some unfathomed natural cause, Eil-oran

248

is quite unlike the rest of the islands, which are mere green mounds in the sea. It is like a little world in itself, with a miniature glen running through it and a lively burn flowing into dark pools fringed with rowan trees and hazels. From the sea Eil-oran is seen to be surrounded by a ring of white sands, merging into bright green turf starred with the salty flowers of sea-pinks and bladder campion. There is a brightness and bloom about the place, rising as it does out of foaming seas, which accounts for some of the mystery and romance that have become woven around this remote little isle. The local legend is that it belongs to the fairies and that mortals are better away from it. It doesn't take much in the west of Scotland to give an island a bad name, and it is always best to be on the safe side in any dealings with the *Sithe*, or Little People. Therefore it has become a tradition not to go to Eil-oran, and only on the rarest occasions does anyone venture there.

The fascination of this island for the MacAlvey children can now be easily understood. The first sight of the island, misty and alluring, sent them into ecstasies, and they could hardly wait to get ashore. The approach took some navigating, for a long low reef lay under their lee, its bubbly black seaweed just awash. A long tack brought the boat clear of the reef, and Hamish paid out the sheet and let her run down channel into a tiny bay. He grounded her, dropped anchor, and began to run down the sails.

"What are you doing that for?" said Elinore.

"Think," said Gavin scornfully. "Use your nut."

Elinore got her feet tangled in the maze of wet ropes amidships, but managed to scramble out with the others.

They all stood, rather awed, on the white sand, looking about them. A few yards away the burn found its way to the sea and the green turf that followed the sand looked invitingly soft. There were rocks too, brilliant with coloured quartz, and not far away the mysterious glen.

"Doesn't it look voluptuous?" said Primrose. "I think it is much the most exciting place we ever went to."

"Couldn't we have dinner before we do anything?" said Archie. "It's about five hours since we had breakfast, and if we don't have dinner we'll be too weak to explore. Explorers always begin by eating."

"I've never heard that," began Gavin, but Hamish was already unpacking the food. He had seen to it himself, and his landlady had the right ideas about picnic food, so it was all particularly good. There were packs of sandwiches, ham, egg, and tomato, wrapped up in separate dozens in paper napkins with pink roses round the border. This novelty added considerably to the success of the feast, especially from the point of view of Elinore, who was faddy about finding bits of the boat bottom in her food. There were also fresh scones, buttered thickly, and chunks of fruity cake. There were tarts with apple inside and biscuits with chocolate on top. Finally everybody had a bottle of fizzy orangeade, the quart size, all to himself. So superior a lunch seemed fitting for such an occasion.

After lunch they still delayed their exploring to have a bathe, and when they were dressed again it was Elinore who said, "Aren't we going to see what's on this island?"

Now that it had come to the point, everybody else showed a strange reluctance to leave the beach. It wasn't that they really believed the fairies would take them, but tradition dies hard and they had been brought up in Highland homes on the kind of story of which *Mary Rose* is an example. It was Elinore's turn to be scornful.

"You utter babies!" she said. "Afraid of the fairies! All right, you can stay on the beach, but I shall go along the glen and see if I can find some new ferns for Cecil."

She stalked away by herself and they let her go in silence. They explored the sands and caught several large crabs, then as an hour had gone by Primrose said, "Elinore is sure to be back in a few minutes. Let's get into the boat and shove off and lie under the overhanging rocks where we can't be seen. When she comes she'll think the fairies have spirited us away, or else that she's come back after fifty years. That will shake her."

"Do you think we ought to," said Gavin, "when she's our guest?"

"Do her good," said Primrose shortly.

"Let's get back into our bathing things," suggested Hamish. "Then I'll take the boat round and drop anchor under the rocks, and you can swim there without being seen."

They did this, except that Hamish himself went to sleep in the boat while the rest swam. An hour went by.

"She must be back now," said Primrose, hauling her dripping form on to the rock where she had placed her towel and clothes. "Funny we haven't heard her calling."

"Let's dress and go back," said Gavin. "It was rather a feeble joke, anyway. She's sure to be on the beach."

They roused Hamish and, leaving the boat at anchor, clambered over the rocks back to the beach. There was not a sign of Elinore, beyond her footsteps on the sand going towards the glen, but none returning.

"She's been gone two hours," said Primrose, beginning to feel a slight coldness round her middle.

"If she's picking ferns, she won't have noticed how the time is going," said Gull. "We'll have to explore the island and find her. It's only small, it can't take long."

With one accord they made for the glen.

"Elinore!" they were shouting. "Elinore! ELINORE!"

Everywhere was the silence of desolate places. The only sounds were the far wash of the waves, the tinkle of the burn, the crying of gulls.

"My Russian rabbits!" said Gavin.

"We've just got to find her," said Primrose. "She must be farther on."

They began to search the island. Separately and in pairs they covered every part of it. They became very hot and hardly noticed how romantic Eil-oran was or how prettily the rowans grew beside the water. They were satisfied that if Elinore was on the island they must have found her or made her hear them, but there was no sign of Elinore.

Gull had a look of genuine awe on her face.

"It's happened," she said. "The *sithe* have taken her."

"Rot," said Primrose, angry as one is when another puts one's secret fears into words. "She's probably trying to put one over on us like we did on her. Let's go back to the beach and pack up the tack as though we were getting ready to leave without her. That'll make her appear. She's probably hiding and watching us now."

They went back to the beach, where they found Archie, who had taken no part in the search, lying on his back in the sand, and spent a long time collecting their things, but no Elinore appeared.

"They've got her all right," said Gull. "What do you think, Hamish?"

"Beats me," said Hamish, who, being the only grown-up of the party, was beginning to feel uncomfortably responsible.

"I'll like to see Granny's face," said Gavin, "when we go

back and say we've left Elinore on Eil-oran with the fairies for fifty years or so."

Primrose looked at him blankly, and all their spirits began to sink. What had begun in fun had now gone far beyond a joke.

But it is time to go back to Elinore herself. When she left the others on the beach she wandered happily along the shady glen, feeling pleased with herself. She knew, for instance, that her hair was nice — much nicer than Primrose's or that horrid little Gull's — and that she had on smart white strapped shoes and her prettiest dress of pale green linen, so that if unknown to her any fairy was watching her, he — or she, or it — would be bound to say, What beauteous mortal maiden is this? Elinore got a good deal of pleasure from thinking of herself as a beauteous mortal maiden.

It was delightful to wander by the shallow burn, amber-coloured and laced with creamy foam as it bubbled over the stones. Hart's-tongue fern grew beside it, with musk and reeds with pinkish flowers, and the cool shade of overhanging rocks was welcome in the heat. There was a great humming going on from millions of gnats and other insects, and Elinore had to keep stopping to scratch her bare legs, for though the Scottish midges are tiny they seem to have enormous teeth. She scanned the ground as she went, and every now and then stooped to pick something and place it carefully with the small bunch of ferns in her left hand. She was a good and conscientious sister, and was happy to think of the pleasure she would be bringing to Cecil with these new specimens for his collection.

Presently she began to feel tired so, seeing that the glen opened out upon sand-dunes, she went and sat down there and was rewarded by a breeze off the sea. In her lap she spread out her slightly wilted ferns. She wasn't anxious to go back and join the others, she felt quite happy alone. Tonight, she decided, she would write a long letter to her friend Pearl Panton and tell her how she wished they were together. Pearl was so poised, so sophisticated, she would make Primrose — who thought so much of herself — look small.

If only, thought Elinore, I could be exactly like Pearl!

That was really what was wrong with Elinore. If she had been content to let herself be herself she might have proved quite a likeable person, but instead of that she spent her whole time in trying to be like Pearl Panton, and the result, as might be expected, was neither Pearl nor Elinore, but an affected little nobody. The pity of it was that Elinore would never see her mistake, but would spend her whole life trying to be what she wasn't, and was already on the way to becoming one of those women who try to be impressive and only succeed in being disliked.

Sitting there upon the sand-dunes in the sun, far away from the others and not caring, gazing out at the misty blue sea, Elinore gave a sigh and as she did so she heard a low rumbling noise like gentle thunder. Almost before she had time to wonder what it was, she felt herself slipping as the sand gave way beneath her. The sand all round her was sliding and falling and Elinore was sliding and falling too. She couldn't possibly stop herself, there was nothing to hold on to. She shrieked as everything began to go dark and the sunlit day disappeared, and then there came a bump and, gasping for breath and spitting sand out of her mouth, she opened her eyes and found herself in a kind of sandy underground cave with a round hole above her head, roofed with blue sky.

"Help!" yelled Elinore. "Help! Help! Primrose! Gavin! Help!"

Her voice only echoed in a hollow way round her prison,

and she realised that barely a whisper of it must have risen to the outer air. Every time she tried to move she slipped and slithered. It then occurred to Elinore that she was in a very tight spot indeed. She was in a kind of underground box with only a ragged hole high above her head leading to the light of day, and unless somebody actually happened to be near the hole when she happened to shout she wouldn't be heard at all. The others would eventually search for her, but they might never come near this place. And the worst thing of all was that they would give up looking for her, because they believed in fairies and would conclude the fairies had taken her, and would sail off home and leave her to her fate — as Simon and the ghillie left Mary Rose.

And then . . . ! Poor Elinore, sick with fright now, could not bear to think of it. Although she was fourteen and a great student of poise and sophistication, she forgot all that and lay in her sandy prison and cried and cried. Then she fell into a panic and shouted again until her voice grew hoarse and weak and she realised that nothing she could do was any use.

As she tried to drag her feet from the clogging sand a worse thing happened, for the rumbling noise came again, and again she felt everything slipping from under her, and again she was swept down, down, this time into complete darkness. All other dismay paled before this. She struck the bottom at last and was really hurt, for the ground she fell upon was hard, and lumps of all kinds of things that had accompanied her in her descent began to fall upon her.

Elinore lay on her face, too miserable to move or stir. She thought she must be at the bottom of a mine.

No use to shout now. She was far, far underground. What would become of her? A long time seemed to crawl by, and then — as usually happens in dark places — the darkness didn't seem to be pitch black, after all. It was greyish, and Elinore could discern something like a rocky wall and other rock shapes. Then she realised that she was lying on pebbles and that pebbles were wet.

She picked one up and smelt its saltiness, touched it to her lips and tasted the sea. Wet, and yet not under water? What could that mean? She groped about with her hands and seized a great bunch of what felt like seaweed. Yes, it was seaweed — loose, wet seaweed. Then the sea must have been in this place, and recently! Could it possibly be a cave into which the sea came at high tide? Because if that was the case, then this must be low tide and there must be a way out!

Hardly daring to pursue this new hope, Elinore struggled to her feet and began groping her way forward. There was just enough of the faint grey light to keep her from crashing into loose rocks. The cave was long, she kept close to the dripping walls, then suddenly the wall ended, she lost her balance and sat down in a pool, in a mess of sopping seaweed.

Choking, she scrambled out of the pool on her hands and knees. She couldn't stand much more of this. But as she lifted her head she found that she had turned a corner, and there before her was a small arch of daylight that was the mouth of the cave. It was still a long way off, but it was the Way Out! Elinore's relief could not be exaggerated. She was not going to die of starvation in the dark, after all. She started at a run towards the light and tripping over some obstruction fell flat, completing the ruin of her dress and shoes. She felt behind her to find what she had tripped over, and discovered that it was a wooden box about a foot square. It was soggy with sea-water but not very heavy, so she heaved it up and staggered along with it to the mouth of the cave.

She emerged into the sunshine of a tiny bay of white sand,

256

and found herself crying again because the nightmare was over and she had come back to life.

Not far away the rest of the party sat in a silent row, too worried to talk. By Primrose's watch it was ten minutes past five. If they sailed for home now, it would be past eight o'clock when they arrived. How could they stay any longer, yet how could they leave Elinore? Hamish was the most worried of all, because he didn't like the look of the sky. It was going to be a rough night, and the sooner they got home the better. *Heather Bell* was slow to windward. Suddenly Archie gave a yell which, coming on top of their suspense, nearly startled the others out of their senses.

"There she is! It's Elinore!"

The figure climbing over the rocks from the farther bay certainly had a look of Elinore — and who else could it be? — but it was plastered with dirt and wet sand and soaked in seawater. Its frock looked like a wet rag and its hair was just a tangled dripping floor-mop.

"It's Elinore all right," said Primrose. "My sorrow!" she added as her cousin came in earshot, "what have you been doing to yourself?"

"Was it the fairies?" shouted Gull excitedly.

"There was a landslide," said Elinore with great dignity, "and I fell miles down into an underground cave. I then crawled for miles and miles till I found the mouth of the cave, and I found this box there. I think it must have been washed up from a Spanish galleon at the time of the Armada. If it's full of gold and jewels, they're mine."

"They're not, you know," said Hamish. "They're treasure trove, the King's."

They all crowded round Elinore, staring at the box.

257

"It's mine," said Elinore. "Who's going to know?"

"Oh, give me one!" cried Gull. "Just one teeny weeny little jewel, Elinore!"

"Why should I?" said Elinore unkindly. "You never gave me anything."

"You needn't worry, Gull," said Gavin. "It says Irish Butter on the box."

"Where?" shouted Elinore indignantly.

"There — it's washed out, but you can still read it."

Elinore went red with annoyance, and Hamish obligingly unsheathed his knife and prised up the lid of the box. What was inside may once have been Irish butter, but now looked very peculiar indeed.

"Washed up from a wreck," said Hamish, "but not the Armada."

"Of all the beastly places," said Elinore, "this is the worst. My dress! My hair!"

"Look," said Hamish. "We ought to be getting away. You stay here and I'll bring the boat round. I left her anchored beyond those rocks when we —— " He stopped in time not to say 'when we were hiding from Elinore.'

"We'll have to wade out," said Gavin when Hamish had gone. "He'll be yards off-shore."

In a few moments Hamish was back from the rocks, looking rather dazed.

"Where's the boat?" he said.

"How do you mean — where's the boat?"

"She's not there."

"She must be!"

"I tell you, she isn't."

"Did you leave her safe?"

"Of course. Have any of you played a fool joke?"

258

"Of course not," they all cried, and suddenly Gavin caught sight of his young brother's face.

"You've been up to something, Archie! What have you done with the boat?"

Archie went white with horror.

"Gavin, I didn't mean to — I —— "

"What did you do? Come on, where's the boat?" yelled Gavin, seizing Archie by the shoulder in anything but a tender manner.

"I only — well, it was while you were all looking for Elinore. I wanted to see if I could take *Heather Bell* out and bring her in again, by myself, and it was a good chance, so I did. But I dropped anchor. Honestly!"

"Dropped anchor, my foot!" said Primrose. "She's dragged her anchor. Archie! You didn't hoist the sails?"

"Yes, I did," blubbered her young brother. "I wanted to see if I could, and I did. I fastened the halyards fast to a cleat too. I —— "

"Archie," said Hamish, "you didn't leave her without lowering the sails?"

Archie made sobbing noises.

"I heard you coming. I meant to go back in a few minutes. I —— "

The others stared at each other in complete dismay. Then they rushed to the beach and stared out to sea, but there was no sign of *Heather Bell*. The wind had by now carried her far to leeward.

"You've done some mad things in your time, young Archie," said Gavin violently, "but this crowns the lot. I suppose you realise that we're here for the rest of our lives? And we've used all the food!"

259

CHAPTER SIXTEEN

WHEN Cleo and Raine came off the train at Inverness that evening, the first person they saw was Neil with the car.

"He's come to meet us!" cried Raine in delight. "Now we shan't have to wait for that incredibly slow train."

Neil blushed slightly as they came towards him, and said, "I had to come into town, so Ian suggested I should pick you up. He told me to tell you, Raine, that you'd better come and use your influence on the plumber. He says you can't have your pipes where you want them."

Chatting ardently about pipes, they walked towards the car, and, still talking, Raine got into the front with Neil, while Cleo struggled into the back with most of the luggage and a lot of stuff that Neil had bought in Inverness. This had a tendency to topple every time the car went round a bend, and Cleo sat with her hands above her head and wondered if she could stand it for three hours.

The two in front were sublimely unconscious of her plight and, having finished with pipes, were now on the subject of pigs, which Neil had decided to go in for on a larger scale.

"I've got a new patent trough in the back there," he observed.

So that's what it is, thought Cleo, thrusting aside some object whose sharp corners had been causing her pain for a long time.

Finishing with pigs — which at the best of times she was not greatly interested in — Raine was off gaily on the subject of pictures. Would Ian, did Neil suppose, feel it *infra dig.* to buy some old ancestral-looking paintings she had seen in Edinburgh? And what was Neil's own reaction? After all, Larrich was his house. She really did have a hankering after those oil-paintings if no one minded. . . .

Does everything they talk about have to begin with P? thought Cleo, shifting her tired shoulders so that something soft and heavy immediately fell upon her head and nearly suffocated her.

"Are you still there?" called Raine cheerfully.

"Only just," said Cleo in a muffled voice. "I'm merely being slowly smothered by that eiderdown you insisted on bringing back with you instead of letting them send it."

"Shove it somewhere else," said Raine carelessly, as though there were anywhere else to shove it.

"Can I do anything about it?" said Neil.

"Not a thing," said Cleo, nettled beyond endurance by their nonchalance. "Just go on talking about things beginning with P."

"But how can we?" said Raine. "P? Why P? All the things I hate begin with P, like plastic raincoats, and pink, and picking fruit, and phoney people."

"Did you have a good time in Edinburgh?" asked Neil, changing the subject, and Raine cried, "Yes, we had a wonderful time and bought everything we wanted. I mean, strictly speaking, everything I wanted. The Edinburgh shops are magnificent, but a lot of the things are meant for English tourists. They had silk nighties in Cameron tartan."

"You didn't ——" began Neil in horror.

"Of course not. Ian would shoot me. But we bought my wedding dress and the bridesmaids' dresses, and we even took a plunge and bought dresses for Mother and Vannah. We knew the sizes, and there's a woman in Dunmaig who's good at alterations, if you can restrain her tendency to sew little bows and bits of lace all over your ensemble."

Neil laughed, and Cleo thought, how lovely to be able to chat carelessly to him like that, about dresses. While she was always racking her brains to think of something intelligent to rouse Neil's interest or something romantic to put him in the right mood, along came Raine prattling about shopping, and he actually laughed.

"Oh, but we haven't told you about going to see Auntie Kat," cried Raine, bouncing with excitement. "You tell him, Cleo. I'm breathless."

"She isn't really our aunt," said Cleo. "She's Mother's cousin. We thought it might be prudent to call on her while we were in Edinburgh in case she found out afterwards that we'd been and hadn't called, as people seem to do in some psychic way."

"It took us several hours," said Raine, "to get up enough strength to ring her on the telephone, but at last we did and were we glad! She ——"

"She said she knew we were in town already," said Cleo, "because her maid had seen us waiting for the tram in Princes Street. Can you beat that? The maid of course has known us from our blameless infancy. She has been with Auntie Kat for forty-five years."

"Forty-six," said Raine.

262

"Forty-five," said Cleo firmly.

"It makes a difference," said Neil.

"Be quiet, Larrich," said Raine. "The point is, she told us she had a wedding present for me, two very valuable articles, and would we call round for them and take them home ourselves, as she had been worrying about how to get them to Strogue."

"So we said yes, we would," said Cleo, "and for the rest of the evening we discussed what they could be."

"Works of art," said Raine. "You forgot. She said they were works of art."

"Oh yes, because we decided they must be pictures. You thought they were a couple of Gainsboroughs, Raine, and I guessed they were *Wedded Lovers* and *The Battle of Bannockburn*. They had to be huge, otherwise she could have sent them by registered post."

"What were they?" asked Neil, manlike, anxious to get to the point.

"Oh, we're not nearly there yet," said Raine. "We went round to her house next morning and had sherry and Bath Olivers in the drawing-room."

"What are Bath Olivers?"

"Very superior English biscuits. The sherry was extremely potent."

"Tell Neil about the cat-pens," said Cleo.

"Oh yes! Round her dining-room Auntie has got eight cat-pens with a cat in each sitting on a different coloured cushion. She has them called after English kings and queens, like Henry Tudor and Farmer George. We could have suggested a few names she hadn't used."

"The main thing we were terrified of," said Cleo, "was that she would want to leave us her furniture in her will. There

263

was a sideboard twelve feet long and as high, made of solid teak, and her bed —— "

"An eight-tonner," said Raine.

"What about these art treasures?" said Neil.

"Don't be so impatient. She talked for ages about declining values in a doomed world. She told us that many of her shares were now valueless, and though she had personally written to the Chancellor of the Exchequer, nothing had been done. She said that what Scotland needed was another John Knox, didn't we agree? And I said, absolutely."

"I was for arguing it out," said Cleo, "but Raine —— "

"I wanted to get on to the presents," said Raine.

"So do I," said Neil.

"Oh, we're not nearly there yet. She said there wasn't a divine in Edinburgh she could sit under; so she went to Leith every Sunday, where there was somebody rather like John Knox, and if only we would stay over next Sunday she would take us. I said we couldn't, though we'd have loved to."

"And then," said Cleo, "she asked us if we had ever been down her cellars and would we like to, they were very old and dark and some Covenanters had once been hidden there. I said no thank you, we both suffered from severe claustrophobia and might go mad, and she said that that reminded her of a friend of hers who got lost in the catacombs in Rome and was never seen again. This brought us to the subject of how most of her friends had met their ends, but the catacomb story was the best value, all the others had very humdrum deaths. Then she told us that she was actually wearing a dress that was made in 1903, but the brush braid wanted renewing and there wasn't a shop where she could buy brush braid. She said the Edinburgh shops had gone down a lot since she was a girl. At last we got to the presents."

264

"What a relief!" said Neil. "What were they?"

"Let me tell him," said Raine. "Marble busts. Two of them, about eighteen inches high, of two very noble-looking men, eighteenth-century types. Only we didn't know who they were and we didn't like to ask."

"What did you say?"

"I said, Thank you very much, and Cleo said, How impressive."

"But what did you do with them?"

"What could we do with them? Brought them with us, of course. They're in the boot, in that case that the porter could hardly lift. I really don't know where I'm going to put them — at Larrich, I mean. Do you think they'd make hat-holders, like the ones in milliners' shops?"

"I'll tell you when I've seen them," said Neil, stopping the car.

He cut the rope on the wooden case with his clasp-knife, and Raine took out one of the busts and nearly dropped it on his foot.

"It's real marble," said Cleo.

Raine dragged out the other bust and stood the pair side by side on the road.

"I'll tell you what," said Neil glowering, "those are not going anywhere at Larrich. They're English generals, Cope and Wade."

"Oh no!" cried Cleo, appalled.

"That's who they are, I tell you."

"I don't believe you," said Raine, "but the more I look at them the less I like them. We'll dump them at our house. Mother can find room for them somewhere."

"Oh no, you don't!" said Cleo. "You know what Mother is, she won't want to hurt Auntie Kat's feelings, and she'll put

265

them in somebody's bedroom, who'll throw them out, and eventually they'll become mine. If they really are Cope and Wade, they've come to the right place to be executed."

"That's easy," said Neil. "We'll be crossing the river in about five minutes."

"Right!" said Raine. "We'll pack them in the back till we get to the river. All aboard."

With Cope and Wade on either side, Cleo found it impossible to move her knees, but it was not far to the river. Neil stopped the car on the bridge, and they all got out and waited rather self-consciously for a lorry and another car to pass. When the road was clear they got Wade out and stood him on the parapet.

"Should we or should we not?" said Raine at the last minute.

"They're your property," said Cleo. "I couldn't care less."

Neil looked furtively from side to side, but there was nothing coming along the road.

"Now or never," he said, and Raine gave a shove. Wade shot over the parapet and vanished. There followed a heavy splash.

"That's one," said Raine. "Give me Cope."

"Quick," said Neil, "there's a car coming."

Over went Cope and splashed to his doom.

The car drew up and two policemen got out.

"What was yon you were clumping into the river?" said the sergeant.

"Only some rubbish," said Neil.

"I'll have to ask for your names and addresses."

"Why?" said Raine.

"These are the Misses MacAlvey of Strogue," said Neil, "and I am Neil Garvine of Larrich." He looked proud and incorruptible.

"I'm sorry to trouble you," said the sergeant, "but we're looking for some stolen jewels, and it's just the sort of way they'll be disposed of."

"That has nothing to do with us," said Cleo.

"You haven't told me yet," said the sergeant, "what you were toppling into the river. It was something big and heavy, so don't tell me it was your lunch paper."

"I'll tell you," said Raine. "It was a wedding present I didn't want, and that's the truth."

"It's a gey likely story," said the police sergeant.

Raine, who was one of those people whom to doubt was to whip into maniacal fury, shrieked, "How dare you not believe me!" and Cleo said, "Shut up, Raine!" and to the sergeant, "What she said was quite true, and we always do unlikely things and we've got a perfect right to."

The sergeant went and looked over the parapet and there in the clear water he saw the two marble busts lying on the bottom, the features foreshortened by ripples on the surface.

"Come here wi' ye, Robert," he said. "There's pairts of two men in the burn. Go ye down and get them up." This sounded so Biblical that Cleo began to giggle and Neil shouted, "Ha! ha!" at the top of his voice.

The young policeman got very wet rescuing the busts, for though he rolled his trousers above the knees the water was deceptively deep and he went in almost to the waist. He came out clutching the heavy things and swearing fiercely.

"What are they?" said the sergeant to Neil.

"They're busts of English generals," said Neil. "Cope and Wade that they sent against us in the '45. Now you know why we were drowning them."

"Why didna you tell us that before?" said the young policeman, disgustedly.

"You'd have said it was a gey likely story," said Neil.

267

"There's something inside of this one," said the sergeant, shaking Wade and looking suspiciously at Cleo, who couldn't stop laughing. He turned the bust upside down and saw a small round hole in the base.

"It wouldna be his dennerrr?" said Neil sarcastically, imitating the policeman's Lowland tongue.

"Gi' us yer bit corkscrew," said the sergeant to Robert.

With a good deal of effort he extracted a rolled-up envelope from the marble interior, and reading the blurred writing said, "It's addressed to Miss Raine MacAlvey. Would that be one of you?"

"It's mine," said Raine, snatching the envelope and recognising Auntie Kat's spidery handwriting, though the ink had run badly in the water. She tore it open and discovered a roll of five-pound notes, so tightly packed that though the outer ones were soaked, those inside were not wet at all.

"Oh, darling Auntie Kat!" she cried. "I am a beast. But why did she do such a fool thing? She must have catacombs on the brain."

"How much is there?" asked Cleo.

"I'm counting. Twelve, thirteen, fourteen. Fourteen! What's fourteen fives, Neil?"

"Is that money hers?" asked the sergeant. "What for would she be tossing it into the water?"

"Thanks to you," said Neil, superbly illogical, "the poor wee girl nearly lost her wedding money."

"I'm sorry, miss," said the sergeant automatically. Cleo giggled, and the constable said to Neil curiously, "Is it you she's marrying on?"

"That's no business of yours," said Neil.

"Is there anything in the other one?'" said Cleo, and she

268

and Raine both began to shake Cope furiously, but there was nothing inside.

"Done again!" said Raine.

"Ye dinna want much, do ye?" said the constable.

"That's finished with Wade and Cope," said Cleo. "Let's bung them back in the river and get along home."

"You'll do no such thing!" yelled Raine. "They're my present from darling Auntie Kat, and I shall keep them as long as I live. It was disgusting of you to try to make me drown them. Give the poor things to me. I'll have little niches made for them in the wall at Larrich —— "

"Not while I'm living!" said Neil. "Not English generals. I'll burn the house down first."

"They're not really English generals," said Cleo. "I think they're actually Beethoven and Mozart. It was you who said they were Wade and Cope. You didn't look properly."

"See here!" said Neil, snatching one of the busts from Raine's tender clasp and flourishing it at the sergeant. "Would you say this was the man they've got a beastly likeness of at Inverness Castle?"

"It's no him," said the sergeant. "There's nae resemblance."

"Darling!" said Raine, beaming at the law. "Give it me back, Neil, and do let's go home."

"I've got all your parteeculars," said the sergeant, "so I'll let ye know if ye're wanted again. The licht-hairted way ye carry on I'd have said ye were English yourselves."

"We asked for it," said Cleo, bustling the others into the car.

"You'll have to have these in with you," said Raine, bundling the busts round Cleo's feet and crushing her into immobility. "Or I'll sit in the back and you can go in front with Neil."

"After all, it is your stuff," said Cleo, extricating herself with care. "Will you have me, Neil?"

"Ha! ha!" guffawed the young policeman. "If he says yes in front of us witnesses you'll be married on him and a dafter wedding I never saw."

"Get in, will you!" said Neil, bright scarlet, but not so embarrassed as Cleo, who dropped her handbag, the contents of which rolled all over the road, while Raine laughed heartlessly.

At last they were off, and as Raine seemed to have gone to sleep in the back of the car and Cleo couldn't think of anything to say, a long silence set in and lasted all the way to Strogue.

In the garden Mrs. MacAlvey was struggling along behind the lawn-mower.

"Calum's got lumbago," she explained, "and I don't seem to be making any headway at all."

It was a beautiful evening. The grass was silvered with dew and all the flowers were giving out their night scents. From the other side of the lane you could hear the peaceful sound that sheep make while grazing, brushing with busy little bites the warm turf. The still air was full of dancing gnats.

"You leave that heavy job, Mrs. MacAlvey," said Neil. "I'll do it with pleasure."

"Now that's sweet of you!" cried Mrs. MacAlvey, seizing both her daughters and kissing them fondly. "Did you have a nice journey? It seems a month since you went away. Daddy and I have had some lovely visits, I must tell you when there's time. Mercy, what a car load! You didn't buy all that?"

"Some of it's Neil's," said Cleo.

"It's nearly dark, Neil," cried Raine. "Leave that, do."

"Not till I've finished."

"You'll be there all night."

270

"There'll be a moon."

Raine and Cleo began to unpack the car, which took a long time, as Mrs. MacAlvey seized each package as it appeared and cried, "What is this?"

"We'll be here till daybreak if you don't let us get them into the house, Mummy," said Cleo.

"Mercy! You didn't buy those?" shrieked Mrs. MacAlvey, catching sight of the two marble busts on the floor of the car.

"Those are Raine's wedding present from Auntie Kat."

Mrs. MacAlvey put her head on one side thoughtfully.

"They'll make door-stops for Larrich."

"I never thought of that. How ingenious!" said Raine. "Who do you think they are supposed to be?"

"Well, they're poets, aren't they? Walter Scott and Robbie Burns?"

"They're all things to all men," said Cleo. "Tell her what was in them, Raine."

"Fourteen five-pound notes, Mummy. Isn't it a silly number?"

"Seventy pounds? You ungrateful girl!" cried Mrs. MacAlvey with incredibly swift mental arithmetic.

"Is it as much as that?" said Raine. "I can't multiply. I had to put down five fourteen times and add up and I made it sixty. Do let's have some supper and then I'll tell you about the dresses."

"We were going to wait supper for the children," said Mrs. MacAlvey, "but they're away somewhere in the boat. It's downright wicked of them to be so late. Oh, look at that poor boy slaving!"

Neil was still working, out there in the falling dark, as though releasing some fierce pent-up energy.

"Call him in for supper, Raine."

"He won't come till he's finished, I know him," said Raine, rushing as if famished to her place at the dining-room table.

"The children," said Mrs. MacAlvey, looking round helplessly.

"Need we wait?" said Cleo, as hungry as Raine. "Do you know where they went to?"

"They said something about going sailing with Hamish McInnes because his boat was big enough to hold them all, but they didn't say where they were going. They never do, and you know how I hate to look interfering."

"You interfered with us in our day," said Raine. "We always had to say where we were going. It's quite true that grandmothers are not fit persons to bring up children. Talk about indulgence!"

"When you come to think of it," said Cleo, "we don't know a single thing the children have done or a single place they've been to these holidays. They're always on the point of slipping away, and so silent at meals! Do they ever talk? I suppose they have some interests of their own."

"I suppose they talk among themselves," said Mrs. MacAlvey vaguely. "But I wish they'd come home. Cecil is in bed with a cold, and he keeps sending Mysie to ask where Elinore is — as if I knew! Those two children fuss too much."

A swish of wind came suddenly in at the open window, and as suddenly died away, leaving a waiting silence.

Neil came in, putting on his coat, and said, "The wind's working round to the south-west. It looks like being a rough night."

"You've said the wrong thing," said Raine, carving him a lavish slice of meat-pie. "Mustard? And a piece? Mother is worried to death because the children haven't come home. They've been out all day sailing with Hamish McInnes."

272

"Well, he's reliable," said Neil comfortingly, eating hard. "But it's past nine o'clock."

Mr. MacAlvey suddenly appeared in his old fishing mackintosh.

"I've been to the village," he said, "to see if anybody knows where the children went — oh, hullo, Larrich. Home again, girls?"

"When they do come back," said Raine, "Cleo and I are going to take them in hand and shape their future lives, aren't we, Cleo?"

"A little discipline," said Cleo, "will do them no harm."

"Is there anything I can do?" said Neil.

"There's nothing anybody can do. Apparently they sailed in Hamish's *Heather Bell*, and it's round the village that they were making for Eil-oran."

"*Heather Bell*'s a big boat and has good sails on her," said Neil. "But it would take them all of three hours to come from Eil-oran. They shouldn't have left it so late."

The telephone began to ring in the hall.

"I'll go," said Mr. MacAlvey.

They heard his voice, enquiring at first, grow full of consternation.

Everybody ran into the hall.

"What is it?" cried Mrs. MacAlvey. "Tell me, Alexander."

He turned round, his face blank with horror.

"Get your father a chair," said Mrs. MacAlvey briskly, keeping her head. "Now, Alexander, what is it?"

"It's *Heather Bell*. A trawler has picked her up at sea. Capsized."

It was Mrs. MacAlvey who sank into the chair. The others stared in silence.

Mr. MacAlvey went on, "Her foresail had been torn away,

273

only a shred of it left hanging from the yard, and her lug was trailing."

"I'm going down to see the trawler," said Neil. "What's she doing at Strogue, anyway?"

"Put in to escape the gale, I suppose."

"We must get a launch to put out from Dunmaig," said Neil. "Don't worry, girls. Cheer up, Mrs. MacAlvey. They'll have been safely picked up, I've no doubt."

"I'm coming with you," said Mr. MacAlvey. "Stay with your mother, girls," he added hastily, seeing Cleo and Raine begin to make a dash to the mack-room.

When the men had gone, the silence was dreadful. The hall was piled with Raine's parcels, which nobody had the heart to clear away, much less unpack. In the midst of this Ian — whom everybody, even his fiancée, had forgotten — rang up to ask if the girls had been duly met and conveyed home, and where was Neil? When he was told what had happened, he said he would go straight over to Dunmaig and see about a launch. He would have to ride. He would go and saddle a horse.

"Oh, don't go to Dunmaig, Neil is doing that, come here and talk to us!" cried Raine. "It's quite medieval to leave the women at home doing nothing."

Ian arrived within the hour, but fidgeted and was obviously longing to be off to any scene of action.

"Go then, go!" said Raine at last. "You're too exasperating."

"Try to get some rest," said Ian fatuously, remembering this phrase from the films.

At that moment the telephone rang, and it was Neil, from the village, to say he was coming up for the car and then going on to Dunmaig, so Ian offered to take the car down to meet him, and duly departed. The hours dragged on. Soon after midnight Neil — who was behaving most conscientiously about telephone calls — rang from Dunmaig to say the storm was abating, and they were just about to set off for Eil-oran in a motor-launch, but he sounded so gloomy that Cleo who answered the phone was convinced that all hope had been abandoned, though Raine pointed out that he was probably only cold and hungry, for nobody in their senses could be pleased about setting out for Eil-oran in the middle of the night in an open launch.

"All I hope is," said Mrs. MacAlvey, "that Alexander has had the sense not to go with them."

Shortly after, Ian rang up from Dunmaig to say that Mr. MacAlvey had insisted on going in the launch; so as there wasn't room for anybody else he, Ian, was waiting with the car, and James was with him, and they had got a bottle of whisky, and practically the whole of the town was down at the pier.

The thought of the excitement that was going on at Dunmaig because her grandchildren were lost at sea took the last spark of vitality out of poor Mrs. MacAlvey and she consented to lie down on the settee and be covered with a rug, but tossed and turned so much that the rug spent most of its time on the floor, while Cleo and Raine and Miss Paige renewed the hot-water bottles in all the beds, made coffee which nobody wanted to drink, and tried not to scream at Mrs. Mortimer and Mysie, who kept popping their heads out of their bedroom doors and asking insane questions like, "Have you heard anything yet?"

"It's nearly daylight," said Raine at last. "How callous of Ian not to ring us during all these hours."

At that moment the telephone bell rang out shrill and sudden through the house. Cleo was the first to get to the phone, but she had barely lifted the receiver when Raine yelled, "This is Kilchro House. What's happened?"

"They're back," said Ian in a completely matter-of-fact voice. "I thought you'd like to know."

"Who's back?" shrieked Raine. "Everybody? The children?"

"Yes. They were marooned on Eil-oran."

"Are they all right?"

"Losh, yes. But drenched to the skin. It rained all the way back in the launch. We're all starting for home in a minute."

"Is that Father? Is he alive?" cried Mrs. MacAlvey feverishly, dragging her rug behind her like a train.

"They're *all* all right, Mummy. They're coming home."

"What a relief. They'll be hungry. Bless them!"

"I'd bless them with a Lochaber axe," said Raine.

The tension relieved, she flopped down on her knees in the hall, ripped open the nearest parcel and held up a length of dress silk.

"I knew it was too blue," she said. "You ought to have stopped me buying it, Cleo. Now you'd better buy it back from me."

"I don't think I want it," said Cleo, bouncing down on the hall floor beside Raine and fingering the despised silk. Life was normal again, except that they didn't usually do this at six o'clock in the morning.

276

CHAPTER SEVENTEEN

Suddenly the house was full of people. Elinore was the first to rush in, crying dramatically, "Please, please don't worry! We're all safe!"

"They're not worrying," growled Primrose, glaring at Elinore for thus seeking the limelight. "They're making dresses on the floor."

"What did it feel like when you thought we were dead?" asked Gavin in a deeply interested voice, while Archie added proudly, "*Heather Bell* got washed out to sea. It was my fault. I'm that hungry!"

"Poor laddie!" cried Mrs. MacAlvey, clasping her youngest grandson to her breast. "My poor wee man!"

"He isn't, you know," said Gavin. "He's a criminal."

"Here's somebody else," said Ian, unwrapping his plaid from Gull who looked like a drowned kitten, while the hall door opened wide to admit a chilly blast along with Mr. MacAlvey and Neil, both purple with cold and filthy with rain after six hours in the open launch. More people arrived, including neighbours who wanted to know if they could 'do anything,' and with everybody milling about or falling over Raine's parcels, it became more and more like a wet day at the Highland Gathering.

Raine herself came out of the kitchen with a tray of steaming cups.

"Take them," she said, "it's as much as I can do to hold the tray up."

The cups were snatched.

"How many more?" asked Raine.

"Dozens," said Primrose, her wet hair plastered like seaweed over her face.

But Raine brought from the kitchen only one cup, large and gaily coloured, with the legend A Present from Ballater, and this she gave to Ian, saying, "This is specially for you. Heather ale!"

Excitedly he sipped, and cried with unconcealed disappointment, "It isn't! It's only cocoa!"

"Have you no imagination?" said Raine.

How like life! thought Cleo. You think you are getting heather ale, that drink of forgotten magic whose secret was buried with the ancient clans, that gave valour to men and beauty to women, that swirled richly in the quaich with its swooning fragrance — and in the end it is only cocoa.

The telephone rang and Ian answered it.

"The police," he said. "They want to know if anyone's dead."

"They're hounding us down!" said Cleo bitingly, and began to relate the story of the busts and the bridge, to which no one listened. She wished she had been the one to think of that old heather ale thing, and had found a brightly patterned cup to present to Neil; but even if she had thought of it, she wouldn't have had the courage. So far as Neil was concerned, she always had behaved like the family half-wit and always would,

278

shooting away like a startled sheep rather than engage him in conversation. Being on the go continuously for twenty-four hours didn't help you to be intelligent, and it was just so long since she and Raine had got up in the hotel bedroom in Edinburgh. Yet somebody had to be talking to Neil, and it was Gavin — who also had been on the go for twenty-four hours without impairing his faculties in the slightest — and the two of them were laughing over some private joke as they tried to beat the wet out of their trouser legs. Gavin's voice rose excitedly as he told how he planned to visit Eil-oran again, in *Minnow*, 'and without any women' — casting a glance over his shoulder to make sure that Primrose was not listening.

"For between you and me, Larrich," he went on, as man to man, "it's women who have ruined these holidays."

"Mercy!" cried Mrs. MacAlvey, catching sight of Gull, who had sat down on Cleo's suitcase to devour hot toast. "There's Malvina! They'll be out of their minds wondering where she is. Somebody ring up the Castle and tell Lord Cronisdale his daughter's safe!"

Primrose grinned with glee as she saw Elinore's unbelieving eyes staring at the despised Gull; and she cried, "I'll do it. I'll go and ring at once."

"You needn't really bother," said Gull. "I don't suppose they've missed me. I'm always popping in and out of windows."

But the Marquess of Cronisdale evidently thought it fun to leap from his bed at 6:30 a.m. to collect his dripping daughter from Kilchro House, and he arrived with his hair unbrushed and the elbows out of his old shooting-coat, and accepting a glass of brandy — which was by now being served to the seniors — seemed reluctant to leave, and told a lot of angling stories to people who were standing round, and by then the wet ones had gone up in relays to bathe and change and had appeared

279

again in the oddest garments, and Raine was still on her knees in the hall absorbed in showing Ian what she had bought in Edinburgh, and the maids were about and breakfast nearly ready, and Cleo having washed her face in stinging cold water was beginning to feel human again and ready for anything.

The gong sounded with deafening gaiety.

There was no hesitating to accept its invitation, and twenty-two packed themselves round the breakfast table where Elinore, who with superb strategy had contrived to slip herself in between Cronisdale and Gull, could hardly eat anything for rehearsing how she would tell Pearl Panton that she had sat at breakfast with a marquess on one side of her and his daughter, Lady Malvina Tordoch, on the other. Minor details, of course, would need to be suppressed, such as the way the marquess ate kippers with his fingers, and the fact that Lady Malvina was dressed in a pair of boy's shorts and a lumber jacket without any buttons. Life in the Highlands, decided Elinore, was quite mad. On the one hand it was steeped in romance; on the other it was sordid beyond the dreams of English respectability. But what a story she would make of it when she got back to school!

The morning sun shone in wicked brilliance straight through the dining-room window into the eyes of Cleo, but the besotted girl gloried in the discomfort, for she had had the nerve to displace Gavin from Neil's side and sit down there herself, and though she couldn't think of anything to say, and up to now Neil had taken practically no notice of her, she felt extremely happy, for there is something comfortable about coping with kippers next to a man you love. The cocoa, Cleo decided, might even be turning into heather ale.

Meanwhile everybody talked at once, while one or two even

burst into song, and it turned out to be one of the best parties ever held at Kilchro.

"What do we do next?" whispered Mrs. MacAlvey to Raine, for she was sixty-six and feeling the strain.

"Oh, just let them drift. They'll probably drop off to sleep after this, and there are plenty of chairs, so it doesn't matter if they stay all day," said Raine cheerfully.

Though nobody knew when anybody else had actually left, they were all gone by lunch-time, and the chairs in the drawing-room were empty, except for a few of the MacAlveys themselves who slept until late afternoon.

The only one who suffered at all was Mr. MacAlvey, who developed a severe chill and was in bed for a week, but after the first three days of fever and misery — worse for the family than for the patient since a man in bed turns the whole house into an emergency hospital — he enjoyed having his friends call at all hours of the day to chat and smoke in his bedroom, and bring him a nice fish or a brace of grouse and the local gossip.

Among these visitors came Inga Duthie, a charming sick-room guest, in pink with mauve accessories. She brought mannish books, purple grapes of the kind one has to be practically dying to get, two bottles of vintage port, and a large Dundee cake of incredible richness and fruitiness, which she said she had made herself. She stayed for an hour, while peals of laughter rang out from the open windows of the sickroom. It was as though the fairies had descended upon Kilchro House.

When Cleo took up her father's supper, he showed her the two bottles of port — one of which he had already opened so that he and Inga could sample it together — and the grapes and the books, for the cake had already been removed lest he eat too much of it, and said, "Sweeter woman ne'er drew breath" — meaning Inga.

"I can't think why she should be so kind to us," said Mrs. MacAlvey, for she, like everybody in the house, could talk of nothing but the glamorous visitor. "It's just sheer goodness of heart."

"Didn't she look wonderful?" said Raine. "A pink tailored suit. That's something I never thought of. Just a pink tailored suit — but how tailored! And her hat! And her bag! And her gloves! And her —— "

At heart, thought Cleo, I must be a beast. She reflected miserably for a few minutes on the deterioration of her character since she came home from America. She had always despised women who hated their rivals and slunk about green with jealousy and grew into curdled old maids with gall dripping from their withered lips, and now she was well on the way to being one of their number. She gazed at herself in the mirror, and wondered if her eyes were too close together, the chief sign of a malicious nature. 'I fear the Greeks especially when they bring gifts' was a hackneyed saying, but horribly applicable to the present situation. And yet — to visit poor Father in his affliction was surely no out-of-the-way thing for a family friend to do, even so exotic a family friend as Mrs. Duthie.

But — 'What's in it for Inga?' Cleo's lower nature kept on saying, and the vulgar sentiment, proceeding no doubt from unplumbed depths of vulgarity in her own nature, shocked and depressed her as she admitted it.

A few days later she said to Raine, "Did you tell Ian about the things Inga brought for Father?"

"Why yes," Raine said. "I took over a chunk of the cake, and we ate it on the stairs because there was nowhere else to sit. Neil said, had Inga really made it herself, and if so, why couldn't *he* be ill?"

"Oh!" said Cleo, who from the arrangement of the almonds was certain that the cake had come from McVitie's of Edinburgh. The sermon the following Sunday morning was on 'Think no evil,' and so obviously divinely inspired for her benefit that the only alternatives left to her seemed to be to love Inga or to stop going to kirk.

There was no escaping Inga either, because on Monday afternoon she turned up with Raine's wedding present, a small round-topped antique chest, heavily ornamented with brass squiggles and said to be the one in which Prince Charlie had carried his personal effects when he fled to Skye disguised as Betty Burke.

"Of course one can't prove it or disprove it," said Inga, "but I do think it has atmosphere. I mean, if you put your hand on it and shut your eyes you can literally feel something."

"Literally," said Raine, putting her hand on the chest and getting a deep scratch from one of the squiggles which had worked loose. "But I think it's awfully romantic, and thank you very much, Inga; I don't know how you can part with it."

"Oh well ——" said Inga modestly. "It suits Larrich much more than it does my house, and I thought you could use it for a slipper-box. And I brought this also, as a little personal gift to you," she added, producing a large cut-glass scent bottle, in which an ounce of Devon Violets, which was Raine's wildest extravagance in the way of perfumery, would look like a halfpenny on the collection plate.

Before this there had been another departure, and so far as the family were concerned Elinore and Cecil had passed away as silently and imperceptibly as they had arrived. Primrose,

Gavin, and Archie, however, made of their cousins' leaving a major event. As if in atonement for the coldness with which they had greeted their arrival, they gave Elinore and Cecil a royal send-off, with promises to write often and send any snapshots which might have come out. One feels this way disposed to parting guests however much of a bore their visit may have seemed while it lasted, and somehow Cecil and Elinore had become inextricably mixed up with heavenly sunshot memories of sea and boats and picnic meals on island shores, and summer holidays regrettably past. Primrose, Gavin, and Archie would never think of these holidays again without thinking of Elinore and Cecil, blots though they had been, yet somehow part of the fun. So, returning from Inverbyne station whence their cousins had just been carried away on the 10:40 train, sharing a bar of rather old chocolate discovered in the pocket of Primrose's coat which she had not had on for several weeks, they all said, "Won't it seem funny without Cecil and Elinore?"

"And without Gull," said Primrose sadly, for Gull had already gone back to school. "Gosh, I wish it was Christmas."

"I wish it would jump every year from September to about December the twenty-second," said Gavin, "and then from the end of the Christmas holidays to Easter and then to July breaking-up."

He sighed, ruthlessly wishing his youth away.

Triumphantly Mr. MacAlvey came downstairs, restored to health, seized rod and line, and slipped out of the back door unnoticed. With her own hands Mrs. MacAlvey prepared a strengthening drink of eggs and milk with a dash of brandy, placed the glass on a tray, and brought it into the morning-room where a chair lined with rugs stood empty beside a welcoming fire.

"Alexander! Where are you, Alexander?"

She put down the tray and looked round helplessly.

"Raine, where's your father?"

"I haven't the foggiest, Mummy. Where should he be?"

"Ask Cleo."

"*She* won't know."

Mr. MacAlvey, coming in two hours later with four grilse, was unperturbed and said he never felt better in his life.

"But it isn't *normal!*" cried Mrs. MacAlvey, struggling between relief and fury. "Can't any of my family be normal?"

She sat down weakly in the chair with the rugs and drank off the strengthening drink — now stone cold.

Raine came back from Larrich, and said that everything was behind schedule. Instead of returning from their honeymoon to reasonable comfort, they would have to pick their way over the entrails of the plumbing system and eat off a card-table in the hall, which was the only part of the house the decorators hadn't got at.

"Do you mean you want to postpone the wedding?" said Mrs. MacAlvey, horrified but resigned to anything.

"Of course not!" said Raine, amazed at the suggestion. A world where people waited for builders and plumbers to finish what they were at was beyond her comprehension. All she wanted was to get married to Ian and live in an easy-going muddle which showed every promise of lasting until Christmas. It was Highland life, where there's always another day.

The only thing she got excited about was that Ian had been in Fort William and had met his father's old piper, Ben Macquarrie, who was out of a job since he left the Army and living on odd pints and very down in the mouth, and Ben had said he would like to come back to Larrich and work on the land; so he was coming and there would be a piper again at

285

Larrich as in the mighty days of yore. It seemed not only to put Larrich on the up-grade at once, but, so far as Neil, Ian, and Raine were concerned, to solve the whole problem of the decline of the Highlands. Ben, who had left Larrich in 1934 to make his fortune, had actually fallen so low as to play his pipes on the tourist steamers between Fort William and Oban for English pennies, but now these degrading days were over, and when they came back from their honeymoon he would meet the bride and groom on the threshold with a tune he was composing for the occasion called *Iain's Return.*

CHAPTER EIGHTEEN

N̲ow, I am not going to stand any nonsense from Mrs. Din-widdie," said Mrs. MacAlvey when she and Raine were settled in the bus. "I shall say to her quite firmly, 'Mrs. Dinwiddie, I want you to make this dress fit me, and by that I mean that you will not alter the style, or add little bows here and there, or remodel the sleeves.' I shall show her that I know what I want, and I am not going to be thwarted. Mrs. Dinwiddie was always too fond of having her own way regardless of her cus-tomers' wishes, and I hear she has got worse since she began to sew for a few of the County people. I do dislike to see any-one spoiled by success. I can remember her when she was Mary Deas and glad to go out to do household mending for half a crown a day and her dinner. I shall find it quite difficult to remember to call her Mrs. Dinwiddie."

"Woodie," said Raine.

"Woodie? Don't be silly! I'm sure there's a Din in it some-where."

"Yes, Mummy. Dinwoodie."

"Well, I shall say to her, 'Mrs. Dinwoodie, I am quite satis-fied with everything about the dress which my daughter has bought for me in Edinburgh, except that I want you to make it fit a little better on the shoulders. . . .' "

Mrs. Dinwoodie lived in an ugly little house which had once been the U.F. manse at Dunmaig. It was a narrow little house, yet had a cramped bay-window on either side of the front door as though determined to be double-fronted or die in the attempt, while the tight net curtains drawn across the lower halves of the windows gave an impression that the whole house had coyly dropped its eyelids. The woodwork was newly painted in a repellent shade of chocolate-brown which jarred with the flaming pink of the Dorothy Perkins standards dotting each section of tiny lawn, and one was not surprised to see that the ornamental shingle hanging from two gilt chains at the lintel and lettered in gold bore the name, *Inverary*. It had to be either *Inverary* or *Dunstaffnage*.

"I haven't been to her for ages," said Mrs. MacAlvey. "I hope she won't think I'm making a convenience of her."

That, unfortunately, was only too clearly what Mrs. Dinwoodie did think. She opened the door herself, wearing a tape measure round her neck, a pin-cushion attached to the front of her blouse, and trailing over her arm a length of sky-blue taffeta. At first she affected not to know who the visitors were, but when she heard the name cried, "Mrs. MacAlvey, of course! And is this your daughter? Come into the workroom, if you don't mind; the girl's just doing up the sitting-room, and you know how it is!"

She led the way to the room on the left of the door, which was the workroom and tremendously littered with the evidences of her industry, and brushing a pile of odds and ends from two chairs said, "Do sit down. Have you come on the bus? Very nice weather, isn't it? Though I must say I'm too busy to notice. Just wait a minute, if you don't mind, and

I'll be with you." She evidently meant to be with them in the spiritual and intellectual sense, for she was obviously very much with them physically. Mrs. Dinwoodie cannot have weighed much less than twenty stone, and the room was tiny, having been originally designed for a very thin minister's study.

"This house is very inadequate, if you know what I mean," she said, unwinding the sky-blue taffeta from her arm and doing something to it with pins. "But I suppose one is lucky to have a house at all in these days, isn't one?"

"I have a little work for you, Mrs. Dinwoodie," said Mrs. MacAlvey. "It won't take up much of your time and I shall be very grateful if you can —— "

"Four inches — no — yes — just a minute, if you don't mind," said Mrs. Dinwoodie.

It was obvious that one was going to have to be tactful and ingratiating, for already Mrs. MacAlvey's promises to be firm and commanding had all faded away, since in these days one no longer conferred a favour by giving work but received a favour in having one's work accepted.

Mrs. Dinwoodie pushed the taffeta aside at last and said, "Well, I suppose I'll have to fit you in somewhere, though I'm very rushed at the moment with this big wedding I'm doing. Miss Christy Platt. You'll know the Platts, of course?" Seeing the politely blank look on her visitors' faces, she went on, "Don't you know the Platts? Big County people. I am surprised! Six bridesmaids — four adults and two tinies. I'll be up all night this week."

"You do seem to be busy," said Mrs. MacAlvey. "Well, mine is only a small thing. My daughter is getting married in a fortnight and —— "

"A *fortnight!*" said Mrs. Dinwoodie with a shriek, "Why,

289

that doesn't give me any time at all. I mean, I'll do what I can but — what was it then?" And the dressmaker pressed her hand to the side of her head and looked as though she was calculating the number of bridesmaids' dresses she could construct in fourteen days.

"It's just a little alteration," said Mrs. MacAlvey nervously. "Nothing at all really. Just the shoulders of a frock."

"Now what frock would that be?" said Mrs. Dinwoodie, in a tone that plainly said she couldn't remember making anything for Mrs. MacAlvey in years.

Mrs. MacAlvey turned pink and fiddled with her gloves.

"Well, you know that coat-frock I bought in Aberdeen during the war, and the hip-line wasn't quite right and you did it for me?"

"Oh," said Mrs. Dinwoodie, with a suggestion of imminent ground-frost.

"It isn't that one I'm talking about now, of course. But my daughter has bought me a frock in Edinburgh to wear for the wedding, and the shoulders want a little —— "

"I see!" said Mrs. Dinwoodie, as though there was very little she didn't see. She pulled up a chair with her toe and sank into it ponderously. "Well, I don't know, I'm sure, Mrs. MacAlvey. I mean, after all, I'm a dressmaker. A modiste, if I may venture to call myself that. I mean, it's all very well buying dresses here and there. Other people's bad work, as you might say. I mean, I *make* dresses, you know, Mrs. MacAlvey, if you know what I mean."

"Oh, I do!" said Mrs. MacAlvey, wishing herself through the floor and looking at Raine's blank face for guidance, which was not forthcoming. "But you used to — I'm afraid I took it for granted —— "

"Ah," said Mrs. Dinwoodie with a discouraging cough. She went into deep thought for a minute, and then said, "If I do it, you understand, it will be just to oblige. I mean, I wouldn't want it to go any farther. It's quite out of my line, altering other people's awkward dresses. It seems a pity you didn't come to me in the first place. I've got some lovely broché, powder blue, I could have made you a very graceful gown. It really does seem a pity. A great pity!"

"I do hope you can see your way," said Mrs. MacAlvey humbly. "You made a splendid job of that coat-frock I bought in Aberdeen —— "

"Ah, that was a long time ago," said Mrs. Dinwoodie, in the tone of a great couturier looking back to his apprentice days. "I suppose there wouldn't be anything else? The brides-maids —— "

"Raine bought those in Edinburgh too. The frocks I mean."

"I see," said Mrs. Dinwoodie coldly. "Well, I suppose I'll have to help you out, though I do hope you'll understand it's just for the once. Have you the dress with you?"

"Yes, it's here." Thankfully Mrs. MacAlvey began to pull the string off the dress-box and to strew tissue-paper on the floor. "This is it. Shall I slip it on? The shoulders —— "

"H'm," said Mrs. Dinwoodie, rising with an effort and picking up a corner of the dress between her fingers. "I can't say I see you in beige."

"It's a very good dress. Raine —— "

"H'm. Well, I suppose you'd better slip it on."

"Oh, thank you!" said Mrs. MacAlvey fervently. "I really am very grateful."

"Tch! Tch! Tch!" said Mrs. Dinwoodie, surveying her customer in the dress, and thereby reducing Mrs. MacAlvey to a state in which the only thing to do seemed to be to tear off the offensive rag and wear her old green to the wedding.

"It's a beautiful dress," said Raine, opening her mouth for the first time. "I got it at the best shop in Edinburgh. You look marvellous in it, Mother. It only wants lifting a little on the shoulders. Vannah could have done it herself."

"And is this the young lady who's getting married?" said Mrs. Dinwoodie, surveying Raine from top to toe with a deeply malevolent smile. "I see lots of blushing brides in here, you know. And who's the lucky gentleman?"

"It's Mr. Ian Garvine of Larrich," broke forth Mrs. Mac-Alvey happily, feeling that all was well and disposed to be chatty. "You'll know the Garvines, of course. They've remade the old house, it's fine now. The wedding's on September the eleventh, and everything's arranged but the weather, so we'll have to hope."

"Oh yes, I know the Garvines," said Mrs. Dinwoodie. "Mr. Ian Garvine! Well, I am surprised! I didn't know he was getting married. But then he's not the first to be caught on the rebound. If I just raise it here — that'll do, Mrs. MacAlvey, you can take it off."

"Rebound?" said Mrs. MacAlvey vaguely, hardly knowing what she said and struggling out of the sleeves of the beige gown.

Mrs. Dinwoodie helped her graciously. "Well, you know how he was over Miss Nona MacKenzie at Mossgiel. Never off the doorstep, right through the war. Everybody thought, but there — one mustn't gossip, must one? Especially in my profession. She got married in the end, and they say poor Mr. Ian took it badly. But that's all over and done with. She wasn't in his class, and class does count, doesn't it? Mossgiel is just a tenant farmer, a mere crofter, as you might say, though he and the girls do a bit of riding and shooting, apeing the gentry. I'm letting my tongue run away with me. Now when would you be wanting this?"

"As soon as possible," said Mrs. MacAlvey firmly.

"I'll get it done some time next week and post it to you. Will that do? And I'll be having some nice woollens in shortly. A two-piece, say? Very becoming to the older lady, Mrs. Mac-Alvey. Perhaps —— "

"Er — yes — perhaps," said Mrs. MacAlvey, back in her own dress and hastily picking up her bag and gloves. "Thank you, Mrs. Dinwoodie. Thank you very much. I'll let myself out — good-bye — my daughter — we're in rather a hurry. My address? Oh, you know — Kilchro House —— "

"I know," said Mrs. Dinwoodie. "I like to do a favour. Good-bye, Mrs. MacAlvey. I do hope I shall see you again soon. It will be two guineas if you care to —— "

"Oh, of course!" Mrs. MacAlvey rooted through her bag and found two pound-notes and a florin. She was past arguing about the extortionate nature of the charge.

She hurried down the path after Raine, who was looking distastefully at the standard roses, and said, "Well, I suppose that will be all right. We've time for a cup of coffee before the bus. I thought she wasn't going to do it. I wouldn't take any notice of what she said about — I mean —— "

"I expect it's true," said Raine stolidly. "We saw nothing of Ian during the war, he had the farm to run with Neil away. And we didn't know him very well in those days."

"Are you upset?" asked Mrs. MacAlvey, anxiously trying to interpret Raine's rather baffling expression.

"Not a bit. It happens all the time."

"Thank goodness. I was so afraid you'd be proud and call the wedding off."

293

Raine smiled. "It's the wrong reaction, Mother. This is 1948, not 1908. I can take it, even being a second-best."

"Oh, don't say that," said Mrs. MacAlvey, leading the way into the Silver Tassie Café. "Any woman knows you have to spend your life making allowances for men. They don't look at things as we do, not at one single thing in life. You'll find that out. And they expect you to understand. You don't understand, but you pretend to."

"Two coffees," said Raine to the waitress, "and some cakes. Éclairs."

"Two coff and plate of mixed," said the waitress in an effortless shout directed towards the back regions.

"Of all the revolting women!" said Raine. "But you won't have to go again, she's posting it. I wouldn't put it past her to ruin it, out of spite."

"Oh, I don't think she'd do that, dear," said Mrs. MacAlvey mildly. "She's got her professional reputation to think of. And she charged me two guineas. I could have got it done by Norman Hartnell for that."

"You need never go again."

"Oh, I don't know. I felt a bit cheeky, going for just an alteration when it wasn't her dress. Are you coming back with me on the bus or —— "

"I said I'd go up to the butts," said Raine, devouring in two bites the only éclair on the plate of mixed. "They're shooting over Praddaside with that English lot that rented the moor."

"That's nice for you," said Mrs. MacAlvey, gathering up her bag and gloves happily. "But do be careful. I hate guns."

"I may not see anybody I want to shoot," said Raine.

She saw her mother off and found her own bus. It took her to within a mile of the shoot, and she began to scramble up the long hillside in the heat. The stony track was unpleasant for walking and the flies persistent, but it was a lovely day, with a blue, unstained sky smiling down on the heather. Raine, who disliked shooting and only showed an interest in it because it was the thing to do, would not have minded if she had never got to the butts. Some sandwiches and a book would have done just as well, but as she had no sandwiches or book she was driven to press on until in the wake of a volley of gunfire she found herself at the first of the butts, which seemed to be full of people. This was only due to the frenzied activity which takes place when everybody is wondering what they have bagged, and by the time a couple of brace had been brought in and things were calmer, Raine saw that the occupants of the butt were Colonel Mayhampton, who was lying on his stomach against the parapet of turf looking along his gun barrel as though it had let him down, his wife, who was sitting on a shooting-stick in pastel-pink tweeds and pearls, and a young man with an eyeshade who was counting the bag in a noisy don't-interrupt-me voice.

"Why, it's Miss MacAlvey!" cried Mrs. Mayhampton. "Or is it?" She put her head on one side, and swept the cock's-feather plume with which her hat was adorned out of her eye. "What a pleasure to see a different face. I don't know why we do this. You know my husband, don't you? Splendid! And Captain Parsons? Ah, I thought so. Are you coming to join us? There isn't much room, but I'm dying for somebody to talk to. Thomas, where's that little folding stool —— "

"Look," said Colonel Mayhampton, "could you be a bit quieter? Chatter puts me off."

"And then you'll shoot a beater," said his wife. "That's what always happens, isn't it, Miss MacAlvey?"

295

"Only in books," said Raine. "Have you got a good bag?"

"I haven't the slightest idea. Thomas, have we got a good bag?"

"So-so," said the young man with the eyeshade. "The birds are a bit furtive. Yes, definitely intricate."

"We got a couple of brace that time," said the Colonel, "so the ruddy thing can't have misfired, but I'd have sworn it did."

"Don't you shoot, Mrs. Mayhampton?" said Raine.

"Now, do I look as if I did?" Mrs. Mayhampton sighed, considering the contrast between her nylons and huge ghillie shoes. "I think as regards entertainment it's the depths. There isn't a bit of comfort, and I hate eating out of doors and beating the midges to it, and the cotton-wool always falls out of my ears just before the bang. Then there's the nervous tension, thinking that a beater is going to be shot."

"Oh, do stop harping on that!" said her husband. "The English may take their pleasures sadly, but the Scots take theirs in absolute misery."

"If you think this is awful, you've never been deer-stalking," said Raine. "Crawling for hours on your stomach through scratchy heather, and then you point like a dog and your nose is pressed flat against a hot rock, or down into a bog, which happens more often. You get home practically unconscious, and sit licking your wounds for days and digging bits of granite out of your scalp. You must try it some time, it's thrilling."

"Could you be a little quieter?" said the Colonel, as he saw the line of beaters advancing and the next moment the birds came over rather spread out and straggling, and a crackling volley ran along the butts. Mrs. Mayhampton shrieked and pressed her hands to her ears.

296

"There!" said the Colonel. "Both the ruddy barrels misfired. You missed too, Thomas."

"I didn't. I definitely winged one."

"Not you. Not a hope."

The two men began to argue violently, and the Colonel ended it by saying, "It was Linda's fault for yelling out."

"I didn't yell till you'd fired," said Linda. "I waited on purpose." She looked at Raine, straightened her pearls, and said, "*Mon dieu!*"

A cloud suddenly obscured the sun, and with the variableness of Highland weather the temperature seemed to drop a few degrees.

"Do they stop if it rains?" said Mrs. Mayhampton hopefully.

"Aren't you shooting today, Miss MacAlvey?" asked the young man called Captain Parsons. "By jove, I never underrate you Scotch girls. Met a girl at Fort William last year who was photographed with forty brace she'd brought down in a day — or was it a day? I forget. But it was prodigious. Perhaps you know her? Her name was Macdonald, it seems to have stuck in my memory."

"I'll have to have my other gun," said the Colonel loudly. "Where's that ghillie of mine? Oh, he's over in the next butt arguing about the birds. Well, he's wrong, I didn't get anything that time."

"I'm supposed to be joining my fiancé," said Raine. "I'm not much of a shot, but I can load."

"Oh, are you engaged?" cried Mrs. Mayhampton. "Practically every girl I know seems to be engaged; I suppose it's getting towards the end of the season. Is he anybody I know?"

"It's Ian Garvine," said Raine.

"By God, so it is!" shouted the Colonel, peering over the turf. "Arguing hell for leather with my ghillie."

"Miss MacAlvey means that she's engaged to our nice land-lord, George."

"I don't," said Raine. "He's the laird's brother."

"The laird's brother!" repeated Mrs. Mayhampton. "Doesn't it sound sweet and quaint and Biblical? That's what I like about Scotland. That and the food. I'm sure I've eaten enough in the last eight days to last me for a year. You never think" — she added, looking reproachfully at Raine — "while you are gorging your enormous Caledonian meals about us poor starving Londoners. Or do you?"

"Oh, but I do!" cried Raine fervently. "I just picture you fainting in platoons in Trafalgar Square."

"Well, that's neither here nor there," said Mrs. Mayhampton. "Oh, here comes our ghillie! Did you ever see anyone so large? I think it must be glandular, though his limbs look firm. We're going to be such a crowd in this little butt —— "

"But I'm going," said Raine, smiling brightly all around and making her farewells, not flattered by the look of relief on Colonel Mayhampton's face.

"Oh, here you are at last!" cried Ian, as she entered the butt where he and his ghillie were counting over a large bag. "I might have known you'd come in time for lunch. How do you like the Mayhamptons?"

"I should think they'd be quite a success in London. Are they paying you a lot of money? Do you want me to load any guns?"

"No, you're too late. In my haversack you'll find a cold grouse pie and a bottle of hock. Rude fare, but appetising. Yes, they are paying me a lot of money, almost enough to marry on."

"Was it being short of money that stopped you marrying Nona MacKenzie?" said Raine.

"No, of course it wasn't," said Ian calmly. "Why bring that up?"

"Listen," said Raine, picking up a dead grouse and ruffling its feathers. "It never occurred to me that you had a Past, Ian. But if you had a Past — and it appears that you had — I should like better to have heard of it from you than from a scruffy little dressmaker in Dunmaig with a tongue like a snake."

Ian put out his hand and took the grouse from her. He laid it down with the others and said, "But it's all so long ago."

"Not really long ago. Not as time goes. Only a few years."

"Long enough," said Ian, beginning to cut the cold pie with what looked like a well-used hunting-knife. "It's all over and done with."

"I'm sorry," said Raine, "that it still hurts you to talk about it. But you ought to have told me, just the same."

"Hurts me — rot!" said Ian with a splutter. "What are you talking about? Have you gone mad?"

"Mrs. Dinwoodie says I caught you on the rebound."

"Who the hell is Mrs. Dinwoodie?"

"That's beside the point. And stop swearing, Ian, it's a sign of emotional instability. You should have told me about Nona MacKenzie. You'd better tell me now."

"But there's nothing to tell. I liked her, but she liked another chap better."

"When you say you liked her, I suppose you mean you were madly in love with her?"

"All right. What of it? It died out years ago," said Ian cheerfully, adding, "Have some pie, it'll do you good."

"You don't deceive me," said Raine, "by being casual. I'd rather you didn't pretend, honestly I would. It's a blow to know I'm second-best, but I can take it."

"Thundering hell!" said Ian. "Second-best? What are you talking about? Eat your lunch and have some sense."

"I suppose every time you look at me," said Raine, "you keep thinking what might have been."

"I can't imagine," said Ian, "how girls ever get married at all when they can't realise when a man loves them. One swallow doesn't make a summer."

"I don't in the least know what you mean by that. Is Nona MacKenzie the swallow, or am I?"

"Now, Raine, don't get me tangled up," said Ian apprehensively, looking longingly at the grouse pie and laying it down on the ground. "Let's get back to the beginning again. You say I ought to have told you, and I say there was nothing to tell —— "

"I wouldn't have minded a mere nothing," interrupted Raine dismally, "but a grand passion is so very something."

Ian tugged at his tie and gulped.

"You didn't expect me to tell you about all the meals I ate before I started coming to your house."

"Ian Garvine! You're not comparing being in love to eating meals!"

"It seems to me much the same thing," said Ian stubbornly. "And talking of eating, don't you think we might call a truce on this argument while we have lunch? I haven't eaten since half-past six this morning."

Raine was famished too, and while she was hesitating Ian managed to thrust a huge slice of pie and a plastic mug full of hock into her hand. They both ate furiously and in silence. The sky was clouded over now and a chilly wind blew. Somewhere far off a sheep made plaintive noises and a curlew overhead echoed the sound more eerily. Apart from that, there was a vast cosmic hush.

"I've done," said Raine.

"Would you rather have cake or apple or both?"

"Cake."

Ian passed her a wedge and took one himself. They disposed of this in four or five bites, and cleared up the remains of the feast.

"Now that's over," said Raine, "do you mind if we start arguing again?"

"If I say I'm sorry, will that settle it?"

"No. I know you're sorry, but it settles nothing. I may be a sordid little unloved swallow, but I've got feelings."

"Have you got the nerve to stand there and say I don't love you?"

Rather taken aback, Raine thought for a moment and said, "You've got something there. Yes, I believe you do love me, in a rather second-morn sort of way."

"Second *what?*"

"You know. Emily Brontë. 'No second morn has ever shone for me.' Though I wouldn't go so far as to say I shone for you. I probably gave a sort of watery glint."

"I see! You think I'm hankering after —— "

"There! You find it difficult to say her name. That's a sign."

"You didn't give me the chance to. You were so anxious to get your silly little wisecrack in."

"Now you're getting bitter. That's another sign."

"You're out of your mind."

"That's not a very convincing thing to say."

"Oh! You want to be convinced?"

"I don't know what I want."

"I could try kissing you but we're visible here for miles round."

"That's a man's answer for everything."

301

"Look, who did you say was the woman who started all this? Is she within murderable distance?"

"Oh Ian would you really murder Mrs. Dinwoodie for me?"

"Is that her name? And what was it she said?"

"That I'd caught you on the rebound from Nona Mac-Kenzie."

"The woman ought to be locked up!"

"In olden days that's what they did to people who told the unpalatable truth."

"You *believed* this 'rebound' business? You ought to be ashamed to admit it," said Ian coldly.

"Tell me it isn't true and I'll believe you. Naturally."

"I shall not lower myself," said Ian with that Highland pride which had so foolishly sent his ancestors and forebears to their deaths rather than answer their English inquisitors.

"Then we're back where we started," said Raine, who by now knew that she was beaten and had been rather a fool about the whole thing. "We shall have to go on arguing some day when we've time. But you said a few minutes ago that we were visible for miles round. I can't see anybody or hear anything. Isn't this supposed to be a shoot?"

Ian looked round wildly.

"Good heavens! They were going to move over to the other side of the moor after lunch. They've gone and left us, and we never saw or heard a thing."

"But your ghillie!"

"He's so tactful he'd never interrupt us. He'll have gone with the others."

Raine leaned against the butt and shrieked with laughter. When she recovered she said, "I've spoilt your day's shooting. Oh, Ian, I am sorry. Do you want to go after them?"

"It isn't worth it," Ian said. He laughed and added, "I don't care. Let's go home. You'll have to help me to the car with all these birds."

"I'm truly sorry. It was my fault."

"I don't mind a bit. Look, there seems to be a lot of stuff to carry."

When they were loaded up with guns, birds, haversacks, mackintoshes and gum-boots, they advanced across the heather at a crawling pace.

"Ah, there they are," said Ian as a crackle of gunfire rang out in the far distance. It was followed immediately by a long low howl.

"What was that?" said Ian. "It sounded human."

"Colonel Mayhampton has shot a beater at last," said Raine cheerfully. "Linda said he was going to."

"Said he was going to shoot a beater? You don't mean deliberately?"

"It's an English custom."

"Oh," said Ian.

He tramped on for a few minutes across the shoulder of the moor, his keen gaze ranging far ahead, then with a sudden excited, "Sssh! Down!" he fell flat under his burdens in the heather and dragged Raine down with him.

"Give me my glasses! Quick!"

"What is it?"

"Look!"

Adjusting the lens with hot pricking fingers, Raine saw in the little white circle the tiny picture of a feeding stag, perhaps a mile away. His magnificent head was outlined against the sky, monarch of the wilderness.

"Drop the stuff," hissed Ian. "Keep down. Follow me. We

303

must make that corrie before he gets our wind. Give me the gun — no, the other one, silly — and the unopened box of cartridges. Now don't talk any more. You're stalking."

"Help!" said Raine with a groan, dropping her face into the scratchy heather for several hours of agonised crawling behind Ian's nailed boots. She didn't care. She was utterly convinced that he loved her.

CHAPTER NINETEEN

Aᴏᴛᴇʀ two or three false starts, Cleo awoke to find it actually was The Day. She rushed to the window and looked out. A grey mist was steaming up from the earth towards an ethereal pinkish haze which was the sky, while far away on the eastern horizon she could see orange and crimson stripes where the sun was about to come up.

"A lovely day!" said Cleo, reaching for her watch. It was ten to six.

Incredibly early as was the hour, Primrose and Gavin were already panting up the brae, carrying wet bathing suits. The magic light of dawn seemed to clothe them in mystery, they looked like two slender figures from the morning of the world, timeless and eternally young. Seeing them, Cleo's heart was moved with a queer feeling that between their minds and hers ran invisible threads of sympathy. She knew what they were thinking as they ran lightly up the steep hill, knew that in each young breast burned the thought, This is the end. A solemn rather than a carelessly happy moment for those two. The end of lovely freedom, the end of summer, the end of a boy's dream of becoming the best amateur helmsman in Scotland, the end of all those things one planned to do when time seemed limitless and proved so fleeting. There would be other summers, of course, but to fifteen (nearly sixteen) and fourteen (nearly fifteen) next year seems a lifetime away.

When the holidays began, Primrose and Gavin were thinking simultaneously, there seemed to be time to do everything we'd planned, and somehow it has gone and in three or four days we shall be back at school leaving islands unexplored and a dear little boat wilting in its winter quarters. It was heart-rending.

In the kitchen at Kilchro House Cleo had made tea. The boy and girl came in silently, a little subdued. Their faces brightened at the sight of gay cups and a steaming tea-pot.

"You bathed very early," said Cleo.

"Couldn't sleep," said Gavin tersely.

"Nerves," said Primrose in a rather grown-up way. "But the water was heavenly. School — after this!"

"If it wasn't for the wedding," said Gavin, "we should be having our end-of-the-holidays treat today."

"The wedding *is* your end-of-the-holidays treat," said Cleo, drawing into her lungs the sweet fragrance of a Player's.

Gavin gave her a long, bitter look, and Primrose's hand shot out, whisked away the cigarette and placed it to fresh lips. Primrose took a lung-filling draw.

"Thanks," she said. "I needed that."

The maids appeared with a view to getting something done, and Cleo in her blue silk housecoat rushed upstairs.

Mrs. MacAlvey's head came round the bedroom door.

"Mother! Go back to bed. It's far too early to get up."

"You're up! I can't sleep any more. Oh, I do hope Raine is asleep. I'm going to ring for tea. Mysie will have a fit, but I can't wait any longer. Is it going to be a fine day?"

306

"Magnificent. The sun is struggling out of a golden mist and the sky is turning blue. Gavin and Primrose have been bathing. They looked like the Golden Age."

It seemed hours until breakfast. Archie rushed into the dining-room entranced.

"They're actually putting up the marquee! A huge marquee with red and white stripes like a circus. Supposing," he added hopefully, "that it turned out to be a circus by mistake!"

"Cleo dear," said Mrs. MacAlvey, "would you do a rather special tray for Raine? Something very dainty. I don't suppose she'll be able to look at any breakfast. Brides never do."

"Why?" said Primrose.

Cleo, who knew Raine better, loaded several plates to capacity, and then ran out into the garden and cut a red rose. This she laid on the tray. Sentimental, perhaps, but just that touch of the romantic to offset the sausages.

She looked the tray over approvingly and carried it upstairs.

Raine sat up in bed in her old striped pyjamas, and surveyed her breakfast with enthusiasm. Her eyes fixed themselves on the rose.

"Was that, by any chance, Ian's idea?"

"Mine, I'm afraid."

"He wouldn't have the imagination. Anyway, it looks a bit corny. What a good thing I'll wear long gloves. Look at my scars!"

"It's that day you went stalking. They look awful."

"Five hours of it. And we lost the stag. I prayed we would. What sort of a day is it?"

"Lovely. And the marquee has come. Can you eat egg, bacon, sausage, and mushrooms?"

"Why not? I'll be down in half an hour."

"Oh no. No, Raine, you mustn't. You must stay up here."

"Whatever for? Don't be silly. I want to see them put up the marquee. I've always wanted to see a marquee put up, and I'll never have another chance."

"I ought to see that your packing is done. There won't be much time later."

"There's always time," said Raine vaguely, "and I'm not taking much luggage. You know how I leave things in drawers when I stay in hotels. I'd sooner set off with a cotton frock and a comb. I hope Ian turns out to be good with his own clothes, because I'm hopeless with mine. I feel as though I'm waiting on a station."

"There are several parcels for you downstairs."

"Are there? I wish we had thought to tell the organist — with consummate tact, of course — not to play too loudly. When Ina Stewart was married, she was practically carried down the aisle on the blasts. The vibration from behind shook her orange blossom over one eye."

"Raine! Raine!" called Mrs. MacAlvey from afar, bustling in swiftly on the heels of her cry. "Are you feeling all right, dear?"

"I should be if I was left alone," said the bride.

"I was just thinking that as it's going to be such a fine day you might as well receive on the lawn. It will prevent the guests getting in a jam going and coming through the doors."

"Do I have to shake hands with everybody?"

"Of course. But lightly, then it's no strain. Don't grip. The Queen does it perfectly."

"She has practice," said Cleo.

"Don't distract me, dear," said Mrs. MacAlvey reproachfully. "I'm trying to think of so many things. I found my own bouquet very heavy. Sometimes they put it on a small table, even for the photograph. Have you your labels?"

"Labels!"

"The hotel sent special ones. Printed. I thought you had them. Cleo, could you come down, I'm not pleased with the wedding presents, we'll have to arrange them again."

"Oh, not again!" Cleo followed her mother obediently downstairs to the drawing-room where the presents were laid out for display.

"This is what I mean," said Mrs. MacAlvey. "We shouldn't have put the cutlery canteen there. It was better where it was. Everything caught the light and shone so."

"Oh, Mummy, I don't think the family's presents should have the best places. It looks so self-satisfied."

"But Miss Reay's table-lamp hardly shows at all. We must bring that forward and put the canteen more to the right and . . . oh dear! you can't see Lady Keith's embroidered sheets now and they're so decorative."

"Raine says she thinks they'll be scratchy, but she'll keep them for guests she doesn't like much. Let's put them on the piano with the tea napkins and move that gong arrangement of Ian's aunt. That is much better. The cut-glass looks very impressive with the sun on it. Where is the list of cheques? It ought to be stuck up on the wall with drawing-pins. People read it and wonder how much."

"I don't see it at all. Oh, it's here, almost hidden by that peculiar pewter tray that came without a card. It's dirty. Vannah will have to type another, she will be vexed."

"Shouldn't we leave it now?" suggested Cleo. "Every time we reshuffle, it looks worse."

"Just a minute. If anyone comes round that door in a hurry they'll collide with Mrs. Leigh's pink cups. I'll put the nest of tables in front — so."

"Let's hope none of the guests are impulsive."

309

Primrose wandered in.

"What time is lunch?" she asked. "And do I dress before or after?"

"Oh, I don't think you should eat in that beautiful frock, dear. And there isn't any set lunch. Just ask Mrs. Mortimer for a bite if you feel hungry."

"That's a poor do," said Primrose. "The boys'll take a dim view."

Thankfully Cleo went out to the garden. The huge striped marquee made it look quite different, as though Kilchro itself had been picked up and set down again in some exotic Eastern land. The lawn was dotted with tables and chairs. Cleo looked into the marquee. There was a long table down either side, draped in white cloths and covered with glass and silver dishes, piles of plates and bundles of spoons and knives, and in the middle of the floor which was covered with scarlet drugget, stood a special table, and upon it in its three-tier glory, Raine's flower-crowned wedding cake.

Waitresses in crisp white aprons were dashing about, rubbing up the spoons and polishing the glasses, taking trays of iced cakes out of containers and arranging pyramids of pastry rolls. Such unusual activities for a September morning!

All this terrific busy-ness of so many people! thought Cleo. It made getting married seem important. And this was a simple country wedding. Now if she had married Mr. Pulham that would have been something! For Mr. Pulham was Somebody in Washington, and the reception might easily have been at the British Embassy and one could imagine what that would mean.

She shuddered and felt slightly sick.

"Would you care for a nice cup of coffee, miss?" asked one of the waitresses kindly. "We're just making some and there's a few sandwiches kicking round. I don't suppose you'll be bothering much at the house."

She accepted the coffee. It tasted bitter yet was too sweet. Coming out of the marquee, she caught sight of Raine sitting on the low wall down by the tennis court, a rapt look on her face. Raine was miles away, she looked just like a bride ought to look. She was wearing the blue cotton blouse and tweed skirt she had worn yesterday, and for background she had an autumn border of golden-rod, bronze heleniums, red-hot pokers, white phlox, and purple monk's-hood. She reminded Cleo of a Victorian drawing-room picture called *Where the Brook and River Meet*, banished long since with scorn to a rubbish heap. Cleo looked at her sister uncritically, but decided that she personally would have gone out of sight of the house to think beautiful thoughts on her wedding morning. It was just a bit too obvious, though perhaps natural to Raine who had no self-consciousness at all.

Cleo ran down the slope and joined her sister.

"Come down to earth," she said.

"But I am," said Raine with surprise. "I was just thinking how hard it is really to exterminate rabbits or cockroaches. Some always escape. It reminds me of the few, the happy few, who got away after the Massacre of St. Bartholomew in that book Miss Goodrich used to read to us on Sunday afternoons."

"When are you going up to dress?"

"Oh, must I? Well, in a bit. I just want to say good-bye to the old Me," said Raine in a rather churchy voice, taking a battered block of Fruit and Nut out of her skirt pocket and biting into it.

Cleo wandered back to the house. The bouquets had come and smelt very strongly in the hall.

311

"Do make Raine come and dress," cried Mrs. MacAlvey, appearing at the head of the stairs half in and half out of her new gown. "Why did you have to get me something with twenty-two buttons down the back?"

"There's plenty of time, Mummy."

"Well, get her in her room. It's so unconventional to have her straying about all over the place. She'll be going for a swim next. Oh, and Mrs. Duthie — Inga — rang up. It seems a very old friend of hers, Sir Barry Hinch, has turned up and she wants to bring him. I told her it was all right. He's a widower, and she says we'll like him."

"Why should we like him because he's a widower?" asked Mr. MacAlvey, who was standing about the landing putting off having to dress.

"Now don't be difficult, Alexander, you know that's not what Inga meant."

"Why did she have to say he was a widower at all?"

"Why does one say anything! Will somebody in this house please *start* getting dressed? *Alexander!*"

Looking from her own window Cleo saw that Raine had disappeared from the terrace, just as by tonight she would have disappeared from the house and from the old easy pleasant life of the family. Perhaps all this dressing up and eating and general fuss and bother of weddings was intended to keep you from thinking how dull it would be afterwards without your irritating sister or daughter.

Her face broke into a smile as a very small rabbit suddenly burst out of the kitchen garden and sat for a moment on the lawn staring goggle-eyed at the marquee. Then it whisked away. Out at sea a tourist steamer went chuffing by with its backward plume of grey smoke and its neat white wake in the peacock-blue water. Nearer at hand in the lane a strange young man was tinkering with a motor-cycle. So there were people in the world who were quite unconcerned about Raine's wedding!

The door opened and in came Primrose. A new Primrose with an unfamiliar, carefully disposed face. Her hair was brushed into a shining cap under a snood of twisted turquoise velvet, her long dress of pale grey brocade shot with silver thread gave her height and dignity, her rough schoolgirl hands were encased in frail gloves of palest grey suède, turquoise satin slippers peeped from the hem of her dress.

"Oh!" said Cleo, looking at her transformed niece.

"Not bad, is it?" said Primrose, turning and turning before the cheval mirror. "I look about eighteen."

"You do! I ——"

"Good. I hear the groomsman is in the Scots Guards and an absolute smasher. Francis Macdonald, Younger of Strathpingle. Don't you go chipping in! You stick to stodgy old Neil."

"Oh, is Primrose ready?" cried Mrs. MacAlvey, darting in. "My dear, you look very nice."

"That isn't the point," said Primrose. "Do I look seductive?"

"Go and help the boys with their ties." Mrs. MacAlvey looked at Cleo. "It's dreadful. She's growing up. It's too sudden."

"You can't stop her, Mummy. She'll be sixteen next month, and then she'll cast away boats and sandals and want dances and hair-dos."

"Mercy!" said Mrs. MacAlvey.

Left alone, Cleo proceeded to dress, and felt better when she saw how nice she looked in an outfit identical with Primrose's. Then she went to Raine's room to see what was happening.

The sight took her breath away.

Raine, never particularly good-looking, had taken on a sort

313

of supernatural beauty. She stood in the centre of the room, fully dressed in the plain long dress of ivory satin with its long sleeves pointed on the backs of her hands, and Ian's gift of pearls gleaming in twin rows on the deep square at her throat. Her dark hair went smoothly down like a ballerina's under a tiny coronet of waxen flowers. Her face, creamy pale, had the look of one of her own pearls. Her eyes, shadowed underneath, were brilliant and starry. Over all, from head to feet, flowed the cascade of white tulle that was her veil. She looked fragile, ethereal, fearfully lovely.

"Oh, Raine!"

"I know what you mean," said Raine, gazing at herself in the mirror. "How can anybody who looks as gorgeous as I do ever come down to ordinary life? This is the climax. After today I ought to go straight to the fairies. I'm so beautiful, so beautiful! How wonderful for Ian when he sees me!"

"Don't worry," said Cleo cheerfully. "This time tomorrow you'll be sitting on a bench at North Berwick in your tweed coat and skirt writing postcards and saying, 'You are a dope, Ian, to forget the stamps.'"

"I'm haunted by an awful dread," said Raine. "It was a wedding Mysie once went to. The bridegroom never turned up and the bride swooned at the altar."

"Have you practised swooning?"

"I've told Daddy to leave me in the car till he finds out."

The telephone had been ringing for several seconds, and as no one else seemed to bother, Cleo went to take the call.

"I thought you were all dead," said Ian. "Could I speak to Raine?"

"I don't think Mummy will let you. She's conventional."

"Well, tell her for God's sake to turn up. That's all."

"She has the idea that you're not going to turn up."

314

"What!" shrieked Ian.

"Oh, I'm sure you will."

"Thanks, Cleo. Neil and I have both been ready for about two hours and we're cold sober."

"Well, I shouldn't be as sober as all that, Ian, you sound a bit low."

She thought, wouldn't it be marvellous if he suddenly said, 'Hold on, Neil would like a word with you,' but it was too much to expect and Ian rang off. Cleo went back to Raine and said, "It was Ian. He's worrying in case you don't turn up."

"Don't be silly," said Raine calmly. "I've been working and praying for this moment for years and years and years."

To Cleo the ceremony was like something that happened in a film. The little kirk was packed, and crowds of village people in their Sunday black who couldn't get inside stood outside chattering in Gaelic and wondering if the whole thing was rather frivolous and godless, until reassured by the strains of "O God of Bethel," sung with ponderous solemnity and Drumpegge's mighty bass shaking the pews and half a beat behind everybody else.

Cleo discovered she was nervous; far more so than Raine, who looked as cool as an icicle and as beautiful as a waterfall. Weighed down by the burden of her own bouquet and Raine's, she only had the strength to lift her eyes to the corner of Neil's green, blue and black kilt and then, with an effort, to the silver buttons on his cuff. What were bridesmaids supposed to think of? What was Primrose, for instance, thinking of? Food, probably, and looking nearly eighteen, and boats, and what she'd tell the girls at school.

She must look at him just once, when everybody else was looking at something absorbing. She chose the moment when Ian put the ring on Raine's finger. There was a deep hush in the little kirk. Neil wasn't looking at the bride or the ring, he was staring straight in front of him with a gallant, sad expression. He was probably worrying, thought Cleo, about Larrich Torpedo going off his food.

At last it was over, and swept out of kirk on the deafening peals of the organ, she found herself in a car with Neil, Primrose, and young Macdonald. Wild with excitement, Primrose chattered all the time, while Cleo choked on a mouthful of confetti someone had unwisely thrown.

The car dashed up the lane and spilled them out into the midst of a scene in which Raine and Ian were being posed on the lawn to meet the tide of incoming guests. They looked radiant, drowned in bliss. Raine's white-gloved hand was out. . . . "How do you do? . . . Thank you! . . . Oh, thank you! . . . So pleased — so glad — "

Everyone was kissing Raine, kissing Ian. The photographers clicked frenzied shutters. Those who had shaken hands drifted towards the marquee whence came the attractive tinkling of spoons, but more and more guests arrived. They took possession of the house and garden, they kissed each other, universally congratulating. They told Cleo, "The bride looks beautiful. I never realised how nice-looking your sister was. Your dress is charming, where did you get it? How happy your mother looks! How fortunate to be getting the right son-in-law! To marry in one's own set is so suitable, and so rare. What is she going to do with her bouquet? The whole County is here. What a gathering! So pleasant! Are we going to be allowed to see the presents?"

Gavin was stationed at the drawing-room door to direct the traffic. Rather unnecessarily he pointed out the presents he admired most, and also indicated those he scorned. Other members of the family were busily employed. Neil was helpful, finding chairs for the elderly, and finally attaching himself to Lady Keith, with whom he became deeply engaged in earnest conversation. The Keith girls with other young people stood three deep at the buffet, eating heartily and exchanging adolescent jokes.

Out of the house came old Miss Reay in her odd collection of Shetland woollies and gold chains. Ignoring the bride and groom, she swept across the lawn with outstretched hands to the minister.

"What a cheery service! Thank you, indeed," she cried. "I've just been in there, but there didn't seem to be anything to eat. I meant to give them a cuckoo clock, but I feared it might be misunderstood."

"Dear Miss Reay, I trust you are keeping well."

"So well! I do like the country. Not like Sidney Smith who called it a healthy grave, even if he did found the *Edinburgh Review*, which I sometimes find hard to believe. I've been reading novels lately, though they always end in gloom."

"The food," said the minister's wife, whose new navy shoes were killing her, "is in the marquee."

"In that thing?" said Miss Reay. "Unusual. I had some gloves when I left home."

Cleo, moving about the garden like a graceful little sheepdog, breaking up groups of recalcitrant ewes and driving them before her towards the refreshments, ran headfirst into her brother James with Trina and the children.

"Raine looks very composed," said James. "I've never seen her look better."

"Oh, do go and have something to eat," said Cleo.

"Not in the marquee," said Trina firmly. "The heat. I should collapse." She was wearing a new coat and hat, both blue but inharmonious.

317

"Take the children to the dining-room," said James, "and I'll try to bring you something. Armitage looks a bit green."

"Oh, Daddy!" cried Armitage in distress. "You said that Angela and I could have lunch with Gavin and Primrose. Please let us go in the marquee!"

"Do let them!" said Cleo.

"They can if they like," said Trina. "What a pity not to have had child bridesmaids — though of course I'd have had Angela in bed for a week after."

"Excuse me," said Cleo. "I see some people are getting lost in the kitchen garden."

She set off to the rescue, but stood transfixed. Across the shining lawn came Inga Duthie with a man who must be Sir Barry Hinch. Inga wore a breath-taking dress of flame-coloured silk, a hat laden with osprey plumes, a mink cape, and about eight diamond bracelets. Sir Barry Hinch was a very slim, superbly groomed, faultlessly dressed Englishman of about forty-five, and you had only to look at him to see that he was rich and important.

There was no doubt even to the most casual onlooker about Sir Barry's feelings for Inga. He gazed at her with the drooling look of a pet spaniel, and clasped her arm and hand all the time as though afraid she would be whisked away by the fairies. And if Sir Barry Hinch was all over Inga, Inga was no less all over Sir Barry Hinch. She kept giving him a dreamy smile, and putting her free hand over his as she swept him across the lawn to where Mr. and Mrs. MacAlvey were standing.

Following in a kind of daze, Cleo was near enough to hear Inga say, "Oh, dear Mrs. MacAlvey and Mr. MacAlvey, I'm just longing to have you know my dear friend, Sir Barry Hinch. Sir Barry and I have been very close friends for many years but — well, Fate was unkind. And now by a miracle all

318

our troubles have melted away and we're together at last."

Flinging her diamond-braceleted arms around her host and hostess, Inga bestowed upon them radiant, golden kisses. People turned to look. The wedding reception took on a new sparkle, it was as if another bride and groom had suddenly turned up to relieve the monotony.

"Oh, my dears, I'm so glad, do go and have some champagne and cake, Raine is just going to cut it!" cried Mrs. MacAlvey, kissing Inga for the second time and rebounding against the well-shaved cheek of Sir Barry Hinch.

"Come, darling!" said Sir Barry, extending both hands to Inga, and leading her thus clasped across the lawn towards the marquee, as though in a ballet.

"Well!" said Mrs. MacAlvey. "That's a case if ever there was one. And I always thought she was after Larrich."

"I suppose there was always the chance," said Mr. Mac-Alvey, "that Lady Hinch would get better."

Raine came out of the marquee, looking rather warm and much less ethereal. The kilted Ian following in her wake dealt with obstreperous clouds of tulle while the usual humorist made near-funny jokes. Raine, conscientious, began to do her duty by relatives on both sides of the family, MacAlveys from Glasgow, the Dundas uncle and aunt from Edinburgh — rather towny and restrained — and the Garvines, elderly, stiff, and Braemar-ish. The streams converged upon Raine, then parted and withdrew, finding the looks of the others distasteful. Being forced thus to meet did not mean that one need mingle. Dear Raine! — such a sweet bride! Connections by marriage needed the most careful handling, Raine preened herself over her new-found skill. One hour of marriage had already made her a slightly different person; it was as gratifying as it was surprising.

319

Everyone had been shaken hands with, said the right thing to. They all melted away, and for the first time the bride and groom found themselves alone on an island of green lawn three yards square.

"Mistress Garvine!" said Ian.

"Where?" Raine looked round for somebody overlooked.

"You — silly!"

"Oh." She pulled herself together and said, "All that lace of yours. Do you wear it often? I'm not very good at ironing."

"It isn't washed. It's two hundred years old. It keeps clean, more or less," said Ian simply.

"I wish it would begin again," said Raine. "I don't remember much up to now. I'm just beginning to enjoy myself."

"Where can we go? Sh, they're coming."

In the marquee Cleo stood with a cup of tea spilling over her gloves, feeling slightly dizzy and as though she might wake up any minute to find that Sir Barry Hinch didn't really exist. He was so very much the kind of person you might encounter in a dream, and she found herself gazing rather wildly at him as he accepted a shrimp patty and a glass of champagne from a waitress who had similarly equipped Inga. The two of them tipped glasses, gazed yearningly into each other's eyes, smiled as at a private joke, and drank thirstily as though imbibing one another. So much restrained passion seemed to make itself felt through the marquee, as though golden gnats danced in the air.

Someone pulled at Cleo's sleeve.

"I simply haven't had a chance to speak to you," said Mrs. Aird. "You look charming. It has all gone beautifully. A lovely atmosphere. At some weddings there is simply no atmosphere at all. Where are they going for the honeymoon, or isn't one supposed to ask?"

320

"North Berwick. I don't think there's any secret about it." Cleo wrenched herself back to home and duty.

"Really? That's where I went for mine. Raine must give it my love. Can that be Mrs. Storr — over there with the doctor? I haven't seen her for years. Hasn't she aged? Excuse me — "

Mrs. Aird bustled off in search of gossip. Cleo, looking round, found many pleasant sights to delight her; Angela with another small girl screaming happily as they jumped over the guy-ropes; Armitage with Gavin and Archie leaning up against the farther end of the buffet and knocking back ices as fast as they could fill their plates. She felt light-hearted, as though everything had suddenly become wonderful fun.

Primrose came up like a whirlwind, panting, star-eyed.

"Francis Macdonald has taken practically a whole ciné film of just me!" she cried, and babbled on, Francis says this — Francis says that. She was full of this young god, intoxicated by her first taste of sex-consciousness.

At the gate, in the lane, had halted a party of young people, bare-headed and wearing shorts, with formidable packs, entranced by the free show. They made comments, not always inaudible, on the costumes of a bevy of ladies chatting in a ring, in ancient silks and scarves and the kid gloves that had gone to Balmoral in 1919, all emitting a faint smell of petrol.

"It's a wedding. Where's the bride? The old boy's sporran's too wee for his stomach. Hey, miss, would you have a few cakes to spare?"

"I bar this," said Primrose. "Let's get out of range. I say, why isn't Neil looking after you?"

"He has to talk to people. The best man has responsibilities," said loyal Cleo, who had never for an instant in the afternoon quite lost sight of Neil, while doing her own duty and admiring somewhat ruefully his attachment to his.

"He is talking to that Englishwoman who rents the shoot," said Primrose. "Mrs. Mayhampton."

"Oh, is that who she is?" said Cleo, with a vision of green chiffon and sables.

"She rides and organises things, and has two sons called David and Christopher. Why are all English boys called David and Christopher? Is it a law or something?"

"You do know a lot about Mrs. Mayhampton!"

"Oh, I don't know." Primrose tweaked her snood into position and batted her eyelashes. "I must go back to Francis."

Too young, thought Cleo, to have reserves and diffidences.

"Oh look!" she said. "They'll be falling over those ropes."

It was too late. Angela tripped and fell flat on her face. She rose in silence and surveyed her green knees, then explored her mouth with her fingers and brought them back smeared with red from her cut lip.

She began to scream piercingly. The whole garden was full of consternation.

Cleo gathered up her niece and rushed for the house, colliding on the way with Sir Haris Keith, looking more gigantic than ever in his flaming kilt and streaming plaid of scarlet and yellow.

"What! Little girls crying? That won't do!"

He leered at Angela, waggling his fingers above his eyebrows. Angela rolled up her eyes and went into hysterics. She was bundled into the house and handed over to maternal recriminations.

Mr. MacAlvey was coping with the Garvine aunts and finding them heavy going. They had recently been overcharged by a taxi-driver, a situation from which every ounce of discussion would be wrung. They wore toques, à la Queen Mary, one of violets, one of vague, puce-coloured blossoms, and expressed by sidelong glances their doubts as to their host's right to wear the Macleod tartan.

Mrs. MacAlvey came across the lawn in anxious haste.

"Raine must come and change. She's going to be late."

Raine was gathered up, hustled into the house, brought down at last suitably dressed for travelling, reunited with her husband who had also managed to get into everyday garments. The car was at the door, luggage inside. One suitcase seemed to have been forgotten, there was a wild rush to find it. Everybody flocked round the car.

"Thank you, Mother, thank you, Daddy, good-bye, James, good-bye, Cleo," cried Raine, kissing all in turn, conscious of the dramatic nature of this parting.

"Thank you, sir," said Ian, glassy-eyed, wringing Mr. MacAlvey's hand.

"You'll want some thing to spend," muttered Mr. MacAlvey, thrusting four five-pound notes into Raine's new grey handbag.

One final burst of excited farewells and they were gone, out of sight and sound. As suddenly as that, it was all over. Everybody was saying good-bye and drifting away, cars were being started up, and taxis trying to attract the attention of people they were meeting. Already men in sacking aprons were taking out the pegs of the marquee, and waitresses were stripping cloths from tables and repacking glasses and plates, and other men were slapping chairs into piles and carrying them out to the lorry, and all of a sudden out came the sides of the marquee and were rolled up, and the top collapsed and lay on the ground like an enormous crumpled flower.

This finality could not have been more conclusive. All the gaiety had been ruthlessly flattened out, and with the departure of the bride and groom went every trace of colour and sparkle from the day.

The MacAlveys, bewildered by this swift descent from the sublime to the nearly-ridiculous, stood about and wondered how to bridge the interlude before taking up ordinary life again, while Cleo went into the house to find a bit of Elastoplast for a waitress who had cut her finger on a broken wineglass.

CHAPTER TWENTY

There's an all-passion-spent feeling about here. Would you care for a walk along the shore?" said Neil, suddenly appearing at her side.

Cleo felt as though somebody had knocked her off the top of a very high building. Her knees shook. This was another thing that only happened in dreams, like Sir Barry Hinch who had just driven off with Inga in a huge Buick, splendidly chauffeured, she bestowing little backward waves of the hand, he raising his silk hat from side to side, like royalty.

"What — what did you say, Neil?"

"I said, would you like to come for a walk on the shore — to get away from all this? Don't come if you have other things to do."

"Oh but I'd love to! No, I haven't anything to do. I'll come at once." And Cleo set off promptly, before anything could happen to stop her. A spasm of common sense suggested that it might be advisable to ask Neil to wait five minutes while she changed her dress and shoes, but she was too afraid that if she did so he would change his mind or be whisked away by his relatives, and she had missed so many golden chances, she wasn't going to let this one slip from her.

They walked down the brae looking rather exotic, Neil in his kilt and doublet with silver buttons up to the lace at his throat, Cleo in her grey and silver dress and blue satin shoes.

Those shoes were already beginning to worry her when they reached the rocks, but Neil patiently held out his hand to help her over, and his hand was firm and cool and slightly electric, and she left her fingers in it as long as she dared and thought how wonderfully understanding the poet was who said, 'I will hold your hand as long as all may, or ever so little longer.'

Walking on the sand was extremely painful in those thin, high-heeled shoes which were rubbing a sore place at the back of her foot, but this moment to Cleo was worth any pain. Or was it? It would have been if she could have thought of anything to say. Tongue-tied she walked at Neil's side, nor did he seem able to find a word. Desperately Cleo looked for inspiration at the long white lines of surf creaming up the fawn-coloured shore, at the pale emerald sea, the misty shapes of the islands, the squawking sea-birds fighting over refuse at the sea's edge. All suggested nothing whatever. They had hardly exchanged two sentences since they left the house. Had it always to be like this? It was maddening.

Well, if banalities were all she could think of, then she must utter banalities.

"I haven't seen much of you today," she said.

"I had to talk to people."

"So had I. There seemed to be such a lot of people there."

"Yes, quite a crowd."

"It all went off very well, didn't you think?"

"Yes, very well. Of course I haven't had much experience of weddings."

"Neither have I. Things went very flat when it was over."

"We were lucky to have such a fine day."

They walked on in silence. And now we've used up everything, thought Cleo, except 'I suppose we'll be hearing from them in a day or two' and 'I always think a cup of tea is so refreshing'.

Stabs of agony from her ricked ankles and scraped heels shot up her legs. She put her hand to her lips to hold back a groan.

"Have you swallowed a fly or something?" said Neil kindly.

"Oh no," said Cleo, curling up her toes to get some relief.

"It's beastly when you swallow a fly. I had one in my throat once for two days and I kept hawking like a sick heifer."

"How horrid for you."

"I got it on the moors, shooting, one hot day in August. My factor — it was when I had a factor — said eat dry bread, and I pushed down crust after crust until the indigestion was worse than the fly."

"How awful. Did it come out in the end?"

"It just faded away."

"Oh." Cleo racked her brains to think of some entertaining accident which had once happened to her but couldn't remember one. They walked on dumbly for five minutes. The conversation thought Cleo, should be intimate, personal, free. Why should I bear the burden of this mental paralysis? Why doesn't he start something — or is he perhaps in a kind of trance?

"How are the calves getting along?" she asked wretchedly.

"Fine, thank you."

Another dead end, thought Cleo. She couldn't very well work her way through the stock-yard asking after each animal in turn.

The westering sun flooded them with gold. Neil's buttons glittered like the silver threads in Cleo's dress.

"Doesn't it seem an age since we went to Skye?" he said suddenly.

"Yes, an age."

"We must go again some day."

"But the summer's over," said Cleo sadly, more sadly than she intended, for she couldn't bear her shoes another minute. "The summer's over" she repeated, "and the children are going back to school in a few days, and now Raine has gone, and — oh dear!" She abruptly terminated her catalogue of woe. What a moaner he must think her!

"Oh, do you think we could sit down for a second?" she cried in a tone wrung from the heart.

He gave her a startled look.

"Of course. But the rocks are wet from the tide, and your dress —"

"That doesn't matter," said Cleo fervently, flinging eighteen guineas' worth to the winds and choosing a reasonably dry patch of granite.

Neil remained standing, which gave the interlude an impermanent quality.

"The wind's getting up," he said after a moment. The wind was indeed boisterous, and becoming chilly. "Are you ready to go on?"

"My shoes hurt," said Cleo, in the depths. What a fool he must think her! Men hated girls who fussed about their clothes and feelings.

"I'm sorry," said Neil with gratifying concern. "Do you think we'd better go back?"

"I'm afraid we'll have to."

Cleo got up and began to limp homewards in a state divided

328

between wretchedness and fury. This was the sort of thing that always happened to her. Fate shrieked with malicious laughter every time it got her and Neil together, striking her dumb, putting her into tight new shoes that felt like red-hot vices, making her appear to her hero no better than a half-wit. The walk, the unexpected golden chance which had filled her with hope and expectancy, was ruined.

"Couldn't you take them off?" said Neil.

"I couldn't walk on the shingle without them."

"Have mine. I'll manage. Wait —— "

He took off his buckled shoes and insisted on thrusting them upon her feet. She shuffled along in them, humiliated. It was Neil's turn to limp, choosing the easier patches.

"We do look a sorry pair," said Cleo.

A gust of wind whipped the words from her mouth.

"What did you say?"

"I said we look a sorry pair."

"Sorry, I can't hear you."

"I said — oh, it doesn't matter." A triviality oft repeated sounded so banal.

Cleo came to a standstill. The wind tore off her blue and silver snood, whizzed it across the shingle. Her hair was all over her face.

"Shall I go and catch it?" said Neil. "It's nearly out to sea. Give me my shoes."

"No, no, let it go. This is awful."

"Just one more effort," he said kindly. "We're nearly off the shingle and on to the sand. There!"

"Thank goodness," she said. "Do have your shoes back. I can walk on the sand perfectly well, and I shall only fall on my nose in these shoes."

They changed back. Neil put the blue shoes in his pocket.

Cleo stabbed frantically at her wild locks with a single kirbi-grip.

Round the outcrop of rocks they changed their direction and were out of the wind.

"I just wanted to say," said Neil, "that you needn't worry about Raine. She'll be happy at Larrich."

"I never thought she wouldn't. She's so adaptable," said Cleo, filled with relief. It was easy to talk about Raine.

"More than that. She has great intuition."

"Raine has?" said Cleo in some surprise.

"I've noticed it. You know, Ian is emotionally inarticulate. His moods change rapidly. I don't mean he is moody, but he has many moods. I've noticed how unfailingly Raine senses his mood and adapts herself to it. I've been most struck by it. Ian is going to find himself understood, and without any effort on his part. Therefore Ian is going to be happy, and it follows that Raine will be happy too, and neither of them will wonder why but will accept it as the natural thing."

"I never knew you had such a penetrating way of summing people up," said Cleo, startled into frankness.

"When one is interested in the people concerned, the way they fit together is important."

"Of course. And you say that Raine has intuition? It's strange I've never noticed that, though I've lived with her all my life except for odd bits. I do know that she's very loyal. And courageous and kind and unfussy. And she never whines or nags. And whether Ian prospers or becomes poor she'll stand by him till she drops."

"I think you've always let yourself be overshadowed by Raine," said Neil. "You think her perfect."

"But I don't," said Cleo, her brain reeling a little at the idea that Neil thought she let herself be overshadowed by Raine.

"Raine has faults, but they've nothing to do with you or me, and they're not big enough to worry Ian. And now we've thoroughly discussed my sister on her wedding day, what about your brother? He's your younger as Raine is mine, but nobody could accuse Ian of overshadowing you, you're much too lofty."

Neil blinked rapidly and Cleo's heart sank at her own daring.

"Are your feet still hurting?" he asked.

"No. And don't side-track me."

"I wasn't trying to. Ian is one of the best, and though he has a devil of a temper, he's always the first to offer to make it up after a row. And he'll let Raine have the whole of her own way."

"Raine won't take advantage of that," said Cleo. "She's too honest. I once told her she had the spirit of those Highland wives of old, who hid the cattle and the plate and held the place against the redcoats while their men were away. She'll make a wonderful Lady of Larrich."

The moment she had said it she realised what a spectacular brick she had dropped. Of all the things she might have said, nothing could have been more awful than that.

Neil's face looked like a polar landscape.

"Raine will not be Lady of Larrich," he said in a voice thunderously quiet.

"I'm so sorry, Neil," said Cleo impulsively. "It was such a silly mistake. It slipped out —— "

But it had slipped out only too effectively, and just when they were getting along so well. The old deadly silence engulfed the rest of the walk. Silently Neil helped her over the rocks and up the brae, but his cool hand was no longer electric and she withdrew her fingers from it as quickly as she could.

Oh, what a miserable fool she had been! And these Highland lairds were the touchiest people on earth where their status was concerned. Moreover, she had not only offended Neil, but had possibly made things awkward for Raine by suggesting that she might have ambitions beyond the scope of a younger brother's wife.

When they got back to the house, she said, "Won't you come in and have supper?"

"No, thank you," he said politely. "I have things to do at home, and my aunts are staying the night at Larrich."

"I see. Well, good night, Neil."

"Good night. Say good night to your people for me."

"Of course."

"I hope you won't have any blisters."

Only in my soul, thought Cleo.

Neil's was the last car left in the lane. He started it up and drove away.

Mrs. MacAlvey came out of the drawing-room.

"Is that you, Cleo? Was that Neil going away? Why didn't you ask him to stay to supper? Did you go for a walk?"

Everyone else had changed. Cleo felt like something rather wilted left over from a masquerade.

The presents had been repacked. They had supper and sat in the drawing-room, Miss Paige at her gros-point, Mr. MacAlvey reading *The Scotsman* which had lain unopened all day, Primrose, Gavin, and Archie playing some acrimonious card game.

Mrs. MacAlvey said, "It always goes so flat after a wedding."

Tirelessly she and Miss Paige picked up topics from the day, shredded them conversationally and let them drop. This person. That dress. An Edinburgh cousin's impending law-

332

suit. The unexpected appearance of a niece from Glasgow, "with that extraordinary-looking young man."

The sunset died in the sky almost unremarked. Over hot milk and biscuits Mrs. MacAlvey said, "Raine will be glad she took her warm coat."

"We shall be hearing from them in a day or two."

"Tomorrow the children's things are all to pack. The name-tapes ran out on the last handkerchief."

"I'm tired," said Cleo. "I think I'll go to bed."

"We're all tired. We'll all go early. I hope James and Trina got home all right. Armitage was sick."

"We're not tired," said Archie.

"You must be. Such a long day."

Such a long day! thought Cleo, climbing at last into bed. It felt like two years since she got up that morning. It was a day she would remember with mixed feelings as long as she lived.

And — she told herself, banging the pillows into position and snatching *Barchester Towers* from the bedside shelf — I will read and then I will sleep, and not on any account will I go over and over that silly conversation word for word, thinking of all the things I might have said and the things I wish I had not said. I said what I said and, as Voltaire or somebody remarked, only a fool regrets. I have had my chance and ruined it finally by my own imbecility, and now the curtain has fallen on our little play. I shall not see him again. I shall not see him again. I shall not see ——

She gave a shivering sigh and tilted the lamp so that its pool of light fell on page 140 of *Barchester Towers*. She read, "Early on the following morning Mr. Slope was summoned to the Bishop's dressing-room, and went there fully expecting to find his lordship very indignant and spirited up by his wife to repeat the rebuke which she had administered the previous day."

She frowned and reread the sentence, which still didn't seem to make sense. She decided that if she was at variance with Trollope then she was to blame, and fell to reading *Barchester Towers* with desperate concentration. She failed to become drowsy, sleep was very far away. The battle between reason and impulse was taking its toll. I won't think! I won't think! said Cleo aloud.

In the deep quiet of midnight she got up and found aspirins. They seemed rather dismal things to eat in the night, and fulfilled no purpose. It was one of those hushed nights of early autumn when even the sea made no sound, creeping like oil on the smooth drenched sands. She found herself waiting for some sound, and when it came it was the sad hoot of a far-off steamer.

A white moth was trying to dash itself to death against her lamp. She switched off the light.

"Cleo!"

She sat up in bed, frozen into a listening attitude.

"Cleo!"

It sounded as if someone was calling her from the garden. She got up, pulled on her housecoat, and went to the open window.

This was a mad dream. Under her window, looking up, bare-headed and wearing an old belted raincoat was Neil.

She realised at once that Raine and Ian had been killed in a train wreck. With one hand to her pale and horror-stiffened cheek she leaned out.

"I knew you were awake," said Neil. "I saw your light go out."

"Shall I come down?" she said. "Is there anything I can do?"

"No. Stay there or I can't say it."

"You don't need to," she said sadly. "I've guessed. But need we tell the others till morning? It seems so cruel."

He looked up at her rather wildly.

"Can anybody overhear us?"

"There's nobody's window this side except Raine's. Oh, poor Raine!"

"I had to come," he said. "I couldn't sleep till I'd told you. It's a moment of madness, you'll have to understand."

"It's dreadful, Neil. When did they let you know?"

"Look," he said. "Are you going mad or am I?"

Could grief be driving him crazy?

"You're trying to tell me that Ian and Raine have been killed in a train wreck, aren't you?" she said gently.

He clenched his fists and beat them against the air.

"This is impossible. Oh, Cleo, will you never come down to earth? Train wreck!"

"You mean, it isn't true? Oh, what a relief!" Cleo leaned farther out of the window, longing to see Neil's face, but a cloud was over the moon. If there hadn't been a train wreck, why on earth had he come?

"There are some things," he said with sudden urgency, "that you've got to say in the dark so that if they misfire you can pretend to yourself that they never happened. This is one of them. Are you listening?"

"Of course I am."

"If you don't like it the darkness will hide it. What I'm trying to tell you, Cleo, is that I love you."

He waited. Cleo's fingers slid slowly down her cheek. This was where the dream became a little too difficult to follow.

"Did you hear me?"

335

"I heard what I thought you said, but I —— "

"I'm in love with you. Did you hear that?"

"I don't know whether I did or not."

He seemed to relax a little, thrusting his hands deep into the pockets of his raincoat.

"I can tell you the exact minute I fell in love with you. It was when you came over with Raine to see the house and you wouldn't let her chuck out the old tartan curtains. I've been like a dumb dog with you ever since. I've been avoiding you. I thought you'd think I was just being obvious — I mean, Ian and Raine and you and me. It is obvious when you come to think of it. But tonight, with the old aunts in bed and Ian gone and Larrich feeling a bit empty, I knew I couldn't let things go on any longer as they are. I had to come and tell you. I'm cold sober. This may be insanity, but it isn't drink. I love you! I'm in love with you Cleo MacAlvey. There it is! Now for God's sake say something."

The moon suddenly sprang from behind a cloud and lighted Neil's face. It was unbearably moving. Cleo shut her eyes and gripped the window-ledge.

"Oh yes, Neil! I will, with all my heart," she murmured dizzily.

"You will what?"

"I will marry you."

"I haven't asked you yet. I haven't got as far as that. You should say you love me first."

"But I do!" cried Cleo fervently, thinking she might as well get the last possible ounce of value out of this dream.

"Then you will marry me?"

"I said I would. I got it in first. Oh, Neil, forgive me for being such a fool on the shore. That awful thing I said about the Lady of Larrich. You were furious."

336

"It gave me a shock. It was you I'd always thought of as Lady of Larrich. That's what you'll be."

"How wonderful!"

He took his hands out of his pockets and straightened his shoulders.

"Well, that's that. I'll be back first thing in the morning, and we can talk about getting married in a day or two. What a relief!"

"Such a relief! You don't know!"

"Good night, my heaven, my little shoeless *charaid!*"

"Good night, my darling, *mo chridhe!*"

He went as silently as he had come, with just one backward look, fingers on lips and lifted to her. She watched him out of sight, heard his car start up somewhere in the distance and whine away. The deep stillness fell again.

Cleo looked at her watch. It was twenty minutes past one. She got into bed, banged the pillows into position, and sat up against them, looking at the moonlight on the floor.

It had been the most beautiful dream that anyone ever dreamed. It must be a dream, because nothing of that kind ever happened in real life. How wonderful to be able to dream a dream like that! The very words. Words she could never have thought of in her waking hours, words she would say over to herself as long as she lived.

Dazzled, she covered her eyes with her hands. Yes, it was all very well being dazed with rapture at half-past one in the morning, but how was she going to feel tomorrow in the cold light of a family breakfast-time? And dreams so quickly faded from the memory. How could she keep this one?

And what made her so sure it was a dream?

She suddenly shot straight up in bed. What had he said? What had Neil said in that dream — "I'll be back first thing in the morning, and we can talk about getting married in a day or two."

A day or two! No dream could be quite as mad as that. A day or two! Mummy would have a fit. A day or two! The more you said it the more incredibly real and comprehensible it sounded. And the Lady of Larrich . . . ! What was she doing, lying bemused in bed?

She sprang out and rushed to the window. This would settle it. Dream or sublime reality, this would decide it.

She shut her eyes and opened them again, swallowing hard.

There dark in the dew were his footsteps, coming and departing on the silvered lawn.